A TASTE OF DESTINY

"Give me a taste of your sweetness, Maggie. A single taste is all I want."

It seemed inevitable that they should meet like this, and the very thing Maggie had been yearning for would finally happen. Joe bent down to her. Lowering his hands to her shoulders, he feathered soft kisses down the side of her face to her earlobe, which he took between his teeth and gently nipped. She shivered in helpless reaction, aware of him with her entire body.

Then he was kissing her—a real kiss, mouth to mouth. Her breasts—suddenly full and aching—grazed his chest, but he did not try to pinion her or force her in any way . . . and because he demanded nothing, she gave him everything . . .

TODAY'S HOTTEST READS
ARE TOMORROW'S SUPERSTARS

VICTORY'S WOMAN   (4484, $4.50)
by Gretchen Genet
Andrew—the carefree soldier who sought glory on the battlefield,
and returned a shattered man . . . Niall—the legandary frontiers-
man and a former Shawnee captive, tormented by his past . . .
Roger—the troubled youth, who would rise up to claim a shocking legacy . . . and Clarice—the passionate beauty bound by one
man, and hopelessly in love with another. Set against the back-
drop of the American revolution, three men fight for their
heritage—and one woman is destined to change all their lives forever!

FORBIDDEN   (4488, $4.99)
by Jo Beverley
While fleeing from her brothers, who are attempting to sell her
into a loveless marriage, Serena Riverton accepts a carriage ride
from a stranger—who is the handsomest man she has ever seen.
Lord Middlethorpe, himself, is actually contemplating marriage
to a dull daughter of the aristocracy, when he encounters the
breathtaking Serena. She arouses him as no woman ever has. And
after a night of thrilling intimacy—a forbidden liaison—Serena
must choose between a lady's place and a woman's passion!

WINDS OF DESTINY   (4489, $4.99)
by Victoria Thompson
Becky Tate is a half-breed outcast—branded by her Comanche
heritage. Then she meets a rugged stranger who awakens her
heart to the magic and mystery of passion. Hiding a desperate
past, Texas Ranger Clint Masterson has ridden into cattle country
to bring peace to a divided land. But a greater battle rages inside
him when he dares to desire the beautiful Becky!

WILDEST HEART   (4456, $4.99)
by Virginia Brown
Maggie Malone had come to cattle country to forge her future as
a healer. Now she was faced by Devon Conrad, an outlaw
wounded body and soul by his shadowy past . . . whose eyes
blazed with fury even as his burning caress sent her spiraling with
desire. They came together in a Texas town about to explode in sin
and scandal. Danger was their destiny—and there was nothing
they wouldn't dare for love!

RIDE THE WIND

KATHARINE KINCAID

ZEBRA BOOKS
KENSINGTON PUBLISHING CORP.

ZEBRA BOOKS are published by

Kensington Publishing Corp.
850 Third Avenue
New York, NY 10022

First Printing: November, 1995

Printed in the United States of America

For Jonah Alexander
Born May 15, 1994.
Beautiful, beloved grandson
God keep you safe always.

I am tired of fighting. Our chiefs are killed. . . . The old men are all dead. . . . It is cold and we have no blankets. The little children are freezing to death. . . . Hear me, my chiefs. I am tired; my heart is sick and sad. From where the sun now stands, I will fight no more forever.

—*Chief Joseph of the Nez Perce, on the occasion of his surrender to Colonel Nelson A. Miles in the Bear Paw Mountains, Montana, October 5, 1877.*

Prologue

Oregon Territory, 1877

Something was wrong.

The boy knew it. He could sense it on the soft summer wind even before he arrived at the high meadow where the tribe's horses usually grazed at this time of year. The breeze carried the scent of earth, pine, river, and horse—but it also carried something else. Something that made the fine hairs rise on the back of his neck.

The boy had only seen twelve summers, yet already he knew the smell of death . . . and that was what he smelled now, death mingled with bloodshed and decay. He began to run. Pine needles rustled underfoot as he sprinted toward the clearing rimmed by mountains, where the horses could always find nourishment even when the lowlands no longer yielded much in the way of sustenance.

It was perfect country for raising horses: fresh green grass, clear sparkling water, and enough challenge in the surrounding steep terrain to encourage the development of sure-footedness, sturdy limbs, strong muscles, and good wind. The horses bred by the Nez Perce were coveted for their stamina, as well as their beauty, and nothing so expressed the heart and soul of the boy's people as the sleek, black- and white-spotted animals with their mottled pink noses.

Heedless of the noise he was making, which would surely spook the herd and send it galloping, making a hard job of catching his pony and collecting the others, the boy zigzagged through the pine trees and at last raced out onto the meadow. There were no horses. The broad sweep of bunchgrass stretched away to the distant mountains, and nothing moved upon it. Save for the wind sighing through the grass, all was still and silent.

Yet, the smell. . . . It teased the boy's nostrils, elusive as a wisp of smoke but sickeningly familiar. Every Indian knew the smell of death; lately, the Nez Perce had been stalked by death. One never knew when a bullet fired from concealment would take another life and plunge another family into mourning.

The boy's heart thudded loudly, and his breath came in great gasps as he surveyed the barren meadow. Only three days before, at this very spot, spindly-legged foals had romped at their mothers' sides, and the stallion—a splendid black-coated fellow with a blanket of white spots peppering his hindquarters—had trotted the perimeter of the herd, standing guard over his charges. . . . Where were they now? What had happened to them?

It was up to him to find out. He had been sent to gather the herd—some one hundred and sixty head belonging to his particular small band of the Nez Perce—and bring them down to the lowlands where his people were waiting to join Chief Joseph on his wild flight to freedom.

It was unthinkable that he should return without the horses . . . even more unthinkable that he should return without knowing what had become of them. He must search the meadow, study the hoofprints, and determine what had befallen the herd. He could not go back until he knew.

Dropping to a crouch, fearing that some enemy might even now be watching, he ran a short distance, stopped, and examined the ground. The grass was crushed, the earth churned. Hoofprints indented the soft dark soil. Something had startled the herd and set it running.

The boy followed the trail. He was halfway across the meadow when a slight buzzing sound reached his ears. He raised his head and noticed that the stench of death had grown stronger. He could see it now—a sprawled shape lying at the far end of the meadow where a narrow trail led to a cut through the mountains, one of the few exits out of the meadow.

He knew it well, and the horses also knew it. If the head mare were trying to escape some danger in the meadow itself, she would have led the herd in that direction, with the herd stallion guarding the rear of the bunch, driving the slower moving members ahead of him.

And suddenly the boy knew what the shape was; still, he hurried to investigate. The buzzing sound grew louder, the stench overpowering. He held his breath as he approached the decaying carcass of the herd stallion, lying in an attitude of stiffened agony in the high grass.

The magnificent animal had been shot—and not cleanly. He had been able to run a long way before falling, as indicated by the trail of dried blood he had left behind him. Lying not far from his bloated body was a single white glove, the fingertips dirtied, but the rest as pristine white as if it had just fallen from a man's hand.

The boy had once seen such a glove worn by a white man in a blue uniform who had come to tell their people that they must leave their ancestral lands and go to live in a strange, distant place the whites had picked out for them. His people didn't want to go; that's why they were joining Chief Joseph, so they could run away and live in freedom.

As the boy snatched up the glove, rage burned in his heart. The Blue Coats had killed the herd stallion, and run off—or killed?—the rest of the herd. He must discover which, so he followed the trail leading away from the meadow and into the depths of the mountains.

He had not gone far when he found the trail blocked by newly cut trees and logs hauled across the entrance to the narrow pass. The Blue Coats had done this, too; tracks on the beaten-down earth revealed that horses wearing metal shoes had been ridden here, and there were deep ruts also, indicating wagon wheels. Apparently, the wagons had been used to block the entrance to the pass until the logs could be dragged into place.

The boy gazed up at the high walls on either side of the pass. He would have to scale one of them in order to see into the pass itself. He set about it at once and climbed to a high, rocky ledge.

When he had sufficiently regained his breath after the long hard ascent, he crawled to the edge of the ledge and looked down into the pass. The sight that greeted him was like a knife thrust to the heart. In the bottom of the pass lay the pride of the Nez Perce, their speckled coats crusted over with dried blood, their bodies stiff and bloated, their mouths and eyes swarming with flies.

Mares with spring foals at their sides, yearlings and two-year-olds, old horses and young ones. . . . The Blue Coats had spared not a single one. They had slaughtered the entire band.

Tears welled in the boy's eyes as he spied his own pony with its distinctive leopard markings. Not worth much in a trade, the old gelding had still been fleet of foot and gentle of manner. He had never minded a long wild gallop or standing still for many hours to be painted with experimental patterns as the boy dreamed of manhood and riding to war with his elders.

Now, his old friend was dead, his life cruelly ended by the enemies of the Nez Perce. First, the whites had stolen the Indians' lands, now their precious horses, and soon their freedom. . . . It was more than the boy could bear.

Tilting back his head, he let out a great shout of mingled grief and rage that bounced off the walls of the canyon. Immediately thereafter, his gorge rose, and he was violently sick to his stomach. Several moments passed before he recovered, and then—a boy no longer—he made his way back down the side of the mountain to go and tell his people the terrible news.

Their beloved spotted horses, the wealth and pride of their nation, were gone. The whites had taken all that was precious to them. Naught but their freedom remained, and without their swift horses, that, too, would soon be only a distant memory. It was only a matter of time.

The Indians had meant to flee peacefully, but now, surely, they would kill many white people along the way. Or else they would stand and fight. At long last, they would finally fight.

And I will fight with them, the boy swore. *I will fight until the very end.*

One

Broken Wheel Ranch, Idaho Territory, June, 1878

"Mama, Mama!"

The cry split the night, and Nathan Sterling snapped upright in bed the moment he heard it. Beside him, Lena, the young Mexican woman whom he had recently hired as a cook and to help care for Maggie, also stirred.

"Dios! What is it?" Lena exclaimed, clutching the bedsheets to her naked breasts.

"Maggie. . . . It's Maggie havin' another one of her nightmares." Nathan stumbled out of bed and fumbled to light the kerosene lamp on the bedside table. "Stay here. I'll see to her."

"Are you certain you do not want my help, *señor?*"

Despite the fact that they had begun sleeping together, Lena still called him *señor*. That was one of the things he liked about her; she knew her place. Considering it an honor to share his bed, she demanded little in return. She would never tell anyone of the true nature of their relationship if he didn't—and he never intended to do so. He needed feminine comfort but not another wife, and *definitely* not a Mexican wife.

"I can handle it, Lena. I been handlin' her nightmares for the past two years, ever since her Ma died and she . . . she became a cripple. I don't need yer help with this part of raisin' her."

"Whatever you say, *señor.*" Lena sounded hurt, but Nathan couldn't help it. He didn't want Lena intruding on the special relationship he had with his seven-year-old daughter. Lena's job was to teach Maggie domestic arts and how to grow up to be a lady. He himself would take care of his daughter's emotional needs. . . . Goddam! It had been a long time since Maggie's last nightmare; he had thought the bad dreams over and done with.

Tugging on his trousers, he hoisted the lantern, hurried to the door, opened it, and padded out into the darkened hallway in his bare feet. Maggie's cries were louder now, "Mama! Mama!"

They wrenched his soul. He paused outside her room to pull himself together. The plank floors were cool on his bare feet, and he let the coolness seep upward to calm his racing heart before he faced his little girl. Then he opened her door.

Maggie lay in a bundle of twisted bedclothing, her small oval face contorted, her body stiff, her hands clutching at the mattress. He knew that pose; it was exactly the way she had looked two years ago when she was thrown from the wagon. He had found her bruised, broken body beside that of her mother's. Maggie had survived the mishap; her mother hadn't.

"Maggie . . . Maggie, honey," he crooned, setting down the lamp on the chest near her bed. Lowering himself to sit next to her stiff little body, he gathered her into his arms. "There, there, honey. It's all right, baby. Papa's here. There, there now, don't cry."

Tears were pouring soundlessly down her pale cheeks and making her thick, honey-colored lashes stick together. He held her and rocked her in his arms, and she clung to him as if her heart were breaking. He knew better than to ask what her dream had been about; she would not tell him, and anyway, he already knew. In her dreams, she relived the terror of riding in the spring wagon with her mother and arriving at the high pasture, bringing supper to him and the ranch hands who were busy with the branding of the new calves. . . . He could see the scene so clearly in his own mind. Maggie had been sitting up there on the seat beside Crystal, waving to him and calling his name. "Papa! Papa! We brung blackberry pies!"

"Brought, Maggie, not brung," Crystal had gently admonished in her cultured voice. "Just because we live in a near wilderness doesn't mean we can't be civilized."

Nathan had straightened from his work and waved back at his wife and little girl, and that was when he saw the half-naked figures galloping down from the mountainside. There were a dozen or so, mounted on their distinctive spotted horses, whooping and yipping, purposely spooking the cattle gathered together in a bunch so the ranch hands could cut out the calves.

It had all happened so quickly. The cattle had stampeded, jumping over each other to flee. The team of horses pulling the spring wagon had bolted. Panicked cattle had engulfed the wagon. It had turned over, tossing Maggie, Crystal, blackberry pies, and everything else high into the air.

All Nathan had been able to see was that surging river of brown and white flesh, and those wicked horns flashing in the sunlight. The Indians had disappeared as quickly as they had come. The ranch hands—miraculously unhurt in the commotion—had mounted their horses and galloped after the cattle and the Indians together, leaving Nathan and his buddy, Gusty Williams, to assess the damage to Nathan's wife and little daughter.

Crystal had never regained consciousness. Maggie had, but teetered between living and dying for several days. Eventually, she recovered, but her right leg, mangled and broken, remained twisted and misshapen, finally healing to be two inches shorter than her left leg . . . and she had nightmares, reliving the incident over and over, and calling pitifully for her dead mother.

Nathan's throat clogged with the old familiar grief as he held and rocked his daughter, his only child, his pride and joy. His marriage to Crystal had been a good one, full of laughter, passion, and sharing. Crystal had been a petite woman with blond hair, dancing green eyes, and a zest for life that infected everyone around her. Accompanying an aunt and uncle bound for

Oregon, she had come west for excitement and found it in Nathan.

Nathan loved her still—and until Lena, had been true to her memory. He just wished his wife were there now to tell him what to do about a child who was still having nightmares two years after the incident had happened.

He wished he knew what had set off the dream this time. Maggie snuggled closer to him, her arms around his neck, and he realized that she had stopped weeping. He leaned back to look down at her. Her huge hazel eyes, still glistening with tears, gazed back at him with only a vestige of her earlier terror.

"Y'all right now?" he gruffly inquired.

She nodded, and he stroked the tousled hair back from her face to better see her expression. The lamplight made the tumbled, honey-colored curls gleam like spun copper. His own brown hair had mixed with Crystal's blond to produce a shade the exact hue of wild honey. Crystal's green eyes and his brown ones had resulted in Maggie's hazel orbs with golden flecks, though they could look pure green in a certain kind of light.

At first glance, she was a plain child, her face usually sad and serious, older than her years, her eyes reflecting a sorrow no child should ever know. Only when she smiled—the rarest of miracles—was she beautiful, the way God meant her to be.

Nathan loved her more than anything on God's green earth. For perhaps the hundredth time, he wished he had had the satisfaction of murdering the red bastards responsible for Crystal's death and Maggie's twisted, imperfect leg. The Indians had never been found—no more than the ones who had killed his younger brother, Matt, the year before Crystal's death. . . . Matt had been out looking for strays and never come home again. Nathan had found his body with a single arrow straight through the heart.

Goddam, how he hated the redskins! They had brought him nothing but grief. Despite these tragedies, he had managed to achieve a degree of normalcy and contentment in his life, especially now that the Indian menace was over. But his precious little Maggie would always have a limp, and it looked as if she was going to keep right on having these nightmares he had hoped were over.

Nathan had sent back East for special shoes with a built-up heel on the right one, but it helped only a little. The leg was still thin and frail, preventing her from running, jumping, riding a pony, and doing so many of the things she had done before the accident.

He didn't know what he could do about the nightmares—except keep comforting her when she had them, and maybe find out what was provoking them, so he could prevent it the next time.

"Anything upset you t'day?" he asked, rubbing his thumb along her velvety cheekbone. She had skin as soft and delicate as rose petals, just like her mother's.

Maggie gravely shook her head. "I helped Lena make tortillas. I like making tortillas."

Nothing there, he thought. "You like Lena?"

The small head nodded again. "She's pretty."

Yes, Lena was pretty, he silently agreed. And she had been eager to come to his bed. They had a good arrangement between them, so long as Maggie never found out about it. He would have to be careful about that; he wanted his daughter raised with the same high moral standards as her mother, who had been a true lady despite her adventuresome spirit. Since Maggie couldn't have a more active life anyway, he wanted her to be pampered, sheltered, and protected, the way Crystal had been as a child, before the urge to see the world had enticed her into convincing her indulgent parents to let her go west with her aunt and uncle. He'd find Maggie a good husband one day; after all, he had the ranch to hold out as bait, just in case no man was interested in a crippled woman, even one as sweet as his little Maggie.

Maggie suddenly reached up and touched his jaw to get his attention. He realized that his mind had wandered off in the middle of their conversation, and he hadn't made the slightest progress toward finding out what had precipitated this latest nightmare.

"What is it, honey? Ya' ready t' go back t' sleep now?"

She shook her head, her wide-eyed gaze never leaving his face. "Papa? What are you gonna do with them horses you brought in from the range today?"

The horses! The damn spotted Indian ponies. *Of course.* How dumb could a man get? Maggie had seen those pitiful, gaunt excuses for horses he'd found out on the range, and they had reminded her of the accident and brought on her nightmare. . . . He should have shot them himself instead of bringing the flea-bitten, half-starved animals back to the ranch. But something inside him had rebelled against taking out his anger and resentment on poor, dumb beasts who couldn't help it that they were once owned by Indians.

Evidently, they had been chased off everybody else's grasslands, too, for their ribs were poking out of their mangy spotted hides.

"Why, I'm gonna turn 'em over to the army, honey, and let the army take care of 'em."

Immediately, she was up on her knees in front of him, listing a little to the right and earnestly grabbing his bare shoulders to steady herself. "No, please, Papa, don't do that! The army'll kill 'em."

"How do you know they'll kill 'em?" Goddam, the cowhands musta been a-jawin' in front of her; it was the only way she could have known about the army's policy of destroying all the spotted horses—the Appaloosas, as they were called by some folks.

"I heard Gusty tell Will that's what would happen to 'em once the army got a hold of 'em."

So, he was right. Damn Gusty *and* Will.

"Baby, we can't keep 'em. They belonged t' the Injuns once, and now that the Injuns have all been put on a reservation far away from here, they b'long to the United States Government. The army'll have to decide what t' do with 'em. As long as the horses are runnin' loose, the Indians will think they still got a chance—that one day, they can come back here and start raidin' and fightin' again."

"But Papa! The horses didn't do anything wrong. And they're so skinny and sad and scared. Why can't we keep 'em? There's only four of 'em. They won't eat much grass."

"Honey, we don't want no Injun ponies around here. All they'll do is remind you of what happened to your Ma and make you have bad dreams, like you had t'night."

"The horses didn't make me dream of Mama and the Indians again. Gusty and Will did. I heard 'em talkin' about how the army will shoot the horses once they get 'em, like they did all the other horses that belonged to the Indians, and I jus' got a scared feeling, that's all. It was the scared feeling that made me have the bad dream again."

His hands tightened around her waist. Wait until he got hold of Gusty and Will tomorrow. He'd give 'em what for. "Well, maybe the army won't shoot 'em after all, Maggie. Maybe they'll sell 'em instead."

"Oh, Papa. Who around here will want Indian ponies? Everybody hates the Indians as much as we do. Why can't we just let 'em eat grass and get strong again? Why do we have to do anything with 'em?"

" 'Cuz they'd be eatin' grass that should go for own horses and cattle, that's why."

"But Papa, it ain't fair."

"Don't say ain't. Yer Ma would have a conniption to hear you talkin' that way. It ain't—it's *not* ladylike."

"Then why do you always say it?"

" 'Cuz . . . *be*cause I'm a man, that's why. But ladies have to learn to speak proper . . . properly. And that's what you are—a lady."

"I don't want to be a lady, Papa. I want to be a cow-puncher . . . maybe a wrangler like Will. I want to do what you do—ride horses and work cattle, and . . ."

He clapped his hand over her mouth. Godawmighty, he

hadn't hired Lena a minute too soon. Even Lena might not be enough to ensure his daughter was raised to be a lady. He might have to send Maggie back East to her grandparents to get the right education and put the right polish on her. Maggie couldn't ever do those things anyway—not crippled like she was.

He removed his hand from Maggie's mouth and tried to explain. "Honey, you know you can't ever ride and rope—not with your bad leg. Besides, you're a girl. You have to learn female things—not ridin', ropin', and wranglin'."

Tears filled her eyes again. "I wish I had two good legs like everybody else," she whispered. "And Mama. I wish I had Mama. I can't remember Mama's face anymore, but I surely do miss her. She always smelled like rose water, didn't she, Papa?"

He could hardly swallow the lump in his throat. "Yes, baby, she did." He could smell Lena's scent on him—a spicy, musky thing mixed with the odor of recent sex—and he felt a stab of guilt. "I'm surprised you remember what your Mama smelled like."

"Sometimes . . . sometimes, when the window's open, and Mama's roses are bloomin', I lay awake smellin' 'em and think of her up in heaven. Are there roses up in heaven, Papa?"

He blinked to clear the moisture from his eyes. "I don't know, Maggie. I expect so."

"Are the Indians' horses up in heaven, too, Papa?"

"What?"

"The horses the army shot and killed. Are they up in heaven, too? They must be 'cause God wouldn't let innocent horses go down to hell, would He, Papa?"

Down to hell is exactly where they've been, Nathan thought, thinking of the poor specimens out in his corral right now. "No . . . no, He wouldn't, Maggie. I suppose we could turn the damn—durn—things out in one of the upper pastures. As you said, they wouldn't eat up too much grass."

"Oh, yes, Papa!" She clapped her hands together. "Please let's do that. They could be *my* horses, couldn't they, Papa?"

"*Your* horses?" Nathan narrowed his eyes as he studied Maggie's excited face. "But what would you do with 'em, honey, since we've already agreed that you'll never be able to ride an' rope?"

"Why, I'd go up there with you in the buckboard just t' look at 'em sometimes, Papa, and know they belonged t' me and nobody else. They're so pretty with all them spots on 'em. One of 'em has spots that look just like snowflakes all over his back."

Nathan was amazed; he had had no idea that Maggie had taken such careful note of the horses when he brought them in.

"I'm going to call him Snowflake. That's a good name for him, don't you think, Papa?"

"Maggie . . ." he began, but the expression on his daughter's face stopped him.

Her eyes were lit up like Christmas candles; for once, there wasn't a trace of sorrow or sadness in them. Why, she was actually smiling! She babbled on with great enthusiasm. "I haven't thought of names for the others, but I will, Papa. They'll be my special friends . . ."

Then and there Nathan decided that no matter if he didn't want to keep four Injun ponies on the place, he would—if it would please Maggie and make her happy. The child didn't have many friends. There were no other children on the ranch, and when she did see youngsters in town or among their neighbors, she wasn't usually included in their play. Because of her disability and general shyness, the other children didn't know what to make of her—yes, he would keep the damn spotted ponies if they made her smile like she was doing now.

Nathan kissed Maggie's forehead. "Well, you can think up names for 'em t'morrow, 'cuz it's late an' you gotta get some sleep now."

"Yes, Papa." She crawled back under the sheets and let him tuck her into bed. When he reached out to pick up the lamp, she grabbed his hand. "Thank you, Papa. Thank you so much for letting me keep the spotted horses . . . for letting them be mine. I always wanted my own horse, and now I've got four of 'em. Does that make me a rancher like you, Pa?"

Nathan didn't know what to say. He hadn't known she had ever wanted a horse of her own—or to be a rancher like him—not that she could ever actually be one, of course. Pride and love swelled in his heart. His Maggie was one in a million. Crippled or not, she wasn't going to let life pass her by. He just hoped and prayed he would always be there to look after her and keep her safe.

"Reckon it does, Maggie."

She grinned impishly. "Good, 'cause I don't ever wanna leave the Broken Wheel, Papa. I want to live here with you forever an' ever."

"Well, don't forget, you gotta be a lady, too."

"Yes, Papa," she agreed with much less enthusiasm.

He bent and kissed her quickly again so she wouldn't see the flood suddenly filling his eyes. "G'night, sweetheart."

"G'night, Papa."

After her father had left, Maggie pushed back the bedcovers in the darkness. Limping and dragging her twisted leg, she made her way to the window overlooking the corral out back. There was enough moonlight for her to see the distant shapes of four horses standing close together, their heads drooping down to their knees.

"G'night, Snowflake!" she called out softly, pressing her nose to the raised windowpane.

The warm night air blew softly through the partially open window, billowing her nightgown. Never taking her eyes from her horses, she smoothed it down with both hands. *Her horses.* They actually belonged to *her,* now. Papa had said so—and oh, she was going to take such good care of them!

She would make certain Papa took them up to a pasture rich in good green grass, and where there was plenty of fresh, clear water for them to drink. They were so pretty—and they would be prettier still once they got fat from eating good grass . . . and someday when she was bigger, she would learn to drive a cart so she could go up to the pasture all by herself to check on her horses. Maybe the spotted horses could be taught to pull a cart, and then she could drive one into town. . . . Oh, wouldn't that be something! Maggie Sterling driving a beautiful spotted horse into town all by herself.

She wouldn't feel so bad about all the things she *couldn't* do if she had her own horses trained to do things she *could* do. Maggie leaned her elbows on the window sill and balanced her chin in the palms of both her hands. She let her thoughts soar into the warm August night. . . . Finally, at long last, she had something of her very own, something no one else had. She had four spotted horses saved from being shot by the army. Their spots set them apart just as her limp set *her* apart.

That was why she had to save them—why she didn't want them to be killed, even though they had once belonged to the Indians. Just because something was different didn't mean it was bad. . . . And Papa was the best Papa in the world for letting her keep them.

My horses, she sighed, *my beautiful spotted horses* . . . and for the first time in two long years, she was full of plans, hopes, and dreams for the future.

Quapaw Reserve, Kansas Territory, August 1878

Heart-of-the-Stallion leaned over the small wasted woman on the cornhusk pallet and searched for some sign of life. He found it in the slight rise and fall of her sunken chest and in the moisture beading on her forehead and upper lip. His mother still lived, but she was clearly losing the battle to the fever the whites called malaria.

Camas Lily's skin was a sickly shade of yellow. Each miserable day of heat here in the *Eeikish Pa* or "Hot Place," where the U.S. Government had forced the Nez Perce to live after stealing their lands and destroying their magnificent horse herds, had sapped his mother's strength and robbed her of health and vigor. The Nez Perce were mountain people and could not adjust to these hot, flat lands; one by one, they were dying—succumbing to the fever that was slowly killing them.

Now, his own mother lay stricken, and thirteen-year-old Heart-of-the-Stallion could only watch helplessly. He picked up her slender hand and clasped it tightly between his fingers. When he spoke, it was in a formal manner, using the polite, restrained tones of a full-grown man, not a blubbering, frightened child.

"I swear to you, Camas Lily of the Nez Perce. Your only son will avenge your death. He will never forget what the whites have done to you, and one day, he will make them sorry."

Camas Lily frowned. Her eyelids fluttered open, and she gazed up at Heart-of-the-Stallion with censure in her dark brown eyes. "No, my son. You must do nothing to harm the whites, for in the end, you will only be harming yourself. Better you should think about your own survival."

"I will survive. And I will remember this awful place. I will never be able to forget it."

The boy waved a hand to encompass the dingy, dark hut where his mother lay on her pallet. Aside from her pallet and his, in the opposite corner, there were no other furnishings except a barrel and two stools that served as a table and chairs. The ever-present dust lay thick on the dirt floor and covered the few baskets and clay jars that held their only food supplies, a bit of moldy cornmeal and some greenish-tinged dried beef.

Half-sick himself, Heart-of-the-Stallion had not eaten in two days, and no one had come to check on them. All of the other tribe members had their own similar problems—poverty, illness, and most of all, despair. Initially confined to a swampy slough on the Missouri River near Fort Leavenworth, they had been herded by train and wagon onto this barren, hot land and given little or nothing with which to survive. Hardly a family among them did not have someone ill, and more than two dozen had already died since the onset of their captivity less than a year ago.

"I will make them pay for this!" he repeated, clenching one fist and raising it before his mother's eyes. "When I am a man and a great warrior, I will seek my revenge for all they have done to us."

"You must not!" Camas Lily insisted, half-rising in her agitation. Too weak to sustain the effort, she moaned and slumped back on the single thread-bare blanket they possessed. "You must not, Heart-of-the-Stallion, for you alone of all our people have the best chance of escaping the reservation, returning to our homeland, and reclaiming our birthright."

"How can I do that!" he scoffed. "I cannot even prepare food that your stomach can tolerate, nor find herbs to ease your fever. It seems I can do nothing but kneel here and watch you die."

"My son . . . my son. You are not like the others among our people. You do not look like an Indian—not with the red glints in your hair and your gray eyes that sometimes glow as if a torch burned inside your head. You can pass for a white man. You look more like your father than you do like me."

"My father!" he spat. "I curse my father."

Camas Lily closed her eyes and grimaced. "You never knew him, my son. He was good to look upon, and he was gentle and kind. If I do not hate him, you should not."

"I have never understood *why* you do not hate him; he abandoned you and returned to his own people. He must not have wanted me either, or he would have stayed and become one of us."

His mother reopened her eyes and gave him a long, sad look, full of sorrow and remembrance. "He did not know about you when he left me. I have told you this, my son. He spent only a summer among the Nez Perce, hunting and trapping, and then he went away. He thought he was doing the right thing, leaving me behind. We knew our love could never last; he could not fit in my world, and I could not fit in his. Still, he was a good man. You would have been proud to call him 'Father.' "

"I call him nothing, for I am Nez Perce. I will not acknowledge a white man as my father," Heart-of-the-Stallion insisted.

Camas Lily squeezed his fingers, but so weakly it reminded him of the slight pressure a newborn babe might make. "But you *are* half-white, my son, and because you are, you may be able to regain all that our people have lost."

"I want only the chance to kill white soldiers! To draw my bow and send my arrows winging into the hearts of as many whites as I can find."

"No . . . please! Listen to me." His mother's plea was weak and breathy, and he had to lean closer to hear her. "I am dying, but before I begin my long journey to the spirit world, I want you to promise me something.

"What? Do not ask me to forego my vengeance; I cannot be like so many others among our people—sick and sad and too miserable to fight any longer. I will be like Chief Joseph, fighting until . . . until . . ."

"My son, this is the end, and even Chief Joseph no longer fights. Like the rest of us, he must go where he is told and live as he is forced to live."

"It is not the end for me! It is only the beginning. I will run away from here and continue fighting. I will never agree to live in this wasteland, where the only things that can survive are insects." He slapped at a mosquito on his arm, then rewound his fingers through hers. "This is not a healthy place. That is why they have sent us here—so we will all die of fever. They intend to make us suffer and die."

"Then take your revenge in regaining what our people have lost, my son—land in our beloved mountains and spotted horses . . . our beautiful swift horses who used to run free even as we did."

"I would not know where to begin."

His mother sighed. "First, you must learn all that the missionaries can teach you—how to read and write. How to talk and act like a white man. Make no enemies among the whites, and when you escape, perhaps they will let you go and not come after you."

"I already know a little English from the missionaries. I can write a few words. I have no wish to learn more."

"You will need to learn a great deal more if you are to pass for a white man and have a white man's freedom to go where he pleases, earn the yellow metal he treasures, and own land and buy horses. Think about it, my son. The whites have driven us from our lands so that they may own them. As a white man, *you* can return to our mountains, buy land, and own it."

"Our people have always believed that no man can own the land."

"The whites believe differently. You must learn how they think. You must discover their secrets. Promise me that instead of killing them, you will learn all you can from them. Then you will have a good life. You will have your freedom. No man will be able to take it from you, as they have taken it from the Nez Perce."

"But I cannot do this!" The youth jumped to his feet and began to pace the tiny enclosure.

He stopped and gazed up at the pitiful rooftop of the dwelling, which did little to keep out sun, rain, snow, and wind. Wide cracks admitted the late afternoon sunlight beating down upon the hut and heating it like sun-baked pottery. Flies buzzed in the silence.

Camas Lily said nothing, but he could feel her gaze upon his back. He paced some more, and by the time he turned around to look at her, her eyes had drifted shut, and she was lying very still, exhausted beyond her meager endurance. He returned to her side, took a piece of cloth, dipped it in a gourd filled with warm water, and began to wipe the beads of perspiration from her forehead.

He wished he could do more, but there was no medicine for her illness. He had heard the whites speak of something called quinine, but so far none had arrived at the reservation. As with food, clothing, blankets, tools, and everything else they needed to survive, help was slow in coming, and when it did come, it was always too little too late.

The Indians had arrived on the Quapaw in midsummer and found no shelters awaiting them. They had struggled and sweated to build even these rude huts. To Heart-of-the-Stallion, it seemed as if the whites were united in a singleminded effort to see the Indians all dead. Only the missionaries had ever shown consideration to the Nez Perce; but the missionaries, both here and in his homeland, preached that the Indians should give up all their customs and adopt the ways of the white man. With every breath he took, Heart-of-the-Stallion rebelled against such a notion.

He was just coming into manhood and longed to prove his courage and bravery as young men of his tribe had always done—by hunting game, taming horses, fighting his enemies, and being true to his *wy-ya-kin,* or spirit guide who had first appeared to him during his tenth summer. His *wy-ya-kin* was the spotted horse, and as long as his belief was strong, his power would be strong. . . . How could he do as his mother asked and still be true to his heritage?

He thought about it all the rest of that long hot afternoon and into the evening, while his mother alternately slept and drifted in and out of delirium, saying foolish things, and talking to people long gone from the world of men. She spoke to his grandmother, who had died three years ago, and she called out to several warriors who had been killed fighting the whites.

Kneeling beside her pallet, Heart-of-the-Stallion felt the presence of the spirits she conjured. His flesh crawled, and his stomach muscles clenched in dread, but he would not leave her. Instead, he clutched the medicine bag that hung from his waist and drew courage from his *wy-ya-kin,* the spotted horse. His medicine bag held a few strands of hair from the tail of a spotted horse, a powerful talisman against evil that would protect him from all harm—he hoped.

When it grew dark, he lit a fire in a ring of stones near his mother's pallet; the flames cast flickering shadows on the walls of the hut. He chanted in a low, sing-song voice—struggling to remember the proper words that would ease her passage from this world to the next. He dribbled water into Camas Lily's parched lips, bathed her repeatedly, and simply held her hand when nothing else seemed to soothe her.

He longed for company, but at the same time wanted no intrusions on these last moments alone with his mother. So many had died since Chief Joseph had surrendered at the Bear Paw! One more death would neither shock nor excite the defeated Indians. He himself had grown accustomed to death— but not to the death of his own mother.

Camas Lily had done nothing to deserve this; she had never raised a hand against the whites. Instead, she had always spoken for restraint and peace, counseling other tribe members to overlook the depredations of the settlers and try to find ways to live in harmony with them. Probably because of the love she had borne for his father, his mother had never uttered a word of accusation or bitterness against white men.

But everything she had never said, he felt and thought in her place. He despised the whites. Since the day he had found the tribe's horses dead in the canyon, his hatred had been a glowing red coal in his breast. Thoughts of revenge filled his mind and fanned the coal to white-hot intensity. He could never do as his mother asked—forsake his own people to live and prosper among his enemies. Even if it were possible, and he did not believe it was, he could not bear the duplicity, the deceit of pretending to be white when his heart and soul were pure Indian.

Somewhere in the darkest part of the night, his mother regained consciousness and became lucid for several moments. "Heart-of-the-Stallion," she whispered, her voice sounding like the wind blowing through dried grass. "What we spoke of . . . promise me . . . promise."

He bent over her. "I . . . I cannot . . ."

"Promise . . ." she begged, gripping his arm with surprising strength.

"But I . . ."

"Promise!"

He sensed that she was summoning every last bit of her strength to make this plea, and he could not refuse her.

"Yes," he finally agreed. "Yes, I promise."

She sank back on the pallet, and a deep groan escaped her. Spirits hovered in the air around him, not hostile, not friendly either. He knew they had come to take her.

"Wait! Please wait . . ." He seized both her hands, as if by holding her he could make her stay. "I . . . I will call myself Joseph, after Chief Joseph. I will make it my white name, for it *is* a white name. And my second name will be . . . will be Heart, but only *I* will know it stands for my Indian name, Heart-of-the-Stallion."

His mother did not appear to be listening. She lay still and silent in the dim light cast by the dying embers of the fire. Her face was peaceful, her eyes slightly open, her breathing indiscernible. Heart-of-the-Stallion released her hands and grabbed a small stick from the little pile of tinder he had used to start the fire. He began writing in the dust beside her.

"See here? I can write my new name. I remember enough of what the missionaries taught me at Lapwai, before we began fighting the whites."

If he just kept talking, she would not leave, he thought. She would stay and listen to what he had to say; she would watch what he was writing. Squatting beside her pallet, he completed the laborious task of writing his new white name: Josef Hart.

He printed it the way it sounded, using the letters of the English alphabet he had learned several years ago on visits to the missionaries before they fled Lapwai in the Idaho Territory, following the first outbreak of hostilities between whites and Indians. They had told him he was the smartest Indian boy they had ever encountered; they had only needed to show him something once, and he remembered it forever.

He stared down at his new name written in the dust; the act of having written it seemed to make his decision irrevocable.

Josef Hart. That was who he was now. Heart-of-the-Stallion no longer existed.

"Do you see?" he asked Camas Lily. "Do you see my new name? Is this not what you want?"

His mother did not reply. Heart-of-the-Stallion plucked a feather from his long dark hair—the soft hair with the red glints in it that did not resemble Indian hair in either color or texture—and held the feather beneath his mother's nose. It did not move. . . . How could she have gone so quickly, with so little disturbance to mark her passing?

Tears flooded his eyes, but he refused to shed them. A white boy would not grieve over the death of a woman of the Nez Perce. He must begin now to conceal his emotions and bury his feelings so deeply that no one would ever know what he was truly thinking or feeling. He was Josef Hart, now, and he must not forget it. From this day forward, he would live his life so that he could one day keep his promise to his dying mother—to think, act, and become a white man so that one day, he could reclaim his birthright.

His own children would grow up free—owning the land of their forefathers and riding the spotted horses bred for speed and beauty that his people had always cherished. He, Josef Hart, would accomplish what Heart-of-the-Stallion could never gain.

"I promise," he whispered. "Before *Hanyawat,* the Creator, I promise."

Two

Clearwater Plateau, Idaho, 1893

"Easy, little one, easy now. . . . I won't hurt you. Just let me touch you, that's all." Maggie slowly extended a hand toward the wary foal standing spread-legged in front of her. It was a white-coated, black-spotted filly with a pink nose and large, wondering, brown eyes.

The filly watched her hand as if it might be a monster coming toward her. Her short, expressive ears flicked back and forth, indicating she was interested in both hand and voice. The rest of the small herd of spotted Appaloosas grazed peacefully on the tender spring grass. Maggie knew them each very well, but the newborn was making her acquaintance for the first time.

"It's all right, little one. Don't be afraid." Stretching out her fingers, Maggie caressed the downy soft skin on the side of the filly's neck. The filly trembled but didn't jump away, and Maggie smiled to herself. She had spent several moments stroking and petting the foal's mother before trying to touch the foal, and her patience was paying off.

The little one had learned from watching that it was all right to be petted by a human, and her natural curiosity had done the rest. The filly wanted to learn all about this mysterious creature in the long brown skirt and ruffled white shirtwaist who had come into her meadow driving a noisy contraption pulled by a strange horse.

"What a pretty little thing you are," Maggie crooned. "What a beauty!"

With infinite patience, she accustomed the filly to having her neck stroked before slowly running her hands all over the foal's body. Several times, the filly jumped away—but then returned, lulled by Maggie's voice and her own curiosity.

Maggie laughed softly at the baby's antics; she loved gentling new foals. It was such a thrill to meet them for the first time, discover their sex and markings, and teach them that humans were not to be feared. Each spring, there were several foals born to the little band of mares. Maggie kept the best and sold the rest—usually to folks who wanted to use them in Wild West shows back East; men like Buffalo Bill Cody were the only ones willing to pay a decent price for them.

Maggie became aware of another baby standing behind her, sniffing the back of her neck. This one she had first seen on her last visit to the meadow. It had been born several weeks earlier. Very slowly, still in a squatting position, she turned around and confronted the young fellow nose to nose. The stud colt promptly shoved his muzzle in the ruffles of her blouse. Caught off balance, Maggie fell back laughing. The sound startled both babies, and they leapt away, nimble as deer, and galloped in circles around their dams.

The grazing mares lifted their heads and eyed her placidly, while the herd stallion whinnied from fifty feet away, then plunged his nose back down into the grass. Maggie sat back with a contented sigh. It was heavenly to be here this spring afternoon, with the sun shining brightly, the sky a benevolent shade of blue, wildflowers perfuming the air, and the mountains finally greening in the distance; now only the peaks of the Bitterroots were still snow-covered.

Blue windflowers carpeted the mountain meadow, along with purple shooting stars and yellow bells. Her father and her fiancé would be angry she had sneaked out of the house and come up here on her own, but Maggie didn't care. She had to see the new foals. The men were each too busy to accompany

her anyway, so they had no right to complain that she had come
by herself.

She intended to come as often as possible now that she need
worry no longer about abrupt changes in the weather. She was
twenty-two and soon to be married—long past time to insist
upon more independence. The two important men in her life,
Nathan and Rand, her father and her fiancé, must stop trying
to mollycoddle her. She had a mind and goals of her own, and
they had better get used to it.

The stud-colt, Billy, as she had named him, had regained his
courage and was now sniffing the tip of her built-up, patent
leather, high-top shoe, which had come all the way from Bos-
ton, a present for her last birthday. She wiggled her toe and
giggled as the colt jumped backward.

But she made no move when the filly inched closer and
curiously nuzzled her cheek. Instead, she inhaled the foal's
sweet baby smell, certain she could detect the faint odor of
mother's milk on the baby's silky nose.

"And what shall I call you, little one? I must think of an
elegant name, for already you move like a princess on your
dainty feet. . . . Hmmmm. Princess. I'll have to give that one
serious consideration."

The filly crow-hopped away, then ran around to the other
side of her dam and peeked around to look at her. Maggie
laughed out loud, stretched languorously, then rose to her feet.
She scratched Billy along his withers and began to inspect the
other horses, limping from one to the other, searching for any
cuts or sores that might need tending. Her grooming tools were
still back on the cart, where old Preacher, the only gelding her
father believed quiet enough for her to drive, stood in the traces,
head lowered, tugging at the grass.

She would inspect first and groom later, she decided, running
her hand down the leg of a big-boned, two-year-old colt who
would soon have to be separated from the herd or risk being
run off by his sire. Dusty had several bite marks and some
swelling along one hock—probably from a well-aimed kick.

He was at an age where he was too full of himself for his own good and thus received frequent disciplining.

"Time you were gelded, my friend, and sold off. But first you must be introduced to saddle and bridle. You should be ridden a bit this summer to get you used to it, and maybe in the fall . . . ," she trailed off, frowning, thinking of how Rand would insist upon breaking the colt.

He or one of the other ranch hands would simply saddle Dusty and get on, then whip and spur him until he pitched himself into exhaustion, and all the fight had gone out of him. Bronco-busting, it was called.

"But you're no wild bronc, are you? Given half a chance, you're nothing but a big pussycat."

Maggie ran her fingers through Dusty's tangled mane. Having handled him since he was a baby, she had already taught the colt to wear a halter and walk quietly beside her on a lead rope. Pretending she had a rope in her hands, she put one hand under his throat and held the other off to the side, as if ready to take him somewhere. When she started walking, he walked along beside her, following her shoulder and the cue of her hands.

"Good boy! Oh, good boy, Dusty." She speeded up, and he speeded up. She slowed, and he slowed. She walked him around in a half circle, and he kept pace like an obedient puppy. She was so pleased she hugged him, then picked up each of his feet in turn, anticipating the day when he would be trimmed and shod by Burt Lyman, the ranch blacksmith.

"Yes, I think you're ready to learn something new," she told him. "Only I wish you could learn it without having to be thoroughly terrified and maybe even hurt in the process."

It was her main disagreement with her fiancé, who was also the ranch foreman. She kept begging him to try some new, gentler method for breaking green horses, and he kept insisting that this was the way *all* horses were broken. Though probably true, she still wasn't happy about it. Sometimes the horses—or the men—were injured, and the best anyone could say about the procedure was that it was a fast, efficient way to get a young animal under saddle in a hurry. Neither Rand nor anyone else on the ranch had the time or patience to teach one small skill at a time and give the horse a chance to learn it. If it weren't for her darn leg . . .

She sighed, gave Dusty another pat, an started back toward the cart for her brush and curry comb . . . and that was when she chanced to look up at the rocky ridge overlooking the meadow.

A man on a spotted horse stood silhouetted against the blue expanse of sky. Inhaling sharply, Maggie brought up her hand to shade her eyes, so she could see him better. Folks around here simply did not go around riding Appaloosas; the old hatred toward the Nez Perce Indians was still too strong.

Yet this man was mounted on a magnificent stallion with a coat pattern she immediately envied. While her horses were mostly all white with black spots, this one was mostly black with a blanket of white spots over loin and hips. He had a white star in the middle of his forehead and reminded her of one of the original four horses from which her little band had grown. Unfortunately, the young stud's distinctive coat pattern had not repeated itself in the herd's offspring. The coloring of the mares had predominated, and eventually Maggie had sold him.

The horse this man was riding had the typically mottled pink, white, and black nostrils of the breed and also its short, somewhat sparse tail—what the hands called a pestle-tail. He was sturdy-limbed and beautiful, and Maggie wondered where in the world he had come from, since she was the only one in the region who valued and treasured these horses. After the relentless slaughter of years before, very few of the horses were left, and even fewer of the local inhabitants would stoop to riding a hated "Injun pony."

The man must be a stranger to these parts, Maggie decided, finally directing her attention to *him*. As she lifted her eyes to study him, the world seemed to shudder to a halt. He sat tall and erect on his unusual mount, a black Stetson shading his face, one hand resting on a sturdy thigh encased in brown Levi's. He wore a faded blue flannel shirt, brown leather vest, a blue bandanna knotted at his throat, and ornate silver spurs that undoubtedly jingled when he walked.

There was nothing unusual about his attire—it was typical cowboy. But the way he sat so straight and still in the saddle told Maggie he was no ordinary ranch hand. Pride and grace emanated from every muscle in his wide-shouldered, narrow-waisted body. Lean and sleek as a cat, he reminded her of a puma or some other predatory animal.

Her eyes skimmed his tack and discovered an excellent saddle, well-oiled and maintained, probably custom-made for him—the mark of an expert horseman and top ranch hand. A bedroll was lashed onto the saddle's cantle, and fringed leather saddlebags bulged with his other belongings.

She dared to look directly at his face. During her open-mouthed perusal, he had sat silent as a stone, watching her every move. His hat brim shaded his features, making them appear unnaturally dark, but his eyes were some startling light color—could they be gray?—and he wasn't smiling. Instead, the hint of a scowl hovered around the downward slash of his lips. His straight, finely chiseled nose and slightly flared nostrils conveyed haughty disapproval. As the cowboys would say, he looked "on the prod" or spoiling for a fight.

A chill rippled down her back; what was he doing on Sterling land?

She cupped her hand around her mouth and boldly called out to him. "Hello, up there!"

He didn't answer, but his scowl deepened, as if the very sight of her angered him in some mysterious way. She waved, thinking maybe he hadn't heard her or was actually staring at something else. He didn't wave back.

Annoyed by the obvious rebuff, she straightened her spine and lifted her chin a fraction. "Where are your manners, cowboy? Can't you answer a lady when she calls out to you? After all, you're trespassing on my father's land."

Still, no response. Then, very slowly and deliberately, he touched his hand to his hat brim and nodded slightly in her direction. The action was simultaneously polite, rude, and challenging, as if daring her to do something about his presence. Maggie knew that many cowboys were so shy in front of a woman that they couldn't think of a thing to say, but she found it difficult to believe of this one. . . . He was simply too arrogant—both in the way he sat his horse and in the way he watched her with an expression that bordered on outright hostility. Yet she had never seen him before, so how could she have said or done something to offend him?

"Where are you from? What are you doing up here? Where are you going?"

She waited for answers but he didn't offer any. With an almost imperceptible nudge, he urged his horse along the rocky ridge. Maggie had been right that he knew how to ride; his lithe body seemed to flow right into the body of the horse. Even at a walk, the horse's legs appeared to be a mere extension of the man himself, as if he and the horse were one entity, one being.

"Wait!" she hollered in an unladylike fashion. "Aren't you even going to say hello?"

He didn't answer but continued to ride along the ridge, no longer paying the slightest attention to her. Turning his horse, he began to descend the other side and a moment later, disappeared from sight. Maggie clambered into the cart in her usual awkward fashion, picked up Preacher's reins and clucked to him. The old gelding leaned into his breast collar and plodded forward.

Maggie drove him around one side of the ridge, thinking she might catch up to the cowboy as he descended on the narrow rocky path she knew was there. She couldn't drive up the incline, but she could meet him riding down, and when she did, she intended to demand some answers to her questions. The man had no right to refuse to identify himself when he was riding on Sterling land. Actually, he had no right to be there.

Halfway around the ridge, she began to wonder at the wisdom of her actions. She was alone, and her father had repeatedly warned her about the dangers of a young woman driving out unescorted, even on her family's land. Being in a cart put her at a severe disadvantage; that she was crippled besides made her twice as vulnerable.

She urged Preacher into a reluctant trot, but by the time she rounded the elevation and could see the other side of it, the cowboy had disappeared. She drove as far as she could along the rocky trail, bumping along uncomfortably, then gave up, turned Preacher around, and headed toward home.

The stranger was probably just passing through, and she had nothing whatever to fear—but she no longer felt comfortable remaining in the vicinity. Why hadn't the man responded to her greeting, introduced himself, and stated his business? Why had he watched her so unnervingly, then ridden away without so much as a "howdy?"

She had no idea how long he had been spying on her, and that fact made her nervous. Where had he gotten his horse? One would think that if a man riding an Appaloosa came upon a woman in the midst of a herd of Appaloosas, he would at least ride down and talk to her. Considering that spotted horses, once numbering in the thousands, had all but disappeared from the region—except for these few—a body would think they could find *plenty* to talk about!

Unless he were up to no good.

All the way back to the ranch house, Maggie relived the disturbing incident in her mind. Too dark and sullen-looking to be called handsome, the man had nonetheless been striking. Had his shoulders really been that wide—wider even than Rand's? And nobody really had silver-gray eyes, did they?

The horse had impressed her more than the man, she told herself. She would love to cross that stallion with a couple of her mares. It was a wonder the herd stallion had not issued a ringing challenge to the potential rival. The wind must have been blowing in the wrong direction. . . . Still, it was all very strange, and Maggie couldn't decide whether to mention the incident to her father or not.

It would only worry him and fuel his arguments over why she should go nowhere alone. And it would probably instigate another diatribe against the Severalty Act, passed a half dozen years ago in 1887. Over the protests of area ranchers, a hundred or so Nez Perce Indians had been permitted to return to Idaho and take up residence at the nearby Lapwai Reservation. The act gave them the right to own land—up to eighty acres apiece—on the reservation. It did not, however, give them permission to move freely about the countryside, and *no* rancher would consider selling land *off* the reservation to an Indian.

Maggie's father had been furious about the act's provisions. Once again the region would be unsafe, he had predicted, because no one could trust an Indian to stay in one place and keep out of trouble.

The thought crossed Maggie's mind that the stranger *might* be an Indian; he reminded her of one in the way he had sat so proudly on his spotted horse. His bearing had recalled the Indians she had seen in her youth, but those light-colored eyes of his were definitely *not* Indian.

By the time she arrived home, Maggie had made up her mind to say nothing. There was no sense upsetting her father and Rand, who shared her father's sentiments about Indians. Rand had lost his father and older brother to Indians, and his mother had grieved herself into an early death. Since the stranger hadn't done anything except be rude, it seemed foolish to stir up a hornet's nest over nothing.

She drove the cart into the front yard near the house and called, "Whoa!" Preacher was only too happy to obey. Immediately, a tall good-looking blond man detached himself from a group of cowboys unloading a wagon near one of the outbuildings. It was Rand, and from the determined way he walked toward her, she knew he was angry even before she saw his face.

He came around the side of the cart and reached up to lift

her down. "Hello!" she said cheerfully, hoping to forestall whatever comments seemed ready to burst from his lips.

"Goddam, Maggie!" he erupted, sounding exactly like her father. "Where in hell have you been?"

His grip on her waist was almost hurtful as he swung her down to the ground in front of him. Beneath the brim of his tattered tan Stetson, his blue eyes crackled with fury, and the mouth under the blond mustache looked ready to bite.

"You been gone for hours, and nobody, not even Lena, knew where you went."

Maggie brushed back a strand of unruly hair and smiled— still trying to be pleasant. "Well, as you can see, I'm perfectly fine, so there's no cause for worry, is there?"

She was acutely conscious of the men gathered around the buckboard unloading sacks of feed and other supplies. They were pretending not to notice her and Rand, but she knew they must be able to hear everything.

"I *asked* where in hell you been! I wuz worried outta my skull, wonderin' if Preacher had run away with you, or the cart had overturned, or you run afoul of a maverick steer or got set upon by renegade Indians . . ."

The latter remark brought a flush to Maggie's cheeks as she remembered the stranger mounted on the magnificent Appaloosa. "There are no Indians around here, Rand, except on the reservation, and they wouldn't *dare* step off it knowing that people like you and my father might put a bullet through them. Now, if you'll please move out of the way, I'd like to go inside and freshen up."

Rand kept his hands on her waist, his big body blocking the path to the house. "You drove up t' the high meadow to see them damn Injun ponies, didn't you?"

Maggie refused to meet his eyes. Instead, she concentrated on the thatch of golden hair poking out of the top of his white cotton shirt. Rand was all blond hair and work-hardened muscles, the kind of man women swooned over. *Some* women, that is. He could have any girl he wanted, yet he had chosen *her*, a cripple, to be his future wife. The thought never failed to amaze her—but that didn't mean she would take any abuse from him.

"I don't have to account to you or anybody for how I spend every minute of my time, Rand," she said in a low even tone. "I'm an excellent driver, and Preacher couldn't run away from anybody if he tried, so I don't see why you should get so riled about it."

"You *know* yer Pa an' I don't like you drivin' all over hell and creation by yerself. It just ain't safe, Maggie." A muscle worked in Rand's lower jaw. His face was such a ruddy hue and his expression so irate, he looked more like a puffed-up bullfrog than the catch of the region.

"Just because I'm crippled doesn't mean I'm helpless, Rand. I can take care of myself."

"With what?" he sneered. "Your parasol?"

Maggie did not normally carry a parasol; therefore, the sarcastic comment highly annoyed her. Tilting back her head, she glared at Rand. "I'm not a child anymore. I'll go where I please when I please. You might trust me to have some common sense."

"Common sense!" he bellowed. "Don't think you'll be drivin' up t' see those damn Injun ponies by yerself after we're married! If I have anything to say about it, I'll shoot the things first."

Maggie's temper snapped. "There won't *be* any marriage if you think you can boss me around, Rand. And you just try shooting my horses, and I'll . . . I'll shoot *you!*"

With that she whirled and flounced toward the house—at least, she flounced as much as a crippled woman was capable of flouncing. No sooner had she stumbled up the steps, across the porch, and into the sprawling clapboard house, when she met Lena, nervously twisting her apron in her plump fingers.

"Oh, *Señorita* Maggie, your Papa has been asking where you been all day. I didn't know what to tell him so I lied and said you'd driven into town. From what I overheard outside . . ." She rolled her expressive black eyes, pursed her full rosy lips, then made a clucking sound of dismay. "Oh, your Papa will be angry too, when he hears you went to the high meadow by yourself."

Maggie sighed and patted one of the plump bare shoulders that rose above Lena's lacey white blouse. "It's all right, Lena. You won't get in trouble. I'll tell Pa I lied to you."

"Querida, you don't have to lie to protect *me;* you are the one I am worried about. I lied to *Señor* Nathan to protect you."

Lies, Maggie thought. We are all so very good at telling each other lies. Lena and her father were lovers but had hidden their relationship for years. Maggie in turn had never let on that she knew what went on late at night after everyone had gone to bed. She wished Nathan and Lena would just get married and be done with it. They obviously cared a great deal about each other. Women—or "calicoes" as her father called them—had been throwing themselves at Nathan for almost as long as Maggie could remember. Her father never appeared to notice . . . while Lena had rebuffed every cowboy on the ranch, letting them know she wasn't interested in their attentions. Quite a few calf-eyed cowboys over the years had brought her flowers or praised her cooking or simply hung around until she sent them packing in no uncertain terms.

"Leave Papa to me, Lena," Maggie advised the little Mexican. "Since I've just had a fight with my fiancé, I might as well take on my father, too, while I'm in the mood."

"Querida, they are simply concerned about you." Lena touched Maggie's cheek in a gesture of fond affection. With her jet black hair and eyes, dimpled features, and generous figure, Lena was still a pretty woman—and big-hearted and kind besides. "They do not want anything bad to happen to you."

"But they want to keep me locked up inside a cabinet like you do the good crystal and china. I can't let them do that, Lena. I love them both very much, but I have to live my own life in my own way."

"I understand, but *they* do not. You must be more patient and try to explain how you feel to them."

"I *have* tried to explain, but they are both too bullheaded to listen!"

"But *querida* . . ."

"Maggie? Maggie, that you?" Nathan's voice drifted down the long hallway from the direction of his study where he liked to have a whiskey, put up his feet, and relax at the end of the day.

"It's me, Papa. Give me a minute to wash my face, and I'll be ready for supper."

"Well, jingle your spurs, will ya'? I'm hungry enough to sample a bite from a certain, good-fer-nothin' Mexican lady, if she don't dish up some of her famous *frijoles* in a hurry. Besides, I want to hear what you wuz doin' in town."

"The *frijoles* are almost ready, but if you insult the cook you might not get any!" Lena sang out.

She exchanged another worried look with Maggie before Maggie started for the staircase and her bedroom on the second floor. As she hauled herself up the first step, Lena anxiously hurried after her. "You sure you want to climb all those steps, *Señorita* Maggie? I can fetch a basin and pitcher of water for you to wash your face and hands down here."

Maggie gave a snort of impatience. "No, thanks. I can go up the stairs twice in one day, Lena—not just at bedtime. It won't take me but a minute."

Lena, too, wanted to protect her and make her life easier, but what did they all think would happen when she one day married and had a baby? Did they think she'd let others take care of her family? No! She would drag herself upstairs and down as often as needed, drive Preacher wherever she had to go, and live her life like everyone else, instead of being waited on hand and foot. Didn't they understand how much they were restricting her by always offering to run errands for her and by trying to forbid her to do what she must?

Reaching the top of the stairs, Maggie limped down the hall

to her room, entered it, and went to the washstand. Directly beside it stood a full-length mirror, and the sight of her own reflection momentarily halted her.

She stood for a moment studying her windblown hair, sun-burnished features, and plain dusty garments. At first glance, she looked entirely normal, even slightly attractive. Her long skirt covered her disability, and the built-up shoe lessened the impact of her limp. Only when she moved could anyone tell she was different.

She raised the hem of her brown skirt, but quickly dropped it back down before the full extent of her deformity became visible. She dreaded letting Rand see her bad leg, if—*when*—they married. She was terrified of what he would think the first time he laid eyes on her twisted, misshapen appendage, and hoped she could somehow keep it hidden from him.

Peering into her own hazel eyes, sparkling green in her present irritation, she wished she could be whole and beautiful, so Rand would never have a chance to be repulsed by her or regret marrying her. Plain. She was so damn plain! And much too skinny. What on earth did he even see in her? Her only redeeming feature was her reddish-brown or brownish-blond hair, which didn't even have the decency to be a clearly recognizable color!

Right now, her hair was a mass of tangles. She needed to wash away the grime, then brush out the knots before supper . . . and she needed to think of what to say to her father who would be just as irate as Rand when he learned what she had done with her day.

"I'm not going to tell you what I did or where I went," she muttered to her mirror image. "Because it's none of your business."

Like Rand, her father would probably guess—and then start cussing and yelling. Like Rand. Sometimes the two of them were so alike it frightened her. She dearly loved her father but she didn't want to marry him in a younger version. Yet she genuinely cared for Rand . . . didn't she? And he was the logical choice, also the only man who had ever proposed to her.

She heaved another great sigh and turned away from the mirror. Everything she did seemed to annoy Rand, and he in turn annoyed her. The plain fact was, he *wasn't* her father, and she resented it when he treated her like a child. When were they all going to let her grow up?

Probably never, she groused, splashing water on her face and hands. They expected her to spend all her time in the house, occupied with boring household matters that Lena could do far better than she ever could—and *enjoyed* doing. Maggie never had relished cooking, sewing, or cleaning. Rather, she longed to be out beneath the sun, chasing after the cattle, helping with the branding, working with the horses . . . all things that her bad leg prevented her from doing.

"Damn! Damn!" she muttered, tugging a brush through her unruly long hair. Maybe she ought to have been born a man. No . . . no, that wasn't right. She didn't mind being a woman; part of her actually reveled in her femininity. She loved babies and kittens and fresh-picked flowers. . . . She just wanted to be her own self. If only she hadn't been thrown from that wagon and practically been trampled to death. . . . If only her leg were strong and normal . . .

Three

Joe Hart left his horse happily grazing in a copse of cottonwoods and stealthily made his way toward the cluster of buildings that made up the ranch he had targeted for his next job. Before he rode in and asked to be hired, he intended to thoroughly scout the place; experience had taught him that if he didn't, he would regret it later.

He had worked at more than a dozen different outfits over the years since his escape from the reservation in Kansas—worked, scrimped, and saved every last dollar—and had now reached the point where it was doubly important that he make the right choice for his next place of employment. This was the end of the line, the last place he intended to work for someone else before achieving his life-long ambition: buying his own land in the very region where his forefathers had once lived and died.

Silent as a shadow, Joe slipped toward a patch of thick trees and boulders not far from the cluster of buildings. It was a perfect spot from which to spy on the comings and goings at the ranch itself and to take stock of the men, horses, buildings, and equipment. From studying an operation unobserved, he could determine whether or not the ranch was successful and able to pay decent wages, if the men got along together or spent most of their time fighting and holding grudges, and if the livestock were well-treated or riddled with disease and just barely marketable.

Some things he couldn't stomach, and unless he had no alternative, he wouldn't work at a place where men and animals were abused. He wasn't that desperate—well, yes, he was, but he had learned that a little foresight at the beginning of a job saved him from a whole wagonload of anguish later on. He didn't like to have to wait for his wages, or worse yet, to fight for them. He despised cruelty in any form, especially the mistreatment of horses and cattle. If a man didn't care for his animals properly, it was a sure bet he wouldn't give a damn about the men who worked for him either.

This time, it was doubly important that Joe pick the right place and the right ranch owner. This time, he wanted more than just a job—he wanted the opportunity to buy cattle and horses such as he had seen up in the high pasture earlier today. Since this was the nearest ranch around, he had to assume that the horses belonged here, perhaps to the husband of the young woman he had watched with the herd.

When he remembered the young woman, he felt a distinct stirring in that part of him that sometimes defied his control. The honey-haired girl was a definite improvement on the women who usually drew his interest—whores and the occasional bored ranch wife looking for a little excitement. For one thing, she was far younger, slim and graceful as a doe. Her tumbled amber hair, sweetly curved figure, and innocent playfulness had nearly enticed him to ride down close enough to see what color her eyes were. . . . However, the sight of her among the horses, *Indian* horses, had greatly disturbed him at the same time it had intrigued him.

Nowhere in his travels had he seen so many fine spotted horses gathered together in one place. Indeed, he rarely saw spotted horses anywhere. He had rescued Loser from near death in Montana. Neglected and mistreated, covered with saddle sores and scars caused by spurs, the stallion had been turned out to fend for himself during a particularly harsh Montana winter. Joe had discovered him, skeletal-thin and on the verge of collapse, trying to fight his way out of a snowdrift almost higher than his head.

The presence of so many fit healthy animals in one place was akin to a miracle—and to discover a young white woman who obviously valued them as much as he did had shocked Joe to the core. What he couldn't forget was that the horses belonged to the Nez Perce, not to some spoiled rancher's wife, pretty and winsome though she may be.

Concealing himself among the trees, Joe cast a wary glance around the ranch. He had an excellent view of it, and what he saw aroused his admiration and envy. Not only were the cattle and horses who roamed the nearby range sleek and fat, but the ranch itself displayed an unusual degree of order and prosperity.

The house was a good size—two stories with a porch wrapping all the way around it. Scattered pine trees framed the dwelling, hitching rails stood neatly out front and back, and rocking chairs graced the porch. Sturdy shutters guarded the windows, where ruffled checked curtains revealed a homey elegance not often seen on ranches he had previously worked.

Care and planning characterized every aspect of the corrals and outbuildings, too. The bunkhouse was sturdy and neat, the stable and various storage sheds large and in good repair. There were no broken rails on the split rail fences enclosing the horses and a small group of white-faced cattle. The ranch was exactly what Joe envisioned for himself one day, though he'd probably have to be satisfied with something much smaller and plainer.

A dozen or so good-looking stock horses—all solid in color—milled in one of the corrals, one section of which had been roofed over to provide shelter from the weather. A wooden water trough was filled to the brim, and someone had gone to the trouble to build a feed trough so that precious grain would not get trampled into the ground.

Joe made a mental note of these things so he could add them to the long list of items he wanted on his own spread. The thought of the girl flitted through his mind again, and he couldn't help grinning to himself; should he add her to the list, also? He had never pictured any woman in the role of his wife, especially not a white woman, but if ever he married, a woman with hair the rich color of honey would suit his tastes perfectly.

He hadn't gotten a close look at her face, but her hair alone made her beautiful; why was it only white women were blessed with silky, soft hair that captured all the colors of the sun in varying hues of yellow, gold, amber, and red? Whenever he went woman-hunting, which wasn't often because he hated to spend the money, he would always choose a blond, if possible. His natural aversion to whites could be overcome when it came to women with light-colored hair.

He leaned forward slightly, the better to see the house and perhaps catch a glimpse of the honey-haired female. The old sorrel horse she had been driving was now in the corral, and the little cart stood near an empty wagon. Joe could hear masculine voices inside the shed and also in the bunkhouse. His hearing was better than most men's, but he couldn't make out what anyone was saying. He was too far away.

Once night fell, he could easily cross the wide open spaces between one sheltered spot and another, and learn all he wanted to know before riding in tomorrow and inquiring after a job. It was the time of year for hiring extra hands; ranch owners and foremen usually took one good look at him and his well-oiled gear and decided to give him a chance to show what he could do. Within a week, he normally earned a reputation as a top hand and could stay as long as he wanted.

He had made it a rule to stay in one place only as long as his privacy was respected. If folks got too nosy and started asking too many questions, he would draw his pay and move on. People thought him cold and surly, but he didn't care. When he got too lonely, he found the nearest town and the cheapest whore and indulged himself for a few brief hours. It was the only occasion he ever spent money, and he relished the conversation as much as the sex.

Leaning against a tree, hidden by a screen of tender young greenery, Joe avidly sized up the ranch. Years of sacrifice, self-denial, and loneliness had brought him to this turning point in his life; he finally had enough gold—prudently buried in a rocky crevice up in the mountains—to buy land and horses. And cattle to keep it all going. He could make a modest start toward achieving his dream and fulfilling his promise to his dying mother.

Whoever owned this ranch would not only have to be willing to hire him, but also to allow him to buy horses and cattle eventually, then let them run with the ranch herds until such time as Joe could locate and purchase land of his own. He would start small and slowly build his ranch and his herds until they were as big and fine as this one.

There was only one problem: No one must ever know he was half Indian. Even his children, were he fortunate enough to one day marry, must grow up white, never realizing that Nez Perce blood flowed through their veins. Joe wished it could be otherwise, for he still felt a bone-deep pride in his Indian heritage, but he knew he could never acknowledge that part of himself or all his plans would turn to ashes.

"Heart-of-the-Stallion has returned," he whispered to the soft wind sighing through the trees. "And now that he is here, he will never leave again. This is his home; he will remain forever—a free man, an Indian in the guise of a white man. . . . I only pray his ancestors will understand and forgive his compromises."

The wind made no reply, but to Joe Hart, newly returned to the home of his ancestors, it seemed to be singing a song of sadness and regret.

"Goddam, Maggie, you *know* Rand and I don't want you drivin' around the countryside all by yourself! I don't blame him a bit for bein' mad as a hornet. One of us ought to take you over his knee and whap some sense into you."

Maggie's father speared a piece of beef with his fork and popped it into his mouth. While he chewed, he glared at her. Maggie glared back, not the least bit hungry despite the delicious meal Lena had served and then left them alone to enjoy, while she went about her business in the kitchen.

"I'm too old for spanking, Nathan." She purposely called him by his name rather than by the childish Papa he still relished hearing. "Besides, you've never laid a hand on me before, and it's too late to start now."

Nathan waved his fork in the air and swallowed. "Maybe I should have. That's probably what's wrong with you. I let you have yer own way in too many things. I shoulda sent you back East—to your Mama's family for yer schoolin', but you didn't wanna go, so I let you stay. I forbade you to learn to drive a horse and cart, and you kept pesterin' me 'til I finally gave in and taught you. . . . Now look where it's got me. You want to drive everywhere without me and don't even take Rand along to look out fer you."

"You were both busy. What was I to do? Sit here in this stuffy house on a beautiful spring day when I could be out checking on my horses?"

"Them damn horses! I never shoulda let you keep 'em. If they weren't up there in that high pasture, you'd be content to stay at home like *most* ladies."

"No, I wouldn't. I'm not 'most ladies.' Even if I were, I wouldn't sit home all the time like some porcelain-faced doll in frills and ruffles, doing nothing more important than pouring tea. When are you going to realize that I'm twenty-two, Nathan? I have a right to start living my own life and making my own decisions."

"Look, I'm your Papa, not some man you hardly know, so I'd appreciate it if you called me Pa, not Nathan. Makes me feel like a distant relative." Nathan speared a chunk of potato and pointed it at her. "But you're right about one thing, Miss Maggie-Headstrong-Sterlin'. You're twenty-two. Time to get married, settle down, and start havin' babies. A fine young man keeps tryin' to set the date—but you keep holdin' him off and tellin' him you're not ready yet."

"Because I'm *not* ready. You just want me to marry Rand

so *he* can start making decisions for me, which just happen to coincide with *your* decisions."

Nathan dropped his fork beside a bowl of steaming *frijoles*. He never noticed that the potato was still stuck on the tines and dripping gravy all over the red-checked gingham tablecloth that matched the ruffled curtains at the windows.

"Rand's got your best interests at heart, Maggie. And he's got more sense than you got. It's too damn dangerous for a young woman with two good legs to go runnin' around the countryside by herself, let alone someone with *your* problems. Have you forgot there's a hundred Injuns livin' less than a day's ride from here?"

"They're on a reservation, Pa. I doubt we have much to fear from Indians anymore."

Nathan heaved his blue-cotton-clad shoulders in exasperation and plowed a callused hand through his gray-streaked brown hair. In his agitation, his already dark eyes grew blacker and harder. "You can't *never* trust an Indian to stay put in one place, Maggie. Why, I shudder to think what one of them buggers would do if he came across a pretty young thing like you."

"Pa, I'm not a child anymore! I can take care of myself. You can't protect me from all the bad things that can possibly happen to me. You have to let me grow up and be responsible for my own welfare."

"When you marry Rand, *he* will be responsible for yer welfare. Whether you like it or not, that's the way of it. It's a man's job to look after his wife and young'uns. I looked after your Ma the best I could; it wasn't enough to keep her from harm, but at least, I tried. Just like I'm tryin' to keep you safe, and so will Rand."

"But . . . but I'm not sure I'm in love with Rand."

There. She had said it. The awful truth was out. How *could* she love a man who made her so angry—a man who would probably never think of her as anything but poor little Maggie Sterling, the helpless cripple? She didn't want to be pitied and protected; she wanted *more* than that, but what that more might be, she wasn't certain. The fact remained: She *was* a cripple, nearly helpless, and everybody knew it.

Her father gazed at her with a dumbfounded expression, as if it had never occurred to him that she might not be in love with Rand. He leaned back in his chair, his dinner temporarily forgotten.

"I don't know what the hell you think love is, honey, but I can tell you from experience that it starts with friendship. You *like* Rand, don't you?"

"Well, yes, of course." What girl wouldn't like a handsome virile man like Rand? Wherever he went, he drew feminine attention.

"And you got a lot in common."

"I suppose that's true . . ."

"You *know* it's true. You've both lost people you love to the Indians, and you love the Broken Wheel. You and Rand are both churn-headed, too, always wantin' things yer own way. Jes' like a hoss what don't like t' be told which direction t' go."

"If you mean we both make each other angry, that's certainly true," Maggie agreed.

Her father gave a short laugh. "Everyone on the ranch can attest to it, but hell, that don't mean nothin'. Yer Ma and I used to fight all the time, too. Some people jus' do, but that don't mean they don't love each other. Makin' up after you fight can be pretty durn nice, I can tell you."

"Oh, Pa!" Maggie laughed at the suddenly abashed look on her father's rugged, weather-beaten face, which was still attractive despite the toll of the years.

"Once yer thumpin' the same mattress, yer bound t' fall in love with Rand, Maggie. All you gotta do is give it a chance. You got everything on yer side."

Maggie abruptly sobered. "Do I, Pa? Do I, really? Sometimes, I think . . . I want. . . . Oh, I don't know. I just want to know who Maggie Sterling really is before she becomes Maggie Johnson, wife of Rand Johnson."

Nathan reached a hand across the tablecloth and covered her fingers with his roughened palm. "Maggie Sterlin' is my little girl who's growed into a beautiful young woman. She's got a bum leg that keeps her from doing everything she wants to do, but that don't mean she's gotta be unhappy all her life. A good-lookin', good-hearted cowpoke genuinely cares for her and wants to take care of her just like her ole Papa has always done."

Maggie smiled at her father, reassured but still doubting. "You seem so certain Rand would love me even if I *wasn't* going to inherit the Broken Wheel one day. I wish *I* could be that certain."

Nathan sat up straighter. "Of course, I'm certain—and you should be, too! Rand can't help it he's the foreman and the best cowhand this place has ever had. Why do you wanna hold that against him? I couldn't have picked a better husband fer you myself; I admit that. But the fact is Rand could go anyplace he pleases. Why, there's men who have already offered him more money than I can afford. And there's that good-lookin' widow, Edith Bailey, who all but threw herself at him after her husband died. . . . Why, he could have had hisself an even bigger spread than this one if he'd taken her up on the offer. . . . No, he stayed because of *you,* Maggie. Rand wants you. How can you doubt it?"

"Then you didn't have anything to do with his proposal; is that what you're saying?" Maggie searched her father's face for the answer to the question that had been plaguing her since the day Rand had first proposed to her.

Nathan might not find it such a reprehensible thing to promise Rand the ranch, since it would mean he could keep Maggie under his wing until the day he died. However, her father looked properly shocked by the insinuation that he had somehow twisted Rand's arm to get him to propose to her.

"I'd never do such a thing to you, Maggie. You sure as hell don't need *my* help to find yerself a husband. Any man with only one good eye can see for hisself that you're a beauty—and as sweet and kind-hearted as the day is long."

"Any man with even a single good eye can also see that I'm a cripple, Pa. Don't you think a man might wonder what sort of deformity I'm hiding underneath my skirt?"

"Hush, Maggie! Don't you talk like that. Why, yer limp is hardly noticeable."

"My limp keeps me from living life to its fullest, as you well know. It makes me feel awkward and ugly. The leg itself is ugly. Sometimes I wonder if I'm worthy of a man like Rand, the 'catch' of the whole region. As you say, he could have any woman he wanted, and there's plenty who'd like to drop a rope over his head and draw him in like a fat steer. So why did he choose *me,* of all people?"

"Because he *loves* you! And yes, as yer husband, he'll get the Broken Wheel one day. But if you never married, he'd probably still get it—or get to keep managing it, which amounts to nearly the same thing."

"It's not the same at all, Pa, and you know it."

"Well, maybe not. But I still think you come first with him, Maggie. We've known Rand a long time, and I, fer one, trust him. That's why I made him foreman. He worked his way up to it, and he deserved it. . . . Why, he's like the son I never had. He'll never hurt you. All he wants is the chance to take care of you for the rest of yer life. . . . He'll take care of you just like I would. Hell, he's just like me in a lot of ways. Must be why I've grown so damn close to him."

She couldn't tell her father, but the more he argued, the more she worried. "Pa, you and Rand have to learn to give me some . . . privacy."

"Privacy?" Nathan blinked. "What d' you mean—privacy?"

"I mean the two of you have to let go and allow me to be an adult."

A tinge of red crept up her father's neck. "We'll treat you like an adult when you start actin' like one—and quit doin' foolish things like drivin' up to the high pasture alone to see yer hosses."

"If I feel I can handle something, you have to let me do it," she insisted. "Otherwise, the two of you are smothering me to death with your concern."

"Smotherin' you! Girl, this ain't smotherin'—it's . . . it's *lovin'* you."

"It feels distinctly like smotherin'." Maggie picked up her spoon and began toying with it. "I know you both mean well, but I can't abide it any longer. If . . . if you and Rand really want this relationship to work, you're going to have to . . . to back off and give me some breathing room."

"Back off." The way Nathan kept repeating her words, it seemed he couldn't get them through his head.

"I mean it, Pa. From now on, I will be responsible for where I go and what I do. I'll learn to shoot and carry a six shooter, but I *will* go where I please *when* I please, Indians or no Indians."

Nathan stared at her as if she'd suddenly sprouted horns. When he pushed back his chair, it made an ugly scraping sound. "Aw, Maggie, you act like the two of us are gangin' up on you all the time."

"You are. And I won't stand for it anymore. If it doesn't stop, there will be no wedding. I . . . I may have to . . . to go away. Leave the ranch and sort things out, I guess." The thought had only just occurred to Maggie, but she knew instinctively that leaving would be the right thing—the only way to get through to them.

There was a brief silence. Then Nathan sighed. "All right, Maggie. I'll try to back off and give you more breathin' room. At the same time, I'm askin' you to talk with Rand and tell him all you just told me. He needs to hear it straight from you, or he won't understand. . . . He's just doin' what I would do in his place. He don't want nothin' bad to happen t' you ever again. So he gets all riled up and starts shoutin' an' givin' orders. . . . He don't mean to step on your toes. . . . Hell, why don't you ask *him* to give you shootin' lessons?"

"Maybe I will, just as soon as I can do so without losing my own temper." Maggie drew circles on the tablecloth with her spoon. "Thank you for trying to understand, Papa."

He grinned, then reached out to ruffle her hair. "Aw, Maggie . . . what would I do without you, girl? I don't wanna find out, you know. You been my reason fer livin' all these years since your Mama died. Guess that's why I want so bad fer you t' marry Rand, 'cuz then I won't ever have to give you up. You can stay here forever, and I'll get to see my grandbabies everyday. What more could a man want?"

"Maybe *you* should get married again. If you had a new wife, you wouldn't have so much time to worry about me."

Maggie was thinking of Lena, foolishly eating alone in the kitchen to preserve the myth that there was nothing between her and Nathan. Did they think she was blind as well as lame? Night after night, Nathan visited Lena in her room downstairs off the kitchen, or else Lena would tiptoe upstairs to join him. It was ridiculous, but she hadn't yet found the courage to tell either of them so.

Her father cleared his throat before answering. "After yer Mama, I couldn't be happy with another woman, Maggie. Haven't been able to look at another woman since the day she died," he muttered, shame-faced.

Maggie wondered what Lena would think if she could hear this fraudulent declaration. The way Nathan refused to acknowledge the true nature of their relationship must be painful for her, but if she was hurt by it, she had never let Maggie see it. Instead, the little Mexican was endlessly cheerful, supportive, and loving—making up in every way for the mother Maggie had lost. Lena seemed perfectly content with life as it was. Maggie herself could never be satisfied with mere crumbs, when she longed for the entire cake.

That's what she wanted with Rand—a whole cake. Yet he didn't think of her as a real woman. His perceptions—and hers—were colored by years of a sibling rivalry that had begun the day she first saw him. It was shortly after his mother's death. Rand was sixteen and Maggie only ten. The members of his family were all dead, killed by Indians, so the bank was reclaiming the Johnson ranch, and there was no way young Rand could fight it. Hearing of the boy's plight, Nathan had ridden over and brought Rand back with him to work at the Broken Wheel. All the things Maggie hadn't been able to do with her father—ride and rope and work cattle—Rand had done, provoking her jealousy.

Rand had called her "Pest" for the first ten years he'd known her, and she had called him Stud, because one day she'd caught him peering in a mirror and flexing his muscles out in the bunkhouse. They had fought, scrapped, teased, and disagreed over nearly everything. Then a few months ago, he had grabbed her, kissed her on the mouth, and asked her to marry him. Just like that.

Maggie had thought to herself: *Who else would I marry but Rand? He's the only one who would have me . . . and besides, it'll make Pa so happy.*

Nathan had been overjoyed, Lena had wept and blubbered, and the ranch hands had teased the devil out of both of them. Rand had been growing impatient to set the date . . . only Maggie wouldn't do it. Somehow dreading the day, she kept putting it off. Precisely the way her father kept putting off telling her about Lena.

They were both afraid of making a commitment that might turn out to be a lasting mistake. . . . Or else they were just comfortable with the way things were and didn't want to change them. Which wasn't fair to either Rand or Lena.

"All right, I'll talk to Rand," she sighed.

Her father's eyes brightened. He picked up his fork. "Good girl. It'll all work out. You'll see. T'ain't right to keep a man danglin' too long, Maggie. Once you got your rope on him, why, it's time t' haul him over t' the brandin' fire."

Maggie laughed. "Get your mark on the little doggie while you can. Is that it?"

Nathan nodded, chuckling. "If a critter don't wear a brand, nobody knows who it belongs to. It's a maverick, fair game fer anybody. Be sensible, an' get yer brand on him, Maggie, before some other cute young thing comes along an' gives him the sugar you been holdin' back."

Is that why you never married Lena, she wanted to ask, because you can get the sugar *without* putting your brand on her?

Her father had advised her to be sensible and set the date for the wedding. But was it really sensible to marry a man she wasn't sure she loved? One she doubted truly loved her? Surely, it *wasn't* sensible to let the only man who had ever asked her to marry him get away! She did have some feelings for Rand. If he died suddenly or went away, she would grieve.

Maybe after they married, they would get along better. He'd keep on running the ranch, taking on more and more of the responsibility as her father relinquished it. They did both love the ranch and never wanted to leave it. Rand had never stated it in so many words, but the emotion shone in his eyes.

Like her, he loved the ever-present view of the mountains all around, and the valleys, meadows, grasslands, and wildflowers that lay nestled between the majesty of the rugged peaks. Rand also loved working the cattle—riding, roping, branding, and everything else associated with ranch work. Given the way they both felt about the Broken Wheel, they certainly ought to be able to work things out between them.

Maggie hoped so, because when Rand stopped by the house tonight, as he usually did, she decided she would have it out with him. If he agreed to back off as her father had, she would go ahead and set the date for the wedding. Somewhere around Christmas, after the main work of the year was done, and ranch life had settled down again. They would invite everyone in the territory.

Ah, it would give her a wicked pleasure to flaunt her success at the daughters of other ranchers who had snubbed her over the years because of her disability—particularly Victoria Gottling, of the Lazy G. Younger and prettier, Victoria was always fluttering her long black lashes at Rand. She never failed to address Maggie as "Our poor little Maggie!"

Waiting until Christmas would also give Maggie time to have another wing added on to the house. She didn't want to live on top of her father and Lena. Not that the house wasn't plenty big enough for all of them, but she wanted . . . privacy. It always came back to privacy. She wanted to live life on her own terms, as a grown-up woman, and not as the child she had always been in this house.

The thought of sharing the bedroom she had slept in as a child distressed her. She wanted a new bed, a new bedroom, and their own sitting room with a separate stove and eating area, so she and Rand could be off by themselves. She would decorate it according to her own tastes and take care of it by herself.

Saying not another word, she picked up her fork and began eating her cold beans. Maybe when her father had to eat by himself, he'd invite Lena to share his table. The thought brought a smile to her lips. If he didn't think of it for himself, she would suggest it. Maybe she would even have a talk with Lena and tell *her* to start standing up for herself.

A woman can't allow the men in her life to make all her decisions for her, she lectured herself. From now on, things were going to be different.

Four

Just as it was getting dark, Maggie heard the knock on the door she had been awaiting. Rand stood on the front porch, looking sheepish but still angry as he fingered the brim of the battered Stetson clutched in his large callused hands. His blond hair gleamed with water recently splashed on it to smooth it down, and Maggie noticed a single droplet trickling down his neck into the collar of his clean red shirt.

"Evening, Rand." She kept her voice cool and polite, letting him know she hadn't forgotten their stormy exchange of that afternoon.

"Evenin', Maggie." He nodded to her, equally polite and noncommittal. "Can I come in?"

Maggie was all too aware of her father in the room behind her. "Why don't I come out instead? It's a warm night; we can go for a walk. I'd like to talk to you."

"Suits me." Rand jammed his Stetson back on his head and took her arm. "Sure you feel like walkin'? We can sit on the porch and talk, if you'd like.

The question was one more reminder of the disability she was trying so hard to forget. "I *like* walking. I can manage a little stroll perfectly well, thank you."

"I didn't mean nothin' by the suggestion. Jus' thought it might be easier on you if we sat rather than hoofed it."

"I don't want it to be easier on me. I want it to be like it is for you and everyone else." She bit down hard. This wasn't the way she intended for the evening to go—with the two of them snapping at each other. She wrapped her fingers around his arm and squeezed it apologetically. "I'm sorry. If I get tired, we'll come back and sit."

"I'll carry you back if you get tired," he offered, unaware he was saying the wrong thing again.

She heaved an inward sigh and took the steps one at a time, in her usual careful fashion. "You won't have to carry me, Rand. We aren't going so far that my leg will give out on me altogether."

"I just wish you'd let me help you more, Maggie. Why do you have to be so damned all-fired proud and as prickly as a porcupine when I like helpin' you?"

"Because . . . because . . . oh, that's what I want to talk to you about. Your attitude and the fight we had this afternoon."

"I wanna talk to you about the fight, too." He steered her around the side of the house, in the direction of the corrals and the line of trees out back. "I'm sorry I got so mad at you and shouted, but you scare me t' death sometimes, Maggie. . . . I don't wanna ride out lookin' for you one day and find you with an arrow shot through your chest."

Rand had found his father and older brother exactly as her father had found *his* brother, her Uncle Matt, and neither had ever forgotten it. In those days, it had been a favorite sport of the disgruntled Indians who resented the ranchers for settling on their lands. And the ranchers had retaliated in kind. . . . But all that was in the past now, and she wondered how often she would have to remind folks of the fact.

Maybe it was better to ignore Rand's continued fears and prejudices, and simply focus on the problems of the present. She stopped walking and turned to face him. "Rand, please listen to me. I'm not going to argue with you anymore about this; I'm just going to tell you and be done with it. I want you to teach me how to use a six-shooter. From now on, I'll carry one with me wherever I go. I've already suggested this to Pa, and he agrees with me. As long as I have a means of defending myself if the need arises, he'll stop worrying about me and let me come and go as I please. I'm asking you to do the same. I've got to have my freedom, Rand—or else I'm leaving the Broken Wheel."

"Leavin'! Yer father said *what?* You actually want me to teach you how t' shoot?" He sounded almost slow-witted, and her irritation spiralled.

"Rand, I can't marry you if we continue to argue over every little thing I do. I can't even continue living here if you *and* my father don't give me the right to make my own decisions. . . . I don't want to hurt you, Rand, but we're going to be miserable together if we don't resolve this issue here and now."

She got nearly the same reaction from him as she had from her father. Incredulity. Disbelief. Annoyance. But finally . . . capitulation. "Well, goddam, Maggie! I never knew you were so all-fired bent on . . . on . . ."

"Becoming a woman, instead of a child," she helpfully supplied. "I have a bad leg, Rand, but my brain works as well as anyone's. So do my hands. If you show me how to shoot, that will lessen the danger of my driving out alone. And if you stop being so mule-headed about it, I'll even tell you where I'm going and describe the exact route I'm taking, so you'll know where to look if I don't come home in a reasonable amount of time. Is it a deal?"

"Hell no! Even women with two good legs don't go runnin' around the countryside alone! This is foolishness, Maggie! You can still get shot and killed by someone you'll never see. My father and brother had their Winchesters with 'em, and it didn't do 'em a bit of good, now did it?"

"Then it wouldn't do a bit of good to have *you* with me. I could still get shot, and so could you." She resumed walking and headed toward the trees and big boulders scattered behind the corrals. "A body can get killed anywhere, anytime; I admit to that. But the danger is much less now than it was fifteen or twenty years ago. I'm agreeing to take precautions. That's the best I can do. I don't care how other women behave; I just know I can't live the way you and my father think I should live. . . . If the two of you persist in your demands, the wedding is canceled, and I'm leaving the ranch."

She limped all the way to the trees with Rand walking beside her, stiff and silent with disapproval. Her bad leg was tired by the time they arrived, and she leaned back against a boulder and let her good one bear the brunt of her weight.

"Just where would you go?" he finally asked. "What would you do if you left the Broken Wheel?"

She hadn't really thought that far—had been hoping that the threat itself would be enough. She wouldn't actually have to carry it out.

"I don't know. Maybe I'd go back East to live with my mother's family. My father always wanted me to get to know them, and they've many times invited me. I just never took them up on it."

"You'd never leave the ranch," Rand scoffed. "You love it too much."

"Yes, I do love it. But if I can't enjoy it, I might as well leave it."

The stars had begun to shine, revealing the downward slant of Rand's brows and mouth. "Maggie . . ." He shifted from one foot to another and nervously eyed the ground. "I . . . I don't know what to say to you. I don't know what you want. We're like two hosses hitched t'gether fer the first time an' pullin' in different directions. I think we could be happy together if you'd just give us a chance. Everything I do and say seems to be wrong. I've asked you to marry me, but now you're tellin' me you might be leavin'. All I'm tryin' to do is take care of you. Isn't it right I should want to take care of you?"

He lifted pleading eyes, and she was abruptly sorry she had hurt his feelings. When he wasn't shouting or being belligerent, she really did care for him. "Yes, you should want to take care of me. That's normal and natural. But . . . you go too far, you and Papa both. I'm not as helpless as you two seem to think.

Just teach me to shoot, Rand, and I'll be fine. All I want is a bit of freedom."

He dug the toe of his boot into the rocky soil, reminding her of a little boy, instead of the rough, tough cowpoke she knew him to be. "I . . . I guess I could live with that, Maggie. I could try anyway."

"Oh, Rand!" She seized his hand and carried it to her lips, impulsively brushing a kiss across it.

He didn't seem satisfied with that modest demonstration of gratitude. Reaching down, he wrapped his big strong hands around her waist, and drew her to him, so that she had to lean against his body instead of the boulder to spare her bad leg. She inhaled sharply, unnerved by his sudden boldness. "Maggie, Maggie . . . ," he whispered. "What am I gonna do with you, girl?"

She let him slide his arms around her and hold her close. It felt very nice, and he smelled of soap and leather, a combination she found pleasant. He had washed carefully before coming to call on her; that in itself told her he cared. He tilted up her chin and began to kiss her. His mustache tickled her upper lip, they bumped noses, and she giggled. She couldn't help it.

Immediately, he stiffened. "Are you laughin' at me, Maggie?" His tone was ripe with affront.

"Not at you—just at the way our noses get in the way when we kiss."

"I ain't never had any complaints b'fore," he growled, and she knew she had offended him by laughing at his clumsiness.

She suppressed the urge to ask him about his past experiences and pressed a little closer by way of soothing his ruffled feathers. He made another growling sound, inarticulate but urgent, and began to kiss her harder, in deadly earnest. His mouth was slightly open, and his teeth ground painfully into her lips. She pulled back slightly, but he held her close and continued the pressure—almost as if he meant to punish her.

His arms were like iron bands around her, and her ribs were in danger of cracking. She could scarcely breathe, with her nose mashed alongside his. She wrenched away and gulped a mouthful of air, but his mouth crashed down on hers again. Gone was the little boy; in his place stood an angry, determined man.

He bent her backward until she thought her spine might snap, and still, he kept kissing her. "Rand!" she managed to gasp, but he didn't give her a chance to say more.

Her back collided with the hard boulder, and he pressed her down upon it, pinning her against the rock. She could feel the hammering of his heart where his chest squashed her breasts. Something hard and wholly male intruded between them. He had never kissed her with such hunger and brutality. Usually, he gave her gentle brotherly pecks that made her yearn for a little more warmth and emotion.

But this . . . this was too much. Alarmed, she began to struggle. It was like struggling against a buffalo. Flattened to the rock, she could do nothing but endure the punishing kisses that bruised and savaged her mouth.

When at last he raised his head for a moment, she managed to shout: "Rand, stop it! Stop it at once! What's gotten into you?"

He jerked his body off her as if she'd scalded him. "Goddam, Maggie! . . . Oh, Maggie, I'm sorry." He pulled her to her feet. "Guess I kinda got carried away."

He pawed at her clumsily, trying to straighten her rumpled garments and disheveled hair. She shrank away from him, then raised a trembling hand to touch her lips. They were swollen and tasted salty.

"Rand, you hurt me! You almost didn't stop when I asked you!"

"Well, hell, Maggie. Whadda ya expect? We're engaged t' be married, and I *want* you, girl. I want more than a few polite kisses and a nice little smile now and then. I'm not your damn brother you know; I'm the man you're gonna marry. Don't you think it's time you started treatin' me like the one who's gonna share your bunk fer the next twenty years or so, God willin'? . . . Well, *don't* you?"

So he, too, wanted to get past their sibling relationship and see each other as man and woman! Husband and wife. The thought made her shiver in a way his kisses never had.

"Yes . . . yes, I do. But . . . you have to be more gentle, Rand. You . . . you . . ." She touched her mouth again. "You've made my lips sore. I think they might be bleeding."

"Bleedin'! Geez, Maggie, I'm sorry. Oh, shit! I never meant to hurt you. . . . Here, let me see!"

He tilted up her chin and peered at her mouth. Her sore lips twitched with sudden amusement; what a ludicrous scene this was! She just hoped no one was watching. He whipped off the bandanna from around his neck and dabbed at the soreness. The cloth abraded her lips like a piece of rawhide being rubbed across them.

"Godawmighty, they *are* bleedin'. Maggie, I'm sorry—damn sorry. Do you see now why I want t' git married right away? Yer puttin' me through hell, girl. I want to poke you so bad I can taste it."

"P-poke me?" she stammered, hoping he didn't mean what she was afraid he did.

"Oh, hell, I don't mean to make it sound so crude. That's what the boys call it. Pokin' a girl. I mean . . . I mean takin' you to bed, Maggie. I wanna take you to bed."

"You want to *love* me," she suggested desperately, put off by the image of him mashing her lips and mauling the rest of her in bed.

"Yes, that's it. That's it, exactly. I want to *love* you. . . . Goddam, I'm no good at this, but you know what I mean. I surely never meant to hurt you, and I'll be more gentle the next time, I swear it!"

The next time. She was already dreading it. She moved away from him and fought to get her ragged breathing back under control. Thank heaven, she had decided to wait until Christmas to marry him! Maybe by Christmas he would have learned a thing or two about kissing. She didn't even want to *think* about . . . about getting *poked*. It sounded so brutish, like bronco-busting.

Did he somehow equate the two activities and plan on riding her until she just got used to it? She was reminded of something else they should discuss tonight. Breaking Dusty. While she was settling things between them, she might as well air that disagreement, too.

"About Dusty," she began.

"Dusty? Who the hell is Dusty, and what has he got to do with . . . with what we were jus' discussin'?"

Lord above, they couldn't even hold a rational conversation! She tried again. "Dusty is my two-year-old spotted colt. He's ready to be brought down and broken to saddle. I want him ridden lightly this summer—after all, he's only a baby. But he should be broken so I can think about selling him in the fall. He'll bring more money if he's green-broke, at least."

"Sure. Fine. I'll go up and git him in the morning. Why are we even talkin' about him now? We were talkin' about *us*—and gettin' married. I'll teach you how to shoot and get you a six-shooter, and you can drive clear to California if you want, all by yourself—so long as you quit stallin' and *marry* me, Maggie. Before I do go plumb outta my mind with wantin' you."

"Christmas," Maggie announced, belatedly remembering her plans. "We'll get married at Christmas."

"Christmas! What the hell—that's seven or eight months away! I can't wait that long!"

He started to reach for her again but she stepped sideways out of his grasp—rather nimbly if she did say so herself. "I need time to plan the wedding and to have some extra rooms added on to the house."

"What's the matter with the house just the way it is? It's bigger than most ranch houses, and the only ones who live there now are you and your Pa."

"And Lena. Lena lives there, too, don't forget. I want my—our—privacy, Rand. I want a bedroom and living area to call our own. Indeed, I am going to insist upon it."

"That's ridiculous. Nathan won't like it. It's jus' throwin' away good money."

She was hurt he didn't want a special place to be alone with her. She recalled all the times he had sat visiting and talking with Nathan when he had supposedly come to see her, and she knew a twinge of jealousy. She could just imagine him spending the whole evening with Nathan, and then coming to bed for a quick "poke" before he rolled over and fell asleep, exhausted from the long days that began at the crack of dawn.

"I want our own part of the house," she repeated. "As newlyweds, we'll want to be *alone*—won't we?" She posed the question with just enough sarcasm to make her point.

"Fine. Good. Yer plumb right. I just don't wanna wait until Christmas, for God's sake."

"The time will fly by," she soothed, not daring to move closer but forcing herself to brush her fingertips along his sleeve in what she hoped was a conciliatory manner. "Now, about Dusty. I don't want him hurt or scared, Rand. He'll do anything you ask if you're just patient and gentle with him, until he understands what it is you want."

"We been over this topic b'fore, Maggie. I *know* how to break horses. It's one of the things I'm good at, so you shouldn't oughta be tellin' me how t' do it."

"But Rand, he's just a baby, and I've taught him so much by being gentle and trying not to scare him. I know he can learn the rest of what he needs to know."

"Well, he's gonna have to adjust to doing things *my* way from now on. A horse has to learn who's boss, and the quicker, the better. You know how I feel about them damned Palousies anyway. I hate spendin' any more time on 'em than I have to t' get the job done."

"They're called Appaloosas—not Palousies." She disliked the inelegant term which simply meant that the horses came from the area of the Palouse River, where the Nez Perce had first bred them. To her ear, Appaloosa sounded much better.

"And whether or not you like them, they're clever, sure-footed and swift. Exactly what you do like in a horse."

"I *don't* like 'em too damned clever—an' I sure as hell don't like Palousies. They're Injun ponies."

"But you won't be deliberately mean to Dusty, will you, Rand? Please, for my sake . . ."

He shook off her hand. "I ain't deliberately mean t' hosses, Maggie. I should think you'd know that about me by now. I just differ with you in how to break 'em."

"Earlier today, you threatened to shoot my Appaloosas," she reminded him.

"Shootin' 'em would be doin' 'em a kindness. They're like the Injuns themselves. There's no place left for 'em in the world today—except in Wild West Shows where people back East who never really knew 'em want to gawk at 'em, as if they was cute and harmless. There ain't nothin' cute about Injuns *or* Palousies. I don't know why Nathan ever let you keep them critters. All they do is remind me of everything I've ever lost—my whole family and my family's ranch, which the bank never would've taken if Injuns hadn't killed my Pa and my brother."

The horses had nothing to do with your tragedies or mine, she wanted to say, but didn't. What was the use? She and Rand would never agree on the Appaloosas. All she could do was keep pleading with him, but it wouldn't do any good. He would always hate them and break them as he saw fit.

"Let's go back to the house now, Rand, before my father starts to worry."

He took her arm. "All right. Can we tell him it's Christmas for sure, then?"

"I . . . I guess."

"You could sound a little more willin', like you was lookin' forward to it."

"Yes, yes, of course. It's Christmas, for certain."

"Well, he'll be damn glad about that—and so will I. I just wish we could make it sooner." He slid his arm around her waist and gave her a quick, hard squeeze. The air left her lungs suddenly, causing her to gasp in startlement.

"Ooops, sorry. I keep forgettin' what a little bitty thing you are. You tired yet? You want me to carry you back to the house?"

She *was* tired, but she would never admit it to Rand. She pulled away from him. "I can manage."

She limped back to the house feeling as if she had just swallowed a huge heavy stone; it had lodged in the pit of her stomach where she would carry it forever, or at least as long as she was engaged—and married—to Rand.

Joe expelled a long low breath as the couple returned to the house. He had been standing behind a thick poplar not four feet away the whole time they had been out there and had heard every word. He shook his head, remembering. He didn't treat whores the way that rutting bull, Rand, had treated the woman he was planning to marry. Maggie. Maggie of the honey-colored hair and awkward gait.

In another few minutes, the fool would have torn off her clothes and begun humping her right there on that boulder. Not that Joe couldn't understand the way Rand must be feeling, but a fragile little thing like her should be treated with care and gentleness. She should be wooed with caresses, endearments, and tenderness, not leapt upon and nearly raped.

No wonder white women came so easily into his embrace; Joe knew how to soothe their fears and make them open to him like flowers seeking rain and sun. He imagined himself alone with Maggie just as Rand had been—or thought he had been—moments before. His kisses would have been soft as thistledown, so soft that she would have given him everything eventually.

Instead, she had grown frightened and begged Rand to stop—and this was the man she apparently thought she loved and intended to marry. The white man had realized his mistake

and tried to fix things, but by then it had been too late. He had
lost her trust and therefore her cooperation.

What a disgusting—and revealing—exhibition! It was the
same way white men tried to break horses, with force and cruelty, instead of guiding the animal each step of the way until
it did what was wanted, thinking the activity its own idea.

If he lived to be a hundred years old, Joe would never understand the foolishness, the general bullishness and heavy-
handedness, of white men. Why must they always subdue,
conquer, and destroy the very creatures whose affections they
most desired? It was all so very typical and unnecessary.

But Maggie's and Rand's problems were not *his* problems.
He might someday be able to use what he had learned tonight
to achieve his own ends, but that was all he cared about. Maggie
herself did not interest him in the slightest. True, she loved
spotted horses and had beautiful, honey-colored hair, but she
was still a white woman, the daughter of the man who owned
this ranch—and therefore forbidden to him.

Joe could not afford to become involved with her, no matter
how much he might have enjoyed teaching her how to kiss and
overcoming her maidenly shyness so that she could give and
receive physical pleasure. She was obviously ripe for seduction,
but he must leave this particularly luscious fruit dangling on
the branch for another man to sample—the crude, clumsy Rand
who was going to marry her.

Having made his decision, Joe began to move stealthily toward the bunkhouse where the murmur of male voices held the
promise of yielding the information he had come here to gain
this evening.

Maggie spent a near sleepless night wondering if she had
done the right thing—agreeing to a Christmas wedding or any
wedding at all. In the morning, as she struggled into her chemise, drawers, and requisite two petticoats, one of blue-colored

flannel and one of moreen, which produced a rustle when she moved, she debated her choices.

Marry Rand and hopefully live happily ever after on the Broken Wheel, or become a dried-up old spinster everyone pitied for her sad, dull life as well as her damaged leg. It was really no choice at all! Of course, she ought to marry Rand, even if she discovered she *couldn't* love him. At least, she might be lucky enough to have children, and if she hated getting "poked," she supposed she could endure it long enough to get pregnant.

She couldn't help wondering what would happen to her if she never married and her father died suddenly. The ranch would be hers, but she would have a difficult time finding the right person to run it for her. Before Rand, Nathan had always managed it himself, and if Rand left for some reason—angry because she backed out of the wedding—she would have to choose a new foreman. Her father had never trusted anyone but Rand to take his place, not even one of the cowboys who had worked on the ranch for years and years. Who on earth could ever take the place of her father *and* Rand?

Maggie slipped a dark blue printed calico skirt over her head and paired it with a Swiss embroidered muslin shirtwaist. There would be no driving out alone today, so soon after yesterday's transgression, so she might as well look the part of the lady, she decided.

Planning to find Rand and set a time for her first lesson in using a six-shooter, she made her way downstairs, only to recall that she had asked him to bring Dusty down from the high pasture, and he had said he would do it today. She limped into the kitchen and surprised Lena in the midst of making *tortillas*.

"Oh, *Señorita* Maggie!" The little Mexican woman rushed forward to embrace her, then remembered her messy hands and clapped them together instead. "I am so happy for you and *Señor* Rand! A Christmas wedding—how wonderful! Finally, you have set the date."

Yes, Maggie thought. *I've set the date. I have to go through with it now.*

"I see news travels fast around here. You heard it from my father, I take it."

"He is so happy, Maggie! He swung me around the room today, he was so delighted. When he went out to saddle his horse, he was whistling."

"I'm glad everyone's so ecstatic." Maggie poured herself a cup of coffee from the blackened pot simmering on the stove. "I just wish I could feel better about it myself."

"You are not pleased?" Lena quickly wiped her hands on the broad white apron covering her bright red skirt. "Why ever not, *querida? Señor* Rand is a most attractive man, and anyone can see that he cares for you."

"How can you tell, Lena?" Maggie sat down on a stool drawn up to the rough-hewn table where Lena had been working. "What does he do or say that makes you so certain?"

"He . . . why, he looks at you in a special way, as if he could eat you up like a . . . a sweet juicy peach. And he comes to see you every night. And he frowns and shouts like your Papa when he worries about you. Those are all signs that he loves you, *querida.* Don't you feel the same way about him?"

"I suppose so, Lena. I'm not sure what I feel. Or what I'm *supposed* to feel. What does love feel like, anyway?"

"Oh, *querida*, it is a most wonderful sensation!" Lena's black eyes shone. Her cheeks grew pink. "It's like having the sun shining inside your heart—or frogs leaping inside your belly. It makes you grow warm when you are cold, and cold when you are warm. It turns you upside down and inside out, so that sometimes you want to laugh—or cry—at nothing and everything. It is marvelous confusion and great certainty all rolled into one!"

Maggie had to smile. Could a mere mortal man really do that to any sane rational female? She wasn't sure she had ever felt such internal commotion for Rand—but then she suddenly recalled the way she had felt when she looked up to discover the dark handsome figure on horseback in the meadow the day before. *He* had made her feel something odd and exhilarating, almost frightening in its intensity. But really, it had been more like fear than love or attraction.

"How do you know what love is like, Lena, when you yourself have never married?" she slyly inquired, wondering if she could finally get Lena, at least, to admit to what she had shared with Nathan all these years.

Lena darkened to a shade of red even brighter than her skirt. "Ah, I just know. A woman does not have to be a wife to experience love, *querida*. Many wives never do experience it; I pity those poor creatures, but I suspect they have no one but themselves to blame."

"Why do you say that? Can a woman choose to be in love then? Or choose *not* to, as the case may be?" Maggie gulped a mouthful of strong black coffee and nearly burnt her tongue.

"A woman can choose whether or not to open her heart to a man, I believe. She can choose to let love grow inside her or to destroy the first tender buddings unfolding inside her."

"Interesting . . ." Maggie sipped more slowly, letting the coffee warm her insides.

Lena returned to making her tortillas, talking as she worked. "But love is not all feelings—happy or otherwise. It is also . . . commitment. Being willing to stand by your man even when he makes you angry or disappoints you."

Ah, now we are getting closer to the heart of the matter, Maggie thought.

"It is being loyal and faithful. It is working everyday for the good of the beloved."

You certainly do that, don't you, Lena?

"Passionate, romantic love is not all you think it might be, *querida*. True love is very hard work that brings satisfaction and contentment in one's home and family—perhaps even in children, if one is lucky enough to have them. One does not feel those feelings I described every hour of every day. Otherwise, no work would ever get done."

Lena laughed—a merry sound full of amusement at her own expense. "Listen to me going on as if I am an expert. Believe me, I'm not. But I *have* lived much longer than you, *Señorita* Maggie, so compared to you, I have had many more opportunities to observe life and draw my own conclusions."

"I think you sound very wise, Lena. Do you know that no one's ever talked to me about love before? Perhaps that's why I'm so hesitant about marrying Rand. I can't say I know a thing about it, and I'm terrified of making a mistake."

"Maggie, Maggie . . ." Lena paused in her task to drape an am around Maggie's shoulders and give her a quick hug. "You will make no mistakes when it comes to love, *querida*. When you marry, you will give your husband your heart, and that will be that. Then you won't have to ask me what love is because suddenly you will know. A person who is truly in love doesn't need to ask about it. . . . That person *knows;* there is no doubt."

Maggie returned Lena's hug with genuine affection for this dear little woman who had done so much to make her own life easy and happy. "You should get married, Lena. Any man would be fortunate to have *you* for a wife."

"Yes, that is true," Lena agreed, chuckling. Then she added wistfully, "But the only man I have ever loved still loves another and does not realize how fortunate he would be to have me for a wife. So I must be patient until he comes to his senses, eh?"

It was the closest Lena had ever come to mentioning her relationship with Nathan, and Maggie felt privileged to have had this conversation with her father's cook—and lover. "You have more patience than I would ever have, Lena, if I were in your place. I think I'd be tempted to hit the fellow—whoever he is—over the head with a frying pan right about now."

This set Lena off again, and she laughed until tears trickled down her cheeks. "Oh, yes, yes . . . I must think about that. A frying pan, yes, might be just what I need to make the man I love find the courage to propose to me."

She lifted the hem of her apron and dabbed at her eyes. "Ah, but a woman must find happiness with what she has and not waste the best part of her life complaining over what she has not. That is the best piece of advice I can give you, Maggie. Look for happiness right under your nose; if you cannot find it there, you will not find it anywhere."

"Sounds like excellent advice to me. See you at noon, Lena."

Maggie pushed back her stool, rose, and limped toward the back door to look for her father. She didn't want to think anymore about Rand and her decision to wed him at Christmas. She refused to waste the day in worry. Lena was right. Whomever she married, she would endeavor to love and cherish him until the day she or he died, whichever came first. She would stand by him, be loyal and faithful, and put *his* needs ahead of her own.

Loving a man couldn't be that much different from loving the ranch—or her horses. When you loved something or someone, you resolved to give them the best you could. As long as she kept that in mind and didn't demand the impossible, everything should work out just fine.

She stepped onto the back porch to find her father standing at the bottom of the steps and earnestly conversing with a stranger sitting on a horse with a distinctive blanket of white spots over loin and hips. Its rider was equally familiar and unforgettable; he wore a black Stetson shading his dark handsome face, a blue bandana knotted at his throat, a blue shirt stretched across wide shoulders, a brown leather vest tapered in at a narrow waist, brown denim pants that molded his muscular thighs like a second skin, brown boots, and silver spurs that probably jingled when he walked.

Taking him in from head to toe in a single glance, she lifted her gaze to more closely study his face. Brilliant gray eyes flicked over her like a whip, cutting her composure to ribbons.

"Maggie," her father said. "This here is Joe Hart, an' I just hired him to work on the ranch—take the burden off ole Gusty, who shouldn't be chasin' cows at his age anyway. . . . Maggie, honey, didja hear me? You look like you jus' swallowed a beetle. I said, this here is Joe Hart."

Joe Hart. A plain enough name. So why did the mere sound of it set *her* heart to galloping around inside her chest like a panicked horse confined to a corral for the first time in its life?

Five

"Isn't it Rand's job to hire new hands?" Maggie blurted before she thought.

Her father frowned at her rudeness. "As foreman, he's got the final say, but I don't think he'll arch his back over it, Maggie. We discussed hirin' a new man just the other day."

"Oh, I didn't know." Maggie gazed into Joe Hart's unique silver-gray eyes and wanted to bite off her tongue. There was mocking amusement in the man's expression, as if he relished her discomfort and the awkwardness of the moment. "Rand didn't tell me. Anyway, I just assumed it was his prerogative to choose the men he wants working under him, instead of having them thrust upon him."

Nathan's frown deepened. "Well, now, Rand may be the foreman, but he ain't runnin' this ranch yet, and neither are you, come to think of it. I'm still the Number One Cocka-doodle-do around here, even if I am slowin' down some an' sportin' gray hairs."

Ashamed of her uncharacteristic churlishness, Maggie managed to drag her gaze away from the tall dark man sitting so easily astride the magnificent Appaloosa. "Don't mind me and my bad manners, Pa. Of course, you're still the boss. I . . . I was just surprised you'd hire a new man without first discussing it with Rand. You discuss everything else with him," she added defensively.

At that, Nathan grinned. "Since he's gonna be my new son-in-law, that's only natural, wouldn'cha say? Don't worry. Rand's gonna like Joe. Any fool can tell by his gear that he knows what he's doin' around cattle and horses."

Maggie couldn't help studying the well-oiled saddle and shiny silver that had already caught her eye the day before. Everything about Joe Hart revealed a painstaking attention to neatness and detail that was most unusual in a cowboy. While a man's gear had to be well cared for, it did not necessarily have to be immaculate, as Joe Hart's was.

"Welcome to the Broken Wheel, Mr. Hart, but I'm afraid Rand—our foreman and my fiancé—won't like your horse," she pointed out, drawing attention to the one thing she knew to be true. At the same time, she allowed herself an appreciative glance at the black and white stallion who was standing quietly but eyeing the mares in the nearby corral with interest.

"Hell, neither do I!" Nathan laughed. "But just 'cause I ain't partial to spots don't mean I can't tell quality when I see it. Right before you showed up, Maggie, I was tellin' Joe that this here is one fine-lookin' hoss, Palousie or not."

"Appaloosa," Maggie automatically corrected.

"Whatever. Take away that blanket of spots on his rump, an' I'd be proud to ride him myself." Nathan gave the horse a pat on the shoulder. "Joe says he's a wonderful cutter. Since we got lots of cuttin' facin' us, I'm bettin' Rand will be pleased as all get out I hired Joe before some other ranch got their brand on 'im."

"Undoubtedly. So you've had lots of experience at ranch work, Mr. Hart?" Maggie fought to keep a tremor out of her voice as she shaded her eyes to boldly look up at the tall stranger.

"Yes, ma'am." Joe Hart touched his fingers to the brim of his hat as he had done the day before at their first meeting—a meeting neither of them were acknowledging.

At the sound of his deeply timbered voice, the first time she had heard it, Maggie felt a bone-deep shudder. What was there about this mysterious, uncommunicative man that made her pulse speed up and her palms grow damp? Joe Hart's gray eyes seemed to look right through her, seeing her nervousness at being face to face with him—and her chagrin at having challenged her father's authority in his presence.

Ashamed at having done the latter, she realized suddenly that if she wasn't careful in the future, Rand and Nathan might wind up competing for her loyalty. In taking Rand's side, as a good wife ought to do, she could hurt her father's feelings, which was the last thing she wanted. But if she took her father's side, Rand would be angered.

Never had she anticipated such a conflict, and it did not help her peace of mind that Joe Hart seemed to silently understand her dilemma. Glancing from her to Nathan, he compressed his lips, leaving her unaccountably infuriated.

"Well, Mr. Hart, we'll have to see just how good of a cutter your horse is next to Rand's big gelding, Cricket."

"Cricket?" Joe Hart's dark brows lifted. He managed to pack a huge dose of scorn into the question.

"Cricket's the best cutter I've ever seen." To her own amazement, Maggie found herself bragging about Rand's horse and pitting him against Joe Hart's—an Appaloosa she would have given her right arm to possess! "What's the name of *your* horse?"

Joe Hart never so much as blinked. "Loser."

Loser. Maggie felt as if she'd been kicked in the gut. What an awful name for such a splendid animal! Yet it was appropriate, too, considering what had been done to the breed in the hopes of crushing any last rebellion in the hearts of the defeated Indians.

"The boys'll enjoy seein' them two competin' against each other," Nathan interjected.

"Competing?" A flicker of interest lit the silver-gray eyes.

"Oh, that's just a little somethin' we do on the Broken Wheel to liven up brandin' time," Nathan explained. "We bet on who can cut, toss, and tie a calf the fastest."

"You bet large sums?"

"Yep, the pot gits purty big sometimes." Nathan chuckled.

"Rand usually wins, but if your horse cuts as good as you claim, you might wind up to be his main competition. The rest of the boys refuse t' go up against him anymore, and truth t' tell, brandin' time's been pretty dull the last coupla years."

"Rand is unbeatable," Maggie added, for no particular reason than to prick this man's pride and arrogance. She understood now why her father had hired Joe Hart without consulting Rand; he thoroughly relished the competition between the cowboys and took inordinate pride in having taught Rand most of what he knew. It was rare anyone did beat Rand anymore; as her father had said, no one even wanted to compete with him. Here was fresh meat for the slaughter—a man who didn't know what he was up against.

Joe Hart again brushed the brim of his hat, polite but not particularly friendly. "I'll look forward to meeting—and competing—against your foreman."

Nathan grinned, well pleased with himself. "Your chance to meet Rand Johnson has arrived," he announced. "That's him ridin' in right now on Cricket."

Joe half-turned in the saddle to look. It was a graceful movement, an artless one, that struck Maggie as being oddly beautiful. Every movement the man made was sleek and athletic, reminding her of a big tomcat that had once taken up residence in the barn. She could have—and sometimes had—watched the animal for hours, taking pleasure in its fluid, feline power as it traversed beams, stalked mice, or curled up on an old saddle blanket for a nap. The cat would not, however, allow anyone to touch it. Joe Hart moved the same way, as if he had melted butter in his veins, and she found herself wondering if he would prove equally as untouchable.

In sharp contrast, Rand rode up stiff and grim-faced, his actions jerky and impatient, as if he resented every minute of his long morning. She hardly recognized the horse he had in tow at the end of a long rope. Dirty, wild-eyed, and sweat-streaked, Dusty trembled and shook, his long, still-coltish legs almost knocking together in fright and confusion.

"Dusty!" Maggie started down the steps toward him and would have fallen had her father not been there to catch her.

"Careful, Maggie! Not so fast."

Her father's hand steadied her until she reached the bottom of the steps, where she pushed free of him and limped toward the frightened two-year-old as fast as she could go. The colt stood in the center of a circle of mounted men, and Maggie had to maneuver around them to get to him. She held out her hand and spoke Dusty's name, but he shied away and pulled back on the double lassos around his neck.

The nearest one tightened cruelly against his soft white skin which was already rubbed raw and bleeding. The first rope was dallied around the horn of Rand's saddle, and a ranch hand named Bradley controlled the second. He, too, gave his rope a sharp jerk, fueling Maggie's horror and dismay.

"Rand! What have you done to him? Why, yesterday he was following me around like a puppy, and today he won't let me near him. I can't believe this was really necessary." She gestured helplessly at the ropes, grimacing at fresh cuts and abrasions on the spotted coat.

"All I did was catch him and bring him down like you said, Maggie. Damn fool hoss nearly killed me. Twice I almost drew my gun and put a bullet between his eyes. He's plumb crazy, no good for anything except buzzard meat."

"He's *not* crazy! He's just frightened. You've scared him half to death."

Maggie spoke soothingly to the colt, but Dusty reared and pawed the air in his agitation—until Rand and Bradley sidestepped their horses and hauled back on the ropes, half choking him to death.

"Stop! Oh, stop, Rand! He's fighting because he can't breathe!"

"Maggie, stay back or you're gonna get hurt!" Nathan grabbed Maggie's arm and pulled her out of harm's way. "For God's sake, put him in the breakin' pen, Rand. The rest of you boys help him."

Dusty fought the ropes all the way to the small circular corral where new horses were usually broken. Maggie watched with tear-blurred vision, clenched fists, and sheer anguish in her heart as the baby she had petted, brushed, played with, and taught to lead—the colt who had never demonstrated a mean bone in his body—was manhandled into the corral as if he were a dangerous old range rogue who had already killed a few men.

Once they got him there, the cowboys removed one of the lassos but left the other for Dusty to step on and choke himself. "Take off that rope, Rand!" she called out, but Rand waved a hand impatiently.

"Can't. We need something to catch him with. 'Sides, he needs to learn he can't get it off by hisself."

The cowboys hooted and hollered as the crazed colt galloped around the pen, snorting, bucking, then stepping on the rope and catching himself up short. Twice, he went down on his knees, and Maggie expected at any moment to hear the snap of a breaking bone. Finally, Dusty halted and stood dead center in the pen, panting and blowing, his whole body shaking with terror as he gazed wild-eyed at the cowboys.

Maggie was so upset she could not say another word. She didn't trust herself to speak. Rand had done exactly what she feared most—ruined everything she had achieved with Dusty thus far. Now the colt feared men and would never willingly put his trust in them. He may never trust *her* again. She would have to wait until he settled down before attempting to dress the raw wounds made by the ropes. She wished she could lasso Rand and teach him what it felt like to be choked and dragged around at the end of a rope.

Rand rode back to her and Nathan—and Joe Hart, whom she had all but forgotten—as if he were the conquering but much put-upon hero. "You wanted him, I got him, Maggie. He put up one hell of a fight. That's one more reason why you shouldn't be messin' with them wild hosses all by yerself. They could hurt you."

"Dusty would never hurt me—not before you hurt him anyway. He's always been as gentle as a baby."

"Gentle, hell! He's mean as the devil and wild as the Injuns. You'll never be able to trust him. Might as well kill him now and be done with it."

"We're going to break him and sell him," Maggie insisted. "If you don't want to do it, I'll do it myself or find someone who can."

"Breakin' him won't be the problem. It's *trustin'* him I'm worried about. I've told you before; them Palousies are just plain no good."

Maggie knew better than to argue, especially in front of the ranch hands who shared Rand's view. As did her father. She was the only one on the ranch who truly loved and believed in Appaloosas. They weren't much different from any other breed of horse—except they had certain admirable qualities unmatched by other breeds. Meanness wasn't in their natures; only cruelty could drive them to it. Her glance fell on Loser, and she couldn't resist one last parting sally.

"Our new ranch hand is riding an Appaloosa, and he obviously trusts him."

"Our new what?" Rand reined Cricket up short and stared at Joe Hart who, like her father, hadn't said a word since Rand rode up with Dusty.

Nathan coughed and cleared his throat. "Rand, this is Joe Hart. He rode in this morning lookin' for work. I hired him, no questions asked. If he don't work out, it'll be up to you to fire him."

"New hand, huh?" Rand slowly looked Joe Hart up and down, his mustache curling slightly, as if he didn't like what he saw. "Where'd you get the big Palousie?"

Joe Hart looked Rand straight in the eye and said in a calm even voice: "I found him out on the range in a snowdrift up to his neck. I needed a horse. So I dug him out and we've been together ever since."

Maggie noticed that Joe spoke faultless English, never drawl-ing or slurring his words as most cowboys did. She wondered about that; like his tack, his speech was almost too perfect.

"Know anything 'bout breakin' hosses?" Rand's gaze was almost hostile, while Joe's expression revealed nothing.

"Breaking horses is my specialty."

"Good. If you wanna work fer me, you can go on in there and break that one." Rand jerked his head in Dusty's direction.

Maggie sprang to life. "Rand, no! Dusty's had enough for one day. Pa . . ." She turned to Nathan. "Tell him no. Please, Papa. The colt's so tired he's likely to get hurt. He needs to rest, have some water and hay . . ."

To her surprise—and dismay—her father sided with Rand. "Now, Maggie, it's as good a time as any to teach the colt who's boss. A few bucks, and it'll all be over. The hard part'll be done."

"Nathan!" Maggie sputtered. "Oh, you men are so cruel!" She turned away in utter disgust and frustration, knowing there was nothing she could do to stop them.

"Go back to the house if you don't wanna watch, Maggie," Rand said. "This here will give us all a chance to see just what our new hand can do."

Rand eyed Joe Hart with a slow, challenging smirk. Breaking a green horse was a traditional test for new hands on the Broken Wheel. If a man could stay on the bucking animal and eventually subdue it, he won instant admiration and acceptance from his fellows. But if he gave up before the animal did—got bucked off repeatedly and couldn't wear the horse down—he wouldn't last long on the ranch. He'd be alternately hazed and shunned until he collected his pay and rode out of his own accord.

It was a harsh way to initiate a new hand, but every man present, excepting Joe Hart, had passed this test early on in his career; her father had always said he knew he could trust a fellow to do his job once he witnessed how much grit and determination he had in breaking a new horse to saddle. Because of the danger to both man and horse, Maggie never liked watching, but she usually couldn't resist—especially when the horse was one of her beloved Appaloosas.

"Whadda you say, Joe?" Nathan prodded. "You up to a little bronco bustin' this afternoon?"

Joe Hart never said a word. He merely nodded and dismounted his spotted horse with that same feline motion that made every other man in close proximity look as clumsy as a bear. He flung one rein over the pommel of the saddle and let the other hang down to the ground. Loser simply stood there as Joe removed his saddle then walked away, headed in the direction of the round pen. This was known as "ground tying," and the fact that the new man had trained his horse to it was a good indication of his ability.

Sensing an entertaining show in the offing, the men hurried to untack and release their horses to various corrals. Laughing and talking, they gathered around the pen, vying for the best positions. Maggie joined her father in pressing close to the skinned poles enclosing the corral where Dusty stood motionless, his eyes glinting with fear. Even Lena came out of the house wiping her hands on her apron and hurried over to Maggie.

"Gonna break the young one today already?" she asked. "Who's that handsome *hombre* going in there with him?"

"Joe Hart," Nathan grunted. "New fella' I hired this mornin'. Gonna show us what he can do."

"Oh, my," said Lena. "He's a good-lookin' fellow, that one, isn't he?"

Nathan gave her a quelling glance before turning his attention back to the pen while Maggie twisted her hands together in anxiety—more for Dusty than for Joe. She had a feeling Joe Hart could handle anything, but she wasn't so certain about her poor frightened colt. She knew from past experience that cowboys often chose to show off their prowess by spurring and whipping a green horse into a frenzy so he would buck harder and longer, discovering that no matter what he did, he couldn't dislodge his rider.

This usually resulted in a "well-broke" horse a man didn't have to be afraid to mount, but Maggie hated to see the beaten, defeated look in the animal's eyes. Horses always came in off the range with such a proud look about them; it was one of the things that made them so beautiful. Horses ridden by Indians never lost that look, but those tamed by white men did. It nearly shattered her heart to think of trusting little Dusty being subjected to such harsh treatment on top of what he had already endured today.

On impulse, she hurried over to Joe Hart just as he was slinging his saddle over the rails. "Mr. Hart . . ." She touched his arm to get his attention. The silver-gray eyes nailed her, and she almost lost her nerve to say anything. Swallowing hard, she blurted: "Please don't be unnecessarily cruel. He . . . he's just a baby. He's really very gentle."

He looked at her a long moment, then shrugged slightly, as if to say he knew that already, which he probably did if he had been watching her for long the day before up in the meadow. He would have seen her working with Dusty—leading him about without benefit of halter or lead rope.

Joe ducked under a split rail to get into the pen with Dusty. Just then Gusty Williams called out to him. "Hey, greener! You need any help gittin' that saddle on 'im? I'd be glad t' lend a hand."

"Nope." Joe never even thanked Gusty for the offer.

"Suit yerself then."

Gusty tilted back his soiled misshapen Stetson, the same hat he'd been wearing for almost as long as Maggie had known him which was practically all of her life. When he saw Maggie looking at him, he winked. She smiled tremulously at the thin, lanky, leather-faced old man with the tobacco-stained teeth and wispy gray hair and mustache. Dear Gusty! Some days his rheumatism was so bad he couldn't mount a horse, but he never complained—and he always had a wink or a smile for her. Today, it failed to lift her spirits.

She felt it keenly that she was a woman and therefore, in

the eyes of most men, her opinion didn't count. All the smiles and winks in the world couldn't overcome this basic inequality. Oh, how she wished she had had two good legs so she could ride and break her own horses!

She moved closer to the fence and held her breath, watching. Joe slowly walked to within several feet of the terrified colt, then stopped. He made no move to grab the dangling rope but began to talk quietly in a low sing-song tone, his words indistinct and unrecognizable.

"Want me to catch him for ya'?" One of the cowboys teased good-naturedly.

Joe never took his eyes off Dusty. He acted as if he didn't hear. Neither did he stare directly at the colt, Maggie noticed. Instead, he seemed preoccupied with the raw flesh wounds caused by the ropes. For several minutes, he merely stood there, murmuring soothingly, and gradually, Dusty's terror subsided. His ears pricked forward, and he watched Joe with less wariness.

Very casually, Joe patted and stroked his neck, then calmly removed the lasso and let it fall to the ground. Dusty lowered his head and sniffed the rope cautiously, and Joe idly scratched his withers and up along his crest, beneath his mane. Maggie knew how much Dusty—and indeed all young horses—loved to be scratched, and she whole-heartedly approved of Joe's actions. Not so Rand and the other cowboys.

"Hey, Hart!" Rand suddenly shouted. "You gonna play with him all day or ride him?"

The men guffawed, though Maggie could see nothing funny in the question. Joe ignored the lot of them. Using both his hands, he scratched and rubbed and stroked Dusty all over his still trembling body, searching out the itchiest spots and the ones that gave Dusty the most pleasure. Maggie herself knew that Dusty particularly liked to be scratched low on his chest and in the area between his forelegs.

Discovering that for himself, Joe spent extra time scratching him there. When he had finished, he picked up the fallen rope, again let Dusty smell it, and began rubbing him with the rope. At first, the colt tried to step away, but Joe followed, moving with a grace and speed that reinforced Maggie's initial impression of a cat or a mountain lion—or perhaps even an Indian.

The cowboys muttered among themselves, and even Nathan asked no one in particular: "What in hell does that greener think he's doin'?"

Joe never stopped to explain. His single-minded concentration on Dusty never wavered. He continued talking to the colt, and whatever he was saying sounded almost like a chant. It seemed to soothe Dusty who quickly lost his fear of the rope and allowed Joe to drape and drag it across various parts of his body without protest.

At last, Joe stepped back from Dusty, made a clucking sound, and lightly snapped the rope at him. Dusty leaped toward the fence, and Joe positioned himself at the colt's hip and proceeded to drive him forward into a trot. Dusty trotted around the perimeter of the fence. Whenever he stopped, Joe clucked and drove him forward with the rope.

Joe let him slow to a walk, but using his voice, body position, and the rope, kept him moving around the pen. Then he urged him into a lope. When Joe had him working at a walk, trot, and lope with a few simple commands, Maggie realized she was watching an expert. The rest of the audience realized it, too, because the cowboys had all fallen silent—even Rand and her father.

In an amazingly short time, Dusty was walking, trotting, loping, stopping, and reversing his direction at Joe's softly spoken or clucked commands. Whenever the colt stopped, turned inward to look at Joe, and seemed to be waiting for his next command, Joe lavishly praised him—going up to him and petting and scratching him in his favorite spots.

It was like watching two agile dancers anticipate one another's moves. Maggie had attended several dances and watched jealously as couples whirled around the barn, ranch house, or school room floor, knowing exactly what to do, where to put their hands and feet, how many steps to take, when to stop, and when to dip, whether it was a *quadrille* or a waltz. She had envied them so much, the same as she envied anyone who sat a horse as well as Rand and Joe. Now, she envied Joe his ability to persuade Dusty to do whatever he wanted—using little more than his voice and body.

Joe's catlike walk and sing-song chant were almost eerie. But he *couldn't* be an Indian, Maggie decided, not with those silver-gray eyes and the reddish cast in his dark brown hair and eyebrows. Neither did his features have that distinctive Indian look about them, nor was his skin any darker than Rand's and her father's. . . . Only in the way he moved and chanted did he arouse that ugly suspicion—and the fact that he rode an Appaloosa, of course.

She couldn't help wondering where he had learned all these tricks. By the time Joe turned around and walked over to his saddle, Dusty simply stood and watched him with mild curiosity and not a trace of fear. Joe returned with his saddle blanket, let Dusty smell it, then rubbed the blanket all over the colt's body, as he had done with the rope. He flapped the blanket at Dusty a few times, but Dusty seemed not to care, accepting everything Joe did with calm interest.

Joe settled the blanket into place on Dusty's back, left him standing there, and went back to retrieve his saddle. Dusty twisted his head around to look at the blanket but otherwise did not protest. Joe returned, showed him the saddle, and eased it gently down on Dusty's back. Dusty tensed and bunched his muscles as if he might buck.

"Now, we'll finally see some action," one of the men grumbled, but Joe petted and soothed Dusty until the youngster calmed down, then he loosely drew up the cinch.

Maggie expected Joe to immediately leap into the saddle; again, he surprised her. Backing off, he clucked to Dusty and set him to trotting around the corral as the colt had done before. The stirrups flapped against his sides, and he bucked once and broke into a gallop, but Joe soon persuaded him to forget about the saddle and concentrate on getting his reward—those wonderful pats and scratches.

"Shit. This is takin' forever," somebody muttered in disgust.

Actually, it was about an hour since Joe had first started working with Dusty. Yet Maggie understood the men's impatience. They wanted to see a contest between man and beast, a show of courage and bravery, a fight in which one side lost, and one side won. Instead, they were watching the slow nurturing and development of a partnership . . . and it was wildly exciting to Maggie.

Lena leaned over and whispered into Maggie's ear. "This is not what the men expected, is it? I better go back to the house and see to supper. Maybe he will ride the horse tomorrow, instead of today."

Even Lena did not understood what was happening here! Maggie wanted to grab her sleeve and tell her, but she doubted she could make Lena—or any of the other onlookers—understand, if they couldn't figure it out for themselves. Joe was winning Dusty's trust, building on the foundation Maggie herself had started. He was teaching the colt that there was nothing to fear in any of this; everything would be all right.

Fascinated, Maggie clung to the rail with her heart in her mouth and earnestly prayed that Joe Hart could successfully finish what he had started. All around the pen, the men were beginning to grumble. Nathan walked over to Rand, and the two men stood with their heads together, talking in low, disparaging tones.

Joe brought Dusty to a halt with a quiet "Whoa, boy," though Maggie suspected it was more his body language than his command that made Dusty stop and look at him, waiting for the praise he knew was coming. Joe gave it generously, petting him, scratching him, and then lifting his muzzle and breathing gently into his nostrils.

When he did that, the buzzing voices fell silent, except for Rand's. "You kissin' that horse now, Cowboy? I swear I never

seen the like. I've known men to grow attached to their mounts,
but this sure as hell beats all *I* ever witnessed."

The men burst out laughing, Nathan and Rand loudest of
all. Joe Hart didn't spare them a single glance. He walked
around Dusty's side, put his foot in the stirrup, rose, and leaned
his weight on Dusty's back. Dusty looked startled and twisted
around to see what Joe was doing, but otherwise didn't protest.

Joe took advantage of his elevated position to scratch Dusty
between the ears, and Maggie could see the colt exhale with
pleasure. All the tension went out of him. When he seemed no
longer concerned about the strange weight on his back, Joe
swung his leg over and seated himself lightly in the saddle.

The sudden silence was palpable.

"He's gonna boil over now and git the humps out, I reckon,"
came the grim prediction.

Joe gently squeezed Dusty's sides with his legs and using
the same clucking sounds and soothing chant he had used to
direct the colt while on the ground got him walking calmly
around the perimeter of the corral. With no bit or bridle, Joe
guided Dusty using only his legs and voice and letting him get
used to the feel of a man on his back.

Calm as could be, Dusty walked around the corral. When
Joe urged him into a trot, the cowboys let out a loud cheer,
and Maggie, thrilled with what she was seeing, joined them.
The noise startled Dusty into a lope, which Joe easily rode for
several laps around the enclosure. Dusty dug in his hindquarters
and stopped when Joe told him, "Whoa," and Joe patted and
stroked him with obvious pleasure.

For the first time, Joe lifted his head and appeared to notice
his audience. Spotting Rand and Nathan standing near the rail
a short distance away from Maggie, he rode over to them, and
brushed the brim of his hat in that cool, arrogant gesture that
seemed to be his habitual way of communicating with the world
at large, men—and women—he considered beneath him.

His meaning was unmistakable; the job was finished. He had
broken the green horse to saddle. Maggie had to restrain herself

from applauding. Joe Hart's performance had been magnificent. She waited for Rand and her father to acknowledge Joe's success and congratulate him, maybe even offer him his pick of any of the other ranch horses to make up his string—those horses he would ride when Loser needed a rest from his duties. It was the traditional way of rewarding a superior horseman . . . and to think he had done it without terrorizing or threatening Dusty in any way!

She had waited all her life for someone to come along and demonstrate a different, more humane way of doing things. She wanted to shout, "See? I told you so! I told you it could be done."

But it wasn't necessary to rub it in; Rand and her father had witnessed the whole thing from start to finish, just as she had. She didn't need to gloat. One look at Rand's face doused her elation and filled her with a sense of dread. Her fiancé was glaring at Joe Hart, his blond mustache almost quivering with affront.

"You ain't done yet, cowboy," Rand jealously growled. Pulling out his pistol, he cocked it and fired into the air over Joe's head.

Dusty leapt straight up into the air and came down on all four hooves with a bone-jarring thud that reverberated through the soles of Maggie's feet. Then he started bucking. Muscles bunched, back rounded, he pitched and bucked all around the pen. Joe had no choice but to grab mane and hang on with one hand, while he raised the other to balance himself. Clamping his long legs around Dusty's barrel, Joe rode the twisting, fear-maddened colt through a spectacular bucking fit that had the ranch hands leaning over the sides of the pen, shouting in excitement.

Their hoots, hollers, and hat-waving inflamed the colt further, and he fought desperately to free himself of the weight on his back. The harder he fought, the more Joe had to grip, and the more enraged Dusty became. Everything Joe had worked so patiently to achieve unraveled in the space of a few moments. Cooperation and persuasion were no longer possible; Dusty wanted Joe off his back, and Joe had to ride him into exhaustion.

Considering what Dusty had already been through that day, it wasn't long before exhaustion took its toll, and defeat set in. Tears streamed down Maggie's cheeks, as she watched the colt's bucks grow less animated, with longer spaces in between. His contortions subsided. His head drooped. His sides heaved. He tried to run and nearly fell on his face. He could barely walk, and his eyes were dazed. Maggie had never seen a more pitiful sight in her life.

"Now, you're finished," Rand drawled, jamming his pistol back in the holster at his side.

"I was finished before," Joe coldly informed him. He slid off Dusty's back and ran a finger down the colt's sweat-drenched hide. "This wasn't necessary."

"Yeah, it was," Rand disputed. "You hadda git the buck out of 'im."

"You mean I had to break his spirit." Joe's eyes were smoldering, but his face remained impassive. "If that's the way you want it, that's the way I'll do it, but you'd wind up with a better horse letting me do it my way."

Rand's shoulders stiffened. "On the Broken Wheel, we do things *my* way, or however Mr. Sterlin' here says, since he's the owner. If that sticks in yer craw, you had better ride on. Otherwise, you can stow yer gear in the bunkhouse and turn out yer horse with the others. You've earned yerself a job here."

For a moment, Maggie thought Joe Hart might refuse. She half-wished he would, just to register a protest. But he didn't. He turned back to Dusty, his expression hidden as he unsaddled the trembling animal quickly and efficiently.

Maggie hurriedly wiped away her tears with the palms of her hands, her feelings still in turmoil. She had to get a rein on her emotions before anyone noticed—or she faced Rand and told him what she thought of him *and* her father. As usual, Nathan seemed proud of the way Rand had handled things. Of course, Nathan believed in showing horses—and men—who was boss right from the start.

It was one of his favorite phrases, repeated often over the years to Rand: "Show 'em who's boss, son. Never let 'em doubt it. You wanna run a ranch someday, you gotta show 'em who's boss."

Well, Rand had shown them today—but what a fool he was to deny what he had witnessed with his own eyes! Upset and confused, so angry she wanted to weep or scream, Maggie turned from the corral and limped back to the house and privacy.

Six

"Why you so quiet, t'night, Maggie?" Nathan set down his coffee cup and scrutinized Maggie from across the dinner table.

"She jes' don't like how we treated her l'il spotted bronc, today." Pushing back his chair, Rand smoothed down his mustache with two fingers and eyed her belligerently. "She don't approve of our method of breakin' hosses."

Maggie lifted her chin. "That's right, I don't."

"That why you been sittin' there all night glarin' at us like you got a burr under yer saddle?" Her father flashed one of his charming grins, but Maggie wasn't about to be charmed by this sudden show of interest in her feelings.

Nathan had invited Rand to supper, and the two men had spent the entire evening eating, laughing, and talking as if she wasn't in the same room with them. It had taken all this time for them to notice she was upset; how could they be so blind and inconsiderate? Rand had known; of that, she was certain. He had been giving her dirty looks the whole time, daring her to confront him. Well, the moment had finally arrived. She could keep silent no longer.

"I think it was despicable what you did this afternoon, Rand." Maggie folded her arms across her bosom and met Rand's gaze with a steely-eyed one of her own.

"Despicable," he snorted. "There you go, usin' one of Old Widow Woman Gault's eight dollar words again. What in hell does 'despicable' mean?"

Old Widow Woman Gault was the genteel, Eastern-educated

school marm who had continued Maggie's education when all the resources of the one room schoolhouse in town were exhausted, and she had still refused to go East to her mother's family for the final polish her father had thought she should have.

"It means deserving to be despised. Joe Hart showed you a better way of doing things this afternoon, and instead of learning from it and graciously thanking him, you behaved abominably."

Rand flushed beneath the tan he had already acquired, though it was still early in the season. "Abominably. I s'pose that means the same as despicable."

"Very nearly."

"Now, Maggie," Nathan placated. "Rand only did what wuz necessary. You know he had t' show the new fellow who's . . ."

"Boss!" Maggie snapped. "That's the only thing that's important to you two, isn't it? Showing everyone who's boss."

She rose from the table and balancing on her hands, leaned over her uneaten meal. "Well, I wasn't impressed. If anything, I was disappointed and outraged. You risked a man's life firing off that pistol, today, Rand—and you risked my horse. What if Joe Hart had been thrown and trampled? What if Dusty had broken his leg bucking and twisting all over the place? Did you—for even one minute—consider the possible consequences of your behavior?"

Rand's eyes widened as if she were attacking him with a meat cleaver for no good reason. "Bloody hell! Hart wouldn't be any kind of a cowman if he couldn't sit through a few bucks. And if that damn Palousie broke his leg it wouldn't be much of a loss, now would it?"

"It would to me, Rand! It would to me—and that's the point. Doesn't it matter to you that I care about those horses? Couldn't you have refrained from proving your manhood this one time for *my* sake—because you know how I feel about Dusty?"

"Now, let's not git personal, Maggie," her father cautioned, holding up his hand. "Rand didn't do nothin' today that I wouldn't have done in his place. Yer only a woman; you don't understand these things."

"I understand plenty! And I'm so angry with the two of you that I . . . I . . ."

She clamped her jaw shut and moved away from the table. These were the two people in her life who ought to mean the most to her—and they did. Therefore, it greatly disturbed her that she could detest them as much as she did at that moment. They were two of a kind; she had no doubt of it now. Nathan had molded Rand in his own image. Why, they were both looking at her with the exact same expression! As if she were a foolish, muddle-headed female incapable of understanding the harsh realities of life. But she understood—oh, yes, she did!

Rand and Nathan didn't care who or what they hurt so long as they defended their precious manhoods. They would persist in all kinds of cruelties in an effort to prove they were *men.* Rand simply couldn't abide the thought that Joe Hart knew something about breaking horses that he didn't—and her father was no better. She was heartily sick of both of them. Tears of rage and frustration stung her eyes, making her even angrier, because she had resolved to shed no more of them.

"Maggie, honey, yer gittin' all riled over nothin'." Nathan pushed back his chair and stood. "Come back here and let's talk this out. Why, one minute yer defendin' Rand 'cuz I'm hirin' men behind his back, and the next, yer flouncin' yer petticoats an' screamin' at us just 'cuz he did whut he needed t' do t' keep the respect of the fellows who work for him. How's a man t' make sense of all that?"

"Leave her go," Rand said. "When she gets riled, there's jus' no talkin' to her. I know, I've tried. She don't know how t' be reasonable."

That stopped Maggie in her tracks. Slowly, she returned to the table. "Reasonable!"

"Yes, reasonable." Rand glowered at her. "Is it reasonable t' want t' wait 'til Christmas t' git married? Or t' add on t' the house when there's plenty of room for us just the way it is? I don't call *that* reasonable."

"Who said anything about addin' onto the house?" Nathan demanded. "You all told me you wanted t' git married at Christmas, which seems like a hell of a long time t' wait, but then you never mentioned nothin' about addin' onto the house first."

Maggie shot Rand a look that told him in no uncertain terms what she thought of him for bringing up the subject now. She had hoped to broach it in her own way in her own good time. Now that he had blurted it out like this, she had no choice but to try and explain.

"I want our own living area, Pa, so I can be a proper wife, not merely a daughter. Rand and I will be perfectly happy to share the house with you, but we'll want our privacy. At least, I had *assumed* my new husband would want to be alone with me. I might have been mistaken; it appears he'd much rather spend his time with you than me."

"Maggie . . ." Rand growled. "Shut yer mouth, will ya'? Yer tongue's hangin' out a foot an' forty inches."

"The hell you say!" her father exclaimed. "Don't that beat all! Would it suit you, Maggie girl, if I just died off before my time so's you two could have the whole damn house to yerselves then?"

"I *knew* he'd feel this way," Rand muttered. "I knew addin' onto the house was a bad idea first time I heard it."

If you know so much, then why don't you know how I feel? Maggie silently wondered. *Why don't you care?*

"Pa . . . I don't want the whole house. I just want one small part of it to be our own—a place we've designed and decorated to suit our own tastes. A place where Rand and I can learn to be husband and wife without you interfering like you're doing now."

"*Interferin'!*"

Oh, she was botching this badly. Hurting him as she had never meant to do. But now that she had said it, she knew it was true. She and Rand had so many things to settle between

them, and they could never do it as long as her father kept
taking Rand's side and/or adding his own opinion.

"Yes, interfering. I can't even fight with Rand without you
butting in."

"You wanna fight? Be my guest. Go ahead and holler at
each other t' yer heart's content. I'll jus' sit here calm as a horse
trough an' stay outta it. . . . No, on second thought, I'm goin'
t' bed." Nathan knocked over the chair in his haste to leave the
table and the room. He stomped past her, but paused in the
doorway. "Jus' fer the record, it ain't necessary t' knock out
walls and spend money jus' so's you can be alone with Rand.
All you gotta do is say the word, and I'll make myself good
and scarce. I kin bunk down in the barn, if need be."

"Pa, I didn't mean. . . . You're *determined* to take this the
wrong way, aren't you?"

"What I'm determined to do is git some sleep. But before
I go, I wanna give you some advice, Maggie, and I don't care
if you do call it interferin'. It's plumb foolish t' put this weddin'
off until Christmas. I didn't say nothin' when you first told me,
'cuz I wuz jus' happy you'd finally set the date . . . but I'm
sayin' it now. Marry Rand, and be done with it. Quit stallin'.
He's been patient long enough. Ya' don't realize what yer puttin'
him through. . . ."

"Why don't you ever take *my* side, Pa ? Why do you always
take *his?*"

" 'Cuz he's a man, and I understand 'im, which is more'n I
can say fer you, Maggie! I think the world and all of you both,
and I jus' want you t' be happy—so I'm gittin' out of here. Go
ahead and have at it. But don't be so loud you keep me awake.
G'night, Rand . . . Maggie. Damn it all, maybe you *should*
have yer own part of the house."

Shaking his head, Nathan departed the room, leaving Maggie
alone with Rand. At first, she wouldn't look at him; the pain
was too raw. So she began gathering up the dirty dishes and
cutlery. She had told Lena she'd clean up the mess from supper.
Pleading a headache, Lena had gone to bed early.

"You done it, Maggie. You done it good," Rand finally ground out. "You had t' make him feel like we're shovin' him out of his own nest, now didn't ya'?"

"It's *my* house, too. At least, I thought it was." She picked up a plate and seriously considered breaking it over Rand's thick head. "Anyway, you're the one who brought up the subject. This wasn't the way I had planned on telling him."

"Wouldn't have made no difference how you told him. He still woulda been hurt."

"How sensitive you are when it comes to my father!"

Rand didn't pick up on the sarcasm in her tone. He only sighed deeply. "He's taken the place of my own Pa. Fact is, I'm closer t' him than I was t' my own flesh an' blood. All my Pa ever did was shout at me and tell me how dumb I was. It was Nathan who taught me what I could do and gave me the courage to go ahead and do it."

Rand's honest admiration of her father—which bordered on hero worship—took the edge off Maggie's resentment. "You love him very much, don't you?" she asked softly, touched by Rand's devotion to her father and the sudden softness in his face.

He had been looking in the direction Nathan had gone, but now his gaze cut back to her, and his eyes hardened. "More'n you do, I sometimes think."

The remark jolted her. "No, not more than me. Pa and I don't see eye to eye on everything, but that's got nothing to do with how I feel about him."

Rand thought about that for a moment, and a hesitant grin hovered about his mustache. "Does that mean there might be a chance fer us, after all?"

By now, the anger had all drained out of her, and Maggie was growing weary. She wished Rand would leave. "Maybe. If you stop mistreating my horses."

Irritation rekindled in his eyes. "I don't mistreat 'em. I jus' . . ."

"No, don't say it. I *know* what you're going to say. You just show 'em who's boss. Let's drop it, Rand, shall we? At least for tonight. I'm too tired to argue anymore."

He jumped to his feet, his relief evident. "Yeah, it's gittin' kind of late. I'm ready t' turn in myself."

He came around the table toward her, but since her hands were full of dirty dishes, he couldn't do much but give her a peck on the cheek. "See you t'morrow, Maggie."

She recoiled from the affectionate gesture, and to her relief, he looked eager to leave. Glad he was going, she nonetheless couldn't help wondering why he thought she was too fragile to drive out alone, handle a gun, or take a moonlight stroll, but was strong enough to carry out all the dirty dishes by herself, fill the cast iron sink with water, wash, dry, and put everything away without anyone's help.

Come to think of it, her father never questioned her ability to perform domestic chores either. He probably figured she had Lena to do the heavy things—which she did, but it would still be nice if once in a while he offered his assistance when Lena retired early. . . . *Men.* They were clearly impossible.

"Goodnight, Rand," she bade him as he took his leave, his spurs jangling.

She finished cleaning up the dining room and kitchen, then laid out the wood for the morning's fire in the huge wood stove, so that Lena wouldn't have to do it in the morning. She was physically exhausted by the time she was done, but not sleepy. She had too much to think about—Rand, Nathan, the wedding plans . . . and Dusty.

Oh, how she wished she could learn to do what Joe Hart had done today! She wouldn't dare climb on a horse's back— wouldn't know what to do if she got there—but she might be able to train the animal to the point where a man could safely mount it. However, she would still need someone's cooperation; she'd have to have someone lift the saddle, for example.

The only man with the expertise as well as the inclination to train horses kindly was Joe Hart. But she doubted he'd be willing to assist her. She swept the floor while she thought about him. The way he had worked Dusty suggested he could read a horse's mind! She had never seen anything like it. She relived the thrill of the moment while she opened the back door and swept dust out onto the porch.

It had been a true pleasure to watch him: the graceful, self-assured way he moved, the manner in which he anticipated every movement of Dusty's, the generosity with which he rewarded the colt for every right response, even the small uncertain ones. Yes, it had been like watching two people dance—two very good dancers, or one good one and one just learning.

She clutched the broom to her chest as if it were a dance partner and laughed softly to herself; how fanciful to equate dancing with what Joe Hart had done with Dusty! People would say she was moonstruck if they knew what she was thinking. The porch was dark and shadowed, but the yard beyond was bright with moonlight, silvering the corrals and outbuildings, outlining the silhouettes of the animals within the fenced enclosures.

Had anyone thought to give Dusty hay and water—or had he been left in the breaking pen, sweaty, dirty, and thirsty, thoroughly miserable and alone? Since he was an Appaloosa, he might very well have been neglected. She propped the broom against the side of the house and limped down the back steps to go check on him. She wouldn't put it past Rand to further punish the colt by deliberately ignoring him until morning. There was no water trough in that particular corral, she remembered.

On her way to the pen, she collected a pail of water and slowly made her way around the side of a storage shed. Halfway there, she set down the heavy pail which sloshed water on her built-up shoe and the hem of her skirt. She leaned against the side of the building and rested a moment in the dark shadow of the overhang . . . and that was when she noticed that Dusty was not alone.

A man was with him, and Maggie had no trouble identifying him. Only one person in the world exhibited such casual poise

and moved with such feline grace. Her heart pounded errati-
cally at the thought of spying upon Joe Hart, but she flattened
herself against the shed wall and watched him without making
her presence known.

A huge wooden bucket stood at Joe's feet. Dusty did not
seem too interested in it, so Maggie had to assume that the colt
had already drunk his fill. Now, Joe was washing the cuts and
abrasions on the colt's neck and body. He bent down, rinsed a
cloth in the bucket, and proceeded to gently clean Dusty's
wounds.

When the colt stepped away, Joe followed, crooning softly
and reassuring him. Occasionally, he simply stroked and
scratched Dusty, his voice a soothing murmur. Maggie edged
closer. The warm spring breeze carried bits and snatches of
what he was saying, and she had to concentrate hard to make
sense of the flow of words.

"Easy, my friend. . . . Don't be afraid. I won't hurt you. . . .
Easy now, young one. Don't hold it against me, what happened
today. It was wrong what we did to you, but you must put it
out of your mind now. I'm your friend. . . . You can trust me."

As Dusty nuzzled Joe's sleeve, Maggie heard him say quite
clearly: "That's it. Learn my scent. I'm your master, but I will
not abuse you."

A furry body suddenly curved itself around Maggie's ankle,
and she inadvertently gasped in surprise. It was only one of
the barn cats, but the small sound was enough to alert Joe Hart
to her presence. He glanced in her direction, and she froze,
waiting for him to discover her. But he did not call out and
soon went back to washing Dusty's cuts—only this time, silently. . . . Had he seen her or not?

She could not be certain. Probably not, she decided, for she
stood in dark shadow and he in bright moonlight. She relaxed
somewhat as Joe calmly continued grooming and tending
Dusty and did not look her way again. When he finished, he
effortlessly swung a leg over Dusty's back and mounted him

in a single smooth motion. Then, without saddle or bridle, he
rode Dusty around the ring.

The colt weaved a bit, not steering easily, but Joe managed
to make him walk, trot, and lope without mishap. Maggie could
only stare and marvel. Dusty's legs were Joe's legs, so well did
the lithe body of the man blend into the horse. Joe had become
a centaur—half-man, half-horse—cavorting in the moonlight.
Maggie had seen an illustration of such an exotic creature in
one of Old Widow Woman Gault's many books, and she had
never forgotten it. If only a horse *could* replace the less agile,
imperfect legs of a human!

She longed to step out of the shadows and question Joe about
his prowess and unusual methods—but she didn't dare. She
yearned to ask him to teach her how to do what he did, but
she knew it was a fool's dream, and he would never consent.
Every time his gaze had met hers during their short acquaintance, she had read scorn and dislike in those brilliant gray
eyes. Like an untamed horse, he was wary and distrustful; it
would be no easy task to befriend a reticent wild creature like
Joe Hart.

He *must* be an Indian, she thought. Who else could do what
he does with a horse? Who else would lavish attention on Appaloosas, hated symbols of Indian terror and aggression? But
if he *was* an Indian, why did she feel such empathy for him . . .
such attraction?

She could never hate Indian horses, but she hated Indians.
More accurately, she feared them. Indians had caused her
mother's death and her own impairment. They had killed her
father's brother and Rand's father and brother. She felt no pity
for what had become of them; they deserved it—and she hoped
she would never come face to face with one again in her lifetime.

If they were ever permitted to leave the reservation, she
wouldn't be able to sleep at night. Her feelings lacked the
white-hot intensity of Rand's and her father's, but in her own
quiet way, she hated them nonetheless. Indians had made her

what she was today—a cripple struggling to live her own life, reduced to fighting even those she loved.

Whether Joe Hart was an Indian or not, she had no business admiring him in the moonlight. Feeling guilty, she left the pail where it was and silently inched her way back along the wall toward the house.

Joe brought the two-year-old colt to a halt, patted his neck, and slid off. Darting a glance in the direction of the shed, he saw that Maggie Sterling was in full retreat. Good. She wasn't going to approach him. He wouldn't have to talk to her. She must be as uneasy about him as he was about her.

He wanted no involvement with Maggie Sterling, beautiful or not, winsome or not, gentle and goodhearted or not, unhappy or not. She was going to marry the ranch foreman, and the sooner she did so, the better. He couldn't wait for the wedding to take place. Rand Johnson didn't deserve her, but she had chosen him. As whites were fond of saying, she had made her bed, now she must lie in it.

He had his own bed to make, and he hadn't started out very well. Already, he and the ranch foreman were enemies. He should have put on the show everyone had been expecting, instead of gentling the colt using the methods he had learned from long practice, employing a combination of Indian lore and his own instincts about horses.

It had been a calculated mistake. Knowing the risks involved, he had done it anyway, largely because it galled him to break an Appaloosa the white man's way. The colt was too fine a specimen of his breed to be ruined; he deserved a chance to learn to enjoy his work and form a partnership with man. Despite Joe's best intentions, much damage had been done. Fortunately, he thought he could undo it.

Scratching the colt's face, he murmured, "There. Feel better now? It's really not so bad to submit, young one. Soon the cuts and scratches will heal, and you will forget they ever happened."

He hoped it was true, but doubted it. Young horses rarely forgot their early training; it set the tone for their entire relationship with humans.

"If they won't let me work with you during the day, I'll come see you at night," he promised. "I'll turn you into a wonderful mount, the sort a man can trust. You deserve that much, my brother."

That's what the colt really was—his brother, just as Loser was his brother. He and these spotted horses were one in spirit, and one day, he would own a whole herd of them. He would not let the breed die out as the Indian was dying.

"I will call you Windstorm," he whispered. "In another year when you have reached your full growth, you will run like the wind and carry me with you. No one will be able to catch us, and together, we shall fly over the earth."

He had heard Maggie Sterling call the colt Dusty, but it wasn't an Indian name and was therefore unacceptable. "Heart-of-the-Stallion speaks to you now," he continued, so low that none but the horse could possibly hear him. "We are brothers, you and I. You must remember that and trust I will never hurt you, no matter what I must do to keep my place here."

With a last pat on the colt's withers, he picked up his bucket and left the pen. Windstorm whinnied plaintively and trotted up to the barrier. Joe tossed him some hay he had already taken from a storage shed. Were it not for him—and Maggie Sterling—the colt would have gone without food and water this night. That must have been her purpose in coming out to the corral at this late hour; she alone of everyone on the ranch possessed compassion.

He regretted that he could not get to know her better, but he had to think of his future. Today, he had made an enemy, but had also proven his abilities. By summer's end, he'd be considered a top hand, and it would be the opportune time to ask Nathan Sterling to sell a few head of his cattle—and some of his spotted horses. Joe intended to buy as many animals as he could persuade Nathan to sell. He would convince the man to let him run his stock among the ranch herds until such time as he could look for land and buy his own place.

Every month until then, he would add his wages to the stash of gold buried up in the mountains near the meadow where he had first seen Maggie. Nathan paid fairly, and according to what Joe had overheard in the bunkhouse, he also provided bonuses and special incentives at various times of the year. The thought of beating Rand at cutting brought a grim smile to Joe's lips.

If he couldn't bury a tomahawk in the foreman's head and relieve him of his blond hair, which would make a fine trophy, he could at least shame and embarrass him in front of his comrades—and Maggie—by proving who was the better man. And who had the best horse.

Satisfied with his night's work, Joe sought the meager comfort of his hard bunk. No one heard him enter the bunkhouse; the rest of the ranch hands were fast asleep, their snores loud enough to wake a hibernating bear. Stripping off his boots, hat, and shirt, Joe slipped into his bed like a shadow. Expecting sleep to overtake him at once, he closed his eyes . . . only to have an image appear in his head.

Maggie Sterling dominated his thoughts like a pesky fly that would not go away no matter how much he swatted at it. He pictured himself running his fingers through her fine-spun, honey-colored hair. What would it feel like—that beautiful hair spilling through his fingers and across his naked chest?

What was the texture of her skin? It reminded him of rose petals and must certainly feel as soft to the touch. He had no difficulty imagining the warmth and softness of her breasts— they would be so white! So smooth and tender. And her scent. Inhaling deeply, he fancied he could detect her sweet woman smell in the air around him, blocking out the odor of male sweat, leather, and unwashed feet. White men weren't too particular about bathing, but Joe clung to his Indian heritage by always rising before anyone else and washing in the horse trough if that was all he could find.

When out riding the range, he took advantage of every available stream or river for a quick, bracing plunge into the frigid waters in the hope of washing away his own stench and perhaps even the taint of his deceptions. . . . What would Maggie Sterling think if she knew that he was Indian? Or half-Indian, which amounted to the same thing.

He had noted the admiration in her eyes for his riding skills and could not have misread her approval of his training methods. Up in the mountain meadow, he had watched her unknowingly provide the basis for Windstorm's education. She was partly the reason why Windstorm had responded as well as he had today—before Rand Johnson shot off his pistol.

The colt had been easy to manage because Maggie had already taught him that humans could provide kindness, companionship, and pleasure. It would have taken him much longer to win the colt's trust had Maggie not worked with him beforehand. Joe wondered if she knew that or had guessed it. From what he had witnessed, she had the same instinctive ability to communicate with horses as he had himself. Living so close to nature, Indians were often born with the ability. Only rarely had Joe witnessed it in a white person.

To know that Maggie shared his feelings for horses as unique and wonderful creatures made him feel close to her—but it was a closeness that scared him. He didn't want to feel close to a white woman, especially not the daughter of Nathan Sterling, the man he had marked as holding the keys to his dream. Nor could he forget that she was going to marry his enemy, a man he already hated.

He drew another deep breath and concentrated on banishing her from his thoughts. Finally, he slept, but his dreams were worse than his wakeful musings. Maggie Sterling came running toward him across a mountain meadow and threw herself into his arms . . . strangely, she wasn't limping but was healthy and agile as a young doe. Laughing joyously, she called his name:

not Joe or Josef, but Heart-of-the-Stallion. She *knew* his real name, and it didn't bother her. Her lovely hazel eyes were alight with love and happiness. She didn't care that he was Indian; she loved him anyway and wanted only to be with him.

In the meadow in the midst of the spotted horses, they embraced, and his heart swelled to bursting. He claimed the right to kiss and caress her, to fill his hands with her shining hair, and he tumbled her backward into the tall bunchgrass and took her beneath the burning sun.

Except he didn't quite take her. Before he could complete the act, he awoke drenched in sweat and shivering at the same time. After that, he could not go back to sleep. Instead, he lay awake staring at the beams of the bunkhouse in the darkness until dawn revealed the grain of the whorled and knotted wood.

Seven

Maggie barely saw Joe Hart during the next two weeks. Rand kept him and all the other cowboys busy rounding up the cattle for the spring branding. The men rode out before dawn and returned at dusk or later. Rand himself was so worn out by then that Maggie didn't see much of him either.

This was the busiest time of year on the Broken Wheel, and everyone worked long hours. The cattle had wintered in a huge box canyon protected from the fierce winds and deep snows that usually bypassed the Idaho Panhandle and smote Montana instead. Now they had to be relocated to summer pasture and the nourishing bunchgrass that grew in broad stretches cradled by the Bitterroot mountains that Maggie so loved.

Where no natural barriers existed, barbed-wire fence served to confine the animals, and it was to one such level plain that the cowboys were herding the cattle in preparation for the branding of new calves which would soon take place. Maggie and Lena were laying in huge stores of food and baking for the event; Will Tatter, who had worked on the ranch almost as long as Gusty Williams, would do much of the actual cooking once they got to the site, but as usual, the two women had taken it upon themselves to provide mounds of tortillas, Lena's specialty, as well as pies, breads, and cakes, which would be much appreciated by the hungry cowboys.

The Broken Wheel's good food was one reason why the ranch was able to attract and retain the best cowhands in the region. Beans, bacon, and coffee were just the beginnings of a meal served at the Broken Wheel. Besides all the planning and effort that went into preparing for this event, Maggie had to keep abreast of normal chores and also begin planning for the expansion of the ranch house. Her father had not yet given his approval, nor indeed discussed it further with her, but she was sure she could bring him around eventually—and Rand, too, while she was at it.

She relished the work for it kept her from thinking too much about Joe Hart. From her bedroom window, she had several times watched him work Dusty in the middle of the night, but she had not spoken a word to him or approached him in daylight. She had managed to convince herself that she felt no particular attraction to him, other than admiring his expertise and dedication to horses.

But all that changed one evening when she came around the side of the barn suddenly, looking for Rand and her father, and nearly ran into Joe. With a bunch of lariats over his shoulder, he stood talking to a young ranch hand named Curt Holloway. Seeing her, Curt blushed, tipped his hat, and mumbled: "Evenin', Miz Sterlin'."

"Evening, Mr. Holloway . . . Mr. Hart." Maggie reached out a hand to steady herself against the barn wall. She was suddenly breathless, and butterflies were swooping in her stomach. It required a great effort of will to act as if everything were normal.

"See y'all later, Joe." Curt nodded toward Joe and hurried off, almost tripping over his long spurs in his haste to flee.

The poor young man always turned red as a sunset whenever she appeared. Maggie guessed he had had little opportunity to talk to girls and therefore didn't know what to say to her. Nor was he the only cowboy on the Broken Wheel who was terribly shy around women; it seemed to be a hazard of the profession.

Joe would have walked away, too, without so much as a nod in her direction, but Maggie impulsively intercepted him. "Mr. Hart?"

He turned to look at her, and she was struck by how much

bigger he seemed up close. She had to tilt back her head to meet his silver-eyed gaze. Out of the corner of her eye, she noted the wideness of his shoulders and the play of muscle beneath the fabric of his shirt, which was open part way down his chest. Slim-waisted and narrow-hipped, he wore his brown leather chaps and fringed vest as if they were a second skin. The pleasant odor of leather and man drifted to her. . . . Unlike many cowboys, he did not smell rank, though sweat sheened his jaw and what she could see of his forehead beneath his black Stetson. He did not say a word, but his brows lifted in inquiry. For the life of her, Maggie could not remember what she had been going to say or why she had dared stop him.

Oh, yes . . . it came back to her in a rush. She wanted to ask him about his training methods. "Mr. Hart . . . I . . . um . . . where did you learn to break horses the way you broke Dusty?"

He did not immediately answer, but the directness of his gaze scorched her insides. "Here and there," he offered laconically.

Cowboys were notorious for being noncommunicative and revealing little about their pasts—but this was ridiculous. She had not meant to pry, only to learn.

"I . . . I admire the way you handled Dusty before Rand shot off that pistol. I've been meaning to tell you that. Your way of breaking horses is a great improvement over how it's usually done, and I would like to learn more about it."

The silver-gray eyes glinted. "Planning to break some horses, Miss Sterling?"

His mocking tone raised the fine hairs on the back of her neck. "If I weren't lame, I would be, yes. I'd train all my own horses."

He failed to looked chagrined, as she had intended he should be. "There's no reason why you *can't* train them yourself." He scanned her slowly from head to foot. "If you can walk, you can ride."

She was shocked to the core. "I . . . I can't ride. I've never even tried it. I . . . I have a bad leg."

She couldn't believe he hadn't noticed. Maybe he really was mocking her—for her disability as well as her boldness in approaching him. Well, what had she expected—that he would offer to teach her all he knew? Or to break all her horses from now on? Rand and her father would have to agree to that, and she knew they never would. He must know it, too.

"I've been told how things are done here on the Broken Wheel," he clipped out. "So that's the way I'll do them from now on. If you don't intend to train the green ones yourself, there's nothing I can do or say to help you. Good afternoon, Miss Sterling."

He left her leaning against the barn wall and feeling like a fool. She wanted to shout that she had watched him working with Dusty in the moonlight, so she knew he could not be as rude and unfeeling as he seemed; it was just that his good will did not extend to humans. Maybe it simply did not extend to her. Why he should dislike her so much she could not fathom; it made no sense. Yet he clearly did. He had refused to talk to her that first day up in the high pasture, and he was *still* refusing. Maybe he hated *all* women, not just her.

Early the next morning, everyone on the ranch set out for the high pasture where the branding was to take place. Maggie had assumed that either she or Will Tatter was to drive the chuck wagon, but to her surprise and annoyance, Rand ordered Joe to tie Loser to the back end and assume the lowly task.

Maggie was already sitting in the driver's seat, with Lena beside her, and she was not about to move over to let Joe take her place. Joe himself showed no displeasure at the assignment, though it was the sort of thing most of the hands would have protested. Her own father would never condescend to drive a wagon instead of riding a horse; Will himself, with his creaking bones, would have grumbled. . . . Why had Rand picked Joe for the unwanted position?

One glance at Rand's face told Maggie the reason: Rand meant it as a deliberate insult, a less than subtle way of reminding Joe "who was boss" and that he was still at the very bottom of the pecking order of the cowhands. Driving the chuck wagon—or acting as wrangler, the man who looked after the horses on a roundup—branded a man as being too old, too young, too inept to sit his horse for so many long hours or to handle the more strenuous, dangerous tasks.

Maggie suddenly had no doubt that Joe would also be serving as wrangler during this outing. Rand had probably been assigning him the lowest, dirtiest jobs all along. However, Joe Hart showed no resentment—no emotion whatsoever—as he tied Loser behind the wagon, came around the side, and with his usual agility, climbed up beside her.

Maggie's own protests died on her lips as she moved over to make room for him and handed him the reins to the team of placid horses, which consisted of Preacher and another steady old gelding. Just then, her father rode up beside the wagon.

"Got everythin', ladies? We'll be up there for damn near a week you know, by the time we get everything done."

"We are ready, señor," Lena answered saucily. "Do not worry. Maggie and I have thought of everything."

Nathan grinned and tipped his hat at the plump little woman in her bright red skirt, white blouse, and lacy black shawl. She looked like she was headed for church instead of a grueling week out on the range.

"I hope so, Lena, or I jus' might have t' fire you."

"Fire me! Nonsense! You could not get along without me, señor, and you know it."

The two exchanged fond glances. Nathan then loped off to join Rand who was already riding out, leaving them to follow in a cloud of dust.

The last two weeks had been both drier and warmer than usual, presaging an early, hot summer. Maggie felt overdressed in her sturdy black woolen skirt with its matching ruffled sunbonnet—or perhaps her sudden sense of sweltering heat derived from Joe Hart's nearness. He neither looked at her nor spoke to her, but she was excruciatingly aware of his muscular thigh

so close to hers and his hands holding the lines of the team as
he expertly guided the horses around the rough spots in the
trail. He had very nice hands—with strong, graceful fingers
and neat, clean nails, another thing that set him apart from
other cowboys.

Rand always had grime under his fingernails, and her father
often did, too, but not Joe Hart. He kept his hands and nails
as clean as his gear. They rode in silence for a long while, the
rumble of the wagon wheels making conversation difficult anyway.

Maggie tried to take pleasure in the bright sunshine, blue
sky, and general fecundity of the land during this season—
knowing that as the year progressed, the grass would turn sear
and golden, the flowers would wither on their stems, and even
the trees would lose their fresh, vivid greenness. She tried hard
not to think about Joe Hart and wonder where he had come
from, how he had learned what he knew, and why he was so
unfriendly.

The harder she tried not to think about him, the more she
thought. She couldn't stop watching his hands and feeling the
heat radiate from his body. He made her feel very small sitting
next to him on the wagon seat. If Rand had any idea how much
Joe Hart disturbed her peace of mind, he would never have
ordered Joe to spend so many hours sitting beside her in this
blasted chuck wagon.

She wondered if Joe Hart had ever loved a woman or grown
close to one; she could not imagine any female in the place of
his mother. Could not picture him hugging and kissing his
mother, or letting her ruffle his hair, as mothers were wont to
do with their sons. She could not even picture Joe Hart smiling!
His mouth probably had no experience with that activity, since
all he ever did was scowl or wear that infuriating expressionless
mask—though she did recall a time or two when a mocking
grin had curved his lips.

If he would consent to give her lessons in horse training,
maybe she could teach him how to smile in exchange. She

grinned at the thought and was startled when Lena suddenly asked: "What is so funny, *Señorita* Maggie?"

"What? Oh, nothing." Maggie sat a little straighter on the uncomfortable seat. "I . . . I was just thinking, that's all."

"I wish I knew how to ride a horse." Lena waved her hand in front of her face, then lifted the edge of her shawl to wipe her mouth. "All this dust is making my throat dry and my eyes water. It would probably be much more comfortable in a saddle than sitting up here on this hard bench. Is that not true, *Señor* Hart?"

Maggie peeped around the ruffle of her bonnet to see if Joe Hart had heard the question. She found the proximity of his silver-gray eyes disconcerting. "That's true, " he responded. "But only after you get accustomed to the saddle. The more you ride, the more comfortable it becomes."

Three whole sentences! He had actually uttered three sentences—more than was necessary to answer the question. "How long must one ride before it becomes comfortable?" Maggie demanded, fastening her gaze on the distant horizon.

"Everyday," he said. "All day." He expertly maneuvered the team around some deep ruts in the trail. "Do that for a few weeks, and you'll soon feel right at home on a horse."

"Madre de Dios! Then I do not want to learn if it takes that long. I would have no time to get my work done." Lena rearranged her shawl and sighed. "At what age did you start riding horses, *Señor* Hart?"

Joe Hart stared fixedly at Preacher's ears as if they possessed some unusual fascination. "Can't remember."

"Was it your Papa who taught you?" she persisted.

"No."

"Who then, *Señor?* An uncle or a brother, perhaps?"

"Don't know."

"Where does your family come from?" Lena fired off her questions with relentless curiosity, and Joe Hart avoided revealing anything about himself with equally relentless determination.

"Can't say for certain."

"But everyone must know where they come from." Lena gave Maggie a puzzled look.

"Not everyone," Joe Hart said.

Maggie shrugged her shoulders in answer to Lena's unasked question: Why wouldn't Joe Hart tell them anything about his past?

"Mr. Hart obviously has his secrets, Lena," she informed her friend. "I doubt he appreciates you prying."

"I am not prying!" Lena denied. "I am just . . . just making conversation. Is that not how you say it?"

"But Mr. Hart doesn't wish to be friendly and make conversation. Do you, Mr. Hart?"

Joe Hart never took his eyes from the trail ahead. "I like women who know how to be quiet and respect a man's privacy."

Lena's black eyes widened. "My, but you are a difficult *hombre,* are you not?"

"Some people say so," Joe Hart agreed.

A silence fell after that, and it proved to be a long, tiring day with no one speaking all the way to the pasture where the cattle were gathered for the branding. Maggie grew sleepy from the constant jolting and swaying, most of it uphill, but she struggled not to doze off. It would be thoroughly humiliating to accidentally lean against Joe Hart's broad shoulder.

But Lena dozed. And she leaned heavily against Maggie, her breathing deep and slumberous. Maggie's muscles began to ache from the strain of holding her up. She did not blame Lena for the discomfort; the fault was all Joe Hart's. This could have been a pleasant trip, a chance for all of them to become friends. Joe's silent animosity made it a nightmare.

By the time they arrived on the flat level plain hemmed by the mountains and a fork of the Clearwater—the place where the cattle had been herded and prevented from wandering by judiciously placed barbed wire—Maggie was exhausted and in need of some privacy. She and Lena got down from the wagon and immediately sought relief from overfull bladders behind a screen of young willow trees growing along the river.

By the time the two women walked back to the wagon, Joe Hart had disappeared, and Will and Gusty were setting up camp. Plans called for the two women to sleep under the wagon in good weather and inside if rain threatened. They hurriedly pitched in to help fix supper and empty the wagon of bedrolls and blankets, because it was already late in the day, and darkness would soon be upon them.

Maggie saw Joe setting up the remuda, driving the horses into a rope corral where there was plenty of grass, and she knew that indeed, he had been given the job of wrangler. Despite the lack of prestige, he was an excellent choice, she thought, for he would take good care of his charges. And as everyone knew, without the use of the horses, they might as well all go home; no work would get done. She never had been able to figure out why the job was considered so demeaning, when horses were so vitally important to any ranching operation.

After a hearty supper of beans and tortillas crowned by thick wedges of dried apple pie with cheese and coffee so strong that a horseshoe could have floated on top of it, Rand invited Maggie to go for a stroll in the shadowy darkness to watch the stars come out.

As they walked off together with Nathan's approval, Will Tatter elbowed Gusty Williams and laughingly called out: "Now, you two behave yerselves, and don't do nothin' I wouldn't do."

"Hell, Gusty, you ain't up to doin' nothin' no more," Will taunted his old buddy. "Why, I bet you can't even remember what it is a man's 'sposed t' do when he gets alone with a purty girl."

Amidst much laughter, Gusty responded: "Why, he's 'sposed t' compare her eyes t' stars, an' her cheeks t' roses, an' if that don't soften her up, he's sposed t' go down on one knee and propose to her."

"But Rand done already proposed, an' she said yes. So what should he oughta do now?"

"Hell, I know what I'd do—especially with a gal as pretty as a red heifer in a flower bed!" someone else called out.

"Now, boys," Maggie heard her father good-naturedly protest, "Don't git carried away with yer teasin'. That's my daughter yer talkin' about."

"They better all shut up or I'm gonna bust a few heads," Rand growled, seeing no humor in the comments.

"They're just having fun," Maggie defended.

Rand looped his arms through hers and all but dragged her into the darkness away from the light of the big campfire behind them. In the distance, Maggie could hear the lowing of the cattle as they settled down for the night. A man rode past them, humming softy, as he circled the herd; Maggie knew he was on the first shift to keep watch over the spooky animals and quiet them. Should something alarm the cattle, it would be the job of the two night riders to head the herd away from camp, for the threat of a stampede was an ever-present danger.

Rand steered Maggie toward the river, and the soft murmur of water immediately soothed and relaxed her. She wrapped her black woolen shawl more tightly around her shoulders. At this elevation, the nights were still cold—much colder than down in the valley at the ranch house. She shivered slightly. Feeling it, Rand stopped and pulled her into his arms.

Encircling her waist with his hands, he brushed his mustache across her forehead. "You all right? You ain't too tired, are ya'?"

Why did he always assume she was tired? She was, of course, but the coffee had revived her, and after the long day on the hard seat of the wagon, she had been eager to stretch her cramped muscles. Now, she wanted Rand to make her forget she had ever met a man named Joe Hart.

"I'm not tired," she whispered, pressing closer.

Her willingness to be held emboldened him, and he roughly tilted up her chin and clamped his mouth down upon hers. The kiss was hard and clumsy; this time, she got a good taste of mustache before his lips found the right angle. She endured it as long as she could before pulling away and gasping for breath.

"Rand! Don't you think we should talk first before you . . . you kiss me like that?" She stepped back from him and rubbed her mashed mouth. Why, oh why, couldn't he be more gentle?

"So what do you wanna talk about?" he demanded in a surly tone.

"Well . . . the wedding. Our plans. And the plans for the house."

"Has Nathan given his permission yet?"

"You mean for the expansion? No, we haven't had time to discuss it. We've all been too busy. Actually, I was hoping *you* would bring it up with him. If you were to point out the advantages, I'm sure he would agree much faster than if I alone take up the issue."

"But I still don't see the point of it. Now, if you wanted t' talk about movin' up the weddin', I'd be the first t' take it up with Nathan."

Their conversation was going nowhere again. This was the first time they'd had a chance to talk in weeks, and Rand had not moved one inch off his original position. All he wanted, it seemed, was the right to stow his boots under her bed. He'd be perfectly satisfied with that. But she wanted much more from this marriage—much, much more, only she didn't know how to ask for it.

"Rand, we really don't know each other very well," she began. "We need more time alone together before we finally tie the knot, so to speak."

"Aw, hell, Maggie!" He leaned one hand against a tree and looked out over the river, gurgling quietly in the darkness. "What's there t' know? I been livin' on the Broken Wheel fer years. We've seen each other damn near everyday of our lives for the past how ever many years it's been." He straightened and turned to her. "How can ya' say ya' don't know me very well?"

"Because I don't. I don't know you as a man—only as the boy who came here angry, grieving, and resentful of the way the world had treated him. Since you got here, your life has improved, and for a while you seemed happy. Lately, for some reason, you're angry and resentful again."

"Maybe I'm just stewin' 'cuz I don't understan' the change that's come over you since I asked you t' marry me."

"Changed? Changed how?"

Rand took off his hat and self-consciously brushed a speck of dirt off the brim. "For one thing, you used to laugh an' joke an' tease me—callin' me Stud an' all that. Yer face used t' light up whenever you saw me, and sometimes, you even followed me around when I wuz doin' my chores."

"I really was a pest, wasn't I?" Maggie smiled at the remembrance.

"I called you that, but I didn't actually think of you that way. Truth is, I liked it, and I kinda miss it, Maggie." His little-boy earnestness grabbed at her heart, stoking the guilt already simmering there.

"But I've grown up, Rand, and stopped being a foolish young girl. I've become a woman. Someone you no longer know—or seem to care about knowing."

His hand crumpled the brim he had been brushing. "I care about knowin' you! Hell, Maggie, if there's something you want t' tell me, jus' go on an' spit it out! I'm listenin'."

She sighed, not at all sure of what to say to him or what was wrong with their relationship. She had no other relationship against which to measure it—except her father's and Lena's. And that was what she did *not* want: a love never openly acknowledged, a commitment never sealed, a furtive thing where the participants sneaked around in the dead of night to be together, but pretended nothing existed between them during the daylight hours.

She wondered if she and Rand would ever truly share their hopes, dreams, or emotions. Could they learn to express their feelings in bed at night? Or would it always be awkward and uncomfortable between them?

"Rand, what do you *want* out of life? What's the most important thing in the world to you?"

She waited for him to claim that it was her love and the desire to have children and for the two of them to be happy together. His face was difficult to read in the darkness, but she could hear his accelerated breathing . . . and his hesitancy to answer.

"Maggie, I wanna marry ya' first, and then I want t' make the Broken Wheel the biggest, best damn ranch in all of Idaho, Oregon, or Montana. That's all I ever wanted—since the day I lost my family's place and yer Pa come an' got me an' fetched me home with him. . . . I wanted t' make yer Pa proud of me, so he'd never think he made a mistake takin' me in."

"Is that why you're marrying me, Rand—to get the ranch?" She had feared as much, but it still hurt·to hear him say it.

"Not only that, Maggie. I want *you.* Ya' know I want you."

"But do you love me?"

"Hell, yes! Leastways, I think it's love. I ain't sure what love is, Maggie, but I know I got strong feelin's fer ya', if that's what you want t' know. I don't like other men lookin' at ya', an' I hate like hell that you'll be sleepin' underneath that wagon t'night with Lena, instead of with me."

Those weren't exactly the reassurances she wanted. She didn't know what she wanted, unless it was to feel safe, happy, and content being alone with Rand—to *want* to be alone with him, instead of dreading it. What was wrong with her? She had thought all this time that it was *him;* something was wrong with Rand. But actually, it was her. She didn't have the feelings she ought to have. She didn't even like his kisses!

"Maggie, what do you want from me? Tell me, an' I'll try an' do it."

In the absence of any sudden inspiration as to what she should say, she fell back on her original desire. "I . . . I want to have our own place, our own privacy. And I want you to want it, too. You should be more anxious to be alone with me, Rand, after we're married. I know you love my father and hope to avoid hurting him; well, so do I. But we should be desperate for a little corner of the world to call our own. We . . . we're so awkward together, Rand. Can't you see that? Something's wrong with us, but I'm not sure what it is."

He jammed his hat back on his head and gripped her by the shoulders. "Nothing's *wrong,* Maggie—unless it's you bein' too stubborn t' see that we really oughta marry right away. I'm sick o' waitin'. I can't take it much longer, Maggie. Every time I touch you, ya' pull away like some little scared rabbit, while I'm so on fire for ya' I'm afraid t' be near ya' or I'll go up in flames! It's crazy t' go on like this!"

She supposed he must love her if he felt like that. "Rand . . . could you kiss me again—but more gently? Don't . . . don't be so rough, this time."

"I'll try, Maggie . . . but damn it, yer so sweet and soft. I've told myself before t' be more gentle, but once I start kissin' ya', I fergit all my good intentions."

"Then try harder. Come on, Rand . . . kiss me." Maggie closed her eyes and leaned forward.

Rand's mustache tickled her nose, then his lips found hers, and the kiss was gentle and actually quite nice. It gave her a pleasant feeling. If he kissed like this all the time, she might learn to like it—even to look forward to it. Then his hands began to tighten on her shoulders, and he pressed his lips harder against hers. She sensed his control slipping and quickly broke the contact of their mouths.

"That was much better, Rand!" She smiled at him shakily. "Much, much better!"

His hand suddenly shot out and closed over her breast. The unexpected action shocked her speechless. He squeezed once—quick and hard. Without thinking, she slapped his hand. Immediately, he let go and sheepishly backed up against the tree.

"Sorry, Maggie . . . but that's what I mean. When I'm alone with ya', I plumb lose my head. You want me t' talk to Nathan about the house, I guess I'll talk to him. I'll do anythin' t' earn the right to touch ya' whenever I please. I want t' touch you so bad, Maggie. All over. Without your clothes on. Some days it's all I can think about. . . . Please. Kin I try it again? An' this time, I won't grab ya' so hard."

His passionate declaration frightened her, and she hated the idea of him touching her again. Nonetheless, she stood rock-still while his hand reached out for her a second time. "Gently, Rand . . . gently," she reminded him in a ragged whisper.

This man would be touching her for the rest of her life, and she desperately wanted to know if she could endure it—even learn to enjoy it. She thought she should feel something wonderful and marvelous—it was such an intimate act, this touching of her breast! But all she felt was a vague warmth, nothing particularly special. Then she thought of Joe Hart doing the same thing to her, and her heart nearly leapt out of her chest. A wave of heat and shame cascaded over her; where had that forbidden thought come from?

"I kin feel yer heart beatin'," Rand said hoarsely. "You see? You want me too, Maggie. It's gonna be all right between us. More than all right. It's gonna be real good."

Unable to endure his touch even a moment longer, she pulled his hand away. "We'd better get back to camp. Pa will be worried."

Rand laughed. "No, he won't. Not when yer with me, Maggie. He knows I'll take care of ya'—an' if somethin' *was* t' happen between us, I don't think he'd mind that much. We'd just be a little ahead of schedule. A damn silly schedule, too, if ya' ask me."

"It's not a silly schedule. . . . Oh, do come on. We both need some sleep."

They walked back toward the camp in silence. Most of the men had already unrolled their bedrolls and found places near the warmth of the fire. Maggie spotted Nathan stretched out on the ground with his head pillowed on his saddle. Lena was nowhere in sight, which meant she had retired to their bed under the wagon.

Only one man still sat in the shadows some distance from the fire. Maggie did not have to look closely to see who it was. Cradling a tin cup in both hands, Joe Hart sat on a log, his attention on the crackling wood as it slowly turned to ash and fell apart. He glanced up as she and Rand approached.

"Everything all right with the horses, Hart?" Rand's tone had a blunt edge to it.

Joe nodded, his eyes on Maggie. He seemed to know exactly what she had been doing and thinking out there in the dark with Rand. Her whole body heated with embarrassment. She could hardly draw breath. Head held high, she walked past him toward the wagon. She dared not trust her voice to say good-night to Rand; it might come out all wobbly.

"Night, honey . . . sleep well," Rand called after her.

She almost stopped and turned around. He had never called her anything but Maggie or Pest before—and Pest had been a long time ago. Their recent intimacy out there in the dark must have made him think he had the right to start calling her "honey." The endearment sounded so strange and inappropriate. Honey. But she was his honey, wasn't she?

"By the way, Hart, Will an' the ladies'll be needin' some firewood in the mornin'. Rustle some up, will ya'?"

Maggie did not hear Joe's reply. Very likely, all he had done was nod. Gathering firewood was another demeaning task for a top hand like Joe Hart; it was something only the greenest young men were usually asked to do on a roundup. Something for a youngster like Curt Holloway.

Maggie remembered well the day when Rand himself had vehemently protested the assignment, and Nathan had finally agreed with a laugh: "All right, son. If you think gatherin' wood is beneath you, I guess yer right. Can't waste a fine cowpoke like you on firewood, now can we?"

Rand had never collected a single stick after that, even on those occasions when every man in camp pitched in to do the tedious job of gathering, cutting, and splitting wood. Men like Rand who excelled at riding, roping, and working cattle weren't generally asked to do much else. What they did was more than enough.

Tomorrow, she and everyone else would find out just how good Joe Hart was at all of these important activities. Tomorrow, Maggie would get to watch Joe Hart and his Appaloosa cut cattle. Tired as she was, she could hardly wait.

Eight

The sun rose the following morning in fiery splendor, cutting a golden swath through the steamy tendrils of vapor entwining the legs of cattle, horses, and people. Everyone rose early and ate a hearty breakfast while they watched the glowing red orb conquer the crest of the snow-capped mountain peaks.

It was the sort of morning that humbled a person, making him or her feel small and insignificant in the face of such majesty; it certainly humbled Maggie. She savored her coffee in awestruck silence. Everyone else must have felt the same, for there was little talking around the chuck wagon. The men ate with single-minded purpose and gulped several cups of the fortifying brew that took the nip out of the misty cold morning air.

When everyone had eaten, Maggie and Lena tackled the mess left behind, while the men roped their horses and led them out of the remuda to be saddled. Will and Gusty started a second fire a safe distance away from the main camp. This would be used to heat the distinctive iron with its logo in the shape of a broken wheel.

After the calves were branded and the bulls castrated, the men would also notch the left ears of the young stock, so that even at a distance when the brand was unreadable, anyone in the region could tell which cattle belonged to the Broken Wheel. There was still a lot of open rangeland on the Clearwater Plateau, though more and more ranchers were putting up "bob-wire" fencing and cutting hay to support their stock through the winters.

Maggie's father still clung to the old ways as much as possible, but he had been buying land in anticipation of the day when he would have to confine his cattle to his own holdings. He now owned a big chunk of property, and very little land contiguous to that which they already owned was available.

As she washed tin cups and plates in a big iron kettle, Maggie wondered how much longer they could continue doing things in the old way, which did make for plenty of back-breaking labor. Many cows in the herd were wearing the brands of neighboring ranches; these must be cut out from the rest and together with their calves be driven to join the herds where they belonged. In exchange, Broken Wheel cows would eventually be returned to them. In the past, the ranchers had often joined together for one big roundup to sort and brand their calves, but now that fences were appearing everywhere, it wasn't done as much anymore.

Maybe folks were right to fence their ranges and confine their herds to one place where they couldn't mix, Maggie thought, but oh, she would miss days such as these at roundup and branding time! This morning, the air was so crisp and fresh that it made her lightheaded; she felt so giddy she wanted to laugh out loud. She did laugh when Curt Holloway nearly got bucked off his horse trying to "git the frost outta 'im," as the men called it. On these cold mornings, the horses were as fresh and eager as the cowhands to get moving.

Curt's misadventures caused the onlookers to let loose a string of softly spoken insults, taunts, and wagers about who would outdo the other today, cutting and throwing the calves. Maggie noticed that Joe Hart did not take part in any of the teasing. He was calmly and quietly saddling Loser, while Rand challenged all comers in a voice loud enough to spook the cattle.

What did Joe think of the Broken Wheel's custom of holding a competition at branding time? Usually, the calves were roped by the forefeet by the best roper on the spread, then dragged to the fire and held by two flankers while the iron was applied in a process known far and wide as "burnin' an' bootin' 'em."

Competitions involving cutting, roping, and hog-tying by a single man or a team of men were normally limited to those times when the cowhands wished to amuse themselves. Only on the Broken Wheel did the men mix work and pleasure this way—and that was largely due to her father's competitive nature and desire to keep his men sharp so they could beat all the other ranch hands for miles around when they did get together and compete.

Nathan stood by now, eagerly fingering his gold pocket watch and approving Rand's assignments for the first half of the day's work. Some of the men would remain on foot to do the actual branding, castrating, and ear notching and then to free the bawling calves so they could go running back to their frantic mothers.

While one man cut and roped his calf, another on horseback would make certain the mother did not interfere. It was Nathan's job to keep track of the time it took each man to down his calf and truss it for branding. As soon as Maggie finished at the chuck wagon, she was to help her father keep track of the wagers.

Raising her hand to shield her eyes from the brightness of the early morning sun, she studied the cattle some distance away. Unaware of what was to come, they were placidly grazing. Once the actual work began, the men would ride slowly and quietly toward the herd. In the order called by Rand, each man would cut out a cow and work her over near the branding fire, where he would then rope her calf. Once his rope had settled over the calf's head and been drawn tight, the cowhand would jump off his horse, throw the calf on its side, and hog-tie it. Meanwhile, his horse had to maintain enough tension on the line to enable him to get the job done.

The branding crew then converged on the bawling little creature and finished the whole procedure in a matter of minutes.

All of the men would have their chance at cutting, but no one was forced to accept a wager. However, the best and fastest cowhands usually did, especially if they owned or had been assigned a good cutting horse in their string—one who knew exactly how to play this game.

As Maggie had expected, no one wanted to compete against Rand. She watched as he challenged one man after another, but none accepted. "Aw, hell, Rand," one man complained. "Y'all can't expect me t' bet a month's pay that I can beat ya' when yer ridin' Cricket, an' I'm ridin' a bench-kneed ole hoss like Buck. He's the best cutter in my string, an' I still ain't got a chance."

A month's pay! Maggie hadn't realized that the stakes had gone so high; normally, the wagers were more modest—sometimes as little as a bottle of red-eye or as big as a night on the town. A month's pay was an incredible amount, and she was suddenly ashamed of Rand for taunting the men when he clearly had a superior horse, one who had been born with "cow sense."

"It's all in how ya' ride and train' em," Rand boasted. "Come on now. Surely, you boys've been practicin' t' git ready fer today. Why, I've seen you tossin' loops day an' night for the past coupla' weeks."

Maggie had seen them practicing, too, roping fence posts, horses in the corral, each other, and whatever else caught their fancy. The Broken Wheel was known for the number of its ranch hands who could handle a rope. Of course, it was always a different proposition altogether to loop a calf on the run while your own horse was twisting and turning underneath you trying to keep the calf from racing back to its mother and/or the herd.

Nathan strode up to big Burt Lyman, who did all the "platin' " or trimming and shoeing of horses on the ranch, as well as a good bit of everything else. "Burt? How 'bout you? You gotta good horse. Ain't you gonna accept Rand's proposition? If you ask me, a month's pay is a damn good incentive for tryin'."

Burt Lyman straightened slightly on his little dun gelding.

The horse looked as if he couldn't carry Burt's weight, and he was roman-nosed and ugly besides. But Maggie knew that his appearance was deceiving. Beans, as Burt called him, could maneuver like a jackrabbit when he was turned loose on a cow or calf—and he never let any slack in the rope when he had to hold an animal while Burt got down and tended to it.

The trouble was that Burt himself was simply too heavy to move as quickly as Rand—and he was also older. Beans would do his job in good time, but Burt couldn't hold down his end of the deal. The big man sat there a minute, saying nothing, but his frown revealed his indecision. Burt hated to let a challenge go by without responding. Burly and tough, he took pride in himself and in his work. He had worked with horses and cattle all his life and become a top hand. There was precious little he didn't know how to do on a ranch, even if he did do it slower than some men.

"Better late than niver," he'd drawl when prodded to go faster.

He finally nodded, and Maggie's father grinned and gestured toward another cowboy. "What about you, Luke? You gonna sit back and watch today, or you gonna show us how it's done?"

"I ain't goin' up against Rand, but I'll stand a bottle of red-eye at the Pink Garter that I can beat the time of any other man here."

The Pink Garter was a saloon in the nearest town of Bitterroot—the place where the cowboys headed every payday. On trips to town, to the general store, or the dressmaker's, Maggie had many times heard the raucous laughter and the loud music and wished that just once she dared venture inside the place to get a look at the "calico queens" who danced there and enticed the cowboys into parting with all their hard-earned cash. She never had worked up her courage, but one day she might.

Half the cowboys present pounced on Luke's offer, whether it was because they doubted his big roan could beat them or they were just glad to accept a less risky wager, Maggie could not be certain—but Nathan was delighted. He waved her over.

"Maggie, git over here an' be our stakeholder! You know I'll only forgit who bet what."

Lena handed her a dish towel to wipe her hands. "Go ahead, *Señorita* Maggie. I'll finish here."

Maggie limped over to join the gathering, and her father began rattling off the names of the cowboys and who had bet what. She did not need to write anything down; she had been blessed with an amazing memory—or else she had simply been doing this for so many years that it had become second nature.

When everyone had placed their bets, Nathan made her repeat them back to everyone. "Yer all agreed?" he inquired. "This is what you've wagered?"

The men nodded among themselves. Aside from a month's pay, the biggest wager was a pair of only slightly worn red boots with intricate stitching on the sides in the shapes of stars and flowers. They had cost as much as a month's pay, and since they were already broken in, the man who put them up insisted they were worth more, not less. However, Rand did not agree.

"Ya' mean t' say Burt's the only one with enough guts t' take me on?" he sneered. "The rest of you sissy pants ain't got enough faith in yerselves or yer mounts?"

These were fighting words to a gathering of cowhands—sissy pants being a man who acted like his sister—and Maggie was again embarrassed that Rand would taunt the men the way he did. He was not normally so callous of their feelings, and since he did work as hard, if not harder, than any of them, they did not seem to mind the high-handed way he sometimes gave orders . . . but they looked resentful now.

Will Tatter shook his head, and Gusty Williams spat a long stream of tobacco juice right next to Rand's boot. "Rand, I don't care if you *is* the Number Two Cocka-doodle-do on the Broken Wheel, I gotta tell ya' that yer bein' a hoss's ass about this—an' so are you, Nathan. Me an' the boys don't appreciate bein' leaned on fer a month's pay."

"Now, Gusty, it's all in fun," Nathan said. "Nobody's gotta

do it if they don't want to. We're jus' tryin' t' make a dull job interestin'. . . . Ain't that right, Rand?"

Rand seemed about to argue the point, but apparently decided against it. "Hell's fire, I'll ride another hoss, if y'all insist," he agreed with a self-deprecating grin.

"Why, in that case, I'll take you up on the bet," Luke called out. "You can fork old Sam here, a whey belly if there ever was one, an' I'll take Cricket."

"I'll ride Sam," Rand agreed. "But nobody but me rides Cricket. He can stand and watch fer a while."

The men began buzzing among themselves, debating the wisdom of taking on Rand if he rode a different horse. Several placed bets, and Maggie had to pay close attention to remember who was making them. Then a new voice suddenly spoke up.

"I accept the foreman's original offer," Joe Hart said.

It grew so quiet one could hear the cattle switching their tails and the breeze soughing through the cottonwoods along the river. With a slow, insolent grin, Rand faced the newcomer. "Yer willin' t' bet a month's pay you can beat me on Cricket?"

"As long as I can ride Loser here." Joe Hart gave the spotted stallion a negligent pat on the shoulders. "He's partial to cutting."

"I wouldn't put my money on no spotted, pestle-tailed Injun pony." Gusty Williams delivered another contemptuous stream of tobacco juice to a spot somewhere near Loser's front hooves. "You sure you wanna take a risk like that, Joe? Rand ain't lost a bet in a month o' Sundays, an' neither has Cricket."

Joe nodded. "I could use an extra month's pay."

"I could use a month of free labor," Nathan interrupted. "Make yer bet with Rand and then make it with me if yer that sure of your mount."

"But that wouldn't be fair!" Maggie burst out. "You're keeping track of the time, Pa. You can't be placing bets on your own."

Nathan fixed her with a steely-eyed gaze. "Yer suggestin' I'd cheat, Maggie? You—my own daughter?"

"No, Pa . . . I'm just saying it wouldn't be fair."

"She's right, Nathan," Gusty agreed. "You can't be holdin' that pocket watch and callin' the time if you're gonna be placin' bets yerself."

"I withdraw the offer," Nathan grunted. "If there's one thing I am, it's fair."

"Well, let's jingle our spurs then, boys. Luke, you go first, and then you, Curt . . ." Rand finished making the assignments, and the men rode off to get started.

Maggie assumed a spot off to one side of the branding fire, all the while going over the list of wagers in her mind so she was sure she had them all memorized. The prospect of seeing Joe Hart in action again had rattled her composure. There were at least twenty other men out there on the plain, but none of them affected her so strongly; for some reason, this one single man made her achingly aware of his every move, word, and gesture. . . . It was downright unnerving.

Nathan rubbed his boot over a sandy area nearby, then handed her a small stick. "Maybe you better write this all down in the dirt," he said to her. "We got a heap more bets this year than last. You might forget one of 'em."

"You don't trust your own daughter?" Maggie tossed back at him.

That brought a grin. "I'm just sayin' you might fergit somethin', Maggie girl."

"I won't forget." She threw away the stick. *Even if Joe Hart does seem to make me lose sight of the fact that I'm engaged to another man.*

The branding began with a good fast run by Luke Wilson on his leggy gray gelding, Shadow, or as Luke called him "Shader." The horse had good cow sense and easily cut out a bald-faced cow and calf from the herd and worked them over near the branding fire. While he turned his attention to the calf, Curt Holloway headed off the mother. In no time at all, Luke had the calf trussed and tied, ready for the red-hot iron.

The little creature bawled lustily as the men worked over

him, but it did not take long before they were done, and he
scrambled back to his mother as fast as his short stubby legs
could take him. The smell of fresh blood and burnt hair tainted
the air. Gusty William tossed the bull calf's newly missing parts
into a wooden bucket. Lena would make "calf fries" out of the
bucket's contents, which some of the hands regarded as a deli-
cacy, but Maggie had never been able to stomach them. Gusty
wiped his bloody hands on his pants and sharpened his blade
on a stone in preparation for the next victim.

"That was a good time." Nathan called it out, and Maggie
memorized it. "Next!"

So the morning went, with Maggie keeping track of who
had already won what. Rand still won but didn't do as well
when he rode any other horse but Cricket, and the taunts were
fast, furious, and funny. After a time, the men seemed to forget
she was there and no longer guarded their speech in front of
her.

Burt Lyman called Rand a "goddam rotgut-pisser" for making him lose a month's pay, and Rand promised to take only a
third of it if Burt agreed to shovel less chow in his mouth from
now on. If his pants were no longer too tight by the end of the
month, Rand wouldn't hold him to the original bet. Burt readily
assented, conceding he was "wearin' out poor Bean before his
time with all the extra lard the poor critter's packin' these days."

The work did not stop even for a noon meal; Nathan and
Rand hoped to finish a large section of the herd in one day
then cut out the next bunch for the following day's work. By
late afternoon, they were almost done; Rand and Joe were the
only two remaining men who hadn't yet competed against each
other.

"Let's get this over with, Hart." Rand mounted Cricket and
headed toward the cattle. "I'll go first, then you."

Joe, who had taken a turn at everything but cutting and
throwing his calf, nodded. Rand picked his cow and calf, expertly maneuvered them into position, then roped the calf. Dal-
lying the rope around the horn of his saddle, he leapt off

Cricket's back, ran to the calf, tossed it on its side, and trussed its feet in a single smooth blur of motion. Cricket performed as he always did, with speed, grace, and enthusiasm—making the job look easy.

Nathan called out the time with obvious glee. "That might be a record even for you, Rand. Damn fine piece of work."

Maggie felt a warm swell of pride in her husband-to-be. Rand really was a superb rider, able to sit still and quiet in the saddle while Cricket worked the cow. Joe would be hard put to beat his performance, and she suddenly didn't want him to be able to beat it. She wanted Rand to keep his reputation of being the best, so she could admire him whole-heartedly, knowing he was better than Joe Hart.

"That was marvelous, Rand!" she congratulated the grinning blond man.

Rand surprised her by blowing her a kiss. "I did it for you, honey," he boasted. "Now let's see what the greener can do."

Everyone knew he meant Joe Hart, the new man, the greenhorn, and heads swiveled to watch Joe approach the herd on Loser. The big Appaloosa looked suddenly intent, all his muscles coiled and ready to chase his cow. Joe pointed him toward the animal he had selected—the signal for Nathan to start keeping track of the time. What happened next took Maggie's breath away.

Joe sat down deep in the saddle and turned the stallion loose. He went after the chosen cow, moving with such speed and agility that Maggie was afraid to blink lest she miss the whole thing. Loser was much faster than Cricket, and Joe was much faster than Rand. His catlike grace stood him in good stead as he vaulted out of the saddle and brought down the calf with an economy of effort. The animal was ready for branding almost in the space of a single long breath. Maggie realized she had been holding that breath and slowly exhaled.

"I don't believe it," Nathan muttered. "I must've made a mistake."

"How much faster was he?" Maggie peered over her father's

shoulder at his gold pocket watch as if the timepiece itself could answer.

"Twenny seconds—at least. He was a good twenny seconds faster."

The men broke into cheers, except for Rand. "Hell of a ride, Joe!" they congratulated the tall, graceful figure as he walked back to Loser.

"Wouldn't believe it with mah own eyes if I hadn't seed it," Gusty drawled. "Guess you've done yore share of calf ropin', ain't ya, son?"

The smallest of grins quirked Joe Hart's slash of a mouth; he did not appear at all surprised by his victory—only amused by the other men's reaction to something he had known he could do all along. "Loser did the hard part," was all he said in acknowledgement of the adulation being heaped upon him.

"Luck. Dumb luck," Rand growled near Maggie. "Double or nothin', Hart. Let's do it again, and this time, I'm bettin' double or nothin' that I can beat ya'."

Joe paused in the act of collecting his rope. "I've had enough. No need to wear out my horse. He's been working hard today as it is."

Maggie silently agreed. Loser had been galloping back and forth for the last two hours, keeping the mother cows from following their calves to the branding fire.

"Double or nothin'!" Rand shouted. "And if you refuse, you can draw your pay tomorrow an' ride out."

"Rand!" Maggie gasped, shocked.

"Now, Maggie, you keep out of it." Nathan stepped in front of Maggie. "Rand's got a perfect right t' demand a rematch. He's the foreman; his reputation is on the line."

"But, Mr. Hart already said no! And *he* has a perfect right to refuse."

"He's reconsidered. Ain't that right, Hart?" Rand's gaze flicked over Joe Hart with undisguised contempt. "He knows he wuz jus' lucky, and he's afraid he can't repeat his li'l performance."

"I can repeat it," Joe quietly responded, but his silver eyes glittered. "Go ahead. We'll try it again."

Rand swung into the saddle and jabbed his spurs viciously into Cricket's sides. Unaccustomed to such harsh treatment, Cricket pitched, nearly unseating Rand, then galloped off. Rand hauled back cruelly on the reins to slow him down before they reached the cattle. He signaled his choice of cow, then dropped his hands down low, letting Cricket have his head.

The big sorrel horse quickly worked the cow and calf out of the herd. Rand tossed his loop and was out of the saddle running almost before the rope tightened around the little fellow's neck. Burt Lyman on Beans had a difficult time keeping the mama cow from charging Rand before he had a chance to toss and tie the baby. Rand did it with breathtaking speed, then raised his fist and punched the air in a gesture of triumph, certain no one could beat him, especially not Joe Hart.

Joe patiently waited until the calf had been branded and freed. Then he mounted Loser, leaned forward in the saddle, and grasped his horse's bridle at the crown. Deftly, he slipped the bridle off Loser's head and let it fall to the ground. Maggie watched in disbelief. . . . Joe intended to make his run without even a bridle on his horse!

Silver eyes glittering, Joe rode toward the herd, selected his cow, and sat deep in his saddle. Loser gave the same amazing performance as he had before—this time without benefit of even the mildest of restraints or direction from Joe's rein hand. Joe swung his rope, looped the calf, tossed and tied it faster and more efficiently than Maggie had ever seen it done in her life.

The cowhands evidently thought so too, for they whooped and hollered and yipped in glee and admiration—until Nathan called out the time. "Five seconds slower than Rand! Guess you both won one, boys—and that cancels out the debt. Neither one of you gets an extry dollar."

"Rand won?" Gusty inquired disbelievingly. "Goddam! I coulda sworn Joe was faster. Must be I'm goin' blind as a snubbin' post. If I git any worse, I won't be able t' see through a bob-wire fence.

"You sure about that time, Nathan?" Burt Lyman gruffly demanded.

Nathan held up his pocket watch. "Sure as I can be, 'lessen something's gone bad with my timepiece." He held the watch up to his ear. "Nope. It's still tickin' good 'n regular."

Maggie watched her father closely, scarcely able to believe that he would actually lie about a thing like this. Nathan looked as innocent as a newborn lamb, which only made her more suspicious. For years, he had been lying—or not telling the truth—about Lena, so how could she trust him now?

She couldn't. She looked at Joe Hart who was paying no attention to anyone and indeed seemed to have accepted the verdict that he had lost this second run. Then she glanced at Rand. He wasn't behaving as he normally did when he knew he had won, which meant he wasn't grinning from ear to ear and rubbing his victory in his opponent's face. Instead, he seemed subdued—almost angry.

"Well, that's it fer the day, boys. Time t' think about fodderin' our tape worms," Nathan said jovially. It was a typical cowboy joke about eating, only no one laughed.

But no one argued or challenged Maggie's father any further either. He was the ranch owner, the Number One Cocka-doodle-do, the highest authority on any subject, and his word was law. If he said Rand had won, then the men must accept it. However, *she* didn't necessarily have to accept it.

As the men dispersed, she walked with her father back toward the chuck wagon. "Pa? Are you *certain* Rand won this last run?"

"I said so, didn't I? Rand won it fair and square. As the future Mrs. Rand Johnson, I should think you'd be real proud of 'im."

"I am proud of him. He did a fine job. But I'm not so proud of the fact that he feels he *has* to win all the time and pressures the other men into competing with him. Nor am I proud of *you* for pushing them into it. I think we should just cut and brand the calves the way other ranches do—have the best cutter do the cutting, the best roper do the roping, and let the men take their turns flanking and branding."

"Well, Maggie, you don't know a damn thing about it, so you shouldn't oughta express an opinion on the matter. We do things my way on the Broken Wheel, and it also happens t' be Rand's way. . . . Ya' honestly wanna see some greener beat the ranch foreman—the man yer gonna marry?"

"Joe Hart proved today that he's no greenhorn, Pa, and if he won, he should get the credit for it as well as double a month's pay. Why, he did it the second time without a bit or hackamore to control his horse! Nobody else on the ranch can ride like that, and you know it."

"Humph! I wouldn't have said it at first look at him, but now I'm beginnin' t' think Joe Hart's the sort of man t' get calluses from pattin' his own back. He was just showin' off, that's all. He didn't have no call t' shuck that bridle, now did he?"

"Well, what does Rand do every chance he gets? *He shows off.* Rand made it impossible for Joe to walk away and quit. He had to go against him again or risk losing his job. Do you think that's fair, Pa?"

"I think if you got a beef with Rand, you oughta be talkin' with Rand, not me. I'm suddenly dry as bone. I sure hope Lena's got some of that brown gargle she calls coffee awaitin' on the coals."

"Pa!" Maggie wailed as her father increased his pace and stomped off, faster than she could limp. Maggie stopped and stared after him, deciding that she certainly would talk to Rand about his behavior today. She was proud of his prowess on horseback but ashamed of his swaggering around all the time; if anyone was going to get calluses from patting himself on the back, it was Rand, not Joe Hart, who barely spoke a word if he didn't have to. Why, Rand was beginning to sound like a "flannel mouth," the range term for a braggart!

He had been graceless even in victory; at least he could have
congratulated Joe or complimented him upon his ability to ride
Loser with no other guidance but his legs and the shift of his
weight in the saddle. Whether Joe won or lost, it had been an
outstanding performance, worthy of recognition by the ranch
foreman. . . . Maggie decided to confront Rand that very night
after supper—and to congratulate Joe herself the first time she
had the opportunity.

Nine

All through supper, Maggie watched for an opportunity to get Rand alone so she could talk to him, but he seemed to be deliberately avoiding her. If she sat down next to him, he got up and walked away to get another cup of coffee or go check on the cattle or have a word with someone. He was surly and uncommunicative, calling to mind that he always had taken it badly when someone could do something better than he could.

As a boy he would spend hours practicing with a rope until he could toss a Mother Hubbard, a hooleyann, a figure eight, a washerwoman, or dog loop as needed. Even then, he hadn't been satisfied, especially after Nathan took him out on the range to find some wild maverick cattle and showed him how to throw a *mangana de pie* and a Blocker loop, fancy roping not much used in regular range work.

No matter how hard Rand tried, Nathan was always hazing him, challenging him to go a step further—and Rand had almost killed himself on any number of occasions trying to live up to Nathan's expectations. Maggie supposed that was why Rand himself hazed the other cowboys, and why he was so jealous when a man came along and earned compliments doing something at which Rand had always been the best. Nathan may have declared Rand a winner earlier that day, but every cowboy present knew who had really won. By working his horse without a bridle while he did his cutting, Joe had earned the respect of the Broken Wheel hands—and Rand's everlasting envy.

Joe sat off by himself as he ate his dinner, but every now and then, a man would stop by or call out to him. "You done good t'day, greener. Guess we can't call you a greener no more, not when you can outride and outrope the lot of us."

Joe would only nod as if the praise meant nothing to him— but Maggie could see what it was doing to Rand. As the night wore on, he got more and more "on the prod," finding reasons to bark or snap at people, and when he wasn't doing that, he just sat and glowered. Nathan went out of his way to make conversation with Rand in their usual joking fashion, but Rand's responses were all brusque and ill-mannered.

Maggie withstood it for about as long as she could. Then she got up from the blanket where she had been sitting with Lena, walked over to Rand, and said quietly, "Rand, could we walk out for a bit?"

"Whooooee!" Gusty exclaimed. "Looka here, boys. The heifer's ridin' herd on the cowpoke t'night, 'stead o' the other way around. What y'all think about that?"

"Quit yer jaw-flappin', Gusty, 'fore Rand puts a fist in yore mouth," Will counseled. "Rand don't look amused."

Rand didn't. His face was blood-red. It could have been the warmth from the campfire, but Maggie didn't think so. "I jes' wanna set here, Maggie," he growled. "Maybe Lena'll walk out with you."

"Goddam! He's turnin' her down! I may be old and rusty, but I still remember what's it's like t' be young an' have a good dose of 'calico fever.' I'll walk out with ya', Maggie honey," Gusty volunteered. "An' hold yer hand whilst I do it."

Only Gusty could have gotten away with such an outrageous offer—but then Maggie had known Gusty all her life. And Gusty had known Rand since the day Nathan had brought him home. Gusty, as much as Nathan, had taught Rand his skills, and it was Gusty who always smoothed things over when Rand rode the men too hard.

"You kin walk out with her, but if you hold her hand, I'll

give you a good dose of lead right in the backside," Rand muttered.

"Thanks, Gusty, but I've changed my mind," Maggie said. "I think I'll just sit around and scowl at everybody like some bad-tempered grizzly bear. If it's all right for some people, it must be all right for me."

With a flounce of her skirts and a last furious glance at Rand, who wouldn't meet her eyes, Maggie limped over to the log where Joe Hart was sitting all by himself. She sat down a polite distance away and smoothed her skirt, as if she weren't aware of the fact that Joe Hart occupied the other end of the log . . . but she was aware.

She furtively watched him as he finished his coffee, set down his cup, took out his "makin's," and rolled a "quirly." She had never seen him smoke before and was faintly surprised to see him do it now. Most of the cowboys did indulge from time to time—but her father didn't, nor did Rand, and since she hadn't witnessed Joe smoking in the time he'd been there, she had assumed he didn't either.

He scraped a match along the bottom of his boot, lit up the cigarette, then took a long deep draw. When he expelled the smoke, it wafted in her direction. Hardly thinking about it, she waved her hand in front of her face. Immediately, Joe Hart stubbed out the quirly, wasting nearly the whole thing.

"You didn't have to do that," she remarked. "The smoke wasn't really bothering me."

"Maybe not, but it was suddenly bothering me," he responded. "A foolish way for a man to spend his money anyway."

She didn't know how to take the cryptic comment; why had he lit up in the first place if he didn't like to smoke or found it too expensive? It was one more mysterious thing about an already incomprehensible man. She inched a little closer to him on the log, determined to find out more about him—especially since Rand had refused to walk out with her and embarrassed her by saying no in front of everyone. . . . It wouldn't hurt for him to see that she could strike up a conversation with a potential rival.

"You rode magnificently today. I never saw anyone rope a calf while riding a horse with no bridle."

Joe Hart leveled a long look at her that turned her insides to mush. "All it takes is a little practice."

"I wish you would tell me more about how you learned to ride and train horses. I don't understand why it's such a big secret."

The silver-gray eyes softened with some inner amusement. "It's no secret. I just worked at it 'til I learned."

"But that trick with the bridle? Why would you want to ride a horse without the usual means of controlling it?"

"Because I can control it just as well with my body and my voice, and sometimes I like to have my hands free for other things."

That made sense to her, especially since a good cow horse worked best without interference. "I think you won today. Both runs," she said softly.

His unique silvery eyes reflected back the light of the campfire, and she thought she read agreement in them, but he said nothing. He merely shrugged, the set of his mouth and shoulders conveying that he already knew he was the best; it didn't matter what a pocket watch—or her father—claimed.

"I'm afraid you've made an enemy though." She nodded toward Rand. He was too far away to hear what they were saying but was watching them with about as much friendliness as an old bull standing guard over his cows.

"I'm surprised he's allowing you to sit here and talk to me," he drawled.

She adjusted her shawl more closely about her shoulders. "I doubt it bothers him all that much. I was referring to the way you rope and ride. He doesn't like it when someone's skill matches or exceeds his."

"I hardly think that's all that's bothering him. Is that why you came over here—to make him jealous?"

She couldn't help smiling at the ridiculous accusation. "I wish I *could* make a man jealous, Mr. Hart. However, I'm not the sort of woman men are given to fighting over. I'm twenty-two years old and have only recently received my first proposal of marriage. Considering the scarcity of unattached females in this area, that's hardly a testimonial to my feminine appeal. Most women my age have been married several years and already have children."

"Are you fishing for testimonials, Miss Sterling? All right, I'll give you one. I'd forfeit my Stetson just to wrap that honey-colored hair around my fingers, pull you close, and bury my nose in it."

"Mr. Hart!" Maggie drew back in shock, her eyes searching his face then lowering in acute embarrassment.

Joe Hart calmly reached down, picked up his empty coffee cup, and ran one finger around the lip of it. "Do you smell as sweet as you look, Miss Sterling? Does your hair feel like silk against a man's skin? And what about *your* skin? I bet it's softer than the ear of a newborn calf—touching it would be worth a whole month's pay."

She couldn't believe he would actually be willing to pay thirty dollars for the privilege. She had thought him blunt and plain-spoken to a fault, possessing none of the colorful way with words to which some cowpokes could lay claim. Gusty, Will, and her father, for example, had unique ways of "augurin'." Indeed, they sometimes competed to see who could "augur" the best and the most outrageously. Rand himself tried to keep up with them, but with only modest success.

With all the "augurin'" she had been subjected to over the years, Maggie had never heard a man talk like this—or put such a suggestive spin on his words. Yet all the while he had been doing it, his face had shown no emotion. He might have been discussing the weather.

"You shouldn't be saying such things to me," she primly scolded. "Why, I hardly know you, and I'm engaged to be married to another man."

"Then why did you come over here, Miss Sterling? You must have had some good reason for sitting down on my log and telling me what a great rider I am. You've already told me that once before."

"I . . . I was just trying to be friendly. I think you should have won, today, that's all, and I wanted to tell you. I certainly didn't come over here to entice you into making lewd comments to me."

"I think you'd better keep away from me. I'm not one of those cowpokes you can toss a loop over, have your fun with, and then turn loose when you've tired of the game. I'm a man with a man's needs. Bees buzzing around an old stump means there's a fresh honeycomb dripping honey inside. When I see them, I start to think about getting a taste of it. . . . If you never intend to give me a taste of your sweetness, you had better not come buzzing around me, Miss Sterling."

"All I came over here for was to talk to you about riding!" she protested, stung by his assumption—which came too close to the truth for comfort—that she found him in the least bit interesting as a man or intended to flirt with him as some girls might.

"You sure are mighty interested in riding then." He shook his head mockingly. "If you really want to ride, you can learn, Miss Sterling. Your bum leg shouldn't be used as an excuse not to try. Plenty of cowhands have bum legs from fallin' off a horse or havin' a horse or steer fall on top of them. I don't know how you got yours, but it shouldn't keep you from doing anything you've set your mind on doing."

"That's easy for you to say, when you have two sound legs to walk around on, and you've been riding for years and years!"

"Maybe so. But it's been my experience that the only rope corral that can hold a horse is the one he *thinks* can hold it. Otherwise, he can bust right through the rope—and maybe even the wood poles used to confine him."

"Thank you very much for your interesting lecture on animal

behavior, Mr. Hart! I'm so glad you condescended to give it to me."

"Condescended?" His brows rose questioningly.

"It's an eight dollar word that an illiterate cowpoke like you couldn't be expected to understand. Think about it, and maybe the meaning will come to you." She rose and dusted off her skirt. "Goodnight, sir."

As she rounded the campfire, Maggie became aware of an awkward silence. All eyes were upon her, but as she glanced from one onlooker to another, they averted their gazes and began talking to each other. Her confrontation with Joe Hart had not gone unnoticed! She had kept her voice down until the very end, and Joe had never raised his, so maybe no one had overheard the whole thing. At least, she prayed they had not.

She started toward the chuck wagon, intending to go to bed, but Rand suddenly got up and joined her, walking her over to the wagon and around its other side—where it was dark and private, and the stars formed a diamond-studded vault overhead.

"What was you two talkin' about?" he demanded, his fingers closing painfully on her wrist.

"Nothing of interest. I don't know why I went over there. That man is . . . is insufferably rude and ill-bred!"

"He was disrespectful? Why, I'll go on back there an' . . ." Rand started to turn away.

"No! No . . ." She grasped his arm. "He didn't say anything wrong, really. I . . . I just don't like him is all."

There was a short awkward pause while Rand studied her flaming face. "You shouldn't oughta be sittin' and talkin' with other men, Maggie," he finally grumbled. "You belong to me. I've already staked my claim on you."

"Then why didn't you come and get me? I asked you to walk out with me, and you refused—embarrassing me in front of everyone."

He was immediately contrite. "Goddam, Maggie, I'm sorry.

I didn't realize. . . . I'll walk out with you tomorrow night, if you like."

"Yes . . . well . . . I would like that. I know you were upset about this afternoon, Rand, but you didn't have to take it out on me. I'm on your side."

"Upset? Hell, I wasn't upset. All right, maybe I was, but I still won all but one, didn't I?"

"Yes. According to my father, you won all but one." *Only you didn't, not really. My father lied, and you know it, and that's what's got you so angry.*

She wished he would admit it—would trust her enough to admit it—but he didn't. Instead, he demanded: "How about a kiss fer the best rider and roper in the whole damn Idaho panhandle, Maggie girl?"

A kiss for Joe Hart? Feeling guilty for the traitorous thought, Maggie slid her arms around Rand's neck. "Will you be gentle?"

"I'll try," he promised.

He lowered his head and kissed her—not as roughly as he usually did, and she melted into him in relief and gratitude. Tonight, the kiss was not half-bad. Actually, it was half-good. Until she thought of Joe Hart burying his nose in her hair. Deeply disturbed by the image and her own reactions to it, she pulled back in Rand's unyielding arms.

"You do think I'm the best, doncha', Maggie?"

"Does it matter so much if you're the best, Rand? After all, there are other things besides ridin' and ropin' that a man can be good at."

"But them two are the most important things—at least t' me. I'm the foreman, an' I'm gonna be yer husband. So I gotta be the best. I ain't much fer slick tricks like shuckin' my horse's bridle an' gallopin' off, but I can do the job of a cowman better'n any other man on the place. Can't I, Maggie?"

"Of course, Rand," she lied to appease him, then wished she didn't have to lie. Actually, it was more important to her at this moment that he be a better kisser, a better lover, than a better roper and rider. She wished that his kisses had the power to blot out the image of every other man on earth from her mind—especially the image of Joe Hart touching her hair or body.

She dared another kiss, another embrace, and tried to put her whole self into it . . . but little things continued to distract her. Rand could have used a good "slickin' up"—the cowboy term for bathing and shaving. Tonight, he reeked of leather, horse, sweat, and cow. Of course, so must Joe Hart and every other man present after the day they had just spent.

Even knowing that, Maggie was unable to overlook it. The ripe smells blunted her ardor; she was sure she would smell as bad as Rand after he was finished hugging her. . . . Somehow, whenever Rand touched her, something always stirred her distaste. As usual, she blamed herself, this time for being too persnickety. If she truly loved the man, she ought to be able to overlook a little honest sweat! She herself couldn't smell that enticing.

Fatigue set in next, and she found herself pushing away from Rand and pleading exhaustion. Still, he clung to her, murmuring into her hair. "Can't wait 'til next year when you and me can find a private spot and lay out our bedrolls side by side under the stars."

Next year she would have to smell him all night long! And from the sound of it, he didn't intend for them to get much sleep, even after a long day like today. She shuddered slightly.

"You cold? Maybe you better get t' bed, now. Might be this night air is bad for you."

There's nothing wrong with the night air! she wanted to shriek at him, but instead, she just smiled and said goodnight, glad for a chance to be rid of him. Later, beneath the chuck wagon, she lay still and listened to Lena's even breathing. Her mind was racing, and she could not make it calm down. Marrying Rand might be the biggest mistake of her life. She didn't love him, so she really shouldn't do it. They would only wind up making each other miserable.

On the other hand, she shouldn't toss aside her one and only chance for marriage and children just because another man lit a fire inside her that *should* be burning for Rand alone. She didn't know Joe Hart very well, and she certainly didn't like him. He obviously didn't like her . . . so what was the problem?

The problem, she finally conceded, was that she wished Joe Hart *would* bury his nose in her hair and touch her skin and kiss her. She had a bad case of "cowboy fever." A lot of women had it for Rand, and why *she* didn't, she could not explain. She had never thought of herself as fickle, but perhaps she was—or perhaps her experience with men was just so limited that nothing should surprise her.

At long last, she finally slept and dreamed that Joe Hart was laughing at her. He had "plucked her fiddle strings" and made her feel forbidden yearnings, and now he was laughing at her for being so weak and foolish. And while he laughed, Rand stood in the background watching and growing angrier and angrier. She felt herself rushing toward some violent confrontation, some explosive blow-up involving herself, Rand, and Joe. Powerless to stop it, to avert whatever disaster awaited, she gritted her teeth, and her heart began to hammer with dread.

Sometime during the night, she snapped upright and cracked her head against the axle of the wagon. That effectively ended her dreaming, and she passed the rest of the night with a throbbing headache, certain she would find a swelling the size of a goose egg on her head come morning.

In his bedroll not far from the chuck wagon beneath which Maggie Sterling slept, Joe lay awake a long time, staring up at the stars and castigating himself for not ignoring Maggie Sterling completely. He never should have opened his mouth when she came over and sat down beside him. He sternly reminded himself that she could make trouble for him and spoil all his plans.

At the same time, he couldn't help wishing he could follow his instincts and take Maggie away from the arrogant foreman.

As he had known from the very first, Rand Johnson had no idea how to woo a beautiful, sensitive, high-spirited young filly like Maggie—no more than he could conceive of breaking a horse in any manner but roughly.

It was a damn shame that Maggie was promised to a man who would try to dominate her instead of earning her respect and eventually, her love. . . . She had said she admired him— *him,* Joe Hart, an Indian. But would she admire him half as much if she knew what he really was? Impossible. He had been on the Broken Wheel long enough now to learn that the Sterlings—and all the cowhands, too—hated Indians and weren't happy that the Nez Perce were now living on a reservation within easy riding distance.

The fools! They didn't even realize that the Indians living at Lapwai were the most pacified members of the defeated tribe. They were the ones willing to cut their hair, become Christians, and accept white ways. The rest of his people, Chief Joseph and others like him who insisted upon wearing their hair in the Dreamer style that symbolized a longing for the old beliefs, were confined to a different reservation at Fort Colville in northern Washington.

Through the occasional newspaper, Joe had managed to keep track of Chief Joseph's continuing efforts to persuade the United States Government to allow the Nez Perce to return to the Wallowa Valley in Oregon, where many of them had originally made their homes. Joe doubted that old Joseph would ever get his wish, because the whites had never forgiven the Indians for fighting for their lands and property. They feared that if the old rebel was given his freedom, he might yet incite another rebellion.

Joe still did not know the family history of the Sterlings, but in order for Nathan Sterling to have amassed a ranch this size, he had to have been living in the area during the time of the Indian conflicts . . . and from the occasional bitter comments Joe had overheard, he deduced that the Sterlings had good reason for hating Indians, just as he had good reason for hating whites.

A relationship between himself and Maggie Sterling was clearly out of the question—unthinkable. Yet more and more lately, he found himself thinking about it, and tonight, he hadn't been able to resist baiting her. He wished she would keep the hell out of his way and let him do his job. That's all he wanted, to win Nathan Sterling's respect, not his daughter's.

He probably should not have torn off Loser's bridle today and demonstrated yet another facet of his abilities, but Rand's attitude had roused his temper and made him want to prove something. In the end, all he had wound up proving was that Nathan Sterling did not play fair. Joe was sure he had had a better time, but Maggie's father had refused to acknowledge it.

In doing so, the man had revealed a great deal about himself, as well as about his feelings toward Rand, the foreman. Nathan Sterling looked upon Rand Johnson as a son, not just a future son-in-law, which was all the more reason why Joe could not afford to alienate either of them. He must fight to keep his own temper under control and avoid souring the situation beyond repair.

He dared not allow himself to become obsessed with a woman he couldn't have. He just wished he could talk to her about horses, at least, and feed the hunger he knew she harbored. He could teach her so much! She was the first person he had met who wanted to learn the skills it had taken him years to master. Most people dismissed his methods with a scornful sneer, especially other cowhands who found it unmanly to admit they might be wrong about the way they'd been breaking horses all their lives.

Over the years, Joe had tried to use his skills only to his own advantage when he was working by himself, as cowboys often had to do . . . yet from the moment he had first arrived here and seen Maggie and the spotted horses in the meadow, he had broken his own rules. And why now—when he stood to lose so much if he made a mistake? He had reached a turning point in his life, where everything he did from this moment on could mean the difference between achieving his dream or seeing it destroyed.

Tormented by doubts and the first real confusion he had ever experienced about his purpose in life, Joe tossed and turned on his bedroll. Maggie Sterling touched him in ways he could not begin to fathom; he only knew that he desired her and that every moment he spent in her company was a sweet kind of agony. She loved the same things he loved—the horses and the land, and he sensed that her love ran as deep as his, and she revered them in the exact same way.

He felt drawn to her as he had never been drawn to any woman, but he did not want to feel this way. It was too damn dangerous. He wondered what he would do or say if he ever found her alone again—away from the prying eyes of her father and Rand. He didn't like to think about it—didn't like to admit that he couldn't trust himself to be true to his purpose. But it was *all* he could think about.

Morning came, and he rose before anyone else and walked silently down to the mist-shrouded river to bathe. The river ran close to the campsite, but was still a long enough distance away that he could bathe and swim in privacy. Stripping off his garments and plunging into cold water should take his mind off Maggie Sterling, he thought, but as he slipped through the brush and headed toward the water's edge, he saw that he was not alone. . . . Maggie herself knelt in the mist among the stones. Dipping a cloth into the water, then wringing it out, she held it against her left temple. . . . Had she hurt herself? Had someone attacked her? Unable to stop himself, he rushed to her aid.

"Here, let me see . . . ," a deep voice said to her, and Maggie dropped her cloth in startlement.

Her head had been throbbing so badly, and she had such a huge lump on her brow, that she had finally risen from her pallet beneath the wagon and made her way down to the river in the misty predawn darkness to bathe the swelling in the cold river water. She had thought no one had seen her leave camp and had intended to return before anyone missed her—but Joe Hart was suddenly standing there beside her. Taking her chin in his hand, he tilted her face so he could better examine her.

"What did you do?" he inquired. "That's quite a lump."

He wore no hat, no vest, and no chaps—only a half-opened shirt, denim pants, and boots. His dark hair curled around the collar of his shirt, and a lock of it had fallen across his brows, softening his usual scowl.

"I sat up in my sleep suddenly and bashed my head against the axle of the wagon," she confessed sheepishly.

His teeth flashed whitely in the semi-gloom. "Did you break the axle?"

She could not repress a smile. "I think I might have cracked the wagon bed."

"If the wagon splits in two and falls apart today, then I'll know who to blame." Kneeling on one knee, he picked up the cloth, dipped it in the water lapping at his pant leg, wrung it out, then pressed it to the swelling on her temple.

"You shouldn't be out here alone," he scolded. "Does anyone know you're here?"

Maggie hesitated only a bare second before admitting the truth. "No, Lena was still asleep, and no one else saw me leave. Anyway, I'm perfectly safe now that you're here."

By her tone, she dared him to dispute it, and he adjusted the cloth so he could look down into her eyes. "Ah, but you are *not* safe with me, Maggie Sterling. I thought I made that clear last night."

"You . . . you were being rude last night. This morning, you're . . . different."

She held her breath, waiting for his reaction. Considering how little she knew about this man, she was taking a big risk speaking to him with such familiarity. But then, since she could hardly run away from him, maybe it was best to be forthright and challenge his intentions right at the start of this unexpected encounter.

In his customary silent fashion, he said nothing—either in agreement or dispute. But while he held the cloth to her temple with one hand, he wound the fingers of his free hand through the hair at the nape of her neck. "I was right," he finally murmured. "Your hair does feel like silk. Long curly strands of honey-colored silk."

Beneath the intense scrutiny of his silver-eyed gaze, she could scarcely breathe. Even had she known what to say, she could not have said it. After a long moment, he released her hair and ran his knuckles down the curve of her cheek. She struggled desperately to find her voice.

"And does my skin feel as soft as the ear of a newborn calf?" she mocked.

He grinned—the first real grin he had ever given her, and it was devastating. Her heart slammed painfully against her ribcage as he nodded. "I have felt nothing softer in my lifetime."

She strove for casual bravado. "I'll just bet, Mr. Hart. You can augur quite well when you want to, can't you? At first I thought you were as tongue-tied around women as Curt Holloway, or maybe you were just one of those men without much to say. But that's not true, is it? You're very good at telling tall tales and sweet-talking a female."

"I'm only telling the truth." His tone was as seductive and caressing as his movements. He dropped the cloth and cupped her face in both hands, then smoothed his thumbs across her cheekbones. "Give me a taste of your sweetness, Maggie Sterling. A single taste is all I want."

It seemed inevitable, even predestined, that they should meet like this, and the very thing Maggie had been yearning for would finally happen. Joe bent down to her. His lips brushed her forehead, and light as a butterfly's wing, pressed against the goose egg on her temple. Lowering his hands to her shoulders, he feathered soft kisses down the side of her face to her ear lobe, which he took between his teeth and gently nipped.

She shivered in helpless reaction, aware of him suddenly, with her entire body.

His masculinity seemed the perfect counterpart to her femininity. He was lean, hard, and muscular. She was soft, supple, and at the moment, quivering. Between them shimmered an elemental attraction impossible to resist. His fingers wound through her hair again, twining the strands, learning the texture. Her breath escaped on a long sigh as his lips trailed down her neck.

Then he was kissing her—a real kiss, mouth to mouth, drawing her upward to face him as they both knelt in the water. Her breasts—suddenly full and aching—grazed his chest, but he did not try to pinion her or force her in any way . . . and because he demanded nothing, she gave him everything.

She sagged against him in boneless surrender and let him teach her the way of kissing. Not once did their noses bump. Not once did he cut off her breathing. He simply enticed and tutored her every step of the way. The sweep of his tongue along her outer lip told her to open her mouth, and when she did, he taught her why she should. The kiss was deep and drugging, making her head spin. She had no idea that kissing could make a person feel this wonderful! Had never guessed that tongues could play such an important, suggestive part in it.

When he ended the kiss, he remained breathing into her mouth, prolonging the intimacy, letting her know by the raggedness of his exhalations that he was as affected as she.

"I knew it," he murmured. "Sweet as honey. . . . I haven't tasted that nectar in a long, long time."

First, he had compared her hair to the color of honey, and then rambled on about hives, and now he was back to honey again; the man had an absolute fascination for bees and the result of their industry!

"What will you tell me next?" she murmured, utterly charmed and bemused. "That you're partial to lame women?"

"Might be I am," he said solemnly. "But if we were alone

and not likely to be disturbed, I would beg you to shuck your clothes, and let a real man teach you what loving is all about."

"Oh, my!" she gasped, pushing him away. The full import of what she had just done with this man—still a stranger to her—crashed over her like a thunderstorm, swamping her with shame and remorse. "I wish you hadn't said that, but I'm glad you did. I . . . I don't know what got into me, letting you kiss me, touch me. . . . I can't believe I've behaved this way."

"Wait a minute . . ." His grip on her arms tightened so she could not get away. His gaze compelled her to stay. "I know what's gotten into you. You're a woman who needs love and gentleness, and the man you're planning to marry isn't the one to give it to you. Find someone else, Miss Sterling. Don't let your father make your choices for you."

The gall of the man! Who did he think he was—one moment taking advantage of her and the next lecturing her about her future! "I presume you aren't volunteering for the position yourself!" she bit out.

"No, I'm not. I'm just a cowhand with nothing to offer you—no big fancy house, no ranch that stretches for miles, no herds of cattle and spotted horses. One day I'll have those things . . . but no, *I'm* not what you want and need—and neither is Rand Johnson. You're only marrying him because your father picked him out a long time ago and made him into the perfect husband for you. Except he's *not* perfect. You could do a hell of a lot better for yourself."

"How *dare* you speak to me like this! Whom I marry or don't marry is none of your business. You don't know me, and you don't know Rand."

She began to struggle, wrenching away from him and trying to get to her feet. Her skirts were soaked and heavy, her feet squishing in her shoes. For the first time, she noticed that she and Joe had been kneeling in the shallow water lapping the shore. He helped her rise and kept hold of her arms, his grip tight enough to leave bruises.

"Yes, I do know you, Maggie. A man can tell a lot from the

way a woman kisses. Hell, you wouldn't have let me kiss you in the first place if you were happy with Rand's attentions."

"I never meant to kiss you! It shouldn't have happened. So don't let it give you any ideas. It will certainly never happen again."

"Glad to hear that," he drawled in his infuriatingly superior way. "I can't think why I'd want to kiss a woman who finds it so distasteful to kiss me back."

"It wasn't distasteful—I mean, it *was*—oh, let's just say I'll never do it again. I love Rand Johnson, and I intend to marry him."

"Is that so?" he taunted. "Amazing. You may be able to fool yourself, but you sure as hell don't fool me. You don't love Rand; you just love the idea of living forever on the Broken Wheel, and you need a man like Rand to run it for you."

"I don't need him to run the ranch! I've got my father."

"For now, but not forever. He's getting old. One day, he'll die. When he's gone, what will you do, Maggie Sterling? You, a cripple? Rope the first man you see? Not if you've got handy Randy around to run things for you. You'll be in great shape—except you'll be miserable. . . . Oh, what the hell do *I* care? Why am I even arguing with you?"

"Yes, why are you? And why did you kiss me?"

"Why did you let me?"

"I . . . I don't know."

"Neither do I. I came down here to take a swim in the river. And that's what I'm damn well going to do!"

His hands went to his shirt fastenings, and he began to rip off the garment right in front of her. In the blink of an eye, he was tossing his shirt into the bushes that grew nearby. Then he kicked off his boots and sent them flying through the air to land on either side of her. For one endless moment, she was too shocked to react. When he started on his pants however, she found her tongue.

"Don't you dare take off another thing until I leave here!"

Bare-chested, muscles rippling beneath taut dark skin, his

hands at the level of his navel, he stopped what he was doing and glared at her. "If you don't want to see a naked man, Miss Sterling, you had better turn tail and run."

"Nothing would give me more pleasure."

"Quit lying to yourself. Nothing would give you more pleasure than to stay and gawk, only you won't admit it."

"Oh! You are . . . are . . ." She couldn't think of a strong enough insult to express her feelings.

"A man," he helpfully supplied and yanked his pants down around his hips.

She made an embarrassing little squeak of indignation, spun around, and started limping away. Oh, yes, he was a man all right—but also a monster. Arrogant, dangerous, disturbing, immoral, conceited, moody. . . . She ran out of things to call him but was sure she would think of more later.

As she tromped back to camp, she did think of other words to describe Joe Hart, but they weren't exactly the terms for which she was looking. In addition to all his faults, he was also handsome, seductive, tempting, and the most exciting man she had ever met. Good lord, he knew how to kiss! . . . and his body. She had never had such a response to a male body, but then she had never before given much thought to one. She had seen Rand without his shirt and never had such a reaction; the sight had certainly not given her heart palpitations or made her wonder what the rest of him looked like.

From now on, she must avoid Joe Hart at all costs.

Ten

Maggie avoided Joe Hart for the whole rest of the roundup and branding. It went swiftly, for none of the men could be enticed into making any more bets, no matter how hard Nathan pushed them. Even Rand dug in his heels and refused, claiming he just wanted to get the job done and over with. However, he and Joe wound up doing most of the roping and dragging of the calves to the branding fire. The two men took turns and managed to work so fast that it required two teams of flankers just to tie the calves and keep the irons hot and moving.

In no time at all, Maggie found herself homeward bound in the wagon—with Joe once more handling the team. He brushed the brim of his hat in greeting as he climbed into the conveyance and picked up the reins. She didn't respond, but Lena gave him a broad smile and an answering nod.

As the team set off for home, Joe said: "Glad to be heading home again, ladies?"

Suspicious of this sudden friendliness, Maggie gave him a sidelong glare. He met her gaze with infuriating calm, his gray eyes glinting, and she suspected he was laughing inside at her expense.

"I confess I am delighted, *señor*," Lena volunteered. "Sleeping on the ground makes my bones ache."

"You could have slept inside the wagon, couldn't you?" Joe clucked to the horses to hurry them along.

"*Si, Señor,* but there it is too stuffy. That one night it rained, we—*Señorita* Maggie and I—almost suffocated."

Joe laughed companionably. "Better than getting wet like the rest of us. I forgot to cover up with my tarp when I bedded down and woke up soaked, and so did most everyone else."

"That storm came up fast, *señor.* One moment the stars were shining, and the next, it was raining."

"We were lucky the cattle didn't spook," Joe agreed, amazing Maggie with his unusual loquacity. "Had there been thunder and lightning, we might have had trouble."

"I do not know how you men stand it," Lena said. "I hate to be out on the range when it storms. That is when I miss the comforts of my bed the most."

"If a man has the good sense to climb into his soogan instead of lying on top of it like I did that night, he doesn't get wet. I deserved to get soaked, and I did."

Maggie continued to be silent. She was sure Joe was rambling on like this simply to annoy her, and she felt a deep sense of relief when Rand rode up beside the wagon and demanded to know why Joe was driving.

"What you doin' up there, Hart? I don't remember givin' you orders to see the ladies back t' the ranch."

Joe looked straight ahead, his face completely expressionless. "I drove them out; I assumed I was driving them back."

"Pull up, and I'll get Curt Holloway t' take over. My little cow bunny don't like you much, so I see no reason t' inflict your comp'ny on her all the way back to the ranch."

A cow bunny was a cowman's sweetheart or wife. Until she found the courage to tell Rand that she still had doubts about their suitability for each other, he had a perfect right to call her that. Still, she could not help cringing. She had been avoiding Rand because she felt guilty about what had happened between her and Joe and wasn't sure what to do about it. She had been losing sleep over the issue but was no closer to a solution now than before. She only knew she felt guilty and confused.

Speaking not a word to either man, she twisted her hands together in her lap and wished, for perhaps the hundredth time, that she had never met Joe Hart, much less let him kiss her.

Beneath Rand's watchful gaze, Joe halted the team and swung down from the wagon, then went around back to untie his horse. Rand motioned for Curt Holloway to join them, then he rode closer to Maggie.

"Sorry you had t' put up with him, honey. Was he rude or anythin' while he was drivin' t'day?"

When Maggie didn't immediately answer, Lena answered for her. "No, *Señor* Rand. Today, he was a perfect gentleman. I was *mucho* surprised. On the ride here, he would not stoop to talk to us, but now it seems he has discovered his tongue."

"Today, he was well-mannered," Maggie conceded, unable to explain that she thought his "mannerliness" was actually a way of annoying her.

"Good, 'cause if he don't show you the proper respect, I'll run him off this range faster'n you can say 'skat' to a sachet kitten. He won't last longer'n a keg of cider at a barn raisin'."

"A sachet kitten is a skunk, *si?* That's a good one, *Señor* Rand, I will have to remember it. And a keg of cider would disappear very quickly at a barn raising, wouldn't it?"

Rand grinned, pleased to have impressed Lena, at least, since he wasn't making much headway with Maggie. "I'm glad someone around here appreciates my augurin'. . . . By the way, Maggie, I talked t' yer Pa like you wanted me to, and he gave his say-so for addin' on to the ranch house. What y'all think about that?"

He looked so proud of himself that Maggie felt twice as guilty. "Why . . . that's good news, Rand . . . yes, indeed. Very good news. Thank you."

"Go ahead and draw up what you want, and we'll get started on it right away. . . . Curt, you took long enough gittin' over here." Rand jerked his head toward the empty wagon seat. "These ladies need someone t' drive 'em home. So tie yer hoss t' the back end an' oblige 'em."

"Aw, hell, Rand." Curt looked predictably unhappy. "I thought Joe was drivin' 'em. He's the newest hand on the spread."

"Yeah, but you're the youngest, an' it really oughta be yer job."

"I can do it myself, Rand." Maggie reached for the lines lying on the seat.

"No, Curt'll be happy as a pig in a wallow t' do it, woncha, Curt?"

"Guess so," Curt grumbled.

"See y'all later." Rand tipped his hat and rode off while Curt rode around back of the wagon, muttering in disgust.

"Should be Will or Gusty drivin' this old pie-box—not me. This is no job for a top hand."

Maggie exchanged glances with Lena. "Cowboys," Lena sighed. "They do not complain about driving this wagon when it's full of pies and time to eat, do they?"

"No, they don't," Maggie agreed with a laugh.

"What is this about adding onto the house, Maggie?"

"Oh, it's just an idea I had to give us more room when Rand and I get married. I don't want to be living on top of you and Papa. You two have your own lives; Rand and I need to have ours. Neither of us wants to bother you."

Lena looked surprised and oddly nervous. "You will not be bothering *me*, Maggie. As for your Papa, I cannot say. I . . . I only see him when it comes time to eat, and I serve the meals."

Maggie glanced around to see if they were alone. Curt was still around back, grumbling. She decided to drop the hint that she knew exactly what had been going on all these years. She had been meaning to bring up the matter, and now was as good a time as any.

"If Rand and I no longer take our meals with my father—if we eat by ourselves and Papa has to eat alone—maybe he'll stop pretending he doesn't care for you, Lena. The two of you should eat together. You're both lonely, and you need each other. It's long past time you admit it."

"*Señorita Maggie!*"

Maggie smiled at her friend's reaction. Lena had gone lily-white; her eyes were as huge as wash basins. She seemed astonished by the realization that Maggie was aware of her relationship with Nathan.

"Lena, I've known for a long time," Maggie whispered. "Don't be embarrassed. I whole-heartedly approve. Nothing would make me happier than to see you and my father find happiness together. Why, I think of you as my second mother, and I don't understand why Papa hasn't proposed to you before this."

"Oh, Señorita Maggie!" Lena burst into tears.

At the same moment, Curt came around the side of the wagon, saw Lena's tears, and froze in his tracks.

"What should I do?" he appealed to Maggie. "Is she hurt or sick? Should I go git Rand or Mr. Sterlin'?"

"Just get in the wagon and drive, Curt. Come on . . . get in. She'll be all right."

"Maggie!" Lena sobbed. "You must promise me never to speak of this matter to *Señor* Nathan. You must never tell him that you know about . . . about . . ."

As Curt took his place beside her, Maggie slid one arm around Lena's plump shoulders. "Hush! Hush now, Lena. Don't say it in front of Curt. The poor fellow is embarrassed enough as it is."

Curt did look as if he wished he were somewhere in Oregon right at this moment. "Don't worry, ma'am. I ain't payin' attention. I didn't hear a thing, so don't tell me no more."

He clucked to the horses, and the wagon started off with a lurch, the creaking of the wheels and harness muting the sound of Lena's sobs. Lena threw the flap of her ever-present apron over her head and wept noisily, until Maggie found herself losing patience.

"Lena, why are you carrying on so, when I told you that I approve? . . . Close your ears, Curt. Lena and I have to talk."

"But you do not understand, *Señorita* Maggie!"

"I certainly don't. Can't you explain without . . . without revealing everything?"

"You do not know me, Maggie. Fifteen years I have lived in your house. Fifteen years I have . . . have . . ."

"I think I understand what you mean to say, Lena. Do go on, please."

"Well, haven't you ever wondered why my belly has not swelled with child?"

"Sweet mother Mary!" Curt burst out. "Git on you ole crow-bait hosses, 'fore I trade you in fer maggoty sheep."

Curt—shy, quiet Curt—began to cuss and swear at the team, calling them every bad name he could think of, so that Maggie and Lena had to put their heads together and whisper in each other's ears to be heard. This was obviously Curt's intention; he didn't want to hear anything more. The idea of Lena's belly swelling with child was shocking, the sort of thing women just did not discuss in front of men.

"I have to say I've honestly never wondered about that, Lena—the thought never occurred to me. But if you want to talk about it, you might as well, since you've gone this far," Maggie mouthed into Lena's ear. She bent her head to hear the response.

Lena sighed and dabbed at her eyes. "Once I loved an *hombre* in Mexico—a rich young man whose Papa owned a huge cattle ranch there. Unfortunately, he did not approve of his only son marrying a poor peasant girl. I became pregnant and bore a child—a little girl—but the baby died at birth. It was a hard birth, and I nearly died also. Afterward, I bled for a long time, far more than normal. When I recovered, the midwife told me I would never bear another child. My insides were all ruined. . . . God's punishment for my grievous sin."

"Oh, surely not, Lena! You were young and foolish maybe, but not wicked and evil."

"What I did was a sin, *Señorita* Maggie. The Church says so. And my young man then cast me aside and married a beautiful young virgin from good family, as his father wished him to do. I was outcast, a woman in disgrace and a burden to my family, so I left my home and came north, traveling from one

ranch to another—cooking, mending, sewing, and washing. . . .
But every place I went, I. . . ."

The wagon jolted over a deep rut, and Maggie had to make
Lena repeat what she had said, for it was impossible to hear
her sorrowful whisper. "You what?" she prompted.

"Eventually, I had to leave, for there was always a wife looking over my shoulder, ready to accuse me if I did wrong. I was
very careful to do no wrong, but sometimes, the ranch owner
or his son would smile at me or tease me. And then I knew it
was time to go. I did not wish to make trouble for anyone—and
I was guarding my heart, for I did not want to be badly hurt
again."

"Then you arrived at the Broken Wheel," Maggie added over
Curt's singing.

In his zeal to distract himself from their conversation, Curt
was singing to the team as night riders usually sang to the cattle
to keep them calm on dark, stormy nights. He was, as Gusty
would call it, "punishin' the air with a noise like he was garglin'
with axle grease." All he needed was a mouth organ to accompany himself as he moaned about not getting buried on the
lone prairie where the coyotes would howl over his remains. . . .
Maggie resolved to reward him for his tact, if not his tune, by
baking him his very own dried apple pie at the first opportunity.

"*Si*, Maggie. I arrived at the Broken Wheel and found a
house with no females in it, except for one small girl who had
nightmares and worried her poor Papa half to death over it. . . .
So I decided to stay and be what comfort I could to both of
them."

Maggie grabbed Lena's hand and squeezed it. "And that's
what you've been all these years—a comfort and a joy, Lena.
So I think it's time you knew some joy yourself. You've more
than atoned for one youthful mistake."

Lena's tears welled anew as she vigorously shook her head
in denial. "But I am unworthy, Maggie. And I can bear no
children—what every man wants from a wife. Purity and fecundity. I can give your father neither."

"My father doesn't want any more children, Lena! And I'm sure by now he's guessed that you can't have any. Why, you're both too old even to be thinking of it—aren't you?"

Lena shrugged her shoulders. "I am not so old, Maggie. I was very young when all this happened. Other women my age have been known to conceive, and old men are the worst ones for wanting to prove their virility! The way it is now, no one knows what Nathan and I sometimes do in the night . . . at least, I always thought no one knew. But if we married, then people would begin to talk . . . and Nathan might wish I could give him a son."

"Oh, I'm sure you're wrong, Lena. Have you told my father what you just told me?"

Lena nodded. "*Si*, and he said he understood and did not mind what happened before I met him."

"Then you see? He *doesn't* mind."

"But if he doesn't mind, then why has he not asked me to marry him before this? I think it is because I am a fallen woman—not the sort a man takes for a wife."

"I don't know, Lena, but I'm going to find out. I can't believe my father condemns you for something that happened so long ago, before he even met you. I think he probably just wanted to protect me, somehow. He thought I might object to having a new mother or some other such silliness. But I don't object at all—and anyway, I'm all grown up now and not in the least shocked or upset by what you've told me. . . . I mean it, Lena; you and my father should get married at long last. You've been together fifteen years. If it's lasted this long, it should last another five, ten, or twenty years. My father's getting old, and so are you. Both of you deserve a chance at happiness and companionship before you die. It's time to bring your love out into the open. Why hide it any longer—and from whom? I already know about it, and so does Curt. . . . Don't you, Curt?"

Maggie elbowed the young man in the ribs, and he blushed a deep shade of crimson and bellowed even louder, this time a verse from "The Old Chisolm Trail.

"He knows about it," Maggie said to Lena. "He's just too shy to admit it."

"Oh, I don't know, *Señorita* Maggie! Your Papa could be very angry, too. He is happy with the way things are. Perhaps it is best not to try and change them. Marriage is such a big step; he may not be prepared to marry again."

"No, but the two of you are extremely vocal when it comes to advising me to wed, aren't you?"

"That is different. You are young; *Señor* Rand is young—and he loves you very much. He will be a good husband to you, and you will both have what you want—the Broken Wheel. Your children will grow up loving the same things you love. It is *muy* different for you, *querida*."

"I'm still not sure we love each other, Lena. I have as many—if not more—doubts than you. . . . But I don't want to talk about them right now. Poor Curt has heard enough of our troubles. What I am going to do is speak to my father and tell *him* that I know about the two of you. Once he realizes that secrecy is no longer necessary, I think we'll be planning your wedding along with mine. You wait and see . . ."

Maggie patted Lena's hand encouragingly, then turned her attention to Curt. "Give your lungs a rest, Curt. We've finished exchanging confidences . . . and I can't stand much more of your wailing. You sound like a cat whose tail's been caught under a rocking chair."

Curt abruptly snapped his jaw shut, pulled his hat down, hunched his shoulders, and fixed his gaze on Preacher's long back. Even the tips of his ears where they were pushed out by his Stetson were blood-red. The poor young man was beside himself with embarrassment over what he had overheard. Knowing he would carry no tales, Maggie smiled to herself.

She was glad she had spoken up and ended fifteen years of pretense and falsehood. It was time for the truth to come out— for her father and Lena, of course, not necessarily for her. She didn't want anyone to ever discover that she had shared a steamy forbidden kiss with a man other than her intended, and that she hadn't been able to forget it, try though she might.

That kiss was best forgotten, however, and eventually she would succeed. Joe Hart had made it clear that although he was attracted to her, he wanted nothing more to do with her. So be it. *She must put him out of her mind.* Instead, she must concentrate on Rand and discover if she could *learn* to love him. Just because he didn't arouse the same feelings as Joe Hart, didn't mean she couldn't overcome her petty aversions and develop a lasting relationship with him.

Rand had even spoken to her father about expanding the house, as she had requested! He was doing his best to please her—couldn't she make the same effort? Their marriage would make everybody so happy. If she worked at it, it could make her happy, too.

Thus decided, she rode the rest of the way home in silence, ignoring all her niggling little doubts.

Two weeks after the end of the spring roundup, Joe saddled Loser and rode up to the mountains for a stint of line riding, as ordered by Rand.

Most of the cowhands ranked this task only a step above fence riding, for both were lonely, tedious, monotonous jobs wherein a single man rode the boundary or fence lines of a spread to check on any problems and solve them before they became serious. The fence rider primarily had to mend fences, a boring task involving dismounting and using his hands, while the line rider had to check the condition of everything in his path.

He had to examine the watering holes, grazing land, and cattle, make certain none of the stock were bogged down in mud or quicksand, sick, or injured, and drive any strays from neighboring ranches back to their home ranges, as well as collect wandering cattle wearing the Broken Wheel brand and bring them back home.

Some ranches had lean-tos or shacks where the line rider could take shelter, but as long as the weather held fair, Joe intended to sleep out under the stars. He didn't even mind doing his own cooking. He was planning to trap small game Indian-style and dig some camas bulbs to go with his fresh meat, which meant he would eat better than the usual line rider who had to make do with only coffee, beans, and if he was lucky, bacon.

Actually, Joe was looking forward to keeping his own company; he had had enough of watching Maggie Sterling from afar while Rand Johnson taught her how to load and fire a six-shooter, walked out with her in the evenings, and argued with her over the changes they were planning for the house.

One day, he had heard Rand shouting at Maggie as they stood at the side of the house debating where to knock out the walls for an expansion they were planning. Maggie had won the argument, but not without effort. Joe thought it absurd that any man would want to involve himself with decisions regarding living arrangements. In his opinion, such decisions belonged solely to women.

In the Nez Perce culture, men always decided when and where to make and break camp, but women arranged everything else to their satisfaction. No man would dream of telling a squaw where to put her kettles or cookfire, and this amounted to the same thing.

As he had done so often before, he had silently laughed at the foolishness of white men in general and Rand, in particular. At the same time, he had wished he could pummel Rand into the dirt, sweep Maggie aboard his horse, and ride off with her. Line riding was just what he needed to rid himself entirely of such feelings. Alone in the mountains, he hoped to find peace of mind and freedom from his raging desire for Maggie Sterling.

At least, he wouldn't have to look at her—or Rand—and ponder how wrong they were for each other. He couldn't understand how no one else but him seemed able to see it. Nor could he imagine how Maggie would survive living in the same house with her father *and* her new husband, expansion or no expansion.

The two men together would break her spirit; they were cut from the same leather. They had to dominate and boss others around, and once she was married to Rand—and still under her father's influence—Maggie would lose what little independence and spunk she now possessed. He could see it coming. Joe just hoped he wouldn't have to watch it happen.

By the time Christmas came, he planned to own his own land and be living on it, no matter how rude and primitive the shelter. If Nathan refused to sell him cattle and horses, Joe had decided he would look for land anyway, buy whatever he could manage, and start building his empire. It may be smaller at first than he had planned, but he'd be damned if he would stay on the Broken Wheel and watch Maggie throw her life away marrying the wrong man. . . . It was too much to ask.

Not that *he* was the right man, of course. He knew he wasn't. Yet if things were different . . . if he was white . . . or if half-breeds were accepted in white society . . . Maggie would be the woman he would court. Since he wasn't, and halfbreeds weren't, it was a useless exercise to think about it. She simply wasn't the sort of woman to whom he could lie about his background. Then, too, he was not yet ready to abandon his heritage entirely. At times, when he could indulge himself secretly, he took great pride and a secret joy in reliving some of the old ways, as much as he could remember them.

Line riding should give him the perfect opportunity to clear his head and rededicate himself to his goals. His future was the only thing that mattered. What became of Maggie Sterling was none of his business, and he would rid himself of this unhealthy fascination once and for all.

After three days of his own company, Joe experienced the first sense of peace and contentment he had known in a long time. He doctored several cows for screw-worms, cut out a bunch of steers wearing the wrong brand and drove them off the Sterling grasslands, relocated a bunch of cattle from one meadow to another where the water and grazing were better, and roasted and ate fresh meat he himself had trapped.

Alone beneath the golden sun by day and the bright stars at night, he reveled in a sense of oneness with nature and his horse. The wide vistas of the mountain ranges had a healing effect, and he rejoiced in his own strength and self-sufficiency. This was as close to living like an Indian as he would ever get. It might be lonely, but it was satisfying; such stints as these over the years were what had kept him from succumbing to despair and fueled his hope and dreams.

Swimming in the cold streams, riding the mountain ranges, bearing witness to the beauty of the land and sky, the sunrises and sunsets, convinced him there might actually be a God watching over the earth. He still believed in his *wy-ya-kin,* or spirit guide, the spotted horse, but he had many times doubted the existence of *Hanyawat,* the Creator. *Hanyawat* had either never heard or refused to respond to his youthful pleas for divine vengeance to be visited upon the whites. *Hanyawat* had apparently abandoned the Nez Perce altogether, but Joe could still appreciate His handiwork and marvel at the landscape sculptured by His hand.

On the fourth day of his assignment, Joe had occasion to skirt the mountain meadow where he had first seen Maggie and the spotted horses. He was riding the crest of rock overlooking the meadow, trailing a bunch of cows who had strayed from the main herd. It seemed like the perfect opportunity to stop and get a closer look at the horses with the idea of selecting a few choice mares he would like to buy from Nathan Sterling and breed to Loser.

Excitement swept through him as he mounted the ridge and caught sight of the horses below, peacefully grazing. The stallion lifted his head from the grass and snorted, but did not take alarm, for the wind was blowing in the opposite direction and did not carry Loser's scent.

Joe paused in almost the exact spot where he had first watched Maggie gentling a foal. He recalled his first view of her honey-colored hair, and the first sound of her innocent, joyous laughter. It had done something to him then, and the memory of it did something to him now. He had desired her from the moment he first saw her; she had appeared in that moment as everything appealing in a female—and nothing had changed since then. He *still* desired her.

Sighing to himself, he studied each of the mares in turn, noting their good points and their weak ones, deciding which would nick the best with Loser and produce superior offspring. Then, in the silence of the golden afternoon, a faint sound reached his ears—the jingle of harness and creak of a cart.

No. No, it couldn't be. But it was. The sounds came closer, and a moment later, Maggie herself drove into sight. She was wearing a yellow bonnet and matching yellow shirtwaist over a brown skirt. Brown gloves protected her hands and gave her a good grip on the lines as she expertly maneuvered Preacher around a patch of rough ground and drove almost into the midst of the grazing herd.

She was alone, and Joe's first thought was "good for her." She was refusing to allow her father or Rand to dictate to her yet. His second thought was that he had better get out of there quickly, before she spotted him. He picked up his reins, and Loser's ears flicked back in anticipation, but Joe didn't give the signal. He couldn't. She was a feast for his hungry eyes, and he couldn't bear to leave just yet.

Sweat broke out on his brow, and his heartbeat accelerated as he watched her climb out of the cart, remove her hat and gloves, toss them on the seat, and begin unhitching Preacher as if she meant to stay awhile. The sun turned her hair to burnished copper, and his fingers itched to feel that silkiness again. His groin tightened.

This was madness. He ought to ride away this very minute. She was bound to notice him sooner or later—and then what? He had a good excuse for being there, but he didn't trust himself to be alone with her. He couldn't even stop his body from reacting to the sight of her. His Levi's were painfully tight, and the reins had become slippery in his left hand. . . . He and Maggie were alone again—this time, truly alone.

She suddenly straightened and stood very still, her back to him, and he knew that she knew he was there, watching her. With that peculiar awareness they seemed to have for each other, she had somehow sensed it. Very slowly, she turned around. Her gaze collided with his. He brushed the brim of his hat, then pressed his leg against Loser's side, turned him, and began to ride slowly down the ridge to join her.

I shouldn't be doing this, he thought to himself. But how could he *not* do it? Perhaps his *wy-ya-kin* had led him here and arranged for Maggie to arrive at the exact same moment. He could not discount the possibility, though logic told him he was simply making excuses and allowing passion to rule him, instead of common sense.

Yet he could not stop himself. He would only talk with her for several moments—discuss the horses, perhaps—pass the time of day. There was nothing wrong with that. Then he would leave and go look for his cattle. This was *not* another opportunity to kiss her or a chance to talk her out of marrying Rand. Maybe he would just apologize for his behavior that morning by the river.

Yes, that was it—he would apologize. He had never meant to behave as he had, and he had been regretting it ever since. There would be no more kisses or stripping down in front of her. No more goading or teasing. She was the daughter of his employer, and he would simply ride down and pay his respects.

Eleven

Maggie wanted to run and hide. She did *not* want to stand there and wait for Joe Hart to once again play havoc with her decision to marry Rand. Lately, she and Rand had been making progress—fighting as much as they ever had—but also growing closer as they spent more time together.

Rand had taught her to load and fire a six-shooter, and today, she had one hidden in the cart beneath the seat. This morning, he had even agreed to let her drive into town by herself. She had neglected to tell him that if the weather held fair, she might take a detour to check on her horses; there was no sense upsetting him needlessly. She had simply told him not to expect her before nightfall.

However, she never would have come here had she known that doing so would lead to another encounter with Joe Hart! Now, here she was—and here he was, in the last place she had expected to find him. After nearly three weeks of doubts and confusion, just when she had convinced herself that marriage to Rand was the right thing after all, he had arrived on the scene to renew their tempestuous, disturbing acquaintance and arouse all her doubts once more.

Maggie's hands flew to her hair as she attempted to smooth it down and restrain it. In her haste to tear off her bonnet, she had made a mess of the neat arrangement labored over earlier at home. The day was warm and humid, with clouds gathering on the horizon, and her hair tended to frizz and curl in such weather. Futilely, she tried to brush away the wrinkles on her skirt. Then she pinched her cheeks to give them color and bit her lips so hard they nearly bled.

It finally occurred to her that she was primping for Joe in a way she never bothered to do for Rand, and the realization brought her up short—damn the man for always upsetting her so! It wasn't fair. She had no defense against him and the flustered way he made her feel; all he had to do was brush the brim of his hat in greeting, and she went all fluttery and nervous, like a goose in a hailstorm. Not a single male in her limited experience held such a power over her, and she could only guess at what it might mean. . . . Surely she couldn't be in love with a man she barely knew and didn't particularly like!

Determined to act casually—to ignore him, if possible— Maggie slowly removed Preacher's harness and dumped it in a pile in the grass. The old horse gratefully lowered his head and began munching right where he stood. Catching him should be easy, she decided, and was glad she had turned him loose for a bit, even if it did mean she could not make a quick exit. Well, she had her six-shooter, and if Joe Hart bothered her in any way, she would draw it and take a bead on him; that should straighten him out in a hurry!

Slowly, she got out her brushes and curry combs, neatly arranged in a small basket, and limped over to one of the mares to begin grooming her. No sooner had she started when Joe's deep mellow voice interrupted.

"Need any help, Miss Sterling?"

"No! I can manage perfectly well by myself, thank you." Refusing to look at him, she vigorously brushed the mare's spotted hide, which was streaked with dried mud and grass stains.

"What are you planning to do about that swelling just above the pastern on her hind leg?"

"Swelling? What swelling?" Maggie had been so busy trying to ignore Joe that she hadn't noticed anything amiss with the mare—but now she did.

Bending down to examine the puffy area, she discovered a

small deep wound, crusted over with dried blood and hot and hard to the touch. "Oh, dear. I'm afraid she's injured herself, and now it's infected."

"Here. Let me take a look." Joe was suddenly pushing her aside.

Stepping backward, she glanced around for his horse but didn't immediately spot it, until she caught sight of a slight movement among the rocks halfway up the ridge. So as not to alarm the herd stallion, Joe had thoughtfully tied Loser upwind of the herd and behind a huge boulder and some scrubby trees.

While Joe knelt and examined the wound, she got her first good look at him in nearly three long weeks. He was wearing a red shirt and bandanna today, no vest, but the same brown leather chaps as usual, and the same brown boots and shiny silver spurs. He had pushed his hat back on his forehead, the better to see what he was doing, and a lock of dark hair with reddish highlights dipped low across his brows in a manner that was fast becoming familiar to her.

His brilliant gray eyes were full of sympathy as he gently probed the swelling. The mare lifted her hind leg in protest, and he soothed her with quiet words and a pat higher up on her leg. "Easy, ole girl. Nobody's going to hurt you. If anything, we're going to make you feel better."

To Maggie, he said: "We'll have to clean the wound and make a poultice to put over it to draw out the poison. I've got a halter and lead rope in my saddle bags. Can you get them for me? Loser's up there by that boulder."

Suddenly glad he was there and willing to help—and that he gave her credit for being able to be useful—she hurried to do his bidding. The brief climb up the ridge challenged her, but she managed it without mishap and quickly found the halter. It proved to be a well-crafted affair made of twined black, white, and red horsehair, one of the nicest she had ever seen. She wondered if he had fashioned it himself or bought it from someone. She rather suspected he had done the handiwork, for it had that same meticulous look about it as everything else he owned.

"I have a canteen of fresh water with me," she told him upon her return. Deftly, she slipped the halter over the mare's head and nose, handed him the end of the lead rope, and started back toward the cart. "I'll go get it."

Several moments later, she returned with the leather-covered metal container, then realized she had no cloth with which to wash the wound. Setting down the canteen, she lifted the hem of her skirt and proceeded to tear off a long strip of petticoat.

From his vantage point near the ground where he was kneeling by the mare, Joe Hart eyed her exposed ankles with an impudent interest she pointedly ignored. "Here." She held out the cloth and the canteen, but to her surprise he rose and motioned for her to begin washing the wound.

"I'm going to look for a few plants, any one of which will do the job. Just wash the wound carefully and try not to hurt her."

"If I hurt her, she won't stand still," Maggie replied with some asperity. "So, of course, I won't hurt her."

Joe patted the mare's neck reassuringly. "Just stand here and eat grass, sweetheart. We'll have you better in no time."

With a deep-throated nicker, the mare lowered her head and obediently pulled at the grass, leaving Maggie to wonder what sort of magic Joe Hart possessed. It seemed he could make all horses understand him and lose their fear in his presence. Shaking her head in exasperation and envy, she bent to her task.

Pouring water on the wound, she gently tried to cleanse it, but the cut was so crusty with dried blood and dirt that it was impossible to make much headway. The canteen was only half full, and she soon used up all the water without having succeeded at actually cleaning the wound.

Minutes later, Joe returned clutching a handful of green sprigs. "What's that?" she asked.

"Just an herb that's fairly common in these parts. If we crush it, ball it up, and tie it around the wound, it should help take down the swelling and draw out the poison. . . . Don't look so skeptical. I've tried it before, and it works."

"Where did you learn about it?" she demanded.

"From an old Indian a long time ago. He had a name for it, but I've no idea what it means in English."

"What was the name?" She was fascinated—so he *had* had contact with Indians, just as she had suspected!

He told her, and it sounded like gibberish. She could not even repeat it back to him. "So where did you meet this Indian?"

"Just met him, that's all. It was in . . . Montana, I think. Yeah, Montana." He bent to take another look at the mare's leg. "You didn't get that wound very clean. Where's the water and cloth?" He held out his hand, and she gave him the cloth.

"The water's all gone. I didn't have as much in the canteen as I thought I did," she apologized.

"Then we'll have to find a creek or stream and go stand her in it. Probably a good idea anyway, because the water will help take down the swelling."

"There's a stream down at the other end of the meadow. It's where the horses go to drink. . . . But it . . . it's a long walk from here." Maggie pointed in the direction of the stream and realized it was much too far for her. She would never make it there and back on foot. "I'll have to rehitch Preacher and drive the distance. Maybe we could tie the mare to the back end of the cart."

"Why bother with all that? I'll put you up on Loser, and you can ride while I lead the mare alongside you. It's not all that far."

"Oh, but I can't ride! You *know* that!"

He straightened and gave her one of his heart-stopping grins. "Oh, yes, you can, Miss Sterling. Here, I'll show you."

Before she could quite grasp what he meant to do, he shoved the cloth and herb in his back pocket and put his hands around her waist. "Mr. Hart, don't!" she shrieked.

He didn't listen. He simply picked her up, cradled her as if she were an infant, and started carrying her up the ridge toward Loser. Thankfully, the herd stallion and most of the herd had moved further away and did not appear too interested in what was going on with the human beings in their meadow.

"This . . . this is ridiculous!" Maggie sputtered. "I should stay here while you take the mare to the water."

"What? Deprive me of your company? Forget it, Miss Sterling. Besides, haven't you always wanted to ride? Well, now's your chance."

When they reached Loser, he set her sideways on the saddle. She grabbed the saddle horn and held on for dear life while Loser looked around at her with an expression of mild curiosity. What's going on? he seemed to be saying.

"Don't worry. Loser's not going to buck or run away with you. But you'll feel more secure if you put one leg over the saddle and ride astride; that way you can put your feet in the stirrups."

She was sure he was right; sitting sideways, she might slip off and tumble among the rocks. The ground looked a long way down. "B-but if I do that, you'll see m-my l-limbs. My skirt will ride up."

He slanted her another roguish grin. "I've seen ladies' limbs before. But if it'll make you feel better, I'll turn my back while you do it. Then you can rearrange your skirt, and I probably won't be able to see much more than your ankles—which I've already had occasion to admire, by the way."

She was petrified with fear—as much that he might catch a glimpse of her misshapen leg, as she was that she might fall off the horse. At the same time, she felt exhilarated; she was actually sitting on the back of a beautiful spotted stallion!

While Joe turned away, she managed to lift her good leg over the saddle horn and spread out her skirts to cover as much as possible. Unfortunately, she couldn't reach the stirrups. Joe's legs were much longer than hers, but she was too embarrassed to draw attention to the fact. One simply did not discuss comparisons of anatomy in polite society.

He spun around, grinning, and noticed the problem right away. "Guess I'll have to take up those stirrups, won't I? Then you can put your feet in them and feel comfortable."

He made the necessary adjustments with an economy of motion—the way he did everything else, with his own peculiar ease and grace. As he slid her foot with the built-up sole into the ox-bow stirrup, she held her breath, hoping he wouldn't notice how much it differed from her other shoe.

He did notice. "A brilliant idea." Holding her by the ankle, he studied the alteration to her shoe. "This leg must be shorter than the other, but the raised sole helps you to get around better. I'm impressed. Whose idea was it?"

"My father's," she said stiffly. "And you can let go of my ankle now."

But he didn't—at least not right away. "Is your leg—pardon me, your *limb*—just shorter, or is it also thinner and weaker?" His hand started to move higher, and she slapped at it and almost fell off the horse.

"Hasn't anyone ever told you that you mustn't go around feeling a young lady's limbs—or sneaking peeks at them?"

He laughed and shook his head. "My interest in your *limb* is completely innocent—at the moment. I just want to know what's wrong with it."

It didn't escape her that he had specified *at the moment,* or that he was mocking society's polite euphemism for the unacceptable term, *leg.* "Why are you so interested? I thought you were a cowman, not a doctor!" she taunted in her most sarcastic tone.

His silver-gray eyes caught and held hers as surely as if he'd dropped a lasso over her head. "Because I'm going to teach you to ride, Miss Sterling, and in order to do that, I need to know how severe your impairment is."

He was offering her the moon—the thing she had always wanted—but she knew she couldn't accept. For her, riding wasn't possible; she might as well let him know this very instant. "My bad leg is not only shorter than my good one, but it's twisted and misshapen—about as ugly and useless as a leg can get."

She kept her hand on her skirt, holding it down lest an errant breeze blow it upward and reveal the deformity of which she spoke. Even her undergarments could not hide its ugliness.

"It can't be that bad, or you couldn't walk on it," he said. "May I see it?"

"Certainly not!" A flush crept up her cheeks, and she had the sudden, horrifying feeling that she might faint. "Please. Could we just go get the mare and take her to the stream now?"

He studied her flaming face a long moment before answering. "Yes, but I wish you weren't so ashamed of your disability and shy about showing it to me. If I can fix a mare's leg, maybe I can do something to help a human's."

"Experts have examined my . . . my disability and found they couldn't help. My father once offered a small fortune to a renowned surgeon passing through the region en route to California, and *he* couldn't suggest a thing. So what could you possibly do?"

"Maybe nothing. Then again I might be able to figure out a way for you to ride a horse. If you have any feeling at all in your leg, you ought to be able to strengthen it enough to grip when you need to. If you can do that and also learn to signal the animal, you can learn to ride, Miss Sterling."

"I . . . I'm sure it's not possible."

"Could be you're right, but I thought you might at least want to try."

Yes, oh yes, I want to try! she almost burst out. But then she considered all that would be involved—not the least of which was spending more time in Joe Hart's company. No, she couldn't risk it—and she could well imagine what her father and Rand would say if she suddenly announced she had taken up riding!

"The mare," she desperately reminded him. "We have to go get the mare."

"Yes, we do," he agreed, beginning to lead Loser down the incline.

She had enough presence of mind to ask: "What about the herd stallion? What if he gallops over here and wants to fight."

"He won't. Look how far off he is now and notice the direction of the wind. It isn't carrying Loser's scent to him. As long as I keep the mare between him and Loser, I don't think he'll object."

"Did you learn all you know about horses from that Indian, too?" she asked, hoping to rattle him as much as he rattled her.

He shot her a steady, sober glance. "If I tell you about my past, will you tell me about yours—and what happened to your *limb?*"

"I asked you first."

"All right, I did learn a lot of what I know about horses from an Indian. . . . Now, it's your turn."

"That little bit of information hardly qualifies as telling me about your past," she objected.

"I disagree. It's a straightforward answer to a single question. Now, it's your turn; what happened to your leg?"

"I . . . I injured it when a wagon in which my mother and I were riding overturned and was overrun by cattle."

"What spooked the cattle?"

"Indians," she said, carefully watching him, though she could really only see his profile. "They did it on purpose, and my mother was killed, while I suffered a broken leg that never healed properly."

His face could have been carved from stone for all the emotion it revealed. "So I suppose you hate all Indians."

"In theory, yes . . . but in practice, I've never met one up close, so I can't really say how I'd react if I suddenly wound up in the presence of one."

He did not respond to that, and she wondered how much further to push him. Was now the time to ask him just how well he had once known Indians? Would he admit it if he *were* an Indian or related to them in some way?

"Everyone I know hates Indians," she continued. "And I assume that all Indians must hate whites."

"Sounds like a safe assumption to me," he drawled evasively.

"Did you hate the Indian who taught you about herbs and horses? Or did you count him as your friend?"

"That was a long, long time ago, Miss Sterling. And it no longer matters how I felt about him, now does it? There are better ways to judge a man than by whether or not he wears moccasins."

"Oh, I quite agree! However, we could both be wrong. It might also be true that what a man wears on his feet is an excellent indication of who he is and what he's thinking. It certainly tells *something* about him. If a man's boots need new soles, an observer can deduce he must be down on his luck. If he wears a certain type of spurs, you can often guess his origins. If he doesn't wear boots at all, but favors thick-soled farmer's shoes, you know for certain he's not a cowman and doesn't appreciate steers running on his land."

"All true, Miss Sterling. But I think its a damn shame we can't see past all that and judge a man by his actions rather than his trappings."

"Is that how *you* judge all men, Mr. Hart—by their actions alone?"

He kept right on walking. "No, I reckon I'm as short-sighted and unforgiving as everyone else. I don't want to be, but I am. . . . Guess I was hoping you might be more high-minded than most folks, including me. If anyone's got reason to hate an entire race of people, you certainly do . . . what with your mother and your bad leg."

"And my uncle, too," she added. "And Rand's family. Half the people I know have suffered because of the Indians. The Indians caused a great deal of heartache and loss in this region. I suppose they're paying for it now, and I *shouldn't* feel any sympathy for them."

"Yeah," Joe muttered. "They're paying for it now."

She couldn't tell if there was glee or sarcasm in his tone; it was so difficult to read this man! He hid his thoughts and emotions better than anyone she had ever met. She never knew what to say to him . . . but she didn't believe that he hated Indians like everyone else. He *must* be at least part-Indian. Maybe he was ashamed of it. Or maybe he was proud of his heritage but didn't want to risk showing it. Everything he did radiated an unspoken pride—that straight-backed pride and arrogance she remembered so well from her youth. There was just something about Indians—some indefinable essence or spirit that once witnessed could never be forgotten.

They reached the lower ground, and Joe led her over near the mare. He quietly picked up the mare's lead rope and began walking toward the far end of the meadow, keeping the animal between Loser and the herd. Loser nickered softly at his new companion, but the mare ignored him and docilely followed Joe down the length of the meadow.

After they had gone a short distance in silence, Joe said: "I'm going to let go of Loser's reins. See if you can keep him walking beside me."

Maggie clung like a leech to the saddle horn. "Oh, no! Please don't let go. I . . . I don't know what to do."

"Let go of the saddle horn. Sit up straighter. Ease your weight down into your heels. Now, pick up the reins, and do just what I tell you."

"In both hands?" she squeaked, though she very well knew that cowboys rode with only one hand holding the reins.

"You've seen it done, Miss Sterling. You know how to do it."

She maintained her grip on the saddle horn with one hand and picked up the reins with the other. "Like this?"

"Gather them up a little more. Now, when you want to go right, lay your rein across the left side of Loser's neck and give him a little nudge with your left leg. When you want to go left, do just the opposite."

Maggie experimented, and Loser veered sharply to the right. "What if I want to stop?" she shrieked.

"Sit deep, lean back, and say 'Whoa.' "

"Whoa!" Loser dug in his hindquarters and stopped so suddenly that Maggie fell forward—and then she giggled in delight. "Am I doing this right?"

"You're doing fine." Joe continued to walk in a straight line down the meadow. "Try circling to the right and then to the left. We'll walk slow so you can still circle and keep up with us."

Maggie's heart was pounding, but she did it—a circle each way—and didn't fall off. She kicked Loser's sides to urge him to catch up to Joe, and the stallion obligingly broke into a trot. She had to grab leather again to keep from falling, but she managed to stay on his back.

Joe laughed when she rode up beside him, grinning and triumphant. "I did it! I circled, and then I caught up with you, and I didn't fall off."

"You have to learn to sit deep and grip with your thighs," he told her. "That way you won't fall forward when you stop or bounce around so much when you trot."

"I have to grip with my . . . my . . . what you just said?" She was scandalized he had dared mention such a word as thighs in her hearing.

He only grinned and kept walking. "I know you won't admit to having thighs, Miss Sterling, but most people do have them, and they have to learn how to use them if they want to ride a horse. Would you feel more comfortable if I used the word knee instead—even though gripping with your thighs is a better idea?"

"I . . . I don't think I can grip with either. My bad limb— leg—isn't strong enough."

"It was strong enough for Loser to feel your signal to circle him. It might get even stronger if you worked at it."

"How could I work at it? I don't understand what you mean."

"Miss Sterling, your leg is made up of bone and muscle. When I want a horse to be able to carry me all day without tiring, first I have to build up his muscles and make him strong.

If you want to ride—or even walk better—that's what *you* are going to have to do. Instead of favoring your bad leg and keeping off it, you'll have to go out of your way to exercise it and make it stronger."

She thought about that for a minute as she let Loser walk beside Joe. "I . . . I never thought about it like that before. But of course, it makes sense."

"I could probably show you some exercises to strengthen your muscles," he volunteered. "I used to do them myself when I was a boy."

"You did? What for? What did you do?"

"Oh, I . . . never mind. I'll just show you some things, that's all. Later, after we fix this poor mare's injury."

Maggie rode Loser all the way to the streambed cutting through mountain rock and gurgling among the stones at the far end of the meadow. Heedless of his boots, Joe led the mare right into the water, so that it covered her wound, then proceeded to wash and cleanse the cut. Maggie sat on the stallion, letting him lower his head and drink as much as he wanted.

When Loser stepped closer to the mare and began to nose her, Joe tugged on the mare's lead rope and led her further away. "Don't let him get too close, Maggie. The old girl's not in season, and she may kick him. Besides, he's under saddle and has no business noticing the ladies."

Maggie gathered up her reins and steered Loser a short distance away. She was thrilled she could get him to do anything, and she experimented with walking him up and down the streambank.

"Push your weight down into your heels," Joe called out several times. "Sit up straight. That's better. Don't hunch over his neck like an old woman."

Following Joe's orders felt awkward, even uncomfortable, to Maggie, especially on her bad side, but she tried as hard as she could. She could see she would have to work at strengthening her leg, yet riding was such a thrill! Seated so far above the ground, astride a horse as fine as Loser, she felt as if she possessed power and speed for the first time in her life; she felt on top of the world! He was able to walk much faster than she could, yet he was gentle and obedient, stopping the minute she said "whoa."

While she amused herself testing her limits, Joe worked on the mare. He let the horse stand in the water for a good long time before he led her out, dropped down on one knee, and began applying his poultice, tying it into place with the strip from Maggie's petticoat. During all this, Maggie got into trouble only once—when Loser decided to eat the tender green leaves from some brush lining the stream. He refused to obey her signals to leave the spot and return to Joe and the mare.

"Put more leg on him!" Joe shouted. "Excuse me—more limb! Have to remember who I'm talking to . . ."

"It doesn't make any difference *what* I put on him—he won't move!" she wailed.

"Give him a kick in the ribs. Go on, kick him!"

Maggie marshalled all her strength to do as directed, but Loser still ignored her. Planting all four feet in the ground, he stood motionless and continued snatching leaves.

"Kick him, Maggie!"

Maggie kicked with all her might. Loser finally gave a long sigh, removed his nose from the bush, and rejoined Joe. "There, you made him do it," he congratulated her. "You don't have to be cruel, but you do need to be firm and keep insisting until he responds."

"Yes, I can see that, but I don't have enough strength."

"You will—if you do what I show you. . . . Just a minute." He slipped the rope halter off the mare's head and hung it over Loser's saddle horn. "She'll be all right now. I'm letting her go so she can return to the herd."

While the mare ambled away from them, Joe put his hand on Maggie's bad knee. When she recoiled, he glanced up at her. "Do you want me to show you or not? I promise I won't hurt you or do anything wrong. But I do have to touch you to give you an idea of what sort of exercises you can do—and to see just how weak your leg really is. . . . Relax, Maggie. Trust me."

When had he started to call her Maggie? she wondered, realizing only then that he'd been calling here that for the last several minutes—and had called her that before, as well. Why hadn't she corrected him the first time he addressed her so familiarly?

"Oh, all right . . . show me," she burst out, flustered.

His hand came down on her knee again, and with infinite gentleness, he ran it down her calf muscles. Her skirt, petticoats, and other unmentionables formed a considerable barrier, but she fancied she could still feel the heat of his touch. . . . And she suspected that *he* could feel the thin, ridged muscles, and ugly twisted shape of her bad leg. There was no need for him to actually look at it.

She cringed and glanced away in embarrassment. A wave of dizziness flowed over her, and she had to swallow hard against a sudden lump in her throat. To her great chagrin, tears pricked beneath her eyelids. It took every shred of courage she possessed to refrain from flinching.

"Maggie . . . ," he crooned. "Relax. The muscle is thin and shrunken but I think it could be made stronger. I once knew a man who had suffered a terrible wound in his leg. The muscles had even been torn, but he survived somehow. After the wound healed, he began to stretch the deformed muscles and massage and work them until he could do everything he had done before his injury. See? Like this."

He made her point her toe and swing her leg forward from the knee, then back as far as it would go. He flexed her foot several times and rotated it, gently stretching the shrunken muscles, so that she winced from the discomfort.

"I don't know." she whispered. "I just don't know."

"Let me take a look at it." He began to raise her skirt.

"No! Oh, no, please!" She pushed his hands away. "You mustn't, Joe. I . . . I couldn't bear for you to see it. My leg is ugly. I *never* let people see it."

"Has Rand seen it?" he growled.

She shook her head violently. "No, and I don't intend he ever shall see it. I'll manage to keep it covered somehow."

"Maggie . . . Maggie . . ." Tenderness resonated in Joe's tone, and there was such compassion in his expression that she wanted to weep. "Has no one seen it recently—your father or a doctor, at least?"

"N-no. Not for a long time, not since I was a little girl. And I don't want *you* to see it either. Not now or ever."

His eyes held hers, and she could not look away, no matter how ashamed she felt. "I cannot imagine any part of you that would not be beautiful, Maggie Sterling. You must never be ashamed of your body," he scolded. "You are a beautiful woman; surely, you know that."

How could she know it when she had never been told? Even Rand had never said she was beautiful or looked at her in quite the same way as Joe was looking at her now. His hand still rested on her leg—her ugly, misshapen leg—but his eyes told her she *was* beautiful, and for the first time in her life, she felt beautiful.

"Everyday," he said. "You must go up and down the steps going into the ranch house. I don't mean once or twice or even three times, but ten or more times. You must force your leg to bear your whole weight. . . . And you must climb the rocks and hills near the ranch. You can start by going only a short distance, but each day, you must go a little farther. And at night, you must rub the muscles and knead them, as if you were making biscuits."

"All that will work?"

"I think so. It worked for that man I knew. He climbed rocks and hills all the time. What have you got to lose if it *doesn't* work?"

"If it doesn't work, I won't be able to ride, will I?"

"You're riding now," he reminded her. "But you may have trouble riding faster or staying on a horse that's not well-trained."

"I want to be able to ride Dusty. I'd give anything if I could ride Dusty."

"Then try it, Maggie. Work at it everyday, and I think you'll see a big difference."

"I . . . I will," she said, then added impulsively, "Thank you, Joe!"

He grinned and brushed the brim of his hat. "My pleasure, ma'am." He grasped Loser's mane and suddenly swung up on the saddle behind her, sitting well back, behind the cantle, where it had to be uncomfortable.

"What are you doing?" she asked nervously as he slid an arm around her waist. "If you want to ride him now, I'll be happy to get off."

"No," he whispered, nuzzling her hair. "I don't want you to get off, because now, I'm going to show you what it's like to ride the wind. Are you ready?"

"Joe! Maybe we better not!"

"Don't worry. I'll hold onto you."

With that, he wheeled Loser around, and the stallion leapt into a gallop. Back across the meadow they went, flying over the green grass, with Loser's mane whipping back into Maggie's face and eyes. At first, she was terrified. Then she began to laugh with the sheer joy and exhilaration of the moment. The wind flattened her garments against her body and unleashed her hair from its combs and pins. The wind whistled past her ears and sang in her heart.

She had never felt so free; it *was* like flying! And Joe's arms gave her the security to appreciate every magical moment of it—the wind on her face and hair, the magnificent power of the animal beneath her, the sun gilding the meadow as they flew across it. They raced down the length of the meadow toward the herd of horses, stopped before they reached them, spun around, and raced back the other way again.

Maggie was laughing and crying at the same time when Loser finally slowed down, his warm, sweat-dampened sides moving rhythmically against her legs. He trotted a short distance and finally slowed to a walk, with Maggie leaning breathlessly against Joe's chest.

"Well?" he inquired, his lips near her ear. "What do you think? Did you like it?"

"It . . . it was . . ." There were no words to describe her feelings. She had dreamed of such a moment—had imagined herself galloping across a meadow filled with horses and spangled with wildflowers and rich with the scent of the green earth and growing things. Joe had made her dream come true.

"It was wonderful," she finished breathlessly. "Everything I ever imagined and more."

He said nothing further, just continued to hold her tightly, pressed back against his chest, as once more he turned Loser around and rode slowly back toward the cart.

Twelve

When they arrived at the spot where they had left Preacher and the cart, Joe slid down from the saddle, then reached up to help Maggie dismount. For Maggie, it was an awkward moment. There wasn't much space between Loser and Joe, which meant that her body brushed Joe's as he lifted her down. Her breasts grazed his chest, and her thighs slid along his, setting off sparks between them and making the air itself seem charged with energy.

A cloud scudding past overhead temporarily obscured the sun, and Maggie blamed the strange expectancy she felt on the possibility of an approaching storm. The humidity suggested rain, but the bulk of the clouds were still far off, leaving her with the disturbing realization that the proximity of Joe himself was responsible for raising the fine hairs on the back of her neck.

"I can't thank you enough," she said breathlessly.

He gave her no room to step away from him. "You've already thanked me plenty. It was *my* pleasure to give you pleasure. Your face is still glowing." He lifted his hand to lightly caress her cheek.

"Probably too much sun," she hastened to explain, aware that inside, she *was* still glowing, now from the effect of Joe's nearness and his touch rather than the thrill of the ride. "I should get Preacher hitched to the cart and start for home before everyone wonders where I am."

"And I should get back to line riding. That's what I'm supposed to be doing for another several days, at least."

"Then you'd better go," she agreed.

Yet neither of them moved. In the expectant silence, Maggie studied Joe's face—the tiny creases near his eyes and mouth, the straightness of his nose, the rather harsh, unyielding line of his jaw that suggested inner strength and a stubbornness he had already demonstrated more than once. He looked exactly the way a man was supposed to look, she thought, weather-beaten and sun-bronzed, serious but with a lurking sense of humor, wonderfully handsome but not what one would call pretty.

There was no doubt whatever that Joe Hart was all man. Dark, alluring man—the exact opposite in both coloring and character of the man she was going to marry.

"I really should be going," she murmured, rudely jerked back to reality by the thought of Rand.

Joe smiled in his usual cocky way and stepped an inch or two backward. "I'm not stopping you."

"Thanks again." She made as if to move around him.

"Maggie?"

She paused. He reached out and brushed back a strand of hair from her face, seemed about to say something, then didn't. "What is it?" she prompted. "Go on. Tell me."

A grin quirked the corners of his mouth. "I was going to say you better hurry up, before I . . ."

"Before you . . . ?"

"Do this," he growled, reaching for her.

She didn't resist—couldn't resist—as his arms encircled her waist and hauled her up tight against him. Then his mouth slanted across hers in a hungry, searching kiss that robbed her of all capacity for rational thought. She quite forgot everything but the utter necessity of kissing him back. Her arms stole around his neck, and she instantly recalled every lesson he had given her the last time he had kissed her—how and when to

We've got your authors!

KENSINGTON CHOICE is the only club where you can find authors like Janelle Taylor, Shannon Drake, Rosanne Bittner, Penelope Neri and Phoebe Conn all in one place...

...and the only service that will deliver their romances direct to your home as soon as they are published—even before they reach the bookstores.

KENSINGTON CHOICE is also the only service that will give you a substantial guaranteed discount off the publisher's prices on every one of those romances.

That's right: Every month, the Editors at Zebra and Pinnacle select four of the newest novels by our bestselling authors and rush them straight to you, usually *before they reach the bookstores*. The publisher's prices for these romances range from $4.99 to $5.99—but they are always yours for the guaranteed low price of just $4.20, up to 30% off the publisher's price!

All books are sent on a 10-day free examination basis, and there is no minimum number of books to buy. (A postage and handling charge of $1.50 is added to each shipment.)

As your introduction to the convenience and value of KENSINGTON CHOICE, we invite you to accept

4 BOOKS FREE

The 4 books, worth up to $23.96, are our welcoming gift to you.

Plus as a regular subscriber....you'll receive our free monthly newsletter, Zebra/Pinnacle Romance News which features author interviews, contests, and more!

To start your subscription to KENSINGTON CHOICE and receive your introductory package of 4 FREE romances, detach and mail the card at right *today*.

We have 4 FREE BOOKS for you
as your introduction to
KENSINGTON CHOICE
To get your FREE BOOKS, worth
up to $23.96, mail the card below.

FREE BOOK CERTIFICATE

As my introduction to your new KENSINGTON CHOICE reader's service, please send me 4 FREE historical romances (worth up to $23.96). As a KENSINGTON CHOICE subscriber, I will then receive 4 brand-new romances to preview each month for 10 days FREE. I can return any books I decide not to keep and owe nothing. The publisher's prices for the KENSINGTON CHOICE romances range from $4.99 to $5.99, but as a subscriber I will be entitled to get them for just $4.20 per book or $16.80 for all four titles. There is no minimum number of books to buy, and I can cancel my subscription at any time. A $1.50 postage and handling charge is added to each shipment.

Name _____

Address _____ Apt._____

City _____ State_____ Zip_____

Telephone (____) _____

Signature_____
(If under 18, parent or guardian must sign)

Subscription subject to acceptance. Terms and prices subject to change.

KF1195

We have
4
FREE
Historical
Romances
for you!

(worth up
to $23.96!)

Details inside!

open her mouth, how to use her tongue, what to do with the rest of her.

It was all the same, yet it was stunningly different. This time there was an urgency and such a sense of rightness about it that she could no more have stopped herself—or him—than a calf could resist being swept along in a cattle stampede. Pure instinct took over, and she kissed him with the undiluted enthusiasm of years of yearning and need. All her life she had been lonely; somewhere in the deepest core of her was a great yawning void, a dull, lifeless emptiness. Neither Lena, her father, nor Rand had ever been able to fill it with their love, sympathy, or pity. Now, suddenly, she knew what she wanted and had gone without for so many years—self-affirmation, an awareness of who she was and who she wanted to be.

When Joe Hart looked at her, touched or kissed her, he seemed able to see past her limitations and focus on the *real* Maggie Sterling—the beautiful, whole woman hiding inside the damaged body and longing to get out.

Without breaking the contact of their lips and bodies, Joe lifted her in his arms so her mouth was level with his. He clasped her to him, pressing her against his hard, muscular length. Yet even in his growing passion, he was gentle, holding her as if she were as precious and fragile as fine crystal. "Maggie . . . sweet, sweet Maggie . . ." he murmured into her hair.

"Joe! Oh, Joe . . ." she cried, reveling in the exquisite sensation of desire unfurling inside her like some wild rambling rose reaching for sun.

This was what she had wanted to feel with Rand and never had—this burning compulsion to touch and be touched, to caress a man's warm naked flesh beneath the palms of her hands. She leaned back, laughing, enthralled with the sheer euphoria of her discovery. "Joe, put me down this instant!" she cried. "I'm getting dizzy—or maybe crazy is a better word."

When he did, she cupped his face in her hands and kissed him as if she were printing her brand on his mouth and soul. In a way, she was. She could not remember ever being so bold before. Her hands moved to his chest, searching for the span of muscle rippling beneath the fabric of his shirt. She tore at the fastenings, eager to caress his skin and discover its texture. He let her explore inside his open shirt a moment, but when her fingertips grazed the nubs of his nipples—so different from her own—he seized her wrists and pulled her hands away.

"No, Maggie—no. We shouldn't be doing this. . . . Have you forgotten you're engaged to another man?"

"Of course, I haven't. But engagements can be broken." In her new-found happiness and certainty that this was the right thing—and Joe the right man—for her, she became reckless and brave. "A girl can change her mind, can't she?"

The gray of Joe's eyes turned to flint. "Don't change it on my account. I don't want you to marry Rand, but I'm not offering to marry you either. I can't. And don't ask me to explain because I can't do that either."

Unwilling to accept his rejection, certain he felt the same magic she did when they kissed, she clung to him. "It doesn't matter that you haven't any land or cattle of your own, Joe. I have all we'll ever need. Rand doesn't own land either, but I wasn't going to let that stop me from marrying him—and I won't let it stop me from . . . from . . ." She couldn't quite get out the word "marry," as it applied to her and Joe. It was still too new and radical a thought. Besides, he hadn't asked her yet. How dare she be so presumptuous!

"We can work it out," she finished awkwardly. "If you want to as badly as I do."

"Think what you're saying, Maggie. What will you do—just tell Rand to disappear? What will you say to your father? Hell, you don't even know me."

"I know how I feel when I'm with you—especially when you hold me. I've never felt like this before in my life. . . . Oh, I know it's not proper to say these things or feel this way. I know it's much too soon, and I must be making a terrible fool of myself, but . . ."

"It *is* too soon, and you *are* making a fool of yourself." He removed her hands from his shoulders. "Don't throw yourself away on me, Miss Sterling. I'm not worth it. Let's just pretend this afternoon never happened."

Every word he spoke was a spike driven deep into her heart. "Why? I don't understand. At least, tell me why."

"You're a pretty girl," he said, briefly touching her cheek. "Any man would like to steal a kiss from you. That's all I was doing—stealing a kiss. Nothing more. Don't try to make it into a lifetime commitment. I succumbed to an impulse, and so did you. But that's all it was—just a wild, crazy impulse."

"I don't believe you!" She stepped back from him and collided with Loser's rump. Startled, the horse moved away, and so did Maggie. "What we shared today was . . . was beautiful! The ride, the kisses . . . everything."

"Yes," he agreed. "It was beautiful. I enjoyed showing an over-protected young woman that she could ride if she really set her mind to it—and enjoy kissing. If Rand doesn't make you feel the way I just did, that's all the proof you need that you're marrying the wrong man. That doesn't mean I'm the *right* one. I'm not, Maggie. Trust me when I tell you this. *I am all wrong for you.*"

"Perhaps you are, if you can say such hurtful things without feeling guilty and ashamed!" Blinking back tears, Maggie gathered the shreds of her dignity about herself as best she could. "I apologize for being so forward. This time, the kissing was all my fault. I wanted you to kiss me, and you did. I made it very difficult for you to refuse."

"It won't happen again," he assured her. "I'll keep away from this meadow from now on."

"You needn't go out of your way to avoid it. I won't be coming here myself for a while. There's a great deal to be done at the house. In case you haven't noticed, we're enlarging it—adding another bedchamber and sitting area for me and Rand."

"You and Rand?" One dark brow shot up. "I thought you had changed your mind about that."

"I thought I had, too," she managed to say without bursting

into tears and blubbering like a baby. "But I'm reconsidering. I care for Rand, and he genuinely cares for me. I'm not about to casually toss away the only proposal I've ever had and go to my grave a lonely, childless spinster just because I met a man who's more skillful than he is when it comes to kissing. . . . If you don't want me, he does. A . . . a woman can change her mind any number of occasions. Again, I apologize for my behavior this afternoon. Actually, I should be apologizing to Rand, not to you, shouldn't I?"

An errant tear slipped out and dribbled down her cheek. Clinging to her pride, she steadfastly ignored it. "Good afternoon, Mr. Hart. If you'll excuse me, I must get Preacher hitched."

"I'll do it." He started toward the pile of harness.

"No! I mean, no thank you, but I much prefer to do it myself. We cripples are capable of so much more than most people give us credit for. Indeed, as you've been so kind to point out, I'm capable of even more than *I* thought I could do."

"Sweet Jesus! I . . ."

"Please don't take the Lord's name in vain. It's not at all respectful of *Him* nor of me. I'm the daughter of your employer, may I remind you, and the betrothed of the ranch foreman."

She was gratified to see that *he* was not immune to a few emotional knife thrusts. She hated herself for doing it, but his rejection had cut her so deeply she could not help but respond in kind. She had thrown herself at him, and he had actually rejected her, for whatever stupid, mysterious reasons. The reasons no longer mattered; all that mattered was the rejection itself. Joe Hart wanted nothing more to do with her. Maybe her leg had repelled him after all, and he just wouldn't admit it. Didn't want her to know that her horrible deformity disgusted him—yes, that *must* be it.

He had probably only taught her to ride and kissed her because he felt sorry for her. But she pitied *him!* He disgusted *her!* She had a crippled body, but *he* had a crippled soul. Why else would a man conceal his past unless he was deeply ashamed of it? Unless he had done something terribly wrong and was hiding from the law perhaps?

That was another possibility. Plenty of cowboys were lone wolves, men on the run who sometimes took new names to escape a hangman's noose. Now that she thought about it, the name Joe Hart sounded suspect. He could be a thief or a murderer. She may have hardened her heart toward Rand and allowed herself to become infatuated by a man who was only one step away from the gallows or hanging tree!

"You touch that harness, and I'll get out my six-shooter!" she shouted at him, as he bent over the pile in complete disregard for her wishes.

"Don't make threats you have no intention of keeping, Miss Sterling. If you're actually going to shoot a man, do it and be done with it. Don't warn him ahead of time."

"Put down that harness!" she shrieked as he calmly picked up part of it and tossed it over Preacher's back.

"Make me," he taunted. "If you think you can."

The cart was a good twenty feet away; she couldn't get to it fast enough to retrieve her six-shooter in time to stop Joe. He harnessed Preacher as if he could have done it in the dark of a moonless night with one arm tied behind his back. It would have taken her twice as long to arrange all the pieces and fasten them properly—but then she couldn't walk as fast as Joe Hart.

"You are the most infuriating man I have ever met!" she exploded. "I regret the day my father hired you!"

"Always glad to know where I stand," he drawled.

He drew up the cart behind Preacher and lowered the shafts on either side of the old gelding, then proceeded to hook the traces to the cart. Tossing the lines up on the seat, he motioned to her. "Need some help getting in, Miss Sterling?"

"None whatsoever—especially from you." She limped over to the cart and climbed into it without his assistance.

He stood aside, watching with an expression of grim amusement. "Since you'll be too busy feathering your love nest, I'll come back in a few days and check on that mare as well as the rest of the horses."

"You needn't bother. I'll send Rand—or better yet, I'll ride Dusty up to check on them."

His face darkened. "Don't you dare get on that colt until you've strengthened *both* your legs and learned a lot more about riding. He's coming along nicely, but he's still too green for a new rider. Practice on Preacher first."

"Stop giving me advice, Mr. Hart. I don't want or need it. I was getting along just fine before you arrived on the Broken Wheel, and I'm sure I can survive without your help in the future."

He brushed the brim of his hat in farewell. "I'm sure you can, too. Good afternoon, ma'am."

Maggie snatched the whip out of the whip socket and whacked Preacher on the rump before she realized what she was doing. He surged forward into his breast collar and took off at a smart trot. She expertly steered him around Loser, made a big turn in the meadow, and drove for home without a backward glance.

That night at dinner, Maggie could not find much to say. It was raining, and the steady drumming of the downpour on the roof and the dripping from the eaves did nothing to lighten her mood. She couldn't help wondering where Joe was sheltering; he was probably out in the middle of it. There was a lean-to in the side of a mountain where line-riders usually bedded down in foul weather, but being new to the Broken Wheel, Joe might not know where it was. Even if he did know, the lean-to was a long ride from the meadow.

Rand and Nathan were quiet tonight, too. Nathan normally controlled the conversation, introducing suitable topics and discussing them at length, but this evening, he brooded silently over his dinner and didn't eat much either.

As Maggie poured coffee for him, she noticed a grimace

contorting his features. "What's wrong, Pa? Don't you feel well?"

Her father threw down his napkin and pushed back from the table. "I'm gonna have a talk with Lena 'bout puttin' too damn many spices in her cookin'. Lately, she's been overdoin' it, and I been payin' fer it." He pressed a clenched fist to his chest. "Right here. I got such a burnin' in my chest from all that hot stuff that I sometimes think my breastbone must be afire."

Maggie set down the coffeepot and leaned forward in concern. "Are you sure that's all it is, Pa—indigestion? Why, you've hardly eaten anything tonight, and you've always said that you love Lena's cooking, the hotter, the better."

"I don't like it *this* damn hot! I'm still digestin' what she gave me at noon. That's why I can't eat t'night. What about you, Rand? Don't you think the meat's too spicy t' go down easy?"

Rand shoved a last bite of red beans in his mouth and talked around it. "Tastes fine t' me. Fact is I could use a little more if you don't want yers."

Nathan rose in disgust. "Go on. Help yerself. I'm goin' t' bed."

"I'll look in on you later, Pa, and see if you need anything. By then you might be hungry." Maggie stood and began clearing the table.

"What I need is a cook who understands that a man's insides ain't made of cast iron."

As Nathan stomped up the stairs muttering to himself, Maggie removed all the dirty dishes except for the ones Rand was still using. Scraping her father's food onto his own plate, Rand ate with dogged concentration, and as soon as he was finished, Maggie whisked his plate away before he'd had time to set down his fork.

"In a mighty big hurry, aren't cha?" Rand growled.

"I'm just tired, Rand. I want to get this mess cleared away and go to bed myself."

He poured himself another cup of coffee and tilted back his

chair, eyeing her with a trace of annoyance. "You was gone a long time t'day. Have any trouble in town?"

"None whatsoever. But then I didn't expect any." She picked up the coffeepot and took it into the kitchen so he would not be encouraged to stay and empty it.

When she returned to the table, he grabbed her by the hand and pulled her down to sit on his knee. "Rand, I have a whole sink full of dirty dishes to wash," she protested.

"Leave 'em for Lena. She'll be happy to do 'em in the morning."

"I'm entirely capable of cleaning up the dinner mess," Maggie bristled. "Lena's always the first one up around here anyway, and I hate for her to have to start fixing breakfast in a dirty kitchen. She does so much for me; this is something I can do for her."

"She's the hired help, Maggie. It's her job to clean up after you and yer Pa."

"She's much more than that, Rand, and you know it. She *should* be eating with us. After all, she's family."

"Don't let yer Pa hear you talkin' like that. She's still a bean-eater, an' I don't think Nathan Sterlin' would want to share his table with a bean-eater."

"Rand!" Maggie struggled futilely to get off his lap. "Where did you ever get such an idea? The fact that Lena is Mexican has nothing to do with what my father thinks of her or how he feels about her. Are you blind? He's been in love with the woman for years."

Rand stared at her for a long moment. Then he laughed and shook his head. *"In love with her!* Naw, Maggie, that can't be true. I'm sure it ain't, or I'd know about it. There's not much yer Pa an' me don't discuss."

"Well, it's true, whether you've discussed it with him or not. And what's more, I intend to discuss it with him myself in the very near future."

"What for?" Rand gave her waist a little squeeze and held

her in place when she again tried to rise. "I wouldn't guess it was any of yer business, nor mine either."

"It isn't, but I do know for a fact that Lena's in love with my father, and after you and I marry, there's no reason why the two of them shouldn't eat their meals together, or . . . or even get married, too, if the idea appeals to them."

"Married! Nathan Sterlin' married to a bean-eater? What're you thinkin' of, Maggie?" He shoved her off his lap. "It'll never happen. I don't know what you think's been goin' on between 'em—an' maybe somethin' *has* been goin' on all these years—but I can tell you yer Pa would never give a minute's thought to the idea of marryin' a bean-eater, even if it is jus' Lena."

"How do you know?" Maggie rested her hands on her hips as she stood next to the table and confronted Rand.

" 'Cause he's told me as much any number of times!"

"You and my father have discussed his relationship with Lena? I thought you just said you hadn't."

"No, but we've discussed bean-eaters. You remember that Mexican cowpoke who worked fer us a coupla years back? Name was Raoul Garcia."

"Yes, I remember him. He was a good rider and roper. Did everything well, as I recall."

"Yeah, he did. Come the end of the season, Raoul said he wanted t' come back the next year an' work fer us again. Said he was hopin' t' stay on here permanent. Since he wuz a good hand, I was gonna let him, but yer Pa said no."

"Why would he say no when the man was so capable?"

"Said he didn't trust bean-eaters any more'n he does Injuns. Said they aren't the kind of men he'd be proud t' ride the river with."

A man one could ride the river with was a fellow who could be trusted in even the trickiest, most dangerous situations, such as crossing a swollen river with a herd of spooky cattle. That her father wouldn't trust an Indian in that role was understandable, but Maggie could not fathom why he should feel that way about a Mexican.

"I don't believe it. My father couldn't be that . . . that . . . narrow-minded and prejudiced."

Rand shrugged his shoulders. "He told me t' let the man go and tell 'im not t' come back. I ain't hired any bean-eaters since. Ya gotta admit yer Pa's got a point, Maggie. Mexicans, Injuns, men of any color can't be trusted. They's just different from us, there ain't no way around it. A man shows up with a tan he didn't git from the sun, I jus' tell 'im to keep ridin'. He ain't our kind of people—an' yer Pa agrees with me. So that's how I know he wouldn't ever marry Lena."

"I . . . I can't believe you're saying these things, and that my father feels the same way. Oh, I know you both hate Indians—but then, who doesn't around here? I just didn't realize you extended that hatred to everyone else who's in any way different from us."

"If you don't b'lieve me, ask him, Maggie."

"I intend to. I've been meaning to have a little talk with him about Lena anyway, but I've been so busy lately I've been putting it off."

"You been damn busy all right—like t'day. You sure wuz gone a long time. I was startin' t' git worried. . . . Goddam, I jus' don't like the idea of you drivin' off alone by yerself. You *sure* nothin' happened t' make you so late gettin' back?"

Maggie thought of her chance meeting with Joe and of all that had transpired between them. She was so ashamed of her behavior—and still so mortified and disappointed over the outcome of the afternoon—that she couldn't immediately answer.

"Somethin' *did* happen, didn't it?" Rand demanded with more insight than he normally displayed when it came to her feelings.

Aware that she was blushing, Maggie shook her head and searched her brain for some likely explanation Rand would accept. "Oh, it wasn't anything big, and it had nothing to do with my driving out alone. It's just that . . . that I had a rather nasty disagreement with Mr. Magruder, the shopkeeper of the store where I ordered some fabric for my wedding gown. He refused to guarantee when I would get it, and I said I had to know or I wouldn't order it from him. I could just as well order a ready-made gown from a catalogue; I have seen one I like, but it's more expensive. If I can get the fabric I want, Lena is going to help me make up my own gown, and it will be much nicer—and cheaper, too."

Rand was still eyeing her suspiciously. "Yer sure that's all that happened."

"Of course, that's all. However, if you're so worried, maybe I should try to learn to ride a horse, instead of driving everywhere. Mounted on a good fast horse like Dusty, I could outrun anyone intent on harming me."

"What in hell are you thinkin' of now, Maggie Sterlin'? Ride a horse. Have you got rocks where yer brains oughta be? I catch you anywhere *near* a horse, tryin' t' ride it, and I'll drop a loop over yer head and haul you up so fast it'll make yer head spin. Why, you can hardly walk, let alone ride. You git tired jus' goin' t' the barn an' back. Why, you . . ."

He went on in this manner for several moments while Maggie silently set the dining room to rights. By the time he was finished, he had managed to make her feel so helpless and inept that she wondered how she *could* strengthen her leg enough to succeed at riding. She thought it might be better all around—and certainly far less deflating—if she simply took to a rocking chair and stayed there for the rest of her life.

"Oh, be quiet, Rand. I was merely suggesting it as a possibility, not threatening to leap on a horse and gallop into town tomorrow. . . . I just thought—I mean, I *hoped*—that you might be willing to . . . to teach me. If I can somehow make my bad limb stronger, that is. I . . . I've been thinking a lot about that and wondering if I *might* be able to strengthen my muscles enough to learn to ride."

"Gawdamighty, I ain't never met a calico like you, Maggie Sterlin'. Yer jus' full of surprises. Every time I think I finally got you all figured out, you go and spring something new on me. Ain't I given you everything you asked for lately? Talked Nathan inta addin' on to the house, taught you t' shoot, agreed t' let you drive off alone. . . ."

"Yes . . . yes, you've given me a great deal, Rand. And don't think I'm not appreciative, but sometimes, I wonder . . . I wonder . . ."

"What? What more do you want from me, Maggie?"

Maggie drew a deep breath, then blurted "I . . . I wonder if we're really right for each other, Rand. I wonder if we're not making a terrible mistake getting married. We're so different, you and I. Can't you see it? We don't look at life the same way. I don't want to make you miserable. Nor do I want to *be* miserable. . . ."

Rand jumped up so fast that he knocked over the chair. Then he came after her in a single long stride. "What *is* this, Maggie? What are you tryin' t' say?"

"I . . . I'm not trying to say anything. I'm just . . . just confused, I guess—and afraid. Marriage is such a big commitment. It has to be right for both of us, or it will never work."

His fingers dug into her arms. "It's gonna work, Maggie. It's *gotta* work. You're the only woman I've ever wanted. What'm I supposed to do if you change yer mind? What's yer Pa gonna say? Hell, Maggie, we've torn one wall off the side of the house and started buildin' jus' what you wanted! You can't back outta this now!"

"I know. . . . Oh, I know, Rand! I . . . I . . . oh, forget I ever said anything. I didn't mean it. I'm just tired and I'm not thinking clearly. Maybe I did overdo it today."

"You better go up to bed. Yep, that's what you oughta do. In the mornin', you'll feel better. Could be you and yer Pa are *both* sickenin'. You do look flushed. Yer face is all hot an' red."

He touched her cheek, pawing at it like a bear. With a sharp stab of regret and pain, she remembered Joe's gentle touch. Oh, God, she *couldn't* marry Rand! They were all wrong for each other. But how was she ever going to tell him or her father? How would she ever explain?

"Now you look pasty-white, the color of biscuit dough. I bet you are sickenin'," Rand said. "You want me t' carry ya' upstairs?"

"No, I can get there myself," she sighed wearily. "Anyway, first I have to do the dishes."

"Fergit the damn dishes. Dishes are fer bean-eaters. Hell, if leavin' 'em bothers ya' that much, *I'll* do the dishes."

How like Rand, she thought, to offend her and ingratiate himself all at the same time. "No, please. . . . Will you just go now, Rand? I . . . I need to be alone."

"Only if you're sure yer all right," he muttered, stepping back from her.

"I'm all right. I promise."

No, I am not all right. I'll never be all right again. I have to break off this engagement, but if I do, then I'll have nothing. . . . No, that's not true. I'll still have the Broken Wheel, and I'll have my horses. And somehow I'm going to make myself into a whole person, and I'm going to ride across my land and learn to run the ranch alone if I have to. I don't need any man to run it for me. My father's still fit and strong; I have time to master what I need to know. I can do it. I must *do it.*

"You don't look all right," Rand said doubtfully. "You look . . . I don't know. Different somehow."

I am different. Joe Hart has changed me. He's opened my eyes to a lot of things. I'm not the same person I was before.

"Don't worry about me, Rand. Just go, will you? I'll see you tomorrow."

"Can . . . can I kiss you g'night, Maggie?" He looked so woebegone—so confused and worried—that she hadn't the heart to refuse. Stiffly, she nodded. He took her in his arms and kissed her in his usual gruff manner. She felt nothing—absolutely nothing, and she knew then that she *had* to break off their engagement. It wasn't fair to marry one man when she was in love with someone else. She must think of a way to do it gently, causing the least possible hurt and damage. That much she owed both Rand *and* her father.

Thirteen

Maggie looked in on her father before she went to bed that night, but he was sleeping, and she didn't want to disturb him; there would be time enough in the morning to tell him of her decision to break off her engagement with Rand—and also to find out where her father stood regarding Lena.

She needed to face up to her future, and he needed to face up to his. If Nathan never intended to do right by Lena just because she was a Mexican, it wasn't fair to allow Lena to sacrifice her whole life for the Sterling family. Maggie found it hard to believe that her father would actually treat Lena that shabbily and hold her in contempt while he did it. She hoped Rand was wrong about her father's true feelings. It was one thing for him to despise all Indians because of what they had done to his brother, wife, and child, but quite another to allow his hatred to spill over onto an innocent woman who had done nothing but love him selflessly all these years.

Yes, Maggie thought as she dressed the following morning. It was time to set the world to rights. She had been a coward and a weakling long enough, letting Pa and Rand dictate to her and run roughshod over others. She would stand up to both of them, no matter how painful it might prove to be, no matter if she *did* wind up a childless, loveless old woman.

This morning, she felt much less depressed and scared than she had last night with Rand. She went down to breakfast humming, only to discover that her father had not yet made his appearance. Lena was her normal, cheerful self however, but

Maggie avoided getting into any serious discussions with her, because she wanted to air everything with her father first. She ate a hearty meal, helped Lena clean up, went up and down the front steps of the house a half dozen times to exercise her legs, much to Lena's amazement and protest, and finally decided to see what was keeping Nathan.

Only rarely did he sleep this late, but since he had not been feeling well last evening, Maggie was not too surprised. Though she hated to admit it, her father *was* getting older; a bit of indigestion now and then and a need for more rest were surely no cause for worry.

She made her way upstairs and went quietly to his room at the end of the hallway. The door was tightly closed, the way she had left it last night, and she eased it open so as not to awaken him if he was still sleeping. "Papa?" she said softly.

His answer was a low, deep groan. Alarmed, she flung open the door, and hurried to his bedside. He was lying stiff and gray-faced, one hand clenched upon his chest, the other clutching the bedcovers. "Pa! What is it? You're in pain, aren't you?"

"Got . . . got a big ole ox settin' on my chest. Can't . . . can't move, Maggie."

"Oh, Pa! I'll get help. You need a doctor. Someone will have to ride into town to fetch Doc Rawson. I'll go get Rand and Lena . . ."

"M-Maggie . . . wait." Nathan tried to lift his head and couldn't quite manage it. "D-don't let Lena see me like this. It'll only . . . only upset her."

"You *do* care about her, don't you, Pa? Oh, I *knew* it!"

Her father's eyes registered surprise. "Y-you knew? All these years—you knew all along?"

"Of course, I knew! How could I not know? How foolish you've been, Papa, not to have told me and then acted upon your feelings. How much time you've wasted! But I'm the one wasting time now. I've got to get you some help. We can talk more about this later."

She started to leave, but Nathan managed to raise his hand

to stop her. "M-Maggie . . . wait. I been a b-bigger fool than you know. I-I didn't do nothin' about Lena, because . . . because . . ."

"Papa, this will have to wait. You mustn't exhaust yourself trying to speak, especially when all you're doing is delaying how fast I can summon help for you."

"B-but I may not have time t' tell you, Maggie. This . . . this may be the end of the trail fer me."

"Pa, you don't have to tell me about Lena. As I said, I already know. I know all of it. And I understand everything. I still love you, Pa. I don't care what you've done or meant to do, I still love you with all my heart. And I don't want to lose you, so please let me go and send someone for the doctor."

She was pleading with him, half crying, tears streaming down her cheeks. She had never seen her father this gray-faced, weak, and in pain. If he didn't let her go, she would simply leave him, even if it meant she never got to hear what could be his deathbed speech. His death was what she was trying to prevent. From the looks of him, it might be imminent.

"All right, Maggie, girl . . . go," he sighed.

She ran out of the room as fast as she could drag her bad leg and careened down the stairs, calling for Lena. "Lena! Go find Rand! If he isn't around, fetch Gusty or Will. Pa's sick and needs help at once."

"Madre de Dios! What do you mean—he's sick? How bad is he? Never mind, I will see for myself."

"Lena, there isn't time. We've got to get help immediately." Maggie reached the bottom of the stairs and waved her arms at the frightened little woman. "Quickly, go find Rand. Please hurry! Someone will need to ride into town for the doctor."

"The doctor!" A look of panic crept into Lena's eyes. On the Broken Wheel, a doctor was only summoned in the direst emergencies. *"Nathan!"* she cried, on the verge of hysteria.

"Lena, calm yourself! It won't help to lose control. We must remain calm and . . ."

But Lena wasn't listening. *"Nathan!"* She picked up her skirts and rushed past Maggie, taking the steps two at a time.

"Lena, no!" Maggie called after her. "He doesn't want . . ."

"Nathan!" Once more, Lena's anguished cry tore through the house. It was the cry of a woman about to lose what she had never really possessed, and Maggie's heart ached for her. Nothing short of death itself could have kept Lena from Nathan's side. Maggie could only guess at the pain Lena must be feeling. She would get no help from her in these first few moments of terror and denial.

Maggie limped out onto the front porch and headed for the bunkhouse to ring the chow bell. When the hands were on the ranch, they usually ate at the same time everyday—meals rustled up by Gusty or Will, augmented by Lena's baking. Only occasionally did the bell have to be rung to summon the hands from afar, either for a meal or for some emergency. It had not been rung in a long time for either, but Maggie decided that using it now was the quickest way to get someone's attention—if anyone was there. By now, the men would have scattered and ridden out to tend to the day's chores.

Praying that someone, preferably Rand, was still available to ride into town, she hobbled over to the bell and vigorously began ringing it. It clanged for what seemed like an hour, but could only have been a few moments before Gusty finally appeared around the side of a shed.

"What in thunderation is wrong, Maggie, honey? Yer like to bust my eardrums with all that janglin'."

Maggie saw what had taken him so long. He was limping and shuffling like an old decrepit man, which meant his rheumatism was acting up again. A good heavy rain usually did that to him. She hoped he wasn't the only one available to ride for the doctor; in his present state, he probably couldn't get up on a horse. Dear God, if her father survived this incident, *she* was going to learn to ride no matter what anyone said!

"Gusty, Pa's in a very bad way. I think his heart may be

giving out on him, and I need someone to go for the doctor. Right away, if possible."

"Lord Awmighty, Maggie. That's a hell of a long ride, especially if a man's gotta take the cart instead of a horse. Why, he'd have't go the long way around—the way you go, an' there ain't no guarantee that Doc Rawson is even gonna be there. He could be over t' Moscow or Lewiston or lots of other places b'sides Bitterroot. That man gits around more'n a bee visitin' clover patches."

"I know, Gusty, but we have to fetch him. Is there anyone else here besides you?"

"Nope. I'm the only one. The others all rode out a coupla hours ago. I'd'a gone myself, but mornings like this I can't crawl up into the saddle. Even if I could, I couldn't stand the pain fer long. Guess I'll have t' take the cart. Ain't got no choice."

"Oh, Gusty, would you, please? I'd go myself but I think I should stay here. Just in case . . . in case you and the doc don't make it back in time."

"He's that bad, eh?" Gusty shook his head regretfully. "Who woulda thought it? Hell, I'm older'n he is, an' he's always been twice as healthy as me. Guess there's just no tellin' how it's gonna happen, is there? One day a man's hale and hearty, an' the next he's breathin' his last."

"Gusty—the cart. Come on, I'll help you harness Preacher."

The two of them went to the corral to get the old gelding, but after they had haltered him and started to lead him out, Maggie noticed that *he* was limping. "Oh, no, he's lame! Yesterday must have been too much for him. I had him out the whole day."

It wouldn't have been too much if she had just driven into town and back, with a rest in between—but she hadn't. She had taken him up to the meadow, and because it was so far to go all in one day, had made him trot as fast as he could nearly the whole way. As a result, he could barely walk; why, she ought to be horsewhipped for her thoughtlessness!

"What are we going to do?" she wailed—and the answer came to her. She would have to saddle and ride Dusty. "Gus, go get Pa's saddle, will you? And the bridle he uses."

"What're you plannin' on doin', Maggie? Since neither one of us can ride into town, we'll have to wait 'til one of the boys gets back—or Rand. And that might not be 'til t'night."

"Pa won't last that long without help. I'll have to go myself. Don't look so shocked. I . . . I've had some practice. I think I can make it."

"Maggie, honey, you can't! How you gonna stay on a hoss—especially a green-broke colt? Besides, we just gelded him awhile back, an' he's still sore. He'll pitch ya off fer certain."

"Then I'll ride your horse or Pa's. There must be some horse in the corral that's reasonably quiet and trustworthy. Pick the best one, Gusty, and let's get him saddled."

"Maggie, yer Pa wouldn't approve o' this, and neither do I. Neither will Rand. I cain't let you go, honey."

"You *have* to let me go! If you don't, Pa may die. Now, are you going to help or not? If not, then get out of my way. I'll pick my own horse and get him saddled."

Gusty squinted at her, looked up at the sky as if seeking divine guidance, then let out a long low whistle through his tobacco-stained teeth. "You is either the craziest or spunkiest piece o' range calico in the whole damn territory, Maggie. Come on—I'll help you."

Less than twenty minutes later, Gusty's horse, Pie, was saddled and fidgeting as he waited for Maggie to mount him. Named because he supposedly rode "sweet as pie," he did not seem sweet today; he hadn't been ridden since the roundup, which meant he was full of energy and eager to be off. A wave of fear swamped Maggie as she contemplated riding all the way into town on him by herself. She knew she'd have no trouble getting him to gallop, but without the security of Joe's arms around her, she feared being unable to keep her seat.

She decided not to think about it and put her good foot in the stirrup to mount. Gusty hefted her up, and once in the saddle, she put both feet in the stirrups which were just about right for her.

"Whoa, boy. Easy now," Gusty soothed, hanging onto the reins. "I don't know about this, Maggie. I don't think he'll buck, but he might run off with ya. When I haven't rode him fer a while, he plumb thinks he's a bird instead of a hoss. Just wish I could've ironed the humps outta him first for ya."

Maggie anchored herself to the saddle by holding tightly to the horn, then realized she might still fall off if the saddle should happen to slip sideways. She had seen cowhands hanging off the side and trying to stay on when a bronc twisted its back every which way, and the saddle didn't sit tight on its withers. Letting go of the horn, she grabbed a handful of mane in one hand and the reins in the other.

"You *sure* you know what to do, Maggie?" Gusty's seamed face had grown new wrinkles in just the past few moments.

"Turn him loose, Gusty. At least if he's full of energy, we'll get to town that much quicker."

"Lord, fergive me if I'm a-doin' the wrong thing," Gusty sighed. "I'd never consider this if yer Pa warn't ailin' so bad."

Gusty let go of the reins, and Pie crow-hopped around in a circle. He was a big raw-boned, jug-headed, flea-bitten gray, but Gusty had always prized him because of his speed and sure-footedness over rough ground. Maggie tried to remember his good points as she struggled desperately to control him.

She finally got him pointed in the right direction and touched her heels to his sides. He didn't walk; he jumped. And suddenly, they were galloping—past the barn and other outbuildings, around the side of the house, then down the worn track leading toward town.

"Hang on, Maggie! Hang on tight!" was the last thing she heard as Pie pounded down the track in the general direction of Bitterroot.

Maggie was terrified, but she found a strength she didn't know she possessed as she clung to Pie's mane. She completely forgot she was holding the reins in her other hand. She wrapped reins and fingers around the saddle horn to further steady herself. Her feet came out of the stirrups, and her toes pointed toward the ground, but she clung doggedly to mane and horn. If sheer will power could keep her on, she was determined to stick.

And stick, she did—even when Pie veered off the track and started up a long rise. She nearly panicked then, until she recalled that it didn't make much difference. The track went around the rise, and she and Pie could pick it up on the other side. Maybe Pie would tire soon, going uphill, and by the time they reached the track again, she'd be able to control him.

With tears streaming down her face from the wind, the bright sunlight, and her own fear, Maggie prayed she would make it. Her bad leg was flopping and banging against the fender of the saddle, amply demonstrating just how useless it was. But she refused to entertain the thought that she might possibly fall; she had to stay on, *had* to, all the way to Bitterroot.

Pie raced up to the top of the rise and without slowing his pace, flew down the other side. The ground was rough but firm, and he seemed not to notice rocks or anything else in his path. He swerved twice, almost unseating Maggie, but she didn't see what had made him do it. She had grown so scared she had closed her eyes and put her life in the hands of the Almighty.

Onward, Pie raced—feeling like a crazed rocking chair gone out of control. The drumming of his hoofbeats sounded like more than one horse, and suddenly he was slowing down and snorting, going from the four-beat gallop to the three-beat lope, and then to the two-beat jog. Bump, bump, bump. His jog was worse to sit than his gallop.

Maggie opened her eyes—and found Joe Hart riding beside her, hanging over Loser's shoulder and slowing Pie down by pulling on the reins where they were attached to the bit.

"Joe! Oh, thank God! What are you doing here, this close to the ranch? I thought you were line riding for another few days."

Looking past his angry, dark face, she saw a small bunch of

cows and calves he had been herding toward the ranch. They were behaving in a strange manner, the cows slobbering and drooling. Some of them were unsteady on their feet. Locoweed. They had gotten into some locoweed, and Joe was bringing them in so they could be confined in a corral until their craving for the weed had passed, and its effects had disappeared from their systems. If they weren't kept separated from the stuff, they would keep eating it until they fell down, had fits, and died.

"I hope I'm not the cause of this," Joe said, glowering at her. "What are you doing on Gusty's horse?"

"This isn't what you think, Joe. I'm not out for a pleasure ride. I'm on my way into town to get the doctor for my father who's very ill—possibly dying. Preacher's lame, Gusty's laid up with rheumatism, and there wasn't anyone else at the ranch to go for the doc."

Joe glanced back the way she had come, saw that it was too far for her to walk back alone, and seemed to make his decision on the spot. "Come on, then. We'll double up on Loser but take Pie along for the homeward journey. I assume you're going to Bitterroot. It should only take us a couple hours at most to get there."

"If we go straight as the crow flies and don't follow the track, it'll take less time," Maggie pointed out as Joe lifted her onto the saddle in front on him and dallied Pie's reins around his saddle horn to pony him alongside. "I was planning on doing that once Pie settled down some."

Joe's arms clamped around her waist, and she let out a sigh of relief and leaned back against his hard, muscular chest. She didn't have to worry or be afraid anymore. Joe would take care of everything—at least, he'd help her get the doctor in the fastest time possible.

"You're something rare, Maggie Sterling," Joe muttered as he signaled Loser for a lope. "I've never met a female as brave, courageous, or foolhardy as you."

"I wasn't being brave, courageous, or even foolhardy," she

objected. "I certainly didn't *want* to do this. What I was—and still am—is terrified. I've never seen my father so ill. I'm sure it's his heart. Please hurry, Joe."

They quit talking after that. Whenever the land allowed, Joe let Loser out, slowing him down only when they had to mount hills or other obstacles in the rolling landscape. They made good time to Bitterroot, a small dusty cattle and mining town tucked in the hills. It had a main street lined with shops and more than its share of saloons, including the notorious Pink Garter. In the distance, the mountains rose stark and gray in the early afternoon sunlight. Seen from afar, they sported little evidence of the lush meadows, crystal-clear streams, and towering timberlands hidden in their rocky folds. They looked harsh and forbidding—distinctly unfriendly.

Maggie was so stiff and sore she could hardly walk when Joe swung her down in front of the apothecary shop that also housed Doc Rawson's office. She was relieved to see a horse and buggy tied to the hitching post out front.

"I'll go in and get him if he's here," she told Joe. "That's probably his buggy. At least, I hope it is."

"He must have just come in. His horse looks tired," Joe commented. "We might have to put him up on Pie if we're going to make good time getting back to the ranch."

Steadying herself with one hand on the hitching rail, Maggie mounted the boardwalk that ran along the front of the buildings. A bell clanged as she entered the cool dark depths of the shop and looked around for Iris Rawson, the doctor's wife.

She wasn't there, but Doc Rawson himself stepped out from behind the curtain concealing his "office" from the view of customers in the shop.

"Well, hello, Maggie. What brings you to town t'day? Weren't you just here yesterday? Iris said she saw you over at the dry goods shop lookin' over laces an' such for your weddin' gown."

Doc Rawson was a short, plump, round-faced man with a bulbous nose, red cheeks, and wire-rimmed spectacles. Maggie had known him all her life. He usually maintained his dignity by wearing a black suit, trousers, and vest topped off by a fancy black top hat, but today, in deference to the heat, he was in his shirt sleeves which were rolled up to reveal hairy arms. . . . As he talked, he was rolling the sleeves down again, as if in preparation to reassume his role.

"Doc, I'm afraid I'm here for an emergency." Quickly, Maggie told him of her father's symptoms, and by the time she was finished, he was fully dressed and reaching for his black leather doctor's bag.

"Sounds serious, Maggie. I'd better come at once. My poor old horse will have to wait to be fed and watered. I just came in from the Rocking R ranch where Emma Gladstone gave birth to a baby girl. Had a hard time of it, she did, and her family got scared and called me. Haven't even seen Iris to let her know I'm back."

"I'm just glad you're here. I was afraid you might have been called to Lewiston or Moscow, and then we really would have been in trouble. . . . Can you leave a message for Iris? If your own horse is too tired to make the trip, we've a horse all saddled that you could ride. He's waiting right outside."

"Good idea on both counts, Maggie. Wait here a minute while I write a note to my wife and tell her to take care of Glory for me. Poor old Glory will be right grateful, if he don't have to go out again right away."

Maggie impatiently flipped through a Montgomery Ward and Co. catalogue lying on the countertop, while Doc Rawson stepped behind the curtain for a few moments. More out of habit than anything else, she searched for the section on bridal outfits; she was much too worried to concentrate on gowns while her father was lying ill and in need of a doctor, but the activity enabled her to better endure the wait.

The catalogue fell open to a lovely, appealing gown that briefly distracted her, and she wondered if Joe would like how she looked in it. Then she realized what she was doing—and thinking—and slammed the book shut in total self-disgust.

How could she even be thinking such thoughts at a time like this?

She drummed her fingers on the countertop and called out to Doc Rawson. "Doc? Are you ready yet? We really must hurry."

He waddled out of the back room, nodding in agreement. "Yes, yes . . . I'm comin'. Let's go at once. I'm ready now."

"Thank God." Maggie led him out the front door to join Joe.

Joe leaned over and fastened the doc's black medical bag behind the cantle of the saddle, then handed him the reins to Pie, who was now meek as a lamb. With some difficulty, the portly doctor mounted the gray gelding. However, he raised his eyebrows in surprised inquiry when Joe reached down and hauled Maggie aboard Loser and seated her on the saddle in front of him.

"Are you going to ride all the way to the ranch like that, Maggie?" he asked. "Where's your cart?"

"My driving horse is lame, and this was the only way I could get here. Everyone at the ranch was working somewhere, and I couldn't take time to find them. I was riding to town by myself when Joe came along and . . . and rescued me."

"Rescued you! My word, child, you can't ride with that bad limb of yours. Why, you could have been killed."

"I'm fine," Maggie clipped out. "And I'll soon be riding everywhere. . . . Oh, Doc Rawson, this is Joe Hart. He's a new hand on the Broken Wheel. Hired this past spring. Joe, this is Doc Rawson."

Joe nodded, and then they were off, with Doc Rawson bumping along on Pie almost as badly as Maggie had done. *If he can ride, so can I,* she thought, watching his sorry performance and hoping he didn't fall off and kill himself before they arrived at the ranch.

The sun had already dipped behind the hills to the west when they rode into the front yard of the ranch house. Gusty limped down the front steps and hurried over to them.

"Thank the Lord, yer here, Doc. Nathan seems a heap better, but he's still got me and Lena worried half outta our underpinnin's. You jus' go right on up to him; I'll take yer hoss—*my* hoss, rather. . . . Maggie, I'm glad t' see yer still in one piece, gal. Joe, it's a surprise t' lay eyes on you—but now, I know how Maggie got there an' back so fast without breakin' her fool neck. She musta run into you, boy."

In his usual non-garrulous way, Joe again nodded and silently lifted Maggie down. She had to stretch a moment before she could walk. "You say he's better, Gusty? Has the pain stopped?"

Gusty nodded. "Yep, an' he's sittin' up, eatin', an' jawin' like nothin' happened. Lena won't let him outta bed though. Said he couldn't go nowhere 'til the doc had a look at him. You know Lena; when she's riled about somethin', she can melt icicles with all the hot air she blows. Nathan tried t' git up, but she shooed him back t' bed so fast the house shook."

Maggie almost melted with relief. Having retrieved his black bag from the back of his horse, Doc Rawson waved her toward a chair on the porch. "You better sit a spell, Maggie. You're looking mighty tuckered out, young lady. I'll go up and check on your father, then let you know the results of my examination."

Maggie nodded. "That will be fine. I'll wait on the porch for you." She noticed that Joe was already riding away on Loser. "Joe? Joe!"

He stopped and half-turned toward her.

"Joe, thank you. I'm glad you came along when you did."

Conscious that Gusty was watching her, she didn't say more, but only smiled and waved. Joe touched his fingertips to the brim of his Stetson, nodded once, and rode away. Only then did she think to ask Gusty if Rand or any of the other cowhands had returned.

"Nope," he answered with a grunt of disgust. "Wouldn't you know the one time we really need 'em, they musta decided t' work late. I got supper hot and ready fer 'em whenever they ride in. Don't think Lena's been doin' much cookin' t'day. You want some chuck, Maggie? You must be hungry."

"I'm afraid I'm still too overwrought to eat, Gusty. But thanks anyway. I'm just going to sit here on the porch for a few minutes, like Doc Rawson suggested. If he doesn't come down soon, I'll go on up to my father's room. I need to see for myself that Pa's really better."

"Suit yerself, Maggie, but dinner's there if ya want it. Think I better check on it, now, and make sure it ain't burnin'. The doc'll have t' be fed when he's done. Reckon he'll have t' spend the night, t'night, too. Well, we got an extry bunk in the bunkhouse fer 'im."

"Thanks, Gusty. I'll see you later."

Maggie went up the porch steps and gratefully sank down on a rocking chair displaced from the section of the house where they had torn out one wall. A heavy tarpaulin now hung over the opening, and most of the furnishings had been moved elsewhere until the renovation was complete. She was suddenly glad she did not have to walk a single step farther. All her muscles were protesting the long hours she had spent in the saddle that day, but she felt peaceful and satisfied, too. Nathan was already doing better, and Doc Rawson would soon fix all his problems. . . . At last, she could relax.

She thought gratefully of Joe and how much his presence had meant to her today. Fortunately, he had not allowed his inherent animosity toward her to get in the way of his duty. He could have ignored her plight this morning or made the day awkward and difficult. Instead, he had been a rock of security. . . . She was deeply indebted to him, and regardless of *her* own feelings, would find some way to thank him more adequately—perhaps by persuading her father to give him a bonus.

Her thoughts turned to the cattle Joe had been bringing in, and she wondered if they were all right. There was no locoweed growing near the ranch, so they should be safe until morning. Joe would undoubtedly go after them then, round them up, and bring them into the ranch.

Sitting and rocking, she leaned her head back against the headboard and whispered a silent prayer of thanks that Joe had come to her rescue. What would she have done without him? She just wished she could understand him! How could a man be such a tantalizing mixture of mystery, aloofness, compassion, and . . . and dependability?

Closing her eyes, she rested until a sound behind her made her snap to attention. It had grown dark, she noticed, as Doc Rawson gently touched her arm and smiled down at her, his features barely discernible in the waning light.

"Maggie? I've finished my examination and given your Pa some medicine. He's gone to sleep. I'm ready to talk to you now."

"How is he, Doc? What did you find out?" Maggie started to get up, but Doc Rawson waved her back down, then perched his hefty backside on the railing and leaned against it, half-sitting, half-standing.

"I'm afraid the news ain't good, Maggie. I've got to be honest with you, which means bein' blunt. Your father's heart is plain wore out, and I don't think he's got long to live—no, not long at all."

Maggie heard the words—that is, her ears and her brain both seemed to be functioning—but she couldn't grasp the full import of this startling statement. She sat up straighter and raked her fingers through her windblown hair. The call of a nightbird sounded surprisingly close and clear, and she thought she heard the muffled sounds of a woman weeping inside the house. Lena. It had to be Lena.

"I ain't told him, Maggie. He thinks he's better and will be back to normal by tomorrow. But he's not ever going to be normal again. His heart is weak, his pulse ain't steady, and the next time he has an episode of *indigestion,* as he calls it, I don't think he'll recover from it."

"Lena. Did you tell Lena all this?"

"No, not all of it. She's just the housekeeper, Maggie, and I thought I should tell you first. . . . But I'm afraid she's

guessed. She asked me outside the room if I thought her cookin'
was what made him ill, and I said no. Her cookin's got nothing
to do with it. That's all I said, but . . . well, I think she knows."

"How long? How long has he got?" Maggie managed to
ask.

Doc Rawson shook his head. "Can't say. Could be a year.
Could be two. Then again, could be only 'til next week. Don't
let him work hard, Maggie. Keep him out of the sun. Don't let
him worry or get riled up over things. It ain't gonna be an easy
job keepin' Nathan Sterling quiet, but if you want him to live
as long as possible, you gotta try and do just that. Make his
last days happy ones; that's all you can do. One day, he'll put
too much strain on his heart, and the old ticker will just quit
tickin'. That's as honest as I can be about it. More I can't tell
you, and there ain't much more I can do, except leave you some
medicine to ease his pain if it comes on him again like that. . . .
As I said, the next time'll probably finish him off."

Maggie sat perfectly still, letting it all sink in. The day she
had secretly been dreading had finally arrived. She was losing
her father. He hadn't much time left. She had to make his last
days happy. Had to keep from upsetting him. . . .

"Thank you, Doc. I appreciate all you've done. Gusty's got
dinner for you down in the bunkhouse. You're welcome, of
course, to spend the night, and we'll give you a fresh horse in
the morning. You can leave it at the livery stable in town when
you're done with it."

"Hell, Maggie, I ain't done nothin'!" Doc Rawson slammed
a pudgy fist against the railing. "Why are you thanking me? I
can't fix Nathan and make him better. One day maybe we'll
be able to take broken-down, tired old tickers and make 'em
work like new again, but that day is a long time in the future,
if indeed it'll ever come. Right now, I jus' feel so helpless and
useless. I wonder why I'm even a sawbones if all I can do is
diagnose the problem but can't make it go away."

"You mustn't blame yourself," Maggie soothed. "You're not

God, after all. You're only human, and some things are beyond human capability."

"Hell, times like these I get to wonderin' if there even *is* a God. An' just last night, I was sure of it when I delivered Emma Gladstone's baby. Life is a pure puzzle, Maggie. I sometimes think the only certainties are that folks come into the world, and folks go out. Everything in between is one big damn mystery."

"You're tired and hungry," Maggie sympathized. She herself ached with the pain of despair, but there was also a curious numbness, blunting the sharp edge of her pain. "Why don't you go down to the bunkhouse now and get something to eat? Gusty's got a hot meal and coffee waiting for you. He'll find a clean bunk where you can spend the night. Or you can bed down on the sofa, if you prefer. We haven't much sleeping room in the house; that's why we're adding onto it—so Rand and I will have more room if—when—we marry."

He seemed not to notice her slip of the tongue. "The bunkhouse'll be fine for me, and a hot meal sounds wonderful. Why don't you come with me and get something to eat, too?"

"No . . . I want to go up and see my father first. I'll eat later."

Doc Rawson moved away from the railing. "Then I'll say goodnight, Maggie. I'm just sorry I couldn't have given you better news tonight."

Maggie nodded her thanks and rose from the chair. "If I don't see you before, I'll see you in the morning. Goodnight, Doc."

Fourteen

When Maggie looked in on her father, she found him sleeping peacefully in the lamplit room. Other than a lingering rim of gray around his mouth, he showed no signs of his near brush with death. A red-eyed Lena sat beside him in a chair drawn up to the bed. The plump little woman was holding Nathan's hand, her eyes riveted to his face, but she glanced up when Maggie entered. The two of them looked at each other, and no words were necessary. Maggie could see the pain of knowledge in Lena's tear-filled black eyes. She was sure her own face must reflect the sorrow in her heart.

"I'll sit with him awhile if you'd like to get something to eat, Lena," Maggie offered in a whisper.

Lena shook her head, her ebony-colored hair clinging in damp tendrils to her cheeks and neck. "No, *Señorita* Maggie. I want to stay here. I left him for a little while so he would not see my tears. But I am better now, and I wish to stay. Besides, he will not awaken. The doctor gave him a powder to make him sleep. I . . . I just want to be with him as much as I can. I could feel death stalking him earlier today. It will come again soon—and the next time . . . ," she trailed off, leaving the sentence unfinished, but Maggie knew what she had been going to say.

Lena's instincts amazed her, making her feel humbled and inadequate in the face of the other woman's remarkable intuition. The look of love on Lena's face as she leaned over Nathan and smoothed back a lock of his hair humbled Maggie further and made her realize yet again that she harbored no such all-consuming emotion for the man *she* was pledged to marry.

She could—and perhaps already did?—feel that way about Joe, but since Joe wasn't interested, it was foolish to dwell on such misplaced ardor. She must think about Rand now and plan how she was going to tell him about her father. Rand would be as devastated as she and Lena—and it was important that he hear the news from her, rather than from Gusty or Doc Rawson. She owed Rand that much. Besides, the doc wouldn't tell him the whole story, and Gusty didn't know the truth yet himself. She debated whether or not to tell him or any of the other hands and decided against it. For Nathan's sake, the truth must be kept private from everyone but her, Rand, and Lena.

Assuming Rand was still coming and had not decided to spend the night out on the range, she ought to go out to the bunkhouse and wait for him. If he and the men had encountered some problem that couldn't be resolved in a single day, they might not return until tomorrow. By midnight, she would know. If the men hadn't returned by then, they probably weren't coming.

"If . . . if he should awaken, call me, Lena," she told her friend.

"Si, Maggie. Unless it is very late. I will stay with him tonight. No one needs to know I spent the night in his room."

"I hardly think it matters anymore, does it?" Maggie smiled. "I think you can quit pretending, Lena. After this, it seems kind of foolish. I think my father realizes that now, too."

Lena lifted her eyes from Nathan's face. "You have spoken to your father about me? What did he say?"

"I'll let him tell you, Lena. It's not my place. I just wish you two hadn't wasted so many years apart—or pretending to be apart. What little time is left, you should certainly spend together and not worry about what people might think. Goodnight . . ."

Maggie retreated from the room and softly closed the door. Then she descended the stairs, exited the house, and headed toward the bunkhouse. Halfway there, a figure detached itself from the barn and moved to intercept her.

"How is your father, Maggie? Is he going to be all right?"

She would have recognized that deeply timbered voice anywhere. "Yes, yes, of c-course, Joe . . . ," she stammered with a catch in her voice. Then she broke down completely. "No, he's not! Doc Rawson said he probably doesn't have long to live."

Sobs burst from her throat as if a dam had opened up inside her. Joe quickly closed the space between them, drew her into his arms, and steered her toward the barn. "Easy now, Maggie, easy. You'll get through this. I know you find it hard to believe at the moment, but trust me, you will."

He pulled her into the dark shadows of the stable, where it was so inky black she could scarcely see, and no one could possibly spot them. "Now, you can cry," he murmured. "Go ahead and bawl your eyes out; it will probably make you feel better."

By this point, she couldn't stop. The emotions she had been suppressing all day came gushing forth in a torrent of tears. Burrowing into the shelter of Joe's arms, she wept unrestrainedly. He held and rocked her, crooning words she couldn't understand, but they had a curiously calming effect. It was the same sort of mindless chant he had used the day he gentled Dusty—a cross between a song, a hum, and a prayer. She couldn't be sure he was even speaking words; if so, they were in a foreign language.

She cried until she had no more tears left to shed, and her sobs subsided into a series of erratic hiccups. The outburst had a cleansing effect. Nothing had changed, her father was still in the same situation as before, but somehow she was better able to cope with the idea.

"The front of your shirt is wringing wet," she mumbled into his shoulder. "I've wept buckets on it."

He undid the bandanna at his throat and pressed it into her hand. "Here. Blow your nose."

She had the good sense not to protest the desecration of his bandanna. "I'll wash it and give it back to you clean," she offered instead, then indulged herself in a good blow.

"Better?" he asked when she was finished.

It was probably too dark for him to see it, but she nodded nonetheless. "I don't know why I should be, but I am. This is the worst day of my entire life—about equal to the day my mother died, and I injured my leg."

"I have known the same sorrow," he told her, rubbing her shoulders with his warm strong hands. "So I understand how you feel."

"Your mother is dead?"

"Long ago. She died of fever, and it was the worst day of *my* life. But I got over it, and you will get over this too."

"What—what happened to your father? Is he still alive?"

There was a slight pause before he answered. "I never knew my father. Never wanted to either."

Shocked by the sudden bitterness in his tone, Maggie sucked in her breath. "Why not?"

"Because he abandoned my mother before I was born."

"Oh." Maggie found herself moving swiftly from comforted to comforter. "That must be a hard thing to live with—never knowing your father and resenting him for hurting your mother. I've had my father's love and protection my whole life. I don't know what it is to be without it, but I guess I'm going to find out."

"You are a strong brave woman, Maggie Sterling, not a piece of lace and fluff like so many of your kind. You can survive anything."

Maggie couldn't resist a rueful smile. "I wish I could be as certain of that as you are. You make it sound like I'm as tough as an old oak tree."

"No, you are as supple and bending as a young willow or white pine. That is why you will weather this storm unscathed, because you will bend before it and not let it snap you in two."

"What a poetic thought, Joe Hart! Where did you learn to

speak like that? You don't sound like any other cowboy on this ranch, and some of them are as colorful in their speech as men can possibly be—or so I thought until I met you. Only your 'color' is not at all like theirs."

"I'm *not* like them," Joe conceded. "In my youth, I read and studied everything I could get my hands on—including some moldy old volumes of English verse that fascinated me almost as much as the behavior of horses. . . . But you've pried enough out of me for tonight. That's all I'm going to tell you—now or ever."

"Oh, Joe! I wish you would trust me. Whatever your secret is, I wouldn't tell anyone; I promise."

"Hush, Maggie. No more questions, no more tears, no more prying. It's late, and you should be in bed."

"Joe, wait. . . . If you can't—or won't—allow anything *personal* between us, will you at least be my friend? Would it compromise you too much simply to talk with me occasionally and . . . and help me with my exercising and riding? I *am* going to ride, you know, after I strengthen my legs. This morning, before all this happened, I started exercising, and I'm determined to continue."

"I'm glad, Maggie. I know you can do it. . . . But I don't think it's wise for me to be your friend either. Friendship between us isn't possible."

"Why not?" she demanded, stung. From the way he had held and comforted her, she was sure he could give her that much!

"Maggie . . ." He pulled her closer, his grip on her shoulders tightening. "Are you really that innocent? Don't you understand what you do to me—even when you're drenching my shirt-front with tears?"

She leaned into him, aware suddenly of that spark of attraction momentarily quenched by her sorrow. It flared anew like dry tinder bursting into flame when touched by an ember. She was the tinder and he the smoldering ember—the source of light, heat, life, and warmth—all that she longed for and did not know how to gain for herself.

"What do I do to you, Joe? Tell me. Show me," she said in a voice so husky it didn't sound like her own.

"Don't, Maggie. Don't start it again—not now. I'm only human; I can't endure much more of this."

She couldn't stop herself. With a wantonness she never knew she possessed, she deliberately stepped closer, pressing her suddenly aching breasts against his damp chest. "Hold me, Joe. Comfort me. Love me. Don't push me away. I need you so much. No one will see us. No one will ever know. Just this once . . ."

There could be no doubt it was wrong; she was behaving like a calico queen seducing a cowboy at the Pink Garter. Had she no shame—no pride? Not, apparently, when it came to Joe Hart. A little voice inside her condemned her behavior and urged her to stop, but another more powerful voice drowned out the first and compelled her to continue.

You want this man. You knew you wanted him the first time you saw him, and you haven't been strong enough to overcome that initial attraction. Just this once, forget about duty, propriety, and moral obligation. Seize the moment. Take what you want. You may never have another opportunity. Do it now, or one day you may go to your grave never having known true passion, desire . . . or love.

Was she her father's daughter, denying what she felt and refusing to acknowledge her needs for reasons that meant nothing in the long run?

No, the voice said. *No, no, no . . .*

She cradled Joe's face between the palms of her hands and kissed him with all the expertise he had so recently taught her. To hold him there, to keep him from pulling away and leaving, she took off his Stetson and flung it into the darkness of the empty barn. A cowboy would never leave without his hat, she thought giddily . . . but she need not have worried.

The time when he could still leave had fled. From his response, she could tell that she had kissed it out of him. He wrapped his arms around her and deepened the kiss. He molded his lower body against hers, and she knew she had won. He would love her now—truly love her. There was no turning back.

"Maggie . . . Maggie, sweet . . ." He released her just long enough to lead her farther into the barn, find a pile of sweet-smelling hay, and tumble her down upon it. Then he was ardently kissing and caressing her, plucking at fastenings, lifting petticoats. He was so eager, so avid, he almost frightened her— almost. The intensity of her own feelings and her own boldness frightened her more.

Suddenly, he paused, leaning over her and balancing on his hands, his breathing loud and ragged. "Are you sure you want this—all of it? If not, tell me now, Maggie, while I can still stop."

Disheveled and breathless, swept with pulse-pounding eagerness, she countered the question with a question of her own. "Do *you* want to stop? I hope not, because I'm just getting started. . . . You'll have to . . . to help me. I've never done this before. I'm not sure what I should do."

"Hanyawat forgive me," he muttered under his breath, then added: "I'm going too fast for you. I'll slow down and give you more time."

He seemed not to notice that he had spoken a foreign word, but Maggie noticed: *He's Indian, just as I thought. He must be. That is his secret.*

At this moment, she couldn't find it in her heart to care. She wanted him too much. Later would be time enough to puzzle over the meaning of the word and worry about his past. For now, it only mattered that she should please and be pleased by him, and they should both fulfill the promise of the sweet throbbing inside her body.

"Shouldn't I remove my shirtwaist?" She pushed the garment off her shoulders.

"Yes," he whispered and bent down and kissed each shoulder in turn. She sensed that he was skirting the limits of his restraint, but his mouth and lips were as gentle as the nuzzlings of a newborn foal. He nosed her neck, kissed her throat, and blazed a burning trail down to her partially exposed breasts. Would he kiss her there—on the very tips of her breasts? Oh, surely not! Touch, perhaps—but *kiss?*

With deft fingers, he freed one breast from her chemise, kissed the tip, then—God forbid!—*licked* it! She shuddered from head to foot, jerking beneath him as he took the engorged nipple in his mouth and gently pulled on it. Oh, she had never imagined a man doing that to her! How shameful—how delicious!

The sensation rippled through her lower abdomen as well as her breast. The core of her tightened and throbbed, as if a school of minnows were nibbling at her innermost nerve endings. A raging need flared within her for him to do the same to her other breast.

No sooner had she formed the thought when he freed the second one and gave it the same stimulating attention. She drew a deep breath, fearing she was going to explode. Tossing her head from side to side on the prickly hay, she moaned, and her hands found his hair. Entangling her fingers in the silky strands, she urged him to stop and continue at the same time.

Grabbing her wrists, he stretched her arms above her head, capturing and holding them in one hand, while his other hand went exploring, and his mouth plundered her breasts. His hand found her thighs beneath her hiked-up skirt, and she stiffened, unable to enjoy that particular intimacy.

"No, don't touch me there!"

He paused. "Do you mean here?" His hand closed over the mound at the juncture of her thighs, and a moist heat flowed through her, hinting of pleasure yet to come. Oh yes, she wanted *this,* but the other . . .

"No, I mean . . . my leg." She could hardly get the words out. She was so ashamed! But she simply couldn't tolerate being touched anywhere near her deformity.

"Maggie, let me. . . . I want to caress your leg. As I told you before, it's part of you, so it must be beautiful."

His fingertips played lightly over her upper thigh, while she cringed and flinched away, trying not to cry out. He brushed and stroked—lightly, lightly—and after several moments, she managed to relax. Her thigh grew warm; the tension receded from it, and the nibbling minnow sensations returned to her lower abdomen.

Joe Hart could even do this! Elicit pleasure where only pain had dwelt. Soothe away shame and embarrassment. Make her forget she was—or ever had been—a cripple.

"Joe . . . ," she murmured. "Oh, Joe . . ."

Releasing her hands, he stroked the shrunken muscles of her thigh and calf, then moved lower in the darkness and kissed them through the thin muslin of her drawers. With infinite patience, he made love to a part of her she had always thought ugly and unlovable. . . . And it was all right, because it was Joe, and he *made* it all right.

She was more than ready when his hand once again covered the place she most wanted him to touch. He slid his body upward and returned to kissing her, while at the same time stroking that secret place no man before him had ever been. She writhed beneath his knowing hands and willingly lifted her hips when he sought to draw down her drawers—and that was when she heard the distant jingle of spurs, the whinny of a horse, and the sound of hoofbeats drawing closer.

Her startled brain put the sounds together and arrived at the only possible conclusion. "Joe, it's Rand and the men returning!"

Joe levered himself off her with amazing speed. "Wait! Stay here!" she pleaded. "No one knows we're in the barn. If we're quiet, they'll never notice."

There was no way they could leave without being spotted. They would have to wait until the horses had been turned out into the corral, and everyone had retired to the bunkhouse before risking a departure from the barn.

Kneeling on one knee beside her, Joe yanked up her chemise and pulled the two halves of her shirtwaist together. "Better get dressed just in case."

Fumbling in the darkness to set herself to rights, Maggie couldn't decide which emotion held sway—relief that something had happened to bring them both to their senses or intense regret that they had been interrupted. Joe's lovemaking definitely had the power to banish all her inhibitions, yet now that they had stopped, and she could think rationally. . . .

She doggedly refused to feel guilty; on that score, her mind was made up. She must tell Rand she could never marry him—deliver two punishing blows in one night. No, she had to be more merciful than that. Tomorrow or the next day would be soon enough to break off their engagement. Rand would have plenty to deal with tonight just hearing about her father.

By the time the men arrived at the corral and bunkhouse, Maggie had restored herself to some semblance of order. She joined Joe standing in the deep shadows near the barn entrance, from which vantage point they could hear the men talking.

"Long day, huh?" Will Tatter complained to everyone in general as he climbed down from his horse. "I hope Gusty made hisself useful and kept the grub good and hot."

"I could eat a whole cow," young Curt agreed. "Thinkin' about chow was the only thing kept me awake these last coupla miles. I almost wish we'd a-made camp and stayed out on the range t'night. At least, we could've eaten sooner."

Rand's voice carried to Maggie and Joe over the sound of leather slapping leather, as he unsaddled his horse. "Sorry to keep you up so late, boys, but I wanted t' get back t'night. Didn't wanna worry Maggie an' Nathan, or make 'em think something was wrong."

Burt Lyman laughed in his big hearty way. "You mean you didn't wanna worry Maggie. Nathan wouldn't have wasted any sleep waitin' up fer ya, an' it appears Maggie ain't waited up neither. Leastways, I don't see her out here. Could be she ain't half as worried 'bout *yer* carcass, as you are about hers. But then *her* carcass is a whole lot purtier."

Burt was only teasing, but Maggie could well imagine Rand's scowl. Guilt reared its ugly head again, and she dreaded hurting him by telling him their engagement was off. Yet she *must* do it—and soon. Especially after tonight. What little self-respect she still had left demanded it.

"You boys go see if Gusty's still up," Rand grumbled. "I'm goin' up t' the house first. Give my hoss some hay fer me, will ya, Curt? There's a big pile still left in the barn. Give 'em all some. They worked hard t'day, and they can use the extra chow."

"Right, boss."

Maggie's heart leapt into her throat. Curt would find her in the barn with Joe! She had to do something—fast. Pushing past Joe and stepping quickly out of the shadows, she called out: "Rand! Rand, I'm here."

"Maggie? What in hell you doin' out in the barn so late at night? I was jus' comin' up t' the house t' see if you might still be up."

"I came down to wait for you, but I . . . I was tired and decided to . . . to stretch out in the hay and rest awhile. I must have dozed off. Suddenly, I heard you and the others ride up . . ."

Rand strode toward her, his spurs jingling loudly. "You all right? You seem kinda strange. What's goin' on?"

Maggie prayed that Joe would have the good sense to disappear while she was distracting Rand. Her heart thumped like a blacksmith's hammer beating on an anvil, as Curt—having turned his horse loose in the corral—walked past her and Rand on his way into the barn to get some of the hay on which she and Joe had so recently been entangled.

"Rand, I have bad news," she blurted out. "Doc Rawson is over in the bunkhouse sleeping. He had to come out today to see my father. Pa became ill suddenly, and . . . and . . . well, if you come up to the house with me, I'll tell you all about it."

"Nathan took sick?" Rand stopped in front of her and eyed her with concern. "Is he all right?"

"At the moment, yes. He's had some medicine, and he's resting quietly, but Doc Rawson says. . . . Come to the house with me," she urged, ". . . and I'll tell you what he said."

Rand did not take the hint that she wanted to speak with him privately—or that anything serious was wrong with her father. "Who in hell went t' fetch the doc?" he demanded in his usual blustery way. "The only man here was Gusty, and he's got the rheumatism so bad he can't get up on a hoss. I guess you had to hitch Preacher an' drive into town, huh?"

"No, Preacher was lame, so I couldn't use him. I . . . I had to ride Pie, but . . ."

"Pie! You had to *ride* into town on Pie?" Rand tilted back his hat and stared at her as if she were spouting obscenities. "You made it all the way into town on a hoss that ain't been rode since the roundup?"

"No, not exactly. Joe Hart spotted me when I was having trouble with Pie. He took me up on his horse, and we both rode into town to fetch Doc Rawson."

Rand's head swiveled toward the corral. "Hell, I don't know why I didn't notice that damn Palousie in there as soon as we rode in; but where's the doc's horse? An' where's his buggy?"

"He didn't bring them," Maggie explained. "He had just returned from a call, and his horse was too tired to make the trip. So he rode Pie, and I came back with Joe on Loser, the same way I went."

"Oh . . ." The single word carried a wealth of deep suspicion and jealousy. The mere mention of Joe's name was sufficient to put Rand on the prod. "So where's Joe now, and why wuzn't he out line-ridin' like he wuz supposed to be doin'?"

Before Maggie could answer, Joe's voice issued from the shadows on the other side of the bunkhouse. He must have slipped through the barn and exited from the other entrance, though how he had gotten over to the bunkhouse without being spotted amazed Maggie. He would have had to cross a wide open area in full view of the cowhands.

"I'm over here, Rand," Joe said. "And if you have any questions about my work, you'd better ask me instead of Miss Sterling."

Rand spun around, his concern for Nathan's well-being far less apparent than his hostile feelings toward Joe. "So what wuz you doin' back at the ranch, cowboy? I sent you out to check on cattle, not to rescue my cow bunny from her own foolishness."

"I wasn't being foolish!" Maggie protested. "Doc Rawson had to be fetched from town. There wasn't any other way of getting there, so I had to ride. I had a little trouble, but fortunately, Joe arrived just in time to help me."

Rand whirled back to her. "Trouble? What kinda trouble? You didn't get throwed, did ya'?"

"No—thanks to Mr. Hart for catching my runaway horse."

"I was bringing in a bunch of sick cows," Joe calmly interjected. "And I saw Miss Sterling trying to hang onto Pie. I caught the horse and took her into town. That's all there was to it."

Almost all, Maggie silently added.

"So where are the cows now?" Rand's tone remained surly. "I don't see 'em."

"They're still out there—I was planning to go get them in the morning. They had gotten into a patch of locoweed. I figured they should be kept separate from the main herd until the weed wore off. Didn't want them eating any more of it either."

"You'll go get 'em t'night, cowboy. On the Broken Wheel, we don't let important jobs like that go until mornin'."

"It can wait until it's light, Rand." Rand's vindictive attitude angered Maggie. Considering that he had no knowledge of what had been going on in the barn between her and Joe, there was no excuse for such churlishness.

"I saw those cows," she said, boldly standing up to him. "Staggering like they were, they'll be running into things and breaking them in the dark, maybe even breaking their own legs, if Joe has to bring them in now."

Rand rounded on her belligerently. "I'm the foreman here,

Maggie. If I say he does it t'night, then he damn well does it t'night."

"And I'm Nathan Sterling's daughter and the future owner of this ranch . . . and *I* say it can wait until morning."

Hearing herself, Maggie couldn't quite believe what she was doing, but her courage didn't falter. So much had changed between this morning and tonight. Suddenly, *she* was in charge of the Broken Wheel, at least until her father recovered—*if* he ever recovered and could resume the responsibility—which was doubtful.

A deep silence indicated that everyone present had heard her challenge and was waiting to see what would happen. She had crossed an invisible line, and there was no turning back now. Rand stood stock still, staring at her, his features unreadable in the shadows cast by the brim of his Stetson, but his tension fully evident in the set of his shoulders and the stance of his big body.

Then Joe said: "I guess Loser can stand one more job tonight. He's had a short rest and a good feed, and he's the only horse I'd trust to bring in a bunch of crazed cows at night. I'll open the gate of one of the cattle pens. As long as nobody closes it while I'm gone, it should be no trouble confining that bunch when I get them back here."

"If you need help, Joe, I'll ride out with ya'," Curt Holloway volunteered. "Jest let me grab a cuppa coffee and somethin' t' put in mah belly 'fore we go. It'll take two men at least t' do the job proper."

"Guess I could go, too," Burt Lyman offered. "The more who ride along, the less dangerous it'll be."

"It isn't necessary for *any* of you to go, tonight," Maggie objected. "Besides, in the light of day, it's only a one man job."

"We'll *all* go," Rand muttered. "Burt's right. You men get somethin' t' eat first, while I go up to the house and look in on Nathan."

Maggie mentally stamped her good foot in exasperation. She couldn't understand why Joe had offered to go get the cows in the first place—but she very well understood what had made the others decide to accompany him; they were letting her know that as a woman, she had no say-so. Her opinion didn't count. If she thought it could wait until morning, then of course, they *had* to make an issue out of doing the exact opposite of what she wanted.

Had Joe been trying to send her the same message? Or had he merely been trying to keep the peace between her and Rand? For a brief moment, she wished he had challenged Rand instead. She wished that Joe wanted her enough to fight for her . . . only he *didn't* want her. He had told her that repeatedly. His body and his actions said one thing, but his mouth kept saying another. *He probably didn't want her because he was Indian—or part-Indian—and she was white.*

And if Rand or her father or even the cowhands found out about it, they were entirely capable of throwing Joe off the ranch. Joe would be lucky if that's *all* they did. It was a potentially explosive situation, and she had no idea what to do about it—or even how she felt about it. Joe Hart, an Indian. She needed more time to adjust to the idea, and to accept the fact that she had fallen in love with a man whose people were and had always been her worst enemies.

"Let's go up t' the house now, Maggie. I wanna hear all about Nathan b'fore I see him." Rand took her arm and steered her in the general direction of the ranch house.

In the face of his take-charge attitude and her own confusion and inner conflict, Maggie let Rand have his way. She managed to sneak one last glance over her shoulder at Joe, but he was paying no attention to her. He did, however, have his hat back on his head. That told her all she needed to know. She could never hold him if he didn't want to be held—and from all appearances, he didn't. He had probably already forgotten what had happened between them in the barn. Or if he hadn't forgotten, he was certainly regretting it . . . and he wouldn't allow himself to be caught in that situation again.

Fifteen

With all the unexpected help, Joe had no trouble bringing in the cattle who had gotten into the locoweed. Even so, it was only a couple of hours until dawn by the time the job was done. As he was turning Loser back out into the corral for a much needed rest, Rand approached him.

"Soon as it's light, Hart, you best get back t' line-ridin'. An' this time, I don't wanna see yer face around here fer a good long while. You find another bunch of sick cattle, jus' bring 'em down t' that low pasture a coupla miles from here, an' I'll take care of 'em from there. Take lots of supplies with ya, a coupla spare hosses, and don't come back 'til you've ridden every foot of the Broken Wheel's boundaries and checked all the ranges. Ya hear?"

"I hear," Joe responded, showing no reaction to yet another order most cowhands would resent. He had already been out "a good long while," and it was time for someone else to assume the solitary job, but he didn't complain. He *wanted* to be alone again, to live like an Indian and fill the empty places in his soul with the grandeur of the land itself and the company of his horse.

He obviously needed more time to conquer his growing obsession for Maggie Sterling; the only unfortunate thing about the extension of the assignment was that he would not have an opportunity anytime soon to talk to her father about his ambitions. He had planned to wait until the end of summer, but if Nathan were as bad as Maggie seemed to think, the man could die before Joe had a chance to buy some of his horses and cattle, and to start looking for land of his own.

If something *did* happen to Nathan, Joe had no doubts Rand would fire him immediately. The foreman was behaving like an old bull scenting a rival—or maybe he just didn't like Joe because of the way he roped and rode, and because his horse of choice was an Appaloosa.

Rand clearly couldn't stand the competition, so the only question remaining was how far he would go to make Joe's life miserable. As Joe headed for the bunkhouse and an hour or two of sleep, Rand called after him: "When yer done line ridin', cowboy, I got some post holes that need diggin'. Maybe you can impress my cow bunny with how fast you can wield a shovel."

Digging post holes was considered an even more menial job than line-riding or chopping firewood. Rand was really scraping the bottom of the barrel this time. Top hands were never asked to dig post holes for fear they would be offended and look elsewhere for a job. Rand was probably hoping Joe would refuse. If so, he was bound for disappointment, because Joe simply nodded and kept right on walking.

He reminded himself that he had nothing to gain and everything to lose by responding to the foreman's taunts. Little did Rand know that it would take more than jealousy to force him off the Broken Wheel; he wasn't leaving until he had what he had come for—cattle, horses, land, and the wages that would help buy them.

All he needed to do was restrain his temper, get to Nathan Sterling before he died, and in the meantime, keep his hands off Nathan's daughter. *She* represented more of a threat to his dreams than Rand did. Tonight, he wearily acknowledged, he had come within a hair's breadth of losing everything. Unlike saloon girls for whom a little tumble was all in a day's work, Maggie Sterling would expect a marriage proposal once she gave herself to a man. Whether he proposed or not, Joe knew he'd be facing Rand's fury and her father's, as well. They would kill him for taking advantage of Maggie and luring her away from Rand; ironically, the fact that he was an Indian would have nothing to do with it.

Maggie herself was worth the risk of bodily harm—but not if he could never truly be himself with her. And not if he had to abandon his dreams to have her. No matter how he looked at the situation, he always reached the same dismal conclusion: Maggie Sterling was not for him. He had already told her too much about himself, and if he revealed any more, she would be appalled and wind up hating him. If he *didn't* tell her, she might eventually find out anyway and despise him for his duplicity as well. Yet she could never hate him as much as he would hate himself for allowing the situation to get out of hand.

In the back of his mind, Joe clung to the faint hope that one day he could openly acknowledge his background, at least to the woman who would bear his children, and that she would cherish it as much as he did in the innermost recesses of his heart. With Maggie Sterling, that could never happen; the Sterling family had been hurt too much by Indians.

He thought he knew Maggie well, understood what sort of woman she was and appreciated what she wanted to be—but she did not know him at all. And he could never open himself to her, especially now that he knew what his people had done to her. If he couldn't forgive the whites for their cruelty to the Nez Perce, how could he expect Maggie to forgive the Nez Perce for having made her a motherless cripple?

Stretching out on his bunk, Joe lay sleepless until dawn, then slipped out, saddled Loser, and rode away from the ranch buildings with a sense of frustration so acute it nearly spoiled his appreciation of the dewy morning. He rode all the way up to the mountains without stopping, dismounted, removed Loser's tack and turned him out into a small green meadow for a much needed rest.

Taking a few items from his saddlebags, he climbed to the top of a rocky promontory which boasted a magnificent view of the surrounding countryside. Nearby, a crystal clear stream tumbled down the face of a cliff and pooled on the stones below. The heady scent of pine filled the air. Breathing easier already, Joe stripped naked, washed in the icy cold stream, then donned a breech clout, buckskin leggings, a headband, and a pair of soft, worn moccasins.

He bundled up his white man's clothing, wrapped them and his Stetson and boots in an oilskin, and hid the packet in a rocky cleft. Two days of fasting, chanting, and meditation should purge him of all his weaknesses and unhealthy desires. Another day or two of hunting and living off the land should prepare him to once again take up the ways of a white man and submerge the Indian side of his nature.

He did not usually have to go this far to balance the two halves of himself, but today, it was necessary. For a few days at least, he had to go *all* Indian, shucking even white clothing and speaking only in the ancient tongue of his forefathers. It had been a long time since he had last done this—and to think he had actually managed to convince himself that he might never have to do it again! He had hoped he could live entirely as a white man and be happy just knowing he would eventually own land and raise horses, which was a victory over his enemies in and of itself.

What a self-deluded fool he was! Somehow, a moment always arrived when he could no longer endure the sense of being torn in two, of never belonging, of having no real home and never being accepted for his own self. At such times, he *had* to seek the guidance of the spirits and his ancestors. Had to cast off the identity of Joe Hart and become Heart-of-the-Stallion, if only for a few days or even a few hours. This time, he would enjoy the luxury of several days, because his need was worse than usual, and because he could fulfill his duties at the same time. After a couple days rest, Loser would be ready to be ridden bareback on a silent patrol of the land and herds belonging to the Broken Wheel.

Slipping a necklace of wolf teeth strung on braided horse hair over his head, Joe resolved not to waste a minute worrying that anyone from the ranch would come looking for him; Rand had made it clear they would not. The longer he stayed out, the better—however, he must pray hard that Nathan Sterling did not die before he had a chance to talk with him upon his return.

"Quit fussin' over me, Maggie! I'm fine now." Nathan waved away Maggie's helping hand as he stomped out onto the porch in search of a chair. "If you an' Lena don't let me alone, I swear I'm gonna saddle a hoss an' go huntin' jus' t' git away from the two of you."

Maggie sighed and went after him, determined to keep him from doing anything too strenuous. He wasn't even supposed to be out of bed yet. Before returning to town, Doc Rawson had recommended a week or so of bed rest and then a slow, cautious return to a few but not *all* of his most cherished activities. Ignoring that advice completely, Nathan had gotten out of bed less than an hour after the doctor's departure and kept Lena and Maggie in a state of constant worry and vigilance ever since.

Four days had now gone by, and Lena had circles under her eyes from worry and lack of sleep. Maggie was certain she herself didn't look much better. Her father continually insisted that he intended to resume his normal activities within a week or two, at most, and neither woman knew how to stop him. He just wouldn't listen to their pleas and precautions. Short of telling him outright exactly what Doc Rawson had said, they were reduced to nagging in an effort to get him to slow down and change his lifestyle.

Nathan's only concession to his recent collapse was a willingness to take an occasional short nap, but as soon as he awakened and had a burst of energy, he thought he should get up and start doing everything he had done before—and strangely enough, Rand agreed with him.

Maggie had told Rand how serious her father's condition

was, but he seemed to be denying it as much as Nathan was. Whenever she tried to enlist Rand's cooperation in discouraging her father from pushing himself too hard, Rand would only shrug.

"Maggie, ya' might as well shoot him as tell him he's gotta go out t' pasture like some old lame hoss that can't be rode no more. It'd be a hell of a lot kinder. He ain't gonna listen t' no female advice anyway, so ya' might as well leave him be. His body'll tell him when he oughta quit, an' if it don't, then whatever he's doin' probably won't hurt him."

"Don't you understand? His body won't have a chance to tell him anything!" Maggie had explained more than once. "His heart will simply quit working, and that will be the end of him. You've got to talk some sense into him, Rand. If he won't listen to me and Lena, maybe he'll listen to you."

"I can't, Maggie," Rand finally admitted. "He won't listen t' me neither. I've always been the one takin' advice from Nathan, not givin' it, an' I don't know how t' change all of a sudden, an' neither does he."

That was the problem with all of them, Maggie realized. For years, they had all accepted Nathan Sterling as the prime authority in their lives. What he said went. Just because his heart was weak did not mean his mind was affected; he still possessed the power to persuade and intimidate—and if anyone was going to stand up to him, it would have to be her. She had known for a long time that she had to assert herself—and had been trying to do just that—but she was only just now coming to terms with the idea that she would actually have to assume authority over *him*.

"Pa, would you like some coffee or lemonade?" she asked as he found the chair he wanted, dragged it over to where he could watch several of the men working on the addition to the house, and stubbornly plunked himself down on it.

"Curt!" he hollered. "You mind you get them corners snug and tight-fitting! Do I havta come out there an' show ya' how it's done?"

Three of the cowhands were working under the direction of Lattis Flume, a carpenter who had come out from town, but Nathan still thought he knew more about building—and everything else—than the expert he had hired to oversee the job.

Maggie wished she could put a stop to the whole project, but it was too far along for the men to quit now. She still had not had a chance to tell her father or Rand about her decision to cancel the wedding, but she was hoping to do it soon—and also planning to talk to Nathan about Lena. She had been waiting for him to regain his strength first, but the longer she waited, the harder the task seemed.

Without Joe around to remind her of the way she felt about him, she was in danger of falling into the trap of wanting to fulfill everyone else's expectations but her own. She reminded herself of a salmon swimming upstream while all the other fish were headed in the opposite direction. It would be so much easier to simply turn around and float along with the rest.

"Pa, I asked you if you wanted something to drink," she patiently reminded him. Nathan was drumming his fingers on the railing, just itching to go and show poor Curt exactly how he wanted the corners of the new addition to be done.

"No!" he shouted over the noise. "I jus' wanna be left alone, Maggie—less'n you wanna talk about movin' up the weddin' and fergittin' all this nonsense 'bout waitin' 'til after this damn-fool project gets done. From the looks of it, it'll probably be next spring before it's finished."

"Pa, we've been over this before, but now that you've mentioned it, I . . . I have had a change of heart on the subject."

"Good!" Nathan quit drumming and focused his full attention on her. "So you're finally ready t' ease yer poor ole Pa's mind regardin' yer future, eh? Hell, it's about time. I don't wanna go up yonder and fork a cloud without knowin' that you'll be well taken care of, Maggie—an' the Broken Wheel, too. Let's get this damn weddin' over an' done with, an' I'll sleep a lot easier at night, I can promise you."

Maggie took a deep breath, but the sinking feeling in the pit of her belly would not go away. Dare she be truthful with her father? Would it upset him too much if she told him right now that she wanted to end her engagement to Rand?

"Pa . . . what I really wanted to talk to you about was Lena," she blurted like the coward she was.

"Lena?" Nathan squinted at her in surprise. "What about Lena?"

"Pa, when you were ill, you said . . . well, you mentioned your feelings for her. You *wanted* to talk about her then, and I couldn't take the time because I was trying to get help for you. . . . Anyway, I think we should talk about her now. Whatever time you have left, you should spend wisely, and . . . and . . . marry Lena. After all these years, Pa, you and Lena deserve to live together openly and to be happy."

"We *are* happy," her father said. "We're content as two pigs in a wallow just the way things are. I shouldn't have said nothin' to you about Lena. What's between her and me is private, jus' like it always has been, and I don't see the need fer anybody else t' know about it."

"But Pa! You care about Lena, and she cares about you! So why don't you make an honest woman of her? She *deserves* that much. Why, she's given you the best years of her life, and . . ."

"Keep yer voice down!" Nathan jerked his head in the direction of the men, but there was so much hammering and sawing underway that Maggie was sure they couldn't hear.

She grabbed another chair, moved it closer to her father, and sat down to pursue the topic, but Nathan held up his hand to forestall her. "Did Lena put you up t' talkin' t' me about this?" he gruffly inquired.

"No, of course not! She would never say anything; that's why *I* must. Pa, she thinks she's not good enough to be your wife."

"Could be she's right." Nathan averted his eyes from Maggie, his tone stubborn and unyielding.

"Pa!" Maggie wasn't sure she had heard him correctly. If

she had, she didn't want to believe he had actually said such a thing. Even knowing it might upset him, she could not conceal her dismay.

"What a terrible thing to say! I think of Lena as if she were my own mother. Why, I can hardly remember Mama. And Lena worships you; there isn't anything she wouldn't do for you. How can you possibly say she isn't good enough to be your wife?"

The subject of their conversation crossed the yard just then, with a basket of wet garments under one arm. Glancing back over her shoulder, Lena smiled and waved, then continued toward her favorite spot for drying wet clothes—a huge bush with lots of sturdy branches to support the weight of the laundry. As Maggie watched, Lena began spreading and hanging Nathan's newly washed shirts.

"Maggie . . ." The husky note in her father's voice gave Maggie pause. A suspicious sheen filmed his eyes, and his face was flushed, causing her to worry that she might indeed be upsetting him too much.

"Maggie, honey . . . don't think too badly of yer ole Pa fer bein' honest with ya', but people like us jus' don't marry people like Lena. Even Lena don't expect it. We're too . . . too different, I guess. That don't mean I ain't got feelin's fer her or she fer me. We gotta a heap o' feelin's between us, and when I die, Lena ain't gonna want fer nothin'. I got money set aside jus' fer her, an' I know you won't turn her outta our home or make her leave the Broken Wheel. But the Broken Wheel itself—the land, hosses, cattle an' such—are all goin' to you an' Rand, nobody else. That's why I ain't ever gonna marry again, 'cuz I don't want no disputes about it . . . an' I don't want people gossipin' neither."

"Disputes? What do you mean—disputes? Do you honestly think Lena would challenge your wishes? Pa, that's ridiculous, and you know it. She hasn't got a greedy bone in her body. I don't understand how you can feel this way. A few days ago, when you thought you might be dying, you were ready to marry Lena."

"I didn't never say that," Nathan protested. "An' if I did, it was jus' 'cuz I wuz . . . sick. I've had time t' reconsider, an' I cain't see that marryin' Lena would change anything at all between us. So why do it?"

"Because it would make her so happy, Pa! She'd feel loved and wanted!"

"She already feels that way," he insisted, stubborn as a mule. "She *knows* I love her."

"How would she feel if she knew *why* you won't marry her?"

"You gonna march out there an' tell her?" he demanded. "What exactly are ya' gonna say?"

"Oh, Pa, I'm not going to say anything. She's convinced you won't marry her because of the mistakes she made in her youth—and because she can't bear your children."

"My children! Why would I be wantin' children at my age? Besides, if I had 'em with Lena, they'd all be half-breeds, an' that's even worse than bein' a full-blooded bean-eater."

Tears sprang to Maggie's eyes. "I hope and pray Lena never hears you talk like this. Why, it would destroy her—and it shames me. I never dreamed you were so . . . so . . ."

"Partic-ular? Hell, Maggie, I can't help it, so don't hate me on account of it. In my book, a bean-eater's a little better'n an Injun, but not by much. Guess I been hurt too bad by dark-skinned *hombres* to ever forgive 'em fer it. God knows I never meant to feel the way I do about Lena. Fer years, I fought it, but I jes' couldn't help myself. I was so blamed lonely after yer Ma died . . . and Lena was so damned handy an' willin'. She never asked fer nothin' either. That made it plumb easy. I think if she had, I probably woulda found the guts t' tell her to skeedaddle. But she didn't, an' one day I jus' woke up and knew I couldn't live without her, bean-eater or not. . . . Hell, over the years, she's all but made a bean-eater outta me. I been eatin' like a Mexican fer years. We all have."

"Then you have to tell her that, Pa—not about the food, but

about how you feel about her. It would mean so much. You have to give her something to cling to, something to console her after you're gone."

"I *have* told her how I feel, Maggie. I just ain't mentioned marriage. And I ain't gonna. Marriage ain't in the cards fer us. But you and Rand, now—that's a different story. I want to see you two married b'fore I fork a cloud, so why can't we hold the weddin' next week instead of waitin' all the way 'til Christmas? You don't need no extry rooms right away, an' you sure as hell don't need no fancy gown. A man would rather see his woman naked than all gussied up anyhow."

Maggie sighed in exasperation. "Are you proposing I get married wearing nothing at all then?"

"I don't care what you wear so long as you git to it. That's the thing I want most in the world, honey—t' see you an' Rand git hitched b'fore I die."

"What—what if I said I'm still not ready for marriage, Pa? What if I said I don't love Rand? I hate to disappoint you, but . . . but . . . I'm thinking of calling off the wedding altogether," Maggie blurted in a rush, forcing herself to say it before she could change her mind.

Nathan sat back in his chair, his silver-shot brows knit together in disbelief. "You cain't mean that, Maggie. You couldn't be that fickle and cruel. Yer makin' me feel bad about Lena, an' all the while yer plannin' on breakin' Rand's heart? Hell's fire, I wouldn't never have believed that of ya'."

"I can't help how *I* feel either, Pa. I just can't marry, Rand. I can't promise to be true to him for the rest of my life. I've tried to love him, but the feelings won't come. When he holds me, when he kisses me, I . . . I feel nothing for him. I *care* about him, yes—but not the way I should about my future husband. So how can I possibly marry him? In the end, wouldn't it be more cruel to marry him and make him miserable than to break it off now and be done with it?"

She searched her father's face for understanding and prayed she wasn't hurting him too much—or taxing his already weakened heart. She would never forgive herself if these revelations proved to be too much for him. What good was all her honesty if it put Nathan in an early grave? She began to wish she had said nothing, particularly when he didn't immediately respond.

"Well, Maggie," he finally said, and she was sure he had grown paler in the last few moments. He sighed deeply and plowed his fingers through his gray-streaked hair. "You ain't fallin' fer somebody else, are ya'?"

Joe, Maggie thought to herself. *Yes, I've fallen for Joe.* But she didn't admit it. She didn't dare. It would be too much to dump on her father all at once—especially when Joe didn't reciprocate her feelings.

Nathan was watching her closely. "It's that new fellah, Joe Hart, ain't it? I seen the way the two of you eye each other. 'Course, all the men eye you like that. As I've mentioned before, yer a right pretty piece of calico. But none of the rest of 'em can ride an' rope like Joe, can they? And none of 'em can make yer heart go pitty-pat just by lookin' at ya'."

Should she deny it? What good would be served by admitting it when nothing could ever come of it?

"Joe has no interest in me, Pa. And I don't really know him well enough to say how I feel about him. We were talking about Rand, not Joe. I'm not trying to get out of my engagement so I can turn around and marry someone else. I want to break it off because Rand deserves better than I can give him. He should have a woman who thinks the sun rises and sets on him, the way Lena feels about you. I've tried, but I can't muster those emotions—and I don't think I ever will."

"I see," her father said, but she didn't think he saw at all, and his next words confirmed it. "You ain't said nothin' t' Rand 'bout this, have ya'? No, I don't guess you have, or I'd have heard about it. . . . Well, don't say nothin' yet, Maggie. Don't go breakin' his heart any quicker than ya' have to. In a week or two, maybe you'll change yer . . ."

"No, I won't change my mind. But that's why I haven't told him yet. Because I'm not sure how to do it. I *know* he's going to be terribly hurt, and I dread having to hurt him. Then there's the matter of the ranch. . . . He thinks it will be his someday, but if I don't marry him, it won't be . . . will it?"

Maggie wasn't sure just how deeply her father's feelings for Rand were. He had mentioned leaving the ranch to *her and Rand,* but what would he do now? And what would Rand do when she finally told him? And how long must she wait before telling him?

Well, it was partially out in the open now; could the rest be any worse? She had dreaded telling her father almost more than she dreaded telling Rand.

"I hafta think about all this, Maggie. I got no idea what we oughta do next. Rand *does* expect t' share ownership of this ranch with you someday. Hell, I've told him often enough that he will. We both been plannin' on it."

"I'm sorry," Maggie murmured. "I'm truly sorry."

"Well, you oughta be. If this is just some dumb female notion, I'm gonna be plumb irritated. You sure you ain't gonna come back next week an' tell me you reconsidered?" His eyes lit with hope, and she hated to disappoint him.

"No . . . no, I won't do that, Pa. I've agonized long and hard over this, and I won't come back and say I was wrong."

"But what if you *never* marry? Have you thought about that? What if nobody else ever asks ya'? Not every man would be willin' t' overlook an ugly shrunk leg. B'sides, I want some grandbabies to leave this ranch to—someone t' carry on what me an' yer Ma started. Yer takin' that away from me, too, ya' know, and leavin' me settin' here with nothin'. Who's gonna get this ranch after you die, girl? You got any ideas about that?"

She shook her head miserably. Again, she wished she hadn't said anything yet, though it wouldn't have gotten any easier by waiting. Her father looked so sad and disappointed—so fragile, old, and gray. If she did marry someday, he would not be alive to see her children, assuming she had any. . . . Dear God, was she just being horribly selfish? Was it already too late to back out of this commitment?

"I guess I won't say anything to Rand yet," she agreed in a small voice. "At least, not until I've talked to you again. Surely, we'll think of some gentle way to tell him. . . ."

"Goddamn, Maggie! There ain't no gentle way of tellin' a man he ain't gonna git the only two things he's ever wanted in this world—you and this ranch! There ain't no gentle way a'tall!"

"But what about what *I* want, Pa? Shouldn't you be worrying about *my* happiness, too? What if I did plan to marry another man? How would you feel about that?"

"Not too damn good!" Her father's face reddened in an alarming fashion. "Fact is, I wish you was small enough to take a stick to right now, 'cause a good whuppin' might be just what you need."

"You're not being fair, Pa. The idea that I should marry Rand was always yours and his, not mine. I should have said something long ago, I admit. I shouldn't have allowed things to go this far, but I kept hoping I would learn to love him. Well, I haven't, and I can't keep pretending that nothing's wrong between us."

Her father gave her a sharp look. "Funny, but nothin' *did* seem to be wrong 'til Joe Hart suddenly come along. Guess that was *my* mistake—hirin' such a good-lookin' cowboy."

"Leave Joe out of this, Pa. He hasn't asked me to marry him, so he's not the threat you think he is."

"Humph!" Nathan grunted. "Considerin' that he ain't got a pot to piss in, I can sure understan' why he ain't asked. The only thing he owns in the world is his hoss and his saddle—and his hoss is a damn Palousie."

Maggie said nothing to that; there was nothing to be said. Joe's reasons for not proposing were his own, and they had nothing to do with what he did or did not possess. Without the promise of the ranch, Rand didn't own anything either, a fact her father seemed all too willing to overlook.

"I think we've discussed this matter enough for one day,"

she firmly announced. "Perhaps you had better go in the house and rest for a bit now, Pa."

"No," her father growled. "I don't wanna rest. But I would like t' talk t' Lena. Looks like she's done hangin' up clothes, so why don't you go over an' fetch her fer me?"

"I'd be happy to, Pa." Maggie rose from the chair.

"Jus' don't git yer hopes up. I ain't fixin' on proposin' to her."

"Oh, we are a pair, aren't we, Pa? You want me to marry a man I don't love, and I want you to marry a woman you do love—and neither one of us will do it. We don't make much sense, do we?"

"Don't know about you, but *I* sure as hell do. I make perfect sense t' me."

Before leaving, Maggie leaned over and lightly kissed her father's forehead. "Can you ever forgive me, Pa, for disappointing you?"

Nathan snorted. "Sure, if you can fergive me fer disappointin' you."

"I forgive you," she whispered. "I just don't always understand you."

"Same here." Grabbing her hand, he gruffly squeezed her fingers. "Now, go git Lena, will ya'? I suddenly got a powerful hankerin' t' see that l'il bean-eater up close."

Maggie smiled, shook her head, and left him.

Sixteen

Three weeks passed, and Maggie still had not told Rand, but then he had been exceedingly busy, and she had had no opportunity. By now, the addition to the house was almost finished— at least, the outside work. There was still everything to be done inside, but the shell was complete. Even the planking had been applied to match the planking already existing on the rest of the house.

The cowhands could not spare more than a day or a few hours here and there, and the carpenter had had to quit and help someone raise a barn to replace a structure that had burned down in town, so all work had stopped. Maggie was glad. The more delays, the better. She hoped it was never finished. As soon as it was, Rand would be after her to move up the wedding date, and she would have to tell him that she had changed her mind—no matter if her father was disappointed or not.

She and Nathan had not spoken of the matter again, and he had resumed nearly a full schedule of work. He seemed determined to ignore the fact that he had ever suffered an illness. Other than a daily afternoon nap and getting up later in the morning and going to bed earlier at night, he made no other concessions. However, he was spending more time with Lena and doing so more openly, even being affectionate in front of others, which only seemed to embarrass her. Maggie suspected that Lena had hidden her relationship with Nathan for so long that she was now incapable of acknowledging it in public.

Nor could Maggie bring herself to discuss these things with

her friend, for fear she might say the wrong thing or reveal her father's true feelings regarding why he wouldn't marry again. Despite what Nathan claimed, Maggie knew Lena would be badly hurt if it ever came out, and she didn't want to be the one to make such a devastating revelation.

To avoid awkward moments with Rand, Lena, or Nathan, Maggie spent her spare time exercising and strengthening her legs. When Rand wasn't around and her father was sleeping, she saddled Preacher, climbed up on the fence to mount him, and rode him gingerly around the breaking pen. In her more optimistic moments, she fancied that her bad leg was actually growing stronger, and one day soon she would be able to ride Dusty who eagerly anticipated her daily visits to the horse corral, nickering a welcome each time she appeared.

Twice, she drove into town, but saw nothing of Joe either going or coming. On one occasion, she drove up to check on her horses, but he wasn't there either. That was the day she also picked up the fabric for her bridal gown in town, smuggled it into the house, and then hid it in her room underneath her mattress. As yet unaware that the wedding was not going to take place, Lena was anxiously awaiting the arrival of the satin, lace, and ribbons, so she could get started cutting and sewing.

It was a difficult time for Maggie. By his very presence, Joe would have reinforced her decision not to marry Rand. In his absence, she sometimes doubted the wisdom of that decision. If only Joe cared for her a little . . . if only he was willing to be her friend, perhaps that friendship might lead to something more satisfying. That he desired her was scant comfort indeed, if he would permit nothing further between them.

Sometimes, she dreamed of him—disturbing, erotic dreams in which he came to her as a half-naked Indian, and she gave herself to him anyway, even knowing that he was, or ought to be, her worst enemy. She could picture it almost perfectly; Joe would be magnificent in Indian dress—haughty and proud, possessing that indefinable grace that set him apart from white men. She had sensed that he was different the first time she saw him; she just hadn't realized what she was seeing, but now the memory of how he walked, moved, and rode a horse seemed to mark him as unmistakably Indian.

She would awaken from her dreams, trembling and ashamed, wondering how she could harbor such feelings for a man from the same race of people who had killed her uncle, been involved in her mother's death, and caused so much needless suffering, both for herself and for others.

She wondered what tribe he had come from but doubted that she would ever have the courage to ask him. He *couldn't* be Nez Perce; that would be too cruel of a joke played upon them both by an uncaring deity. God would never do that to them, would He? Besides, the Nez Perce were all confined to reservations now.

Then a new thought occurred to send chills skittering down her spine: Was it possible Joe had escaped from Lapwai, and the authorities there might even be looking for him? The mere thought made her shiver, despite the burdensome heat, and she tried to put it out of her mind and concentrate instead on the weather and her furtive riding sessions.

It was now high summer—hot, dry, and dusty on the ranch. The only respite from the burning sun existed higher up in the mountains. In the lowlands, the grass had turned golden, and the land was colored in shades of ocher, tan, and brown. At this time of year, only the mountain pastures remained cool and green.

Over Maggie's protests one hot morning, Nathan decided to join Rand and the other hands riding up to the mountains to look for Joe. By now, Joe had been out line riding for an unusually long time, and the men were starting to ask questions and worry about him. They well understood the dangers of being alone in rough country; a man could break his leg in a fall from a horse or take sick with a strange malady. He might die out in the wilderness before anyone realized that something was wrong and made the effort to find him.

Normally, line riders were spotted from time to time, or else they rode in to get more supplies, switch horses, or obtain whatever else they might need—but no one had seen or heard from Joe since the night Rand had ordered him to go out and bring in the sick cattle. Worried now herself, both for her father and for Joe, Maggie stopped trying to discourage Nathan from going and begged to be allowed to accompany the men on their search.

"Ya' can't come, Maggie," Rand informed her, glowering as he saddled Cricket out by the round pen. "A cart and hoss can't manage the steep and narrow spots, and we'll probably have to ride high, hard, and fast to find him."

"He's right, Maggie," her father agreed, cinching up his horse. "A cart can't make it, so you better stay here with Lena."

Maggie drew a deep breath and lifted her chin. "I don't have to take the cart. I can *ride* along with you. I've been practicing on Preacher, and I'm sure I can keep up."

Both Rand and her father gazed at her with irritation and astonishment. Her father opened his mouth to say something, but while he was formulating his response, Rand mounted Cricket and swung the big horse around to face her.

"You better *not* have been ridin' Preacher or any other hoss on this ranch. I already told you how I feel about you ridin', an' I thought you had given up on the idea. Now, I find you been sneakin' around behind my back. You jus' go on up t' the house an' wait fer us, Maggie. I'll be up t' talk t' you soon as we get home again. I think it's long past time you an' me had some understandin's."

"That's tellin' her, boy," Gusty Williams chortled, tugging down the brim of his hat. "Only our little filly don't look none too happy about it."

"I'm *not* happy about it," Maggie announced to the entire crowd of cowboys who had been saddling and mounting their horses nearby and heard every word of the exchange already. "And I'm *not* going up to the house to wait for you, Rand. I'm going to saddle Preacher, and I'm riding out with you."

"Now, Maggie," her father placated as he hefted himself

ponderously into the saddle and shoved his feet into the stirrups. "You do as Rand says. It's too damn dangerous fer you t' even think about ridin' along with us."

"It's too damn dangerous for *you* to be going," Maggie countered. "But if you can go, I certainly can."

"Like hell you will, Maggie!" Rand's face was flushed and congested. "I expect my men to follow orders when I give 'em, an' my future wife has got t' do the same. Go on up t' the house. Go on now, git!"

Maggie could feel her own face flame with the heat of anger. She switched her attention to her father's pale features and asked quietly: "Pa, are you going to tell him or am I? It's abundantly clear that someone has to tell him. Things can't go on as they are."

"Tell me what?" Rand demanded.

Her father looked around sheepishly. "Now is hardly the time an' place, Maggie."

Maggie disagreed. It felt like the *perfect* time and place. If she had ever needed a reason why she and Rand were ill-suited to each other, this was it. He thought he could order her around as if she were a misbehaving puppy, and he didn't even realize he was humiliating her in front of everyone. This was the true Rand—the one she would have to live with if she ever married him. And he would browbeat her, wear her down, and disparage her abilities and ambitions until she gave up trying to be anything but what he wanted. Surely her father could see that now.

Unfortunately, Nathan did not look capable of dealing with the matter. He had gone from being merely pale to pasty-white, and she could have kicked herself—and Rand—for upsetting him. "Pa?" She started toward him. "Are you all right?"

"He don't look all right t' me." Rand abruptly jumped off his horse and headed for Nathan's side. "Nathan, maybe you best stay here with Maggie. You can go back t' the house an' rest this afternoon instead of ridin' around in this hot sun."

"Maybe I'd better," Nathan mumbled, pulling off his bandanna and wiping his face with it. "But it's jus' indigestion, that's all it is." He thumped his chest with a clenched fist, lines of determination bracketing his mouth. "It ain't my ticker, I tell ya'. It's jus' Lena's cookin' an' this goddam heat."

"That's what you said the last time." Maggie moved closer to him. "Come on, Pa. Get down. I'll stay home with you today. *Next* time, we'll both go. I've been wanting to show you how well I can ride; I think you'll be pleasantly surprised."

She gave Rand a scornful look as together they helped Nathan to dismount. Gusty Williams and Curt Holloway hurried over to lend assistance, and a worried Burt Lyman crowded closer on Beans, in case he was needed. Nathan scowled at all of them, pushed away their helping hands, and stood upright without support.

"Quit crowdin' me! Hell, if I'm dyin', I need air. Jus' get outta my way, an' I can make it to the house on my own two feet."

Maggie motioned the men back. "Of course, Pa. Go ahead. No one's going to stop you."

Nathan stomped past her, free and unaided, but halfway to the house, he halted and turned, looking from her to Rand and then back again. "When you find Joe Hart, you bring him up t' the house t' see me, ya' hear, Rand? I wanna see him the minute you get back."

"If you say so, Nathan—but all I was gonna do was check t' see he wasn't hurt or nothin'. I wasn't plannin' t' bring him back down to the ranch with us yet. He told me he *liked* line-ridin'."

"He's been out fer weeks," Nathan growled. "Time he gets a chance t' sleep in a bunk again under a real roof an' eat some decent grub. As fer why I want to see him, I got my own reasons. Jes' send him up t' the house soon's he gets here."

"Whatever you say," Rand drawled. "Yer still the Number One Cocka-doodle-do, Nathan."

When Maggie's father got back to the house, he took a nap under Lena's worried supervision, which left Maggie to pace the floor of her room grappling with her own worry. She ought to have spoken to Rand weeks ago; at the same time, she felt guilty for having upset her father by raising the subject before he was ready to deal with it. For his sake, she had procrastinated—and also because she wanted to delay the unpleasantness for as long as possible. However, it was obvious she could delay no longer. Rand had to be told.

It was a sweltering afternoon, and after a time, she lay down on the bed and dozed fitfully. When she awoke, the long blue shadows of evening lay across her bed, and she arose and went down the hall to Nathan's room. The door was ajar, and she could hear voices within—Nathan's and Lena's.

She paused outside, loath to interrupt their privacy but wanting to make certain her father was better. His voice sounded reasonably strong as it carried out into the hallway.

"She ain't gonna marry him, Lena. Maggie has ideas of her own, an' she's gonna call off the weddin' and break Rand's heart."

"But if she doesn't love him, *querido,* perhaps it is for the best." Lena's voice was soft and cajoling as she loyally took Maggie's side of the issue.

"How can she know what's best, Lena? Hell, she's a cripple who's always had me and you t' look after her. What's she gonna do when I pass on—can you answer me that? How's she gonna run this ranch without Rand? And what's *he* gonna do when Maggie dumps him? I know what he'll do; he'll ride outta here like his shirt-tail's on fire. He won't stay if he can't have Maggie an' the Broken Wheel, the only two things he's ever wanted."

"You must not worry so much, *querido.* Rand is a good-looking *hombre,* and he will find someone else. Maggie will, too. Once Rand is gone, she'll be free to look elsewhere."

"Where in hell's she gonna look—toward some two-bit drifter with no money and no prospects? Who else ever shows up here lookin' fer work? Only cowboys down on their luck ever ride in here huntin' fer a job. . . . An' I don't think she'll look at Curt or any of the boys already here. Besides, I wouldn't trust none of 'em t' take over this ranch one day the way I always trusted Rand. I *trained* Rand fer the job. Ain't nobody else in whose hands I wanna leave this ranch."

"It will all work out, *querido*. You must not worry so."

"Why is she doin' this, Lena, why? You think she's got her eye on that new fellah, Joe Hart? Is *he* the reason she's givin' up Rand? I jus' don't understand it. Why, she don't know nothin' at all about Joe Hart or where he come from."

"Por favor, lie back and rest, *querido*. What good will it do for you to make yourself sick with worry? Maggie is not a foolish girl. You must trust her more. She's knows what she's doing, and you must allow her to do it."

"She don't know a goddam thing! Especially about marriage. Why, she's been pesterin' me t' marry you—think of it! Gittin' hitched again at *my* age!"

Maggie held her breath, hoping her father wouldn't say more, praying he wouldn't let slip his real reasons for not marrying Lena.

"You and *Señorita* Maggie have discussed our relationship?" There was a quavery note in Lena's tone.

"Damn right we have. An' I didn't much appreciate her bringin' up the topic. I told her we wuz happy with the way things are. You understand why I can't never marry you, and you don't mind."

"And why is that, *señor?"* Lena inquired in a thin, reedy voice.

"Why . . . 'cuz we're just too different is all. I mean—you bein' a bean-eater, an' me bein' a white man and a ranch owner t' boot."

Oh, Pa! Maggie silently agonized. *How can you say such things to the woman you say you love? How can you be so insensitive?*

"It . . . it is not because I cannot have children that you do not wish to marry me?" Lena clarified. "Or . . . or because I came to you as a . . . a woman who had already borne another man's child?"

"Hell, them ain't the reasons. Goddam, but I was glad you couldn't have more kids. As fer bein' with another man, how could I complain about that when *I* had been with another woman? No, it's as simple as the laws of breedin', which apply to humans as well as livestock. Ya' don't mix a . . . a mustang with a Palousie. Ya' try t' keep the blood pure an' breed like t' like. That's why ya' don't breed whites t' Injuns or Mexicans t' Chinamen. The races was meant to be kept apart—an' it ain't jus' race, it's also class. Folks who own land shouldn't marry peasants. That don't mean they can't enjoy each other once in awhile, if the opportunity comes along like it did fer us, but when it comes t' gittin' hitched . . ."

"You think you're better than me!" Lena burst out indignantly. "Just because of who you are and who I am."

Nathan finally seemed to realize that he might be saying all the wrong things. "Now, Lena, honey, I didn't exactly mean . . ."

"You *do* mean it! *Si,* you do! Oh, you are a terrible bad man, and you want your daughter to be just like you! You think Rand is the only cowboy good enough for Maggie because his parents once owned land, and if they had not died, *he* would have had his own ranch someday. . . . How could I have been so blind, *señor?* How could I have thought you loved me all these years?"

"Why, I do love ya', Lena, honey—I jus' don't wanna marry ya'. Truth is I cain't see the need fer it. I'm happy; ain't you been happy?"

"Si. I *thought* I was happy, but that was before I knew the truth. Now, I am no longer happy, and I doubt I shall ever be happy again!"

"Lena! Where you goin', honey? Lena, come back here!"

Maggie barely had time to step to one side when the door flew open, and a teary-eyed Lena fled the room. She saw Maggie but didn't stop. Instead, she began to sob and ran down the hallway toward the stairs. Her footsteps echoed briefly on the wooden stairs and then faded, until the only sound was the steady hammering of Maggie's own heart and her father's deep sigh within the room.

"Goddam," he said. "Maggie was right. Now I've gone an' hurt her feelin's."

Maggie was torn between the need to console her father and to give him a good tongue lashing. She finally decided that she really did not want to talk to him right now—or even look at him. She turned, and as quietly as possible made her way downstairs to search for Lena. She passed through the kitchen to the backroom where Lena kept her things. The door was shut tight, but the muffled sound of weeping could still be heard.

Maggie knocked on the door. "Lena?"

There was no answer. Maggie knocked again. "Lena, I know you are in there. Will you please come out and talk to me?"

"Go away," Lena finally said in a choked voice. *"Por favor,* just go away."

Maggie sighed and returned to the kitchen. She started a fire in the wood stove and put on a pot of coffee to boil. She washed a few dirty dishes, dried them, and put them away. When the coffee was finished, she poured some and drank it. She lit a lamp for it was getting dark, then listened for any sound from upstairs or from Lena's room. There were none.

She walked aimlessly through the house, stopping in the doorway of the new addition to look at the unfinished walls and exposed beams of the ceiling. What a waste of time and money! She could not remember why she had once been so eager to have this extra space—oh, yes. So she and Rand could enjoy their privacy. So her father and Lena could enjoy their's.

Now, everything had changed—and all because of Joe Hart. If she had never met him, she would never have found the courage to admit that Rand was the wrong man for her. She might never even have realized it. She probably would have gone ahead with the marriage and blamed herself for the rest of her life that they were both miserable.

She glanced toward the open front door of the house and

saw a man standing there in the darkness. A tall, lithe man whose shape she would have known anywhere. She picked up the lamp and moved to the door, then lifted the light so she could see his face.

He looked different—older, darker-skinned, his hair longer—yet he looked exactly as she remembered him. Dangerously handsome. Incredibly masculine. Tonight, he wore no hat and had removed his chaps and spurs. His usual tight-fitting pants and a bright red shirt encased his splendid body, and a red bandanna was knotted at his throat.

His silvery eyes were luminous and compassionate, radiating a wisdom and peace she had never noticed in them previously. She smiled in welcome.

"Hello, Joe."

"Evening, Miss Sterling."

How polite! His good manners struck her as being ludicrous when all she wanted to do was throw her arms around him and kiss him senseless. She had to struggle inwardly to keep calm and cool.

"You've come to see my father?"

He nodded. "What does he want, Maggie? I have my own reasons for wanting to see him, but I can't think of any he might have for demanding to see me."

"I don't know for certain, Joe, but I can guess. I've told him I'm not going to marry Rand, and he suspects that *you* might have something to do with my decision."

A frown wrinkled Joe's forehead beneath the ever-present lock of dark hair falling across it. "You've spoken to him about me?"

Maggie shook her head. "Hardly. There hasn't really been much to talk about, has there? You won't permit anything to happen between us."

"You're right," he bluntly agreed. "I won't."

Maggie looked down at the floor. For some reason, whenever she encountered Joe, she had this overwhelming urge to humiliate herself. She was always much too honest about her feelings, while he managed to hide his emotions all too well. Unfortunately, she had never learned to be coy and devious, as many woman were. She had no idea how to flirt—and until recently, had never practiced deceit or found a reason for doing so.

All that had changed, too, since she had met Joe. She was being deceitful right now—deliberately submerging her desire to throw herself at him and trying to behave as if he had no effect upon her whatsoever.

"My father is upstairs waiting for you," she murmured. "Please try not to tire him too much. He has already had a . . . a difficult evening."

His brows lifted in inquiry, but she did not explain. Her father's relationship with Lena was none of Joe's business, and in any case, she would not have known how to describe what had just transpired. What would Joe think of it all? If his own behavior was any indication, he would probably disapprove of mixing the races as much as her father and Rand did. Assuming he was Indian, of course, and rejecting her because she was white.

Joe nodded and stepped past her, heading toward the stairs. She turned and called after him. "Don't you want to know which room it is?"

"I'll find it," he assured her and kept on going, making no sound as he mounted the steps which usually squeaked when anyone else went up or down them.

Maggie set down the lamp on a small round table near the door and went out on the porch to await his return. She did not intend to allow Joe to depart without telling her what her father had wanted.

Joe paused in the doorway of Nathan Sterling's bedchamber and waited for the old man to notice him. Nathan's eyes were open, but he was staring at the wall, his mouth drawn down in

a thoughtful, unhappy expression. Joe was reluctant to disturb
him.

Quietly, he took in the dark wood furnishings of the lamplit
room, which revealed the same degree of comfort and luxury
found on the first floor of the house. The headboard of the bed
had a carved design on it that matched the design on the partially open double doors of a large piece of furniture that held
clothing, hats, and extra boots.

A thick rug lay on the floor, its red and green colors still
rich despite evidence of fading, and lacy white squares covered
every available surface. Numerous pictures hung on the walls,
and the bed coverings were the finest Joe had ever seen. A
beautiful, delicate, blue and white pitcher and wash basin on a
table in a corner drew his eyes, and he couldn't help wondering
if Nathan Sterling actually washed and shaved in it. Joe would
be afraid of breaking the damn thing.

It looked too feminine; indeed, the entire room seemed feminine. He squinted slightly to make out the features of a woman's
face in one of the framed pictures; could she be Maggie's
mother, the woman who had died when the Indians spooked
the horses and cattle on the day Maggie was injured?

While he was staring at the picture, searching for a resem-
blance to Maggie, Nathan stirred and noticed him. "So how
long you been standin' there gawkin', cowboy?"

"Not long," Joe said, finally entering the room.

Dressed in a white nightshirt, Nathan sat up in bed and
swung his bare, hairy legs over the side. "Hand me my pants,"
he ordered, motioning toward his trousers hanging over the
back of a chair.

Joe did as he was told, then respectfully waited for Nathan
to reopen the conversation. Until he knew why he had been
summoned, he did not intend to say a word about his plans or
to ask for Nathan's help. If Nathan were angry at him for some
reason, it would be futile to mention them anyway.

Nathan tugged on his trousers, took off his nightshirt, and
sat back down on the edge of the bed. He motioned to the chair

where his pants had been. "Pull that up and sit a spell, Hart. Pardon me if I don't put on my shirt, but it's too damn hot in here."

As he retrieved the chair and set it closer to the bed, Joe noted that Nathan Sterling still had a fit body. His chest bristled with a mat of gray hair, but his muscles were well-defined, and he sported only the smallest of hay bellies. Other than a less than healthy color, he appeared to have nothing wrong with him. Joe would have guessed that he had many more productive years ahead.

Then he noticed Nathan's breathing. It was slightly labored, but all he had been doing was resting in bed. This more than anything alerted Joe to the older man's frailty. His heart was obviously not working properly, or he would not find the simple act of breathing to be such hard work.

Joe sat down and again waited. Nathan regarded him silently for a moment before speaking, then sighed and plunged ahead. "You got any interest in my daughter, Hart?" he demanded without warning.

Joe kept his face expressionless, except for a slight lifting of one eyebrow to indicate surprise. "No, sir. Why do you ask?"

" 'Cuz I think my daughter's got some interest in you, an' I wanna know where *you* stand b'fore I up and throw you off this ranch."

"I barely know your daughter," Joe smoothly lied. "And I've been out line riding for weeks. Am I being accused of something?"

"Nope. Not yet. First, I wanna see which way the wind is blowin'," Nathan grunted. "So far you got all the right answers t' my questions."

Joe settled back in his chair, as if he were relaxed and comfortable, not tense as a drawn bowstring, which was the way he really felt. Long practice at concealing his true feelings stood him in good stead now. "Do you mind if I ask some questions of my own?"

"Fire away." Nathan looked suitably surprised, and Joe decided he had nothing to lose and everything to gain by taking advantage of this opportunity while he still could. Tomorrow, Nathan Sterling could die, or Joe could find himself out of a job. Either way, he'd wish he had acted now.

"Would you be willing to part with some of your cattle and horses, if I could pay cash for them?"

Nathan's eyes widened. "You lookin' to buy some beef an' start yer own spread?"

Joe nodded. "If I can find land to buy, yes, I am."

"That's gonna take a heap of cash. How much you got?"

Joe named a figure that was slightly less than what he actually had stashed away up in the mountains. Nathan's jaw dropped, and he sat up straighter. "Goddam! You musta been savin' a good long time t' have that much. That's more'n *I* had when I bought the first parcel of land fer the Broken Wheel an' started breedin' my own herd of cattle off some scrub stock I rounded up on the range."

"It is not as much money as I had hoped to have by now," Joe told him. "But I've been saving a long time, and I'm anxious to get started. First, I want to buy some cattle and run them with your herds until I can purchase land of my own to put them on. I also want to buy horses—spotted ones, since they're all I can afford right now. I'd let the horses run with your herd, as well. That herd of Appaloosas seem to be doing fine up in that high meadow."

He didn't admit that spotted horses were the *only* ones he wanted. He hoped he could persuade Nathan to at least let him have a few mares—and Dusty. Windstorm, rather. He had taken a fancy to that colt. Though Maggie considered the horses to be hers, he suspected that they actually belonged to her father, and Nathan would probably be glad to get rid of a few, since he did not value them for themselves alone.

"You plannin' t' still keep workin' fer me?" Nathan eyed him with interest.

"For as long as you'll let me. I need the wages. I won't be

able to build a house for several years, at least. I figure I could work for you while my herds are building up. I'll sell only the beefs and keep the cows for the first five years. By then, I'll know whether or not I can make a go of it on my own."

"You should be able to—hell, I did it." Nathan grinned. "Worked myself into an early grave, I guess, but I wouldn't have done it no other way. I just couldn't be happy until I had my own place."

"Neither can I," Joe said evenly. "I've been saving for years to get ready, but until now, I hadn't found a place where I wanted to settle down. This country suits me. If there's land available to buy anywhere around here, I'd be interested."

"Oh, there's land, all right—and soon, there will be more land. I been buyin' it a piece at a time myself."

"What do you mean—soon, there will be more land?" Joe asked. "How is that possible?"

"Don't you know nothin' of local politics, son? No, I don't guess you would, if you ain't been long in Idaho. Let me tell you what's happenin' hereabouts."

Nathan went on to explain that on the Lapwai Reservation, the Indians were being given eighty acre land grants under the terms of the Severalty Act. As soon as the Indian claims were all processed, whites would be permitted to purchase the remaining land—and there would be no eighty acre limit for them, as there was for the Indians.

"Soon as it opens up, I'm gonna put in my bid to buy as much land as I can git my hands on," Nathan boasted. "That's what you should do, too. I already own a parcel that abuts the reservation, and I'll start there t' extend my holdin's. Come t' think of it, I know of another piece, separate from my land, that's available right now; if you wuz t' buy that, you'd be in good shape to do the same thing I'm gonna do—extend yer holdin's. Buy all you can, 'cause the day's comin' when there won't be much open range land anywhere, an' if you wanna be in cattle ranchin', yer gonna have to run yer cows on yer own land, an' grow hay t' feed 'em in the winters."

Joe whistled through his teeth. This was the golden opportunity he had been awaiting, but if anyone found out he was Indian, he'd be permitted only a mere eighty acres, which could never support the large herds of cattle and horses he had in mind. Such small plots would be useful only for farming, and then only if the land allowed it.

Of course, he would also be confined to the reservation for the rest of his life and denied the right to breed saddle horses, especially spotted ones. He could just imagine how the surrounding ranchers would feel about an Indian raising the fine animals that had made the Nez Perce such good horsemen and given them mobility and freedom in the past. One day when he wasn't looking, his horses would be shot and killed.

"Where exactly is this land that's still available?" he asked, trying to conceal his spiraling excitement.

Nathan Sterling told him. It was on the other side of a small ranch next to Broken Wheel land, which was why Nathan himself was not interested in it. It did not abut any land Nathan currently owned, though it was reasonably close to the Broken Wheel itself.

"I'd be willin' t' sell ya' fifty head of cattle t' start," Maggie's father offered. "Which ought t' leave you enough money t' still buy that land. As fer the spotted hosses, I'm gonna have t' talk t' Maggie. Them hosses belong t' her. Come fall, she's plannin' on sellin' Dusty anyway, so I don't think she'd mind if you bought him. When it comes t' the mares, however, that's a different story."

"I can understand how she feels," Joe said. "The mares are the foundation of the herd."

"I'm also willin' to keep you on here an' pay you wages—providin' you agree to one condition." Nathan shot him a sly, probing look that made Joe lean forward slightly in anticipation.

"What condition?"

"I want you t' leave my daughter strictly alone. I don't even wanna catch you wishin' her a good mornin'."

Joe straightened, willing his face and eyes to reveal nothing. "I've already told you there's nothing between your daughter and me."

"Maybe not, but if she had her way, there would be. I can see it in her, though she denies it, same as you. I been watchin' you, son," Nathan drawled, eyeing him closely. "An' I suspect you might have a drop or two of tainted blood in you . . ."

"Tainted?" Joe remained seated with only the greatest of efforts. "What do you mean by that?"

"I mean that the way you ride and sit a hoss reminds me of a Mexican . . . or maybe even an Injun."

At that, Joe did spring to his feet. Any white man would. He stood there a minute, glaring down at Nathan Sterling and wondering how far he should go to act insulted. He *was* insulted by the reference to his "tainted" blood, and at the moment, he wished he could demonstrate just how insulted he was.

"Easy now, cowboy," Nathan murmured, raising his hand. "If you are a breed, I'm willin' t' overlook it 'cuz you seem t' be cut from diff'rent leather than most Injuns—an' most cowhands, too. Hell, you got money. . . . But that don't mean I'm willin' t' let you have my daughter. She's promised t' Rand. Leave her be, an' she'll come to her senses an' marry the boy, after all, even though right now she ain't too keen on the idea."

"Perhaps you should allow your daughter to make her own decisions. I've told you I'm not interested, so it won't be me she marries. That doesn't mean it has to be Rand."

Nathan slowly looked him up and down. "Rand's my choice, Hart, an' I think I know what's best fer my own daughter. Cooperate with me on this, an' I'll cooperate with you on buildin' yer empire, which is jus' what I did when I was yer age. . . . But cross me, an' I'll see you run outta this territory with not a dollar t' yer name an' nothin' but the clothes on yer back. Hell, you'll be lucky t' still be breathin'."

For a single long moment, Joe hesitated. Every bone in his body urged him to tell Nathan Sterling to go to hell. He didn't want his cattle, horses, or the chance to buy land, after all. He wanted Maggie, Nathan's daughter—wanted to save her from a loveless marriage, take her somewhere and make passionate love to her, ride with her across a broad green meadow, sleep with her beneath the moon and stars. . . . He wanted to make her his woman, his beloved wife, and forget about the goals he had set for himself so long ago. He could do it, too, if he just kept lying to her, letting her think he was white.

But then he took a moment to think about it. Here was everything he had ever wanted being handed to him at long last. And all he had to do to get it was keep living the lies he was already living . . . and stay away from a woman who wouldn't give him a smile or the time of day if she knew who he really was—a *Nez Perce* Indian.

"I accept your offer," he finally answered, barely managing to say it when his jaw was so tense. "But only because I don't want your daughter. If I did, I would take her, and you couldn't stop me."

Nathan grinned. "Goddam, but you remind me of myself at yer age—all piss an' vinegar, ready t' fight the whole world if need be. I'm jus' glad t' hear you don't want Maggie, 'cuz if you did, I'd have t' shoot you between the eyes instead of offerin' t' sell you my stock an' keep you on here. Now that we know where we stand, you can pick out what cattle you want, an' go take a look at that land I told you about. I'll take care of askin' Maggie about them hosses. Deal?"

He held out his hand, and Joe clasped and shook it. Sadly, he felt none of the elation he ought to have felt knowing that he had succeeded in gaining Nathan Sterling's help. He should have been ready to do a victory dance somewhere, but instead, he felt like mourning, and the feeling grew stronger when Nathan added a last request.

"When you go back downstairs, son, tell my daughter to come up, will ya'? She's been fixin' t' call off her weddin' t' Rand, but I'm gonna make one last effort t' see that don't happen." Nathan lay back on the bed. "A man in my position can be mighty persuasive, don'tcha think?"

"What position is that?" Joe guardedly watched Nathan Sterling as he crossed his legs and settled himself more comfortably on the pillows.

"Why, the position of a man who ain't got much time left t' live," Nathan said, and he was no longer smiling.

Joe nodded. Yes, a dying man—or woman—could be very persuasive indeed. He recalled his own vows to his dying mother, vows that had brought him to this moment, and he did not doubt for a minute that Maggie Sterling would marry Rand Johnson, her father's choice. Hadn't he lived his entire life trying to honor the last wishes of his mother?

Seventeen

When Joe arrived downstairs and walked out onto the porch in search of Maggie, he found her in earnest conversation with Rand, who had apparently just joined her. It was dark on the porch, but Joe had no difficulty detecting Rand's scowl; dislike radiated from the foreman like heat from a stove on a cold winter's day.

Joe paused only long enough to deliver his message for Maggie. "Miss Sterling, your father wants to see you now."

"Oh!" she exclaimed, surprised. "But . . . what did he want with you, Joe?"

"Yeah, what'd he want?" Rand demanded.

"That's your father's business—and mine." Joe stepped around them, wishing as he did so that he could take Maggie with him.

"Just a minute, cowboy!" Rand's hand clamped down on Joe's shoulder. "Miss Sterlin' here asked you a question, and yer answer wasn't very polite."

Joe mentally restrained himself from knocking the surly foreman down the porch steps. He looked down at Rand's hand and then up at his dark, angry face. "If you want a better one, you'll have to ask your boss."

Maggie nervously plucked at Rand's sleeve. "Rand, please! Don't start anything. Joe's right. Pa will tell me everything; it was rude of me to ask Joe—I mean Mr. Hart."

"Hart's the one with no manners. You better jus' remember

that Miss Sterlin's a lady, cowboy, an' if you don't treat her like one, yer gonna answer t' me."

"Rand, stop it! He didn't do anything. You've no cause to make threats to him."

"The hell I don't; I don't like him! That's cause enough."

"I don't like you either," Joe calmly informed Rand. "But I see no reason to fight over it. I'll just do my job, and you do yours, and everyone will get along fine. Now, if you'll excuse me, I've got to attend to my horse. . . ."

He left them standing on the porch, but Maggie's voice drifted after him on the light evening breeze.

"Whatever's gotten into you, Rand? I don't know how you can justify speaking to Joe Hart that way."

"I don't like the way he looks at you," Rand muttered. "There's somethin' in his eyes. . . ."

"Nonsense! You *must* stop this senseless jealousy. It's long past time we talk—about us, the wedding, my father, and . . . and many other things."

"Not now," Rand said. "Didn't you hear him? Yer Pa wants t' see you."

"Then we'll talk *after* I've spoken with Pa."

No, you won't, Joe thought, passing out of earshot. *By the time your father gets finished with you, you'll be making plans to hold the wedding as soon as possible. He'll bully you into it, or make you feel so guilty you won't have the nerve to rebel.*

The realization made him so miserable that he decided to ride out the very next morning to find the land Nathan had mentioned. The land was all that mattered now. He knew he would love it even before he saw it. It could be dry and dusty as an old bone, overgrown with thorns, or completely waterless, but whatever it was, it was going to be his—all his—land in the country of his ancestors. That made it the most precious thing in the world to him. *Nothing else mattered.*

He repeated that thought several times during the night, and then again the next morning when he rode out before daybreak, briefly telling Curt where he was going and that he would return by tomorrow night at the latest. Rand would be angry he had left without permission, but since Nathan had already given it, Joe wasn't about to awaken the foreman and tell him. Let him discover the truth for himself.

Following Nathan's simple directions, Joe headed for the western boundary of the Broken Wheel, rode around the relatively small-sized neighboring ranch, and by early afternoon located a huge stretch of unoccupied land that had to be the parcel—some three hundred and fifty acres in total—described by Maggie's father. Joe was delighted to discover that much of it was rolling open prairie. A small stream, probably a tributary of the Clearwater, flowed through a portion of it, aiding the growth of patches of trees and shrubs to alleviate the monotony of grass and sky.

Lewiston lay to the west and Lapwai further south; if he were able to buy additional land on or near the reservation, he could possibly wind up with a truly sizable spread. Rugged mountains and thick forests loomed in the distance in nearly every direction, and Joe experienced such a sense of homecoming that he had to dismount, remove his Stetson, kneel, and bow his head to the earth in humble gratitude.

This was the land of his dreams, the place he had been seeking for the greater part of his lifetime. This was home, so nearly similar to the vision he had carried in his head and heart since boyhood that he could not hold back tears. Silently, he wept, shoulders heaving, tears splashing down his cheeks to fall unheeded upon the dry welcoming earth.

Never had he allowed himself such a thorough release of emotion, and it cleansed his soul—erasing the memory of all the hurt, pain, sacrifice, and sorrow he had endured to get here. His only regret was that he had no one with whom to share this moment. No one understood what it meant to him. In his mind's eye, he conjured Maggie's image, remembering most of all the pure clear light in her hazel eyes.

He wished with all his heart that those beautiful eyes could hold understanding and acceptance—that he could bring her here, show her this land, and *tell* her what it meant to him. She would especially appreciate what he meant to do with horses on this land. Raising his head, he pictured a large herd of Appaloosas grazing on the prairie around him. He gazed up at the intensely blue sky where a bald eagle floated on the wind currents far above, and he took it as a good omen.

This land would be his; he would buy it even before he bought cattle or horses from Nathan Sterling. He could not take the risk that someone else might purchase it first. Now that he had seen it, he had to acquire it as soon as possible. Reaching down, he clutched a handful of the dry sandy earth, lifted it high above his head, and let it sift through his fingers to fall upon his face and closed eyelids. It was wonderful to feel its texture upon his skin and smell its scent.

Heart-of-the-Stallion is here, he murmured to the spirits of his ancestors, whose presence he could sense in the shimmering golden air. *He has returned to the land of his forefathers, and he will never again leave it.*

A slight movement in the long grass off to one side caught his eye, and he watched a young mule deer emerge from a stand of brush and daintily nose the bunchgrass in complete disregard of his presence. Suddenly, he heard a distinct twanging sound which he easily recognized, though he had not heard it in years. The deer leapt high in the air, took several steps, and collapsed, an arrow protruding from its throat.

Before Joe could react, there came a childish whoop of triumph, and a boy darted from a clump of shrubbery not far away. He sprinted across the prairie toward the fallen mule deer, then came skidding to a halt when he spotted Joe and Loser.

Slowly, Joe rose to his feet and quietly studied the young hunter. The boy was dressed in a faded shirt and torn trousers, white man's clothing, but his straight black hair, snapping black eyes, and dark skin revealed him to be Indian. Joe would have known he was Indian even if he had not been wearing moccasins and holding a short, sturdy bow in one hand and a handful of feathered arrows in the other.

The boy said nothing, but his gaze strayed from Joe to the fallen deer and back again to Joe. Joe could almost read his panicked thoughts. The youngster knew he had no right to be here, on private land, hunting with a bow and arrows. It was against the law, and the look of wild elation he had worn but a moment before was quickly replaced with a shuttered expression. In his younger years, Joe himself had cultivated just such a look to conceal his true thoughts when he was forced to endure the company of white men he hated.

He made a split-second decision to trust the boy, even though the consequences could be disastrous if he was wrong. He called out a greeting in the Sahaptin dialect of the Nez Perce and almost laughed at the youth's astonishment.

After a moment, the boy returned the greeting. Joe then assured him he had nothing to fear, and leaving Loser ground-tied, slowly walked toward him. Midway to the boy's side, Joe switched directions and strolled over to the fallen deer instead. The animal was dead—cleanly killed by the arrow severing its throat, and Joe gave a low whistle of admiration.

"That was a fine shot. You should be proud," he said in the language of his tribe.

Coming up beside him, the youth could not quite hide his satisfaction. "I waited half the morning for him to leave the brush," he boasted. "I found his spoor beside the stream and tracked him here, then hid beneath the shrubs. Fortunately the wind was right, and he did not smell me."

"You did everything correctly—except watch out for intruders. Neither you nor the deer were aware of my presence."

The boy's shoulders slumped; all his pride in his great accomplishment abruptly drained out of him. "My grandfather has often warned me that I must pay more attention to my surroundings. Never must I cease looking and listening, even when I am stalking game. He will be greatly saddened to hear of my failure to heed his advice."

The boy looked so woebegone and ashamed of himself that Joe took pity on him. "No one else need know of this. Just be more careful in the future. If someone else besides me had spotted you here today, you would be in grave danger. As it is, I will tell no one. . . . Only how do you intend to get all this meat back to the reservation?"

Glancing up at him through a fall of blue-black hair, the boy grinned. "I am strong; somehow I will manage. No one will believe I killed the deer if I do not distribute fresh venison to all my relatives. I *must* get it back—and without anyone discovering me. Anyone white, I mean."

Setting down his bow and arrows, the boy gave Joe a long, searching look, full of unasked questions.

"I live as a white man now," Joe offered in explanation for his own clothing. "But in my heart, I am still Indian."

The boy frowned, his black eyes reflecting confusion. "How can that be? How did you escape the reservation, and why have they not come after you, to make you return? You are not from Lapwai, or else I would know you."

"You are right. I'm not from Lapwai." Joe grinned at his inquisitive new acquaintance. "Nor from any reservation near here. However, I escaped very nearly the same way you did; I simply left when no one was looking. It was a long time ago, and I doubt anyone there remembers me now."

"But you speak the language of the Nez Perce. Are you one of us, then?"

"My mother was Nez Perce," Joe admitted. "But my father was a white man."

Hearing himself say the words, Joe wondered at his own rashness. He had never told another living soul what he had just related to this young stranger. Yet he did not regret his hastiness in trusting him; he felt an immediate kinship with the boy who reminded him so much of himself at the same age. Here was a kindred spirit—a child of the Nez Perce who had not forgotten his heritage. He may have been forced to dress in the manner of white men and to live on the nearby reservation, but that had not stopped him from fashioning weapons good enough to bring down a deer.

Absurdly proud of the boy, Joe reached out and ruffled his hair, as he might a younger brother. "Tell me your name, young hunter, and I will tell you mine, but our meeting here today will be known to no one but ourselves and the wind."

"May I not tell my grandfather, at least? I have never kept a secret from Grandfather, but he himself will tell no one if I ask him not to do so."

"All right," Joe agreed. "You may tell your grandfather only."

The boy rewarded him with a white-toothed grin. "I am Red Fox," he said. "But the whites call me Matthew."

"I am Heart-of-the-Stallion," Joe returned. "But the whites call me Joe."

Red Fox's eyes sought Loser, and a deep sigh of admiration escaped him. "That is the most beautiful horse I have ever seen. He looks like one of the old ones I have many times heard about, but I thought they were all slain by the soldiers."

"Most of them were." Joe turned to look at Loser who whinnied a complaint at having to stand there with his reins trailing the ground as a reminder that he must not wander off. "But a few survived. I am going to buy this land on which we are standing, and when I do, I am going to raise spotted horses on it—and cattle, too."

Red Fox's eyes widened. "They will let you do that—you, who are part *Indian?*"

Joe nodded. "They do not know I am Indian. When I do buy this land, you can come here anytime you like, and I will let you ride my horses."

Pure joy lit Red Fox's face. Walking back to Loser, he worshipfully reached up to stroke the stallion's mottled pink nose. "You would permit me to ride a spotted horse like this one?"

Joe joined him. "Of course. But until then, you must be more careful . . . and even then, you must keep your destination secret from everyone but your grandfather. If the authorities should discover that you are occasionally running off and hunting—or riding spotted horses—they will prevent you from doing so."

"They can never stop me from being Indian," the boy fiercely protested. "They can make me go to school, speak their language, wear their clothing, and do most of what they tell me, but they cannot change what's inside of me. Inside, I will *always* be Indian . . . and I will run away to hunt—and ride—whenever I can. Just the way my ancestors did."

A huge lump formed in Joe's throat. He could scarcely believe his good fortune in meeting Red Fox, a son of his own people. Another Nez Perce—and such a proud, defiant one! For the first time in years, he felt a small glimmer of hope. The whites had not succeeded in destroying the Nez Perce nation, after all. Here was one still determined to remember—and preserve—the legacy of his forefathers.

"Would you care to ride my horse now, this very moment—or would you prefer to skin your deer first?"

Joe could see he had offered Red Fox a difficult choice. The boy hesitated, unable to decide. Again, Joe came to his rescue. "Come, I will help you skin the deer and butcher the meat. Then you will ride Loser—but only for a short while. I cannot linger long here. If I am going to buy this land, I must do it quickly, before someone else gets the same idea."

"We are not permitted to purchase land off the reservation—and even there, we are not allowed to buy enough to support the vast herds of horses and cattle we once owned," Red Fox bitterly informed him. He reached under his shirt and withdrew a short-bladed knife to begin skinning the deer.

"You can remember that far back?" Joe asked the boy, unsheathing the knife he himself had worn at his waist today.

Red Fox shook his head. "No, but my grandfather has told me about it. *He* can remember."

"What about your father and your mother? Do they live at Lapwai, too?"

"They are both dead," the boy said with a careless shrug.

Only his eyes revealed his sorrow—and a pain too deep to articulate. "Let us hurry and skin my deer now."

An hour later, the bloody job was done and the choicest portions of meat wrapped in the hide to be dragged back to Lapwai and smuggled to the boy's relatives, piece by piece. Red Fox was now eager to mount Loser. Joe couldn't help thinking of Maggie when he witnessed the youngster's excitement at being allowed on Loser's back. She had been every bit as joyful as he was, and her eyes had held the same look of awe and rapture.

Joe struggled to repress his memories, for they brought him so much pain he could scarcely endure it. Now, having seen his land, he had made his choice, and he knew he would never change it. He would have his dream, Maggie would marry Rand to please her father, and somehow, he would manage to forget her and the way her face had lit up when he first set her on Loser . . . and whenever he kissed her.

He suspected that Maggie Sterling would always be a part of him in the form of bittersweet memories—tormenting him like the recollections of his childhood and his mother's death. He would never forget her.

He gave Red Fox some brief instructions, then turned him loose on the stallion to discover for himself how to manage the horse. Red Fox did not lack courage, and he soon urged Loser to greater speeds than a mere walk. Unfortunately, he did not yet have the skill to steer him, stop him, or stay on, and he tumbled off the stallion's back and landed on his side in the bunchgrass.

Seeing that he wasn't hurt, Joe put him back up on the horse to try again. Not until he succeeded in sitting a fast trot and then a gallop, was Red Fox ready to quit. As he dismounted, his eyes lingered lovingly on the spotted horse; the boy would have gladly traded his successful hunting exploit for a chance to possess such a splendid animal.

"Someday, I will own a horse like this," Red Fox fervently whispered.

Joe doubted it could ever happen. He had heard that the only horses the Indians were permitted to own were draft-type animals—or mules—better suited to plowing fields than racing across the bunchgrass. And they could not afford many of these.

Still, he hadn't the heart to disillusion the boy. "Perhaps someday you will. Now, I must be going—and so must you."

Red Fox touched his arm. "One day I would like to bring my grandfather here to meet you. We sometimes come to this place together and stay a night or two alone beneath the stars. That is when Grandfather teaches me Nez Perce ways, so that they will not be lost. At the reservation, we must do everything the white man's way; we must cut our hair and cannot even pray or chant as we used to do, before the white man came."

"I know," Joe said. "And I would be honored to meet your grandfather. He might remember my mother or others I once knew."

Red Fox stared at him. "Then you were not raised among the whites."

"I was raised among the Indians until we were imprisoned along with Chief Joseph."

"You knew Hin-mah-too-yah-lat-keht?" He used Chief Joseph's Indian name, which meant Thunder Traveling to Loftier Mountain Heights; Joe had almost forgotten it.

He nodded. "Yes, I knew him."

"But he is forced to live somewhere to the north in the land they call Washington."

"I know. I was a boy then. When he was captured, I was sent with him to Kansas. There, like you, I had to learn the ways of my conquerors. I learned them well, and then I escaped. Everyone now thinks I am entirely white, but I have not forgotten my people, Red Fox. . . . No, I have not forgotten."

On what should have been the happiest day of his life, Joe was abruptly conscious of a deep sadness and an aching sense of loss. He bade his new friend goodbye, mounted Loser, and started back toward the ranch just as the sun was setting. Tomorrow, he would retrieve his money from the mountains and go buy his land—but tonight, he only wanted to be alone to think and to mourn . . . and to try to free himself forever of his longing for a heritage he could never claim and a white woman he could never embrace.

Maggie couldn't eat or sleep. She was half-sick with guilt, anxiety, and worry. Her father had once again persuaded her to delay calling off the wedding. He had pleaded with her to reconsider, be a good daughter, and do her duty. He had shamelessly manipulated her emotions and made her resent him, but he was still her father, and she loved him. So how could she defy him and say the words that might eventually cause his death?

She avoided Rand altogether—and Lena, too, because she couldn't bear to witness the silent hurt in her old friend's eyes. There was no one with whom she could discuss this matter, no one to advise her or tell her what was the right thing to do. Good daughters *did* obey their fathers, but did they do so even when they knew their fathers were wrong?

Was her father wrong? It certainly seemed so to Maggie; he was wrong about so many things, she believed, but she dared not argue with him for fear of the possible consequences. Nor could she run to Joe—the only person she instinctively trusted and believed would understand, even if he himself did not want her. Joe had disappeared again, gone to look at some land, Curt had told her. *What land?*

Could he possibly be thinking of getting his own place? But he had told her he had nothing—or at least, he had let her believe that. Why would he want his own place so suddenly, unless it was to have something to offer her? She knew she shouldn't hope, but she couldn't help it. In the midst of her despair, a tiny spark of hope flared brightly, illuminating the darkness.

She wished she knew what Joe and her father had discussed,

but Nathan was no more communicative on the subject than Joe had been. Several days passed, and on the fourth day, Gusty told her that Joe had ridden in late one night, said he had some business to take care of in town, and left before dawn the following morning.

Rand blew up—swore he was going to fire Joe when he finally saw him, then saddled his horse, took Curt and Luke Wilson along with him, and rode out to do a stint of line riding himself. His leaving gave Maggie a temporary respite from her problems, and she breathed a long sigh of relief. Maybe by the time Rand returned, she would have figured out a way to call off the wedding *and* still remain friends with her father.

Later that evening, restless and too hot to sleep, she struggled into an old shirtwaist, then slipped outside to get some fresh air. Heat lightning flickered in the distance, and a long, low growl of thunder promised relief from the heavy, oppressive warmth. A breeze stirred her loose hair, and she wandered toward the corral to visit with Preacher and Dusty.

She was scratching Dusty's withers and crooning to him, when he suddenly pricked his ears toward something behind her and gave a low nicker of welcome. Maggie spun around and saw the shadowy figure of a man on horseback approaching from the direction of the track leading toward town. A splash of white on the horse's rump left little doubt as to the rider's identity.

Her heart slammed against the wall of her chest, and she waited with indrawn breath for him to come closer and notice her. He rode almost all the way to the corral before he saw her standing there motionless and watching him.

"Maggie?" Joe said softly as he halted Loser a few feet away. "What are you doing out here so late at night? Is something wrong?"

"No." She shook her head. *Nothing's wrong, other than that I'm hopelessly in love with you.* "I just couldn't sleep. Now it's my turn to ask you the same question. Where have you been, Joe? Rand is furious that you didn't square things with him first before you rode out."

The darkness could not hide Joe's frown at the mention of Rand's name. "Curt and your father knew where I was. Besides, a man who's been out line riding as long as I have is entitled to a few days off, isn't he?"

His refusal to tell her his whereabouts wasn't lost on Maggie; his rebuff was deliberate and calculated. "Usually, yes. But you didn't clear it with Rand first."

"Then I guess he'll have to fire me, won't he? Where is Rand? Is he here? We can settle the whole matter right now, if he's bent on having it out with me. I had assumed that all I had to do was leave word that I'd be gone for a spell, and no one would object. I should have guessed Rand would take exception."

"Rand isn't here. He took a couple of the hands and rode out to do some line riding since you weren't around to send."

"Well, then, I guess our little confrontation will have to wait." Joe swung down from the saddle. "Can't say I'm too disappointed. I could use some sleep."

Maggie squinted to see him better. The swift glare of lightning overhead momentarily revealed his features, but she couldn't tell much of what he was thinking simply by looking at his face. She watched him unsaddle Loser and toss the saddle over a rail of the corral, then lead the stallion toward a smaller, separate enclosure, away from the other horses.

Silently inhaling the rain-scented breeze, she watched Joe remove Loser's bridle and turn him out. The Appaloosa immediately buckled at the knees, sank to the dusty ground, and rolled—grunting in pleasure. After watching him a moment, Joe walked back to retrieve his saddle and carry it into the barn.

Maggie doggedly followed. Just before they reached the inky-black interior of the structure, he stopped and turned to her. "Why don't you go back to the house before it storms? You shouldn't be out here, Maggie."

More lightning and a loud crack of thunder punctuated the question. While she was thinking of what to respond, a sudden gust of rain-laden wind billowed her skirt. Pressing it down, she begged: "Please, Joe . . . can't we talk? I desperately need to talk to someone."

"Sorry, but I'm not the one you should be talking to. If your father knew you were out here with me right now, he wouldn't be happy about it."

"How do you know? Has he . . . said something to you about me?"

Joe sighed and readjusted his hold on the heavy saddle, resting part of it on one lean hip. "Maggie, go back to the house. If you have any questions, you should ask your father, not me. I need this job, along with your father's good will. So I think it would be best if you and I didn't speak to each other ever again."

Maggie gasped. She could not imagine what her father might have said to provoke such an attitude, but if Nathan had threatened Joe or done anything else that was mean, dirty, or underhanded, she would never forgive him for it.

"Joe, I . . . I need a friend. All I want to do is *talk* to you, to know where you've been and why my father wanted to see you. I . . . I want to ask your advice on something. I know I shouldn't feel this way—and that you don't reciprocate my feelings—but sometimes I think you must be the only person in the whole world I can trust, the only one who understands me, the only—"

"Maggie, don't *do* this! I won't be put in the middle between you and your father—or between you and Rand. I don't want to be involved with you or your problems. I've told you before; I *can't* be. So just leave me alone, will you?"

Thunder boomed directly overhead as Joe stalked toward the barn. Determined to cut through his indifference—rather, his resolve to *behave* as if he were indifferent—Maggie hurried after him. "Why, Joe? Why won't you let yourself become *involved* with me? Is it because you're *Indian?*"

Joe stopped in his tracks. Slowly, he turned to face her. In the bright-as-day flickers of lightning, his fury was plain to see. "Yes, damn it, I'm Indian—and you're white! So leave me the hell alone before we both go too far and get hurt."

His eyes held a demonic light, or perhaps it was only the lightning's glare that made them gleam in a way that quite unnerved Maggie. She stood frozen in place, while Joe swung around and proceeded into the barn to put away his saddle.

The wind whipped her hair around her shoulders and plastered her garments to her body. As the first drops of rain struck her, she shivered uncontrollably, then darted into the barn after Joe. Lit only by periodic flashes of lightning, it was as dark as the inside of a tomb. She paused uncertainly about ten feet down the aisle. A moment later, Joe reappeared without his saddle and started to walk past her.

"Joe—wait!" She reached for his sleeve.

He stopped and looked at her. The air between them crackled with more energy than the storm had generated. "I don't care that you're Indian," she whispered. "I *should* care, but I don't. What has happened between your people and mine has nothing to do with us. That was all in the past. We're living in the present. I won't hold you responsible for what was done to my family, if you don't hold *me* responsible for whatever was done to you and your family."

"I am Nez Perce!" he gritted between clenched teeth. Every muscle in his body was rigid; his hands were balled into fists. But Maggie didn't care. She *couldn't* blame Joe for everything attributed to the Nez Perce—and she would not allow him to blame *her* for everything the whites had done.

It had to end somewhere; why not here? Why not now—at least between the two of them? Joe loved the same things she loved; she had sensed that right from the first. And beneath his haughty, cold exterior, there was a gentleness, a warmth, and a kindness that touched her soul. Surely, they could set aside the hatred and fear that separated them and concentrate on what

they had in common. If *they* couldn't do it, there was no hope
for the world at large. No hope at all.

"Joe," she pleaded more softly. "Do you hear me? I don't
care."

Thunder crashed so close above them that Maggie almost
leapt into Joe's arms which opened as if by instinct to protect
her. He gave a low groan of defeat and hugged her tightly. The
contact of hard against soft was all it took to re-ignite the passion that was never far from the surface whenever they were
together. Joe bent his head and kissed her, and Maggie felt as
if she were being sucked into the very center and heart of the
storm—and Joe was there with her, his arms, his mouth, his
hard, lean body offering the only security available. He filled
her senses, and she strained to know more of him, to get closer
to him, to welcome his maleness in the core of her femininity.

This time, nothing could stop them. They were completely
alone with little chance of discovery, and the emotions she had
been denying herself engulfed her with all the fury of the tem-
pest raging over the barn. She had to have Joe—to know him
intimately, to love him with her flesh and spirit, to become one
with him. . . .

His ardent kisses and caresses left no doubt that he felt the
same. He bent her backward over one arm and lavished hot
kisses down the arc of her throat. Then he lifted her in his arms
and buried his face in her hair. With his lips close to her ear,
she could hear him muttering—his voice a soothing counter-
point to the crashing thunder and pelting rain.

"Maggie . . . my Maggie. *Hanyawat* forgive me, but I cannot turn away from you . . . not now . . . not again. I am breaking my word, my vow, but . . ."

She grasped his face in the palms of her hands to make him
listen. "I love you, Joe. Do you hear me? I love you. Nothing
else matters."

"No, Maggie. You mustn't love me. Don't call it love. All
we can ever have is *this*. . . ." He pressed his lips to hers, and
his kiss stole her breath away. Relentlessly, his mouth moved

over her face, and as he kissed each part—nose, eyelids, forehead, cheeks—he murmured: "And this . . . and this . . ."

She wanted to argue, to assure him that they could have so much more, if they really wanted it and were willing to fight for it. She couldn't see the way right now, but she would think of something; she couldn't think at all with Joe kissing her and fueling the desire she had fought so hard to subdue. In the onslaught of his kisses, with the storm rattling the timbers of the barn, she lost the power of coherent speech and thought.

A whirlwind blew through her mind, scattering her concentration and leaving behind only physical sensation: Joe's hands on her body, his mouth on her skin, his fingers tugging at fastenings, pushing fabric off her shoulders, then tracing the curves of her naked breasts.

He paused long enough to tug off his shirt, then placed her hands flat against his bare chest. She touched him tentatively at first, learning the contours of muscle, the texture of hair, the sleek smoothness of skin. . . . Ah, but he was beautifully, perfectly made! So masculine, so exciting.

He guided her hand lower, and for the first time, she caressed the power and promise of a man's full-blown arousal. "Maggie!" he gasped, even as he pressed her hand down hard against the bulge in his trousers, showing her what he needed.

She stroked him there until he groaned and pulled her hand away, teaching her the power of her own touch. Cursing his weakness, he led her to the pile of scattered hay on which they had lain down to taste the joys of loving the last time, but had been so rudely interrupted.

He knelt before her in the sweet-scented hay and rubbed his stubbled jaw against her bare midriff, then licked and loved her naked breasts, one at a time. Her knees buckled, and she sagged against him, but his strength kept her upright while he teased and tantalized her throbbing flesh.

When she thought she could bear no more of it, he drew her down on the hay, made short work of removing the rest of her garments and his, and gently began to knead and stroke her thighs. Force of long habit made her stiffen when he touched her bad leg, but she reminded herself that this was Joe, and she trusted him completely.

"Beautiful . . . Maggie, you are so beautiful," he murmured, and she hadn't the strength to deny it. She was thrilled he thought so and that he wanted her as much as she wanted him.

Then he was moving over her, parting her thighs, and kissing her once more. She strained upward to receive him, uncertain how to achieve the miracle, but desperate to be joined with him. His slick hard sex probed her gently, and he reached down and opened her with his fingers, then pushed partway inside her.

It was not uncomfortable, but neither was it pleasurable, and she uttered a small cry of frustration. "Now, Joe! Do it now!"

She wanted . . . something, more than what he had already given her, and she lifted herself, clawing at his shoulders in a frenzy of need. He pushed a little deeper, and then she felt it—the sensation of tearing, the sharp bite of pain. She gasped and bit her lower lip, as suddenly, he plunged all the way inside.

"Oh!" It wasn't at all what she had expected, the pain suddenly so intense that she could do little but pant beneath him, as he remained absolutely still, taking his weight on his hands rather than crush her.

"Little dove," he murmured. "Sweet little bird. Forgive me for hurting you, Maggie . . . my Maggie of the green-gold eyes and honey-colored hair. My brave, dear love."

His words were a soothing balm poured over her aching heart, especially his reference to her as his "love." He kissed away the tears that had squeezed out from her eyes and now trickled down her cheeks to pool in her ears.

"Better now?" he soothed.

She nodded. It *did* seem better—almost. But it was still not what she wanted. It seemed as if her body had betrayed her, turning pleasure to pain in the blink of an eye. She thought they must be finished, but Joe was still rigid above her, all his muscles tense, his body sheened with wetness.

"What do we do now?" she asked him on the heels of a loud clap of thunder.

The rain drumming on the barn roof almost drowned out his answer. "Now, Maggie, we begin to enjoy ourselves."

Enjoy herself? But how? All he had been building inside her had ebbed the moment they became fully one. She could not imagine how she might retrieve those magnificent sensations. Joe, however, did not hesitate. With slow, gentle kisses and caresses, he began to build it anew—whatever *it* was.

After a few moments, she began to feel the spiraling excitement, the delicious tension, the first tentative ripples of sweet release deep within her. Joe began to move his whole body. She recoiled in anticipation of the pain she feared was coming—but it didn't come.

Instead, his thrusting motions increased the tension, and something wonderful began to happen. Heat, light, and pleasure blossomed in her center. She wrapped her arms around Joe's neck, her legs around his torso, and surrendered to his mastery over her body. They found a rhythm both ancient and completely new. She followed joyously where he led—to the top of a steep shimmering precipice. They poised there a moment, rocking together, giving and receiving, locked in the sweetest of all labors . . . and then they tumbled into rapturous oblivion.

Neither of them moved for several minutes afterward. Neither of them could. Rain was still drumming on the roof, thunder rolling across the sky. Errant flashes of lightning revealed they were still in the barn, lying naked and entwined on a bed of hay.

Maggie could scarcely comprehend it all. It was beyond anything she had ever experienced—beyond anything she had ever dared dream. Joe was hers now; he belonged to her, and she belonged to him. There could be no other outcome of their glorious joining. They had sealed their fate, for good or ill.

"Joe," she murmured, nibbling his earlobe with possessive pride. "Joe, will you marry me now? We can make it work, Joe. I know we can. I'll talk to my father. I'll make him understand. He *has* to understand. He loves me, so I think he will . . ."

Raising his head to look at her, Joe placed the palm of his hand gently but firmly over her mouth. The fall of his hair brushed her cheek as he gazed down at her, his face alternately dark then gleaming white in the lightning's glow.

"Maggie, you must face it. We can never have a future. Your father will never consent to let you marry me. If he did, it would never work . . . and I could not bear it if one day you came to hate me."

She pulled his hand away from her mouth to protest: "I could never hate you! How can you say that, after what we've just shared?"

"You are who you are—the daughter of a white rancher, and I am who I am—an Indian, a Nez Perce. Your father has already guessed what I am, just as you did. And he has sworn to run me out of this territory if I so much as say good morning to you."

"No! No, he wouldn't . . . he *couldn't,*" she denied, knowing full well that he would and he could.

"Too much has come between us in the past, Maggie. Not only *your* past, but mine. My mother died of fever because of the conditions in which we were forced to live after Chief Joseph's surrender. Can I ever forget that? Can you forget your own mother—or your crippled leg?"

"We can *try* . . ."

"But the effort will be futile. In time, the bloom of our joy will dim. Little things will begin to annoy us. You will not always understand how I behave. I will not always understand how you behave. And then we'll remember that I am Indian, and you are white. The little hurts will remind us of the bigger hurts, and the bigger hurts will begin to fester . . ."

"It doesn't have to be like that! Since we *both* have hurts, we can learn to set them aside."

"Can we, Maggie? Or will they destroy us in the end? I think they will destroy us. If your father knew you lay naked in my arms at this moment, that knowledge would destroy *him*. Can you do that to him, Maggie? How long do you think I will live if he chooses to voice his suspicions to others? He has only to sow the seed—make some mention that I *might* be Indian—and there are men who would shoot or hang me on the mere possibility."

"No! You exaggerate!"

"Do I? I have bought land not far from here. Your father is willing to sell me cattle, and I hope to persuade you to part with a few of your precious spotted horses. But if people knew that I am Nez Perce, would they let me do these things—be a rancher, raise horses, and live off the reservation?"

She knew they would not. "We won't tell them!" she argued desperately. "We'll convince my father to keep it secret."

"He'll kill me first," Joe said. "He agreed to help me only on the condition that I stay away from you. I gave him my word that I would—and now I have broken it, the first time I have ever done so. I *told* you this was all we could ever have, Maggie, and I meant it. Now you must live your life, and I must live mine. *Hanyawat* never meant for us to be together forever."

"Hanyawat? Who is this Hanyawat?"

"The Creator, the Giver of Life. He gave life to us all, yet He made us different. We are not the same."

"I don't believe it! We *are* the same. You just won't see it. Neither will my father. You are both fools, denying what is so apparent. God didn't put these obstacles between us; *we* did. He told us to love one another. That's what I'm doing—*loving* you. If we have enough love, we can do anything. . . . Oh, Joe! Can't you see it?"

He levered himself off her and reached for his clothing. As he tugged it on, he spoke in a cool, passionless voice. "I see that if I let myself love you, I will lose my freedom, my dream of owning my own land, and perhaps even my life. And you will lose the esteem of your father and all your friends and neighbors. You may even lose the Broken Wheel. Is that what you want, Maggie—to cause sadness, heartache, perhaps even violence? . . . Don't think you can keep my true identity a secret. Your father will not permit it; he will never allow his only daughter to marry an Indian."

When he finished dressing, Joe gathered her garments and held them out to her. "Get dressed, Maggie. We're finished here. We were finished before we started. I regret I wasn't strong enough to stop this from happening. I am deeply ashamed. This wasn't your fault. It was entirely mine, and I beg your forgiveness."

"My . . . my forgiveness!" she choked out, sitting up and snatching the clothing. "It was as much my fault as yours! It was *more* my fault. I followed you in here. I begged you to talk to me. I wanted you to make love to me. I've wanted it since the day I first saw you. I . . . I've all but thrown myself at you every time we've been alone together."

"I would not quite say that, Maggie." The lightning's glare revealed his rueful smile. "Let neither of us accept nor relinquish the total blame. What's important now is that we continue as if this had never happened."

"How?" Maggie swallowed a sob and hugged her clothing to her nakedness. "How can we ever do that?"

"Forget me, Maggie. Forget me, and marry Rand. I never thought I would urge you to do that, but I see now that it's for the best. Rand will take care of you. When your father dies, he'll run the Broken Wheel for you. That's what your father wants. That's what Rand wants."

"But it's not what *I* want!"

"What choice do you have, Maggie? Will you go to your father tonight and tell him you have lain with an Indian, and does he mind if you give that Indian the Broken Wheel? Is that what you'll do, Maggie?"

She could find no words to answer him. He *knew* she couldn't do that—or wouldn't do it, which amounted to the same thing. They could always wait until her father died, of course, before marrying, but that was a wicked, selfish thought to contemplate. She would still feel as if she were betraying Nathan . . . and in the meantime, she would still have to deal with the issue of Rand and her father's continued pressure for them to wed.

If Joe didn't want her, maybe she ought to marry Rand. The idea made her sick, but somehow it always came back to that. Did Joe really mean it? After all that had happened tonight, could he honestly stand back and watch her give herself to another man?

"All right," she said, testing him, hoping he would call her bluff. "I'll marry Rand. I'll make my father happy. I'll make Rand happy. Is that what you want?"

A long moment passed before he answered. "I just want you to be happy, Maggie. And I don't think that's possible if you marry me instead of Rand."

Eighteen

Joe knew he was hurting Maggie terribly. The brief glimpses of her face that the storm provided made him feel like a murderer—and in a way, that's exactly what he was. He was killing something bright and beautiful inside her and destroying her trust, idealism, and innocence.

Well, grow up Maggie Sterling, he mentally chided her. We can't always have what we want. . . . But oh, how he wanted to give it to her! He had to fight his own impulse to go to her, take her in his arms again, and make promises he hadn't the slightest chance of keeping. It was better to end it now, before anyone was physically hurt.

"I'm sorry, Maggie," he murmured. "You'll never know how sorry I am."

And it was true. All too true. Considering that she was a white woman, he should be glad he was making her suffer. There had been a time in his life when he would have counted her suffering as sweet revenge for all the suffering he had endured. But he didn't feel that way any longer. The mere sight of her sitting there clutching her clothes to her slender body, her magnificent hair tumbled around her shoulders, moved him in ways he could not begin to fathom.

He loved her; there could be no other explanation for the changes she had wrought in him . . . and because he loved her, he had to insist that she marry among her own kind and live the life she was born to live. If he tried to take her away from the Broken Wheel and make her truly his, they would both have to pay a terrible price. He could not ask that of her; she was too naive and innocent to see it, but he knew what would happen, and he had to spare her.

"I give you to Rand," he said, forcing himself to utter the hated words. "Or perhaps I should say I give you back to him, for he had a claim on you before I arrived here. I'll be leaving before Christmas, Maggie. By the time you wed, I will be gone from here. Surely, that will make everything easier."

"Easier?" she questioned in a tear-laden voice. "Nothing has been easy since I met you, Joe, and nothing will ever be easy again. I am amazed it's so easy for you . . . but then you've never said you love me, so perhaps I shouldn't be so surprised. If you loved me, you couldn't do this. You wouldn't simply walk away."

I do love you, Maggie. I love you as I have never loved anyone.

He could not admit that to her! Let her think he was hard-hearted and opportunistic. Let her hate him and wish him a speedy departure. Then she would be free. . . . Merciful *Hanyawat!* Why hadn't he left her alone right from the start? He had known that first day that she was special—and therefore dangerous. Why hadn't he heeded his own instincts?

"Goodbye, Maggie—and this time I mean it. I won't speak to you alone again. If I see you coming, I'll turn and go the other way."

She lifted her head a notch and did not weep, which made him all the more proud of her, all the more aware of what he was losing. Rand would never appreciate this side of her, the quiet courage and strength that he valued as much as anything. His Maggie would endure and survive. She wouldn't let life beat her down, nor allow Rand and her father to dominate her.

Joe had worried about that, but now he saw that his concern was misplaced. Maggie was strong enough to survive anything; she would keep trying to be her own person. She was stronger now than she had been when he first arrived. It was indeed time for him to go.

"Goodbye, Joe."

That was it; that was all she said, but Joe knew she would not approach him again. He would not come upon her unexpectedly alone; she'd make certain of that. And she would not limp after him, demanding his attention, urging him to stop and talk to her, as she had done tonight. She had too much pride to beg. It was truly over . . . and he could not have felt worse if she had died in his arms, as his mother had.

In the darkness and quiet of the storm's aftermath, he spun on his heel and left the barn.

The following morning, Maggie rose early and dug under her mattress for the paper-wrapped package of fabric and laces she had purchased for her wedding gown. Before she could change her mind, she marched downstairs and gave them to Lena whose eyes widened in surprise.

"You have had these all along, Maggie?" Lena tore open the package and eagerly examined the enclosed satin, ribbons, thread, and laces.

"Yes, but since the wedding wasn't until Christmas, I saw no need for you to start on the gown so soon. . . . Actually, I didn't want you to start it at all, but . . . but I'm ready now."

Lena's eyes met hers across the gleaming white fabric. "Does this mean you are going to change the date and have the ceremony sooner, as your father has been suggesting?"

Maggie nodded, steeling her heart against the shaft of pain that suddenly lanced through her. "I can't think of a good reason why I shouldn't—especially since it will make Papa and Rand so happy."

Lena set the package down on the little work table in the kitchen, next to a bowl of flour. "But *querida*, will it make *you* happy? Are you sure you even want to go through with it?"

Maggie gave a short, brittle laugh and managed to look Lena straight in the eye without shedding a single tear. "Does it really matter if I'm happy, Lena, so long as I can make others happy? Papa wants the wedding to take place as soon as possible. If I wait even a few more weeks, we'll be in the middle of the fall roundup, and there won't be time for a wedding. I think we could finish the gown in a week if we really worked at it, so I was going to suggest a week from this Saturday."

"A week from Saturday! But *querida*, even aside from the gown, there is so much else to do also. Why, the addition to the house is not yet finished. Nothing has been done to the inside."

"I don't care, Lena. I'm sure Rand will be more than happy to help with the house as soon as he gets back from line riding. If it doesn't get done, we'll make do without it. It can be finished after we're married. I'm going out to the barn now to see if Rand has come home yet. Let me know as soon as my father arrives downstairs, will you? I'll give him the good news."

"Maggie . . ." Lena grasped Maggie's arm. "*Querida*, wait a moment! Why are you suddenly in such a big hurry to hold the wedding? All summer long you have refused to consider changing the date. You told your Papa that you didn't think you and Rand should marry, after all. Why, now, are you so eager? What has changed your mind?"

"Let's just say I've grown up, Lena, and realized how selfish I've been. I've kept Rand dangling long enough, and I've threatened my father's peace of mind. If I had a good reason for my recent behavior, I could better explain it. But the truth is, I haven't *any* reason, other than being selfish and afraid."

Maggie kept her gaze steady and unblinking, impressing Lena with the fact that her mind was made up. She had had all night to think about it and had finally realized that Joe was right. She ought to marry Rand. Joe obviously didn't love her. He had made no trembling, dewy-eyed declarations, such as she had done, baring her heart and soul, as well as her body. Instead, he had calmly dressed and just as calmly shattered her girlish dreams. If she was going to be miserable and unhappy for the rest of her life, she might as well be miserable making

Rand and her father happy. She would try hard not to let them know how she really felt—as if they even cared. All the two of them seemed concerned about was the future of the Broken Wheel . . . and by her marriage to Rand, she was doing the best possible thing for the ranch, which *she* loved as much, if not more, than anyone.

Lena's black-eyed gaze was doubtful. "Something has happened, *querida*. Something has changed you. And I fear it is not for the better."

"Didn't you once tell me that a woman shouldn't waste time longing for what she doesn't have—that she should learn to be satisfied with what she does have?" Maggie countered. "All I'm trying to do is follow your advice, Lena."

"But *querida* . . ."

"Don't try and discourage me, Lena. I wish *you* were getting married, instead of me, but it seems we both have our disappointments to bear, don't we? We have to bend, or we'll shatter and break. I'm bending, Lena, just like you."

"Oh, my dearest Maggie!"

Lena enfolded Maggie in a long tearful hug. She patted Maggie's back as if she were still a child in need of comfort. Even then, Maggie didn't succumb to tears. Tears were so futile! Joe had been right when he told her to grow up. Last night, she *had* grown up and become a woman in every sense of the word. She couldn't afford childish dreams any longer. As a result of last night's folly, she might have conceived a child. . . . Was that why Joe had urged her to marry Rand, so *he* wouldn't have to marry her in the event she was pregnant?

She had thought she knew Joe, but now realized how little she did know about him, aside from his being an Indian. The true character of the man quite eluded her; what sort of person would make love to a woman, then urge her to wed someone else? Only the sort she had always been warned about. How right her father had been in saying one could never trust an Indian!

She had trusted Joe and look where it had gotten her.

After several moments, Lena released Maggie and dabbed at her eyes with her flour-smudged apron. "Well, let us see about making this gown, shall we? I will get started on it right away while you go look for Rand. Do you want any changes in the fashion we first discussed?"

"No. No changes, Lena. I want the gown to be basically simple, with only a few elegant touches of ribbon and lace."

It should be black, the color of mourning, she silently added.

"It will be the most beautiful wedding gown you have ever seen. You will be thrilled with it, Maggie."

Maggie doubted she would even notice what she was wearing, but for the sake of her father and Rand, she must try her best to make them proud of her. At least, Rand would be anxious to see her in her wedding gown, while Joe Hart . . .

She dismissed the thought with a quick toss of her head. There must be no more thinking of Joe. That was why she was plunging headlong into preparations for the wedding—so she wouldn't have time to think about him. It hurt too much. If the truth be known, she couldn't stand another moment of the deep, throbbing pain, and the only way to be rid of it was to immerse herself in a new life entirely.

Joe first heard about the wedding from Gusty. "Don't that beat all?" Gusty was saying over coffee at supper several nights after Joe's encounter with Maggie. "Maggie's been holdin' off poor Rand fer months, an' now all of a sudden, she's got a bee in her bonnet t' marry right away—come next Saturday. Nathan's dee-lighted, an' Rand's happy as a toad in a mud puddle, only neither one of 'em can figure out how everything's gonna be ready in time."

"I know," Curt said. "Rand told me I gotta start workin' on the house again t'morrow—an' so does ever'body else. But I thought I was gonna be ridin' around in the mountains all week. We ain't been up t' see that bunch o' cows furthest north of here fer a good long time. No tellin' what shape they're in by now. They really oughta be checked an' doctored fer screw-worms."

Joe stood rooted to the floor, his empty plate and cup forgotten in his hands. He had been on his way to pile them in the wash basin when Gusty had started talking. . . . Saturday? Maggie was marrying Rand next Saturday? He had never expected her to take his advice so quickly. But what *had* he expected after all he had said to her that night?

It was the most natural, inevitable thing in the world for Maggie to rush into marriage; she was simply taking him at his word and running headlong into the arms of the only man who wanted her. After all, Joe had claimed *he* didn't want her.

Burt Lyman let out a belch and pushed back from the rough-hewn bunkhouse table where the men took their meals when they were at the ranch. "Y'know, I'm kinda surprised it's finally gonna happen. Fer a while there, Maggie didn't seem too eager t' tie the knot. Has anybody gone t' find a preacher yet?"

Luke Wilson set down his second helping of beans and tortillas and took over a corner of the bench. "I'm sposed t' go t'morrah—clear to Lewiston or Moscow if I hafta. Rand tol' me not t' come back if 'n I couldn't git a preacher t' ride out next Saturday."

"Whooeee!" Will Tatter whistled. "That boy ain't gonna let this opportunity git away. He'd marry her t'night if he could; guess he's scared she might change her mind."

Just then Rand himself stomped into the bunkhouse. Joe forced himself to calmly walk over to the wash basin, but he couldn't avoid seeing the look of triumph on Rand's flushed, self-satisfied face. "Boys, in case some of you ain't heard, I'm gittin' married next Saturday!"

A chorus of hoots, cheers, and catcalls greeted this statement, and Rand grinned so widely his face was in danger of splitting. "Yep, she's finally come t' her senses an' figured out where her best interests lie."

At this, the men banged their silverware on their cups, plates, and the table—whatever was handy.

"Sure is hard t' believe Miz Sterlin's that anxious to welcome a big ole grizzly like you inta her bed," Gusty chortled, the only one who could get away with such a bold comment. But even he, Joe noticed, respectfully called Maggie by her last name when he talked about her in front of Rand. "Congratulations, Rand. Does that put you in line t' become the Number One Cocka-doodle-do around here one day?"

Rand instantly sobered. "I expect it does, but I don't want that day t' come any faster'n it has to. Y'all know how I feel about Nathan."

Gusty lifted his hand in apology. "Sorry t' be sech a flannel mouth. Ole habits die hard, Rand. Maybe ya better tell us what we gotta do t' help git ready fer this here event. . . . I expect Nathan'll be askin' half the territory t' show up fer it."

"Oh, there'll be plenty of comp'ny," Rand agreed. "An' there's so much t' do I don't see how we'll git it all done in time. Don't know what t' tell ya' 'bout the ranch work, 'cept we won't be doin' whut all I had planned. . . ."

Joe dropped his dirty dishes in the wash pan, which made a discordant clatter, drawing Rand's attention. When Rand glanced over at him, he said: "I don't see that you need me around here. Why don't I ride up to check on that bunch of cattle furthest north?"

He had to get out of there—had to leave the vicinity of the ranch. To have to participate in the preparations for the wedding—even simply to have to watch them—was more than Joe could bear. All the laughter and friendliness left Rand's face as he glared at Joe, apparently still casting him in the role of a potential rival.

"Wouldn't grieve me none if you went, but you might miss the weddin'." Rand narrowed his eyes at Joe. "That what's eatin' you, cowboy? I got the girl instead of you?"

It was suddenly so quiet that the only sound was Curt's indrawn breath. "I was never interested in Miss Sterling," Joe lied. "She was always right there for you, Rand—ripe for the taking. You just weren't man enough to do it sooner."

These were rash words, but Joe couldn't stop himself from saying them. The mere thought of Rand's hands on Maggie filled him with such rage and bitterness that he wanted to pummel the blond foreman into the ground; it was so unfair that he should have her—that he should have everything handed to him on a silver platter—while Joe himself had to fight for mere survival.

"Why, you . . ." Rand's hands balled into fists, and he would have thrown himself at Joe had Burt Lyman not jumped up from the table and intervened.

"Hey, now," he said in his big booming voice. "What's goin' on? This is sposed t' be a happy occasion. A time t' celebrate. Come on now, boss. . . ." Burt steered Rand toward the chow laid out on the sideboard. "Y'all had supper yet?"

Every muscle in Rand's body was taut as a bow string, but gradually, with a quick look around at the faces of the men around him, he began to relax. "No, an' I'm starved. . . . You wanna go look fer that bunch o' cattle, Hart, go ahead an' do it. If I don't say yes, you'll jus' git permission from Nathan t' do whatever you damn well please. . . . All I gotta say is watch out, Hart. When I *do* git t' be Number One Cocka-doodle-do around here, first thing I'm gonna do is fire you."

"You won't have to fire me," Joe responded. "I'll quit. I'll be quitting soon anyway to run my own place."

"Yer own place!" Gusty exclaimed. "Well, ain't that somethin'! I knowed you was diff'rent from the rest of us the day you rode in here. Hot dang, we got us another rooster here, boys! So if Rand don't treat us right from now on, we know where we can go. Jes' how far away is yer spread, Joe?"

"Not far," Joe admitted. *Not far enough.*

Why, oh why, had he encouraged Maggie to marry Rand, when he knew he'd be living close enough to hear the gossip about her and Rand every time one of the cowhands stopped by at his place? In years to come, his cattle would surely get mixed in with the Broken Wheel's, and vice versa. They couldn't possibly share the same open range—assuming it remained open for a few more years at least—without running into each other occasionally. For the first time, he realized just what a living hell he had created for himself—and Maggie.

He would have his dream, but he'd be paying the price for it every day of his life in the years to come.

"We'll be neighbors," he pointed out to Rand. "So maybe we better learn to get along. I apologize for what I just said. I hope you and Miss Sterling will be happy together."

Calling upon his years of training in submerging his true feelings, Joe held out his hand in a gesture of friendship, but Rand refused to shake hands with him. "Git outta here, Hart. Come t' think of it, I don't wanna see ya at my weddin'. Y'ain't welcome. I don't know what ya' got goin' with Maggie's Pa, but whatever it is, it sticks in my craw. I can't pretend friendship with a man I didn't like the first time I met him, an' I ain't found a reason t' change my mind about since. You think yer better'n all of us, doncha? Buyin' yer own spread and talkin' Nathan inta sellin' ya' some cows. Well, you ain't so smart, cowboy . . . or you wouldn't even be inerested in them rag-tail spotted ponies that Maggie loves. I wish she was sellin' ya' the whole damn lot of 'em instead of jus' a coupla mares an' that two-year-old colt."

So she was going to sell him some of the horses. This was the first Joe had heard of it. But then he hadn't spoken to Maggie since that night of the storm, and he hadn't spoken to Nathan either. He had been making himself scarce, trying *not* to see or talk to either of the Sterlings . . . and it was time to ride out and stay out until well after next Saturday.

"Have it your way, Johnson. I've offered you a chance to make peace and get along, but if you prefer to be on bad terms, that's all right by me. I can live with it either way." Joe nodded to the rest of the men and headed for the door. "See you all in a week or two."

"Don't you wanna take along some grub?" Gusty called after him. "There's beans, bacon, and coffee stored in the chuck-wagon. Help yerself."

"I'll get some," Joe assured him and kept on going.

It didn't take him long to make his preparations, and he rode out without a backward glance. He didn't dare look back in case he might see Maggie silhouetted in one of the windows of the ranch house. The next time he saw her, she'd be a married woman. She would belong to Rand, not to him. And it was better that way, he reminded himself—only it didn't feel better. It felt as if a spike had been driven through his chest.

A full moon was rising, silvering the landscape and making it easy to see his surroundings. Joe rode for several miles before finally stopping to think about where he was actually going. He was supposed to be heading north, but something made him veer toward the west.

He had a sudden burning need to see his land again and to console himself with its beauty. He needed to sift the dirt through his fingers once more, drink from the clear stream running through it, and feast his eyes on the intensely blue sky arching over the golden grass. He wanted to witness the morning sun rising over his land, bathing it in a soft rosy glow.

Hopefully, the sight of his land would be enough to banish forever the memory of honey-colored hair, gold-flecked hazel eyes, a sweet winsome smile, and tender soft flesh. After all, he had chosen the land over the woman, knowing he could never have them both. It hadn't been a clear-cut choice exactly, but the only way he could have had Maggie would have been to convince her to run away with him, to leave the Broken Wheel and Idaho itself—and *that* he could never have done . . . nor could he ask her to accept him as an Indian, as the man he really was. He just couldn't believe she was willing to live with the possible consequences.

Keep riding, Heart-of-the-Stallion, he sternly lectured himself. But as he rode, he couldn't help wondering what had happened to his courage. He had never felt *less* like a courageous stallion or more like a coward fleeing confrontation.

He reached his land well before dawn, in time to snatch a few hours of sleep, except that sleep eluded him. When the sun rose, he silently watched it, then again lay down to ease his exhaustion in the shade of some trees growing near the stream . . . and that was where Red Fox found him.

"Joe! Joe!" the boy cried excitedly. "When I saw your horse, I knew you must be here. Look! I have brought my grandfather. I told him all about you. . . . Come, you must meet him."

Joe was still groggy as he got to his feet and followed the enthusiastic youngster across the dried grass toward an old man with a blue bandanna tied around his forehead and white hair hanging down to his shoulders. The old Indian stood beside Loser and reverently stroked the horse's glossy coat as he grazed.

As Joe came up to him, the old man gave Joe a milky-eyed glance of pure joy and pleasure. "He is one of ours," he murmured in Sahaptin. "One of our great ones, and I can die happy now that I have seen him."

His words brought Joe to a halt, and he studied the old man with interest. The Indian appeared to be blind, for a whitish film obstructed his vision, yet he also seemed to be studying Joe with equal fascination.

"I can still see a little," he explained to Joe. "Enough to recognize a horse I thought never to see again in my lifetime. Twice, my grandson has brought me here in search of him and of you, my brother. I am therefore honored to make your acquaintance."

"I am the one who is honored," Joe answered. "May I also call you Grandfather?"

The old man responded with a nearly toothless grin. "You are a son of the Nez Perce, are you not? And I am old enough to be anybody's grandfather. . . . Come, let us find a good spot to sit down together and visit, for the journey here has made me weary. We left while the reservation slept, which is the only way we could do so without being noticed. If we are fortunate, there will be no counting of heads before we return."

Joe led him to the shaded area beside the stream, and Red Fox found a good-sized log for them to sit down upon. At Joe's

request, the boy fetched firewood, so Joe could offer them re-
freshment from his food supplies. In no time at all, they were
sharing a modest meal of bacon, biscuits, and coffee—though
they had to eat and drink from the same plate and cup, for Joe
had brought only a single set of utensils.

Man-Who-Dreams—that was the name of the old Indian,
Joe learned—made much of Joe's hospitality, thanking him ef-
fusively not only for the simple food, but for having allowed
Red Fox to ride Loser. The boy's bright black eyes constantly
strayed to the horse, and after they had eaten, Joe again gave
him permission to ride the stallion.

"Shall I saddle him for you first?" he asked Red Fox. Joe
had removed all of Loser's tack upon their arrival, hobbled him,
and left him to graze while he slept.

The boy shook his head. "No, I wish to ride bareback. That
way I can better feel what he is doing beneath me."

Joe laughed. "Spoken like a true horseman. Go to it, Red
Fox. Use your legs to guide him, and if you have trouble stopping him, just say, 'whoa.' He knows what that means."

Red Fox ran off with a cry of delight, leaving Joe alone with
Man-Who-Dreams. "Tell me more of yourself, my son," the
old man requested, his film-covered eyes staring off into space
as he fingered the nearly empty tin coffee mug. "I know only
what my grandson has told me."

Joe hesitated. He would have preferred talking about the Nez
Perce, asking questions about people he might have known who
were now living on the reservation, either here or in the state
of Washington. He did not remember Man-Who-Dreams, but
was certain they must have many mutual acquaintances.

"You can trust me, my son," the old man added. "I have told
no one about you—nor will I. However, I am curious, so please
forgive me for not waiting longer to question you about your
past. Our time together may be short, and who knows if we will
ever meet again? At my age, I have learned to be direct."

Joe smiled. It had been so long since he'd had the opportunity to speak with another Nez Perce, aside from Red Fox. He

had almost forgotten tribal good manners and the Indian reticence to pry into another's affairs; yet Man-Who-Dreams was right. Who knew when they would have another chance like this? He might as well speak freely and answer all the old man's questions. As the elder of the two of them, it was Man-Who-Dream's right to direct the conversation.

So he began—and once he had started, he was unable to stop. He told the old man everything, about his early life and memories, his mother's death, his long years of working and saving his money, his arrival at the Broken Wheel . . . his purchase of the land they sat on, and the cattle and horses he would one day raise there.

"You have achieved your dream—what no other of our people have managed to gain," the old man said, still gazing sightlessly into space. "You have done as your mother wished. . . . Why, then, are you so unhappy, my son?"

Joe looked up, startled, from his contemplation of the dry earth beneath his boot. "I'm not unhappy," he denied. "I have just told you. All I have ever wanted now lies within my grasp."

"All?" the old man probed. "There is nothing more you seek?"

"Of course, there's more. There's always more. I would like to see the rest of the Nez Perce have the opportunity to achieve the same things I've won. I want Chief Joseph to be permitted to return to his beloved valley in Oregon. I want Red Fox to have his own spotted horse. I want all the land that was taken from the Nez Perce to be given back to them—to us. I want our people to be free. . . ."

Man-Who-Dreams slowly shook his head. "You speak of general things, not personal ones. You echo the wishes of all the Nez Perce. But I am asking about *you,* Joe Hart, also named Heart-of-the-Stallion. What is it that eats away at your triumph and turns it into a shallow, meaningless thing?"

"Nothing! There's nothing. . . ." Joe could not look the old man in the eye. Man-Who-Dreams might be half-blind, but he could see far too deeply into Joe's soul, a place where, until Maggie, Joe had never allowed another person to enter.

"It is a woman," Man-Who-Dreams murmured. "You yearn for the love of a woman, but she has turned from you. . . ."

"She didn't turn from me; I turned from her!" Joe angrily burst out.

A childish whoop of laughter mercifully interrupted their conversation. Red Fox was galloping Loser in a wide circle, his hands twisted in the horse's mane so he could stay on. The joy of his accomplishment lit his face, and he waved to Joe and his grandfather as he sped past them.

"Why did you turn from her, my son? Was she unworthy of you in some way?"

Joe wished he did not have to answer; he would not have done so had it been anyone else asking the question. But he had slipped into the ways of his youth, where younger men showed respect to older men, and he was conscious of how disapproving his mother would have been if he had refused to answer the question of Red Fox's grandfather.

"She is not unworthy of me; I am unworthy of her. But she is white, Grandfather."

"So are you, my son, especially after so many years away from the Nez Perce. So what is the problem?"

"She is promised to another."

"A great mistake if she weds him when it is you she loves."

"But I am still Indian in my heart, Grandfather. *That* is the problem."

"Then you must tell her this and see what she says."

"She already knows, and she says it does not matter. But it *does* matter. Her family has suffered much because of our people."

"And you have suffered much because of her people."

"That is why it can never work between us. Her father already suspects that I am Indian and has threatened to expose me if I interfere in his plans for his daughter. He is dying and intends to leave all he has to her and the man he has chosen to be her husband."

"Then let her delay her marriage to this other man and wait until her father dies before you openly declare your love for each other."

"I can't let her do it, Grandfather! She may lose her land if she defies her father. And there is too much potential for violence. If someone is hurt, she will come to hate me. She can certainly never love me should I one day decide to claim my Indian heritage."

"Why would you do that, my son? You cannot do it and hope to keep what you have gained as a white man."

"I don't know why I would do it, but I might!" Joe rose and began to pace back and forth in his agitation. After a few moments of pacing, he stopped and acknowledged the anguish consuming him. "I am so alone, Grandfather. It's as if part of me is missing. I have lived half my life as an Indian and half as a white man. Yet I am both. If I claim one, I lose the other. This . . . this woman I have told you about. She thinks she loves me, but I do not believe it. She knows me only as a white man. *That* is the part of me she loves. And I . . . I cannot accept that. The fact that I *am* Indian, more Indian in my heart than white, stands between us like a wall. I can never forget it . . . nor can I ask her to sacrifice all she has ever known to come away with me if I choose to be Indian. I could not do that to her."

Man-Who-Dreams gazed at Joe as if he could see to the very heart of him. Wisdom and compassion shone in his weathered old face and milky white eyes. "You will never toss aside all you have won to return to Indian ways, my son. That would be foolish. If you are accused of being Indian, you must deny it and fight to prove otherwise. Make others prove that you are, which is doubtful they can ever do."

"But that would be cowardly. If I have not the heart of a stallion, why am I so named?"

"Perhaps there is more courage in living in two worlds—or

in creating a *new* world—than in clinging to an old and dying one."

"You speak in riddles!" Joe scoffed. "I do not understand. Men do not make their own worlds; their worlds make them."

"I speak with the knowledge of many years of witnessing the foolishness of men," Man-Who-Dreams said quietly. "Listen and hear, my son. Have you given this woman the opportunity to know and accept your Indian side—or have you held her at arm's length and presumed to judge her by your own shortcomings?"

"What do you mean? Tell me what you mean."

"Open yourself to her. Show her your heart. How you do it or when or where is your decision, my son. I cannot advise you on that. Nor can I assure you that your path with this white woman will always be smooth. However, if she loves you, and you love her, it is folly to let her go so easily. Give her a chance to reveal her heart. Give yourselves both a chance to discover a way in which you might be together."

Joe thought about that for a moment, but he could imagine no way for such communication to occur. He needed more time, and there was no time. The old man did not truly understand the constraints of the situation.

"And *you*, Grandfather—will you give me a chance to be Indian?"

The old man's brow lifted in question. "How so, my son? What is it you ask of me?"

"Stay here with me a few days. Let us live the old life. We will hunt and fish and ride in the old ways. You are teaching Red Fox; teach me, too, Grandfather. Tell me the old tales. Sing the old chants. I hunger for them. I know all the ways of the white man—but I have half-forgotten the ways of the Nez Perce. Please, Grandfather, do not refuse me this chance to once again be Indian."

The old man's milky-white eyes sought Joe's. "To what purpose, my son? It will only bring you pain—all this remembering and cherishing of a time that is now dead and gone."

Joe dropped to one knee beside him. "If it is dead and gone, why do you teach Red Fox?"

"So it will live here . . ." The old man touched his heart. "And here . . ." He touched his head. "And so Red Fox will know who he is and where he comes from."

"Then teach me for the same reason," Joe pleaded. "So I can find my way on this earth, Grandfather, and fill the emptiness I feel inside me. So I can decide what to do about the white woman."

Man-Who-Dreams slowly and sadly shook his head. " 'Tis not I who will fill that emptiness inside you, Heart-of-the-Stallion. You search in the wrong place for that which will satisfy you. Nevertheless, I shall do my best. Yes, I will stay with you, for three days only. For such a short time, an old man and a boy will probably not be missed on the reservation—and if they are, there are those who will make some excuse for us. Of course, they will be hoping we return with fresh venison."

"You will!" Joe laughed. "You will."

"What do you think, *querida*, it is going to be beautiful, is it not?"

Maggie peered in the full-length oval mirror she normally avoided. A stranger in shimmering white looked back at her. She ran her fingers down the smooth gleaming satin that hugged her slim waist and hips. Yes, it was going to be beautiful, this wedding gown that Lena was working so hard to have ready by Saturday.

"It's gorgeous, Lena. You must be careful not to go blind sewing all those hours. I should be helping you."

"No, no—you have enough to concern you, *querida*. Do not worry. It will be done on time, and I will not lose my sight. The work goes quickly. Soon, it will be finished."

Maggie stifled a sigh. Saturday was coming too fast. And everyone was being so helpful. Only the day before, the ranch

hands had ridden in all directions to deliver her handwritten
invitations to the wedding to all the neighboring ranches. People were coming that Maggie hardly knew . . . people her father counted as friends, but with whom she herself had never
developed any close relationships.

She wished they would all stay home. The fewer witnesses,
the better. That way if she disgraced herself and refused to say
"I do," at the proper moment, fewer people would know of
it . . . only she wouldn't refuse. She could never do that to
Rand and her father. It would be too cruel. She mustn't allow
her own misery to spill over and make others miserable. . . .
But oh how she regretted giving way to an impulse! She could
have delayed this wedding at least until Christmas, but now she
was committed to going ahead with it on Saturday.

And Joe wasn't even here to see it. Rand had sent him out
to check on some cattle. She hadn't even had time to tell Joe
that she was willing to sell him Dusty and a couple of her
mares. Her father had mentioned it to her that Joe wanted them,
not realizing that Joe had already let it slip that night they made
love in the hay.

Joe wanted her horses, but he didn't want her—not enough
to fight for her, and that realization made every aspect of Maggie's preparations for her wedding day a bitter trial to be endured, like trying on her gown for a fitting. How could she tell
poor Lena that she hated the garment and dreaded wearing it?
That she would sooner slash it to ribbons with a scissors than
don it to wed a man she didn't love?

She couldn't tell her friend that—no more than she could
call off the wedding now that she had agreed to it. "The gown
is truly lovely, Lena," she assured her friend. "Thank you so
much for all your effort. I don't know how I can ever repay
you."

Lena smiled at her in the mirror. "You can be happy, *querida*.
That is all I want from you."

Maggie nodded but could not return the smile, for she was
sure she would never be happy again.

Nineteen

Joe spent three satisfying days with Man-Who-Dreams and Red Fox. He spoke no English, ate no food but what he and Red Fox gathered or killed, and immersed himself totally in the customs, stories, and religious beliefs of the Nez Perce. He felt as if he had returned to the ancient days of his people—a time of innocence, freedom, and the simple joy of living, in which Maggie Sterling played no part.

For three days, he could almost forget her, and his pain seemed to fade away—but on the afternoon of that third day, he was rudely jerked back to reality. Three men came looking for Red Fox and Man-Who-Dreams. Riding around a rise in the hilly land, they drew their six-shooters on the old man and the boy as they bent over a rabbit snare, removing their catch.

"You there!" one of the men called out, a fat man with a bushy brown beard. "Stand right where you are and don't move.

Having just emerged from the stream where he had bathed, Joe stood hidden among the trees, and Loser was grazing out of sight behind a thicket of brambles. While the men advanced on Red Fox and his grandfather who were out in the open, Joe hid his Indian apparel behind a rock and quickly climbed into a pair of Levi's, shirt, and boots, then retrieved his own six-shooter from his saddlebags. Thus prepared for trouble, he moved as close as he could get without being seen and waited to see what would happen.

"Yer in a heap of trouble, Charlie," the bearded man said,

advancing on Man-Who-Dreams. "We been trailin' you fer two days, an' now we finally caught up with ya'. This ain't the first time you been off the reservation, but it sure in hell's gonna be the last."

"We do no wrong," Man-Who-Dreams protested in stilted English. "Only come hunt a little, fish a little." He gestured vaguely toward the stream near which Joe was hidden.

"Yer trespassin' on land belonging to a white man—an' stealin' his game. Yer also off the reservation. We come t' take you back."

"We won't go back!" His hands balled into fists, Red Fox stood tall at his grandfather's side. "Not yet. We have two more snares to check first, and we must get the meat we have already caught."

The bearded man waved his six-shooter. "You ain't checkin' no snares or gittin' no meat. Come on now, Charlie. Tell yer grandson t' git movin' b'fore I fan his toes with lead."

Man-Who-Dreams slowly raised his hands. "We come peacefully. No need shoot."

"But Grandfather!" Red Fox lifted stricken eyes to his grandfather's face. "If we leave the meat, it will all go to waste."

"Then let it waste!" the bearded man snarled. "It warn't yers t' begin with. You got no right t' be out here, huntin' on private land. The reservation's where you b'long, an' we're gonna make sure you stay there."

"Food no good there," Man-Who-Dreams defended. "Game all gone. Need fresh meat. Make boy grow strong. I teach him hunt."

"He don't need t' learn t' hunt. You get rations on the reservation."

"Not enough." Man-Who-Dreams reached down to pick up the dead rabbit. "Not kind of food make boy into man."

"Then take your complaints t' the proper authorities, but leave that game right where it lies, or you jus' might lose a few fingers."

At that moment, Joe stepped out of concealment and leveled his own six-shooter at the intruders. "Let him have the rabbit," he said. "Better still, turn your horses around and ride out of here. The three of you are trespassing on my land."

The men reined their horses around to face Joe, their glances hostile as they eyed him in surprise. "Who the hell're you, mister?" the bearded man, the apparent leader, gruffly demanded.

"My name's Joe Hart, and this is my land. I've got papers to prove it. So maybe you better tell me who you are and what you're doing on my property."

"I got papers, too!" the bearded man cried. "Givin' me authority to find these Injuns, name of Charlie an' Matt, who escaped from the reservation. If they don't come along peaceable, I got the right to shoot 'em, if I have to, t' keep 'em from terrorizin' the countryside."

"An old man and a boy can terrorize the countryside when they don't even have weapons?" Joe drawled sarcastically.

"They got knives. An' the boy's got a bow an' arrows. Them qualify as weapons."

"All they were doing was hunting. I gave them permission to do so on my land."

"Then yer a damn fool, mister, an' breakin' the law t' boot. How long you owned land in these here parts?"

"I just bought it recently, and I don't know of any law that says I can't give permission to whomever I want to hunt on my own land."

"These are *Injuns,* mister. Nez Perce Injuns. And if you had lived here longer, you'd *know* why Injuns have t' stay locked up on the reservation. When I get these two back t' Lapwai, that's exactly what's gonna happen; they'll git locked up fer runnin' away."

"We weren't running away!" Red Fox's English was as good as Joe's. "We just came here to hunt and fish."

"You wuz runnin' away, boy—an' we can't allow that," the bearded man corrected.

"Get off my land." Joe cocked his six-shooter and took careful aim. "Before I blow a hole in you big enough to ride a horse through."

"All right, boys, put yer guns away." The bearded man's eyes were shrewd and hard as he slipped his gun back into its leather holster. "Ya' gonna shoot us when we ain't even drawed our guns on you?" He chuckled grimly. "Can't shoot but one of us atta time, an' whoever's left is gonna ride like the devil fer town an' tell everybody there exactly whut happened. Some damn fool bleedin' heart shot one of us when we wuz jus' doin' our jobs pertectin' the community from runaway Injuns."

"Turn around and ride off, or *you* are the one I'm going to shoot," Joe threatened.

"No!" Man-Who-Dreams exclaimed, stepping into Joe's line of fire. "You not do it, Joe. Is better we do as they say. Leave meat here and go back Lapwai. No good fight."

"Now, yer makin' sense, Charlie," the bearded man said. "After all, we ain't proposin' t' make coffin fodder outta ya'; we're jus' gonna lock ya' up fer a week or so is all."

Despite their assurances, Joe still did not trust them. If Man-Who-Dreams or Red Fox made any suspicious moves on the way back to the reservation, they could wind up dead. In this country, what was another dead Indian or two? No one would mourn them; in all likelihood, no one would even investigate.

"I'll come to Lapwai in a week or two to check on the old man and the boy. They had better be alive and well," Joe said. "If they aren't, I'm coming after *you*." He gestured with his gun at the bearded fellow. "Now, get off my land, and don't let me catch you on it again."

The bearded man gave Joe a long, hostile look. "Sure like t' know what these worthless Injuns are t' you, mister. From the way you act, a fellah could almost b'lieve yer half Injun yerself."

It was on Joe's lips to deny it, as he had been doing for most of his life. But he found he couldn't say the words in front of Man-Who-Dreams and Red Fox. Instead, he simply glared at the

man and said nothing, which struck him as the most cowardly
way out of the dangerous situation. Swept with self-disgust and
shame that he couldn't proudly admit to his heritage, he watched
in silence as the three men herded the old Indian and the boy in
front of them as if they were no more than cattle and started
heading in the direction of Lapwai.

"By tomorrow at this time, yer gonna be a married woman,
Maggie," Nathan said, stopping Maggie as she started to go
upstairs to bed on the evening before her wedding.

Maggie paused and managed a smile which did nothing to
warm the chill around her heart. "Yes, Pa, I suppose I will be."

"Half the folks in Idaho'll be here," he said proudly. "Everybody wants t' see Nathan Sterling's daughter git hitched."

"I don't know why they should, since I barely know most
of them."

"Because yer *somebody,* Maggie girl. One day yer gonna
own one of the biggest ranches in the whole damn state. Why,
as more people settle in Idaho, you an' Rand are gonna have
more an' more influence an' wealth. Any children you two have
are gonna grow up t' be damn important people."

"Is that so wonderful, Pa—that my children should be
counted above others? That they should grow up to be snobs?"

"Why, who said anythin' 'bout makin' 'em snobs? I said
they'd be *important;* that don't mean they have t' be full of
themselves."

"I think you worry too much about appearances. Now, if
you'll excuse me, Pa, tomorrow is going to be a long day."
Maggie turned to start up the stairs again, but her father's hand
came down on hers, pinning it against the railing.

"Maggie? Maggie, honey?"

Maggie sighed and glanced back at him. All she wanted to
do was go to her room and hide there until morning; this was
the last time her bedroom would ever be her private refuge.
Tomorrow night, Rand would be joining her in it, since the

addition was still not finished. With the reality of her wedding night swiftly bearing down upon her, she could hardly bear to spend a moment more in the company of the man who had manipulated and maneuvered her into this loveless marriage. The fact that he was her beloved father only made matters worse.

Standing several steps below her, Nathan was gazing up at her with a mixture of sorrow, love, and regret. "Maggie, honey . . . this weddin' is the best thing fer you. Ya' know that, doncha?"

"I don't know that, Pa, but I'm going through with it anyway."

"Yer a good girl, Maggie, an' always have been. What you got now is jus' pre-weddin' night jitters. One day you'll thank me fer talkin' ya' inta this. Jus' wait'll yer holdin' mah first grandbaby; then you'll be glad ya' married Rand. . . . In the meantime, well, maybe this'll help you feel better about the whole thing. . . ." With a flourish, Nathan handed her a packet of folded papers.

"What's this?" she inquired, taking it, her hand suddenly trembling.

"The deed t' the ranch—made out t' you an' Rand. Call it an early weddin' present. Had me a lawyer draw it up with some special pervisions."

"What special provisions?" Maggie knew she ought to be more excited about this, since it meant so much to her father, but somehow, she wasn't. She had always assumed—and been assured by him—that she would get the ranch on his death anyway. Rather, she and Rand would get it. She wasn't particularly overjoyed to have her father give it to them now, as if he intended to die tomorrow.

"The ranch b'longs to you, first, Maggie—an' then t' Rand only so long as he's your legal wedded husband. Anything happens to you, it passes t' yer kids, if you got any by then—an' if the marriage should somehow not work out, it'll stay all yers. Ain't no way Rand could ever take it away from you, not that

I think he would ever *try,* but I jus' thought you could use the peace o' mind knowin' how things stand."

"I . . . I appreciate that, Pa. But I would rather you just keep these papers and hold onto the ranch until . . . until . . ."

"Until I die? Naw, I ain't leavin' nothin' up t' lawyers t' fuss over after I'm gone. I wanna know—and I want *you* t' know—that everything's all taken care of. Only thing in my will is the money I got set aside fer Lena."

"Have you told Rand about this?" Maggie lifted the papers.

Her father shook his head. "Nope, an' I ain't gonna. Don't want him thinkin' he's the Number One Cocka-doodle-do while I'm still around t' crow. This is between you an' me, Maggie. Git out the papers after I'm gone an' show 'em to him, but until then, this is our secret. An' if ya' take a close look at the boundaries set out in them papers, you'll see that I added more land than even you or Rand knows about. I jus' bought a parcel of the reservation land that came open."

"The reservation land? But I thought that was all going to be divided up among the Indians."

"It has been, but they only git eighty acres each. A section of the rest went up fer sale last week, an' I pounced on it. I been waitin' t' buy it fer a long time," he said proudly. "An' there'll be more openin' up soon. Little by little, we can git our hands on it, even if it is Injun land, set aside fer them."

"Oh, Pa . . ." Maggie wondered if Joe knew about this, if he was aware that white men were scheming to take what little land the Indians had left in the territory. She wondered how he would feel about it. She knew how *she* would feel, if she were Indian.

Nathan mistook her sigh of dismay for one of compliance. He grinned and patted her hand. "Well, you go on up now an' git yer sleep b'fore t'morrah. Come four o'clock in the afternoon, I expect t' see you walk down them stairs lookin' like an angel all in white. I know it'll be the happiest day o' my life, Maggie, an' I hope it'll be the same fer you, too, especially now, when you know yer future is finally secure."

She nodded, holding back tears. Such a high price for security! Leaning over the banister, she brushed a kiss across her father's forehead. "Goodnight, Pa. See you in the morning."

"G'night, Maggie, girl. . . . Jus' remember yer ole Pa loves ya'."

"I'll remember. I love you, too."

She hurried up the rest of the stairs as fast as her bad leg could carry her. Once inside her room, she hid the valuable papers in the bottom of her linen chest, where Rand would be unlikely ever to spot them. Then, to avoid a fit of weeping, she sat down on the edge of the bed in the lamplight to brush out her hair for the night. . . . A few moments later, a discreet knock sounded on her door.

When Maggie opened it, she found Lena standing there, twisting her hands together in agitation. *"Señorita* Maggie!" she hissed in a low whisper. "I don't know if I should be doing this or not, but I . . . I have a message for you—from Joe Hart. He . . . he asked if you would meet him tomorrow morning at . . . at sunrise."

"Meet him! Where?"

"At . . . at the high meadow where you keep your spotted horses. He . . . he wishes to see you one last time before you wed Rand. Since the wedding is at four o'clock, and there is so much to do before then . . . perhaps you should not go, *querida.*"

What could Joe want at this late hour before her wedding? To tell her to call it off? To say he had changed his mind about their relationship and now wished to pursue it? Maggie was vastly annoyed that he had waited so long—but she was also wildly excited. She would rise well before dawn, saddle Preacher, and *ride* up to meet Joe. It was the quickest, fastest way of getting there; driving the cart would take twice as long, if not longer.

"Will he be there waiting for me?" she quizzed Lena.

The older woman nodded, her black eyes filled with worry. *"Si.* He said he will wait for you, and your meeting will not take long. You should have plenty of time to make it back here before the ceremony."

If there's to be a ceremony, Maggie thought to herself. If all went as she hoped . . . she stopped herself from jumping to conclusions. When she considered the idea of calling off the wedding—and explaining why—to her father, Rand, and the wedding guests who would be riding in tomorrow, her stomach muscles began to quiver. . . . Oh, why had Joe waited so long before finally coming to his senses?

Maggie touched Lena's plump arm. "Will you make excuses for me in the morning, my friend? Tell everyone that I'm sleeping late and don't wish to be disturbed?"

"If you go, I suppose I will have to—but Maggie, I wish you were not going! What good can possibly come from a meeting between you and Joe Hart on the very day you are to marry Rand?"

Maggie decided to be forthright and honest. Having never approved of the way Lena and her father conducted their relationship, she could scarcely be less than honest and still respect herself. "Lena, I agreed to this wedding tomorrow only because I had no hope I could ever have the man I truly love. If it should turn out that Joe loves me in return and wants to marry me, I'll follow my heart no matter how much it might upset some people—namely my father and Rand. They will just have to learn to live with my decision. I've been trying to do as they want, and I've only succeeded in making myself miserable."

"But your father's *health, querida!* To do this to him could *kill* him!"

This was Maggie's greatest fear, the reason behind her desire to please her father so much. Yet—if her father truly loved her—he would understand. She would *make* him understand; she simply could not ignore this one last chance at happiness.

"I . . . I know it's a risk, Lena, but we are not just talking about my father's life, we're also talking about *mine.* I thought I could be happy making everyone else happy. Now, I find I have to be true to my own self, or I'll never be happy. If Joe wants me . . ."

She trailed off, allowing Lena to draw her own conclusions, which the little Mexican woman promptly did. "So that's the way of it, is it? You want Joe Hart at any cost."

"I *tried* to love Rand; I really did, Lena. I wanted so much to love him, but the feelings would never come. Whereas with Joe Hart, they were there from the very beginning; there was nothing I could do to stop them."

Expelling a long sigh, Lena sadly nodded. "I understand, *querida*. How can I not? I love a man who considers me too far beneath him to ever marry me. Yet I stay here, waiting . . . hoping . . . watching life slip past while I do nothing. I should have left a long time ago, when I first realized that your father would never wed me. Instead, I stayed, because I could not help myself. I *had* to be near him."

"And if Joe has decided he wants me, I have to be with him—on any basis he chooses," Maggie murmured. "Like you, I cannot help myself, Lena. I did not choose this; it somehow chose me."

"Then go with God, *querida.*" Lena brushed Maggie's cheek with the back of her hand, her eyes glistening with unshed tears. "May God grant your every desire, my dearest child. You deserve a man who will love you for yourself alone—and not out of obligation, greed, or any other reason. Your Papa has been so wrong to try and force you and Rand together. He has abused the love you hold for him, and if he must suffer because of it . . . well, I will try to keep him from suffering too much."

"Goodnight then, dearest Lena!" Maggie hugged her friend, then retreated into her room. "Thank you for bringing me the message, when you could have chosen not to do so, and I never even would have known about it."

"I pray it was not a mistake." Lena smiled ruefully, left the room, and gently closed the door behind her.

* * *

As the sky lightened in the east and blushed a pale rose color, Joe mounted Loser and waited for Maggie in a copse of concealing trees. The herd of spotted horses paid him no heed, except for the herd stallion who trotted anxiously back and forth around the perimeter of the herd, stopping every now and then to snort and paw the earth in the direction of the trees where he sensed Loser's presence.

Watching him, Joe considered anew why he was doing this. He so wanted to be worthy of his name, Heart-of-the-Stallion! Too long had he denied his heritage and lived in fear of the consequences of embracing it. He was sick to death of his own deceitfulness, cowardice, and greed. He was tired of pretending to be something he was not.

Those few brief days and hours with Man-Who-Dreams and Red Fox had opened his eyes to his own foolishness. For the first time since he had rejected his Indian self, he had known a measure of peace and contentment in whom and what he was. He had realized what he was missing by cutting himself off from his own kind for so many long years. He had been able to relax and let down his guard for the first time since his mother's death. . . . And after watching his two friends being herded back to the reservation like helpless sheep, he had known he could not continue like this; he could not keep living a lie.

It was time to come to grips with his identity—to accept his true destiny and abandon false hopes and pretenses. *He was Indian.* And he could no longer turn his back on the plight of his people, ignore their suffering, and live his own life. Maggie as much as anyone had made him question his former goals. She had probed his innermost soul and exposed the ugliness there. Had reminded him that amidst all the evilness and cruelty in the world, there could still be beauty, tenderness, and love. She had offered him the gift of her love, and he could not accept it because he was unclean and self-serving. For years, he had cared for no one but himself, his goals, and his vengeance—until she came along to open his eyes to the good in the world.

Because of her—and Red Fox and Man-Who-Dreams—he
now knew what he must do. He had a new plan and new goals
to pursue, beginning with re-establishing his self-esteem. It
might take years to become someone he could admire and believe in once again, but no matter how long it took, he was
committed to trying. He could not and would not ask Maggie
to wait. But he would see her once more—just one more
time!—to tell her goodbye, to thank her for what she had given
him, and to beg her to be happy in the bosom of her family,
where she belonged.

He wanted her to know that he loved her and would never
forget her—his Maggie of the honey-colored hair, green-gold
eyes, and winsome ways. She would forever haunt his dreams.

Peering into the mist rising from the meadow, he watched for
her and prayed that she would come so he could tell her goodbye
and give her the one thing in the world he valued—the thing that
meant the most to him. He would *insist* she accept it. There was
no one else he would even consider giving it to—and no way he
could ever keep it. Not when it was known he was Indian. Not
when he had finally accepted the limitations and challenges of
his very existence, and the essence of what he was.

Joe Hart would die this day, die as he had been born so long
ago, on the whim of a woman. Heart-of-the-Stallion would be
reborn, taking his place as a leader among his people and fighting to improve their lot and prevent their exploitation. He would
fight as the stallion guarding his herd was prepared to fight—
with courage, bravery, and single-minded purpose.

He knew it now; it was for *this* he had come home, not to
own land and raise horses and cattle like a white man, but to
rescue his people. To give them hope and restore their pride.
To ensure that they were no longer cheated and treated like
criminals. Who better than he could do it? Having spent so
many years studying to be a white man, he understood how to
beat them at their own games. Though unaware of it at the
time, he had spent half his life preparing for this moment.

Three days of fasting and vision-seeking had shown him the

path his life must now take. He was a new man. *Hanyawat* had cured his blindness. His *wy-a-kin* had come to him in his dreams and revealed his future. This very day, he would embrace it . . . but first, he would say farewell to Maggie. If she came . . .

Maggie did come. She rode into the meadow on Preacher just as the sun breached the rim of the mountains, gilding their rugged shapes with molten gold. Nickering a warning, the stallion drove his herd to the far end of the meadow, clearing the way for Joe to leave the trees and approach her without the need for caution.

She watched him come, her eyes widening at the sight of him, and he thought he would never see a more beautiful vision than Maggie lit by a shaft of sunlight, her hair turning to flame around her shoulders. Love and excitement shone in her face— or perhaps it was the mere exertion of her ride that put the flush in her cheeks and the sparkle in her eyes. Maggie. His Maggie!

He stopped in front of her, giving her time to adjust to the changes in him, allowing her to look her fill.

"Joe," she whispered.

"No . . . I am Heart-of-the-Stallion now," he corrected, watching her closely, trying to read the emotions chasing one another across her sweet oval face.

It came to Maggie all in a rush what Joe was trying to do. He was testing her, giving her the opportunity to see him as he saw himself. He wore no shirt or hat and Loser no saddle. He had rejected boots, spurs, and even trousers. His garb was simple, primitive Indian. Breechcloth, leggings, and moccasins. A strip of rawhide tied around his forehead. Black and white paint adorned his face.

Loser had been painted also. Paint, she recalled, indicated war or attack. Perhaps also ceremony. Its use was symbolic, but to her, Joe was simply Joe—lithe and muscular, beautifully masculine, the man she loved above all others.

"Heart-of-the-Stallion," she repeated, trying the name on him for size. It fit; it fit perfectly. Dismounting, she reached for him.

In a flash, Joe was off his own horse and sweeping her into those strong bare arms. "Maggie," he muttered hoarsely, clasping her to his chest. "I did not think you would come."

"You should have known I would. How could I not answer the summons of the man I love?"

"You should not love me. As you can see, I am your enemy. I am Nez Perce."

"No, you are my heart," she gently admonished. "You are my soul, my being. Without you, I am not whole, Joe . . . Heart-of-the-Stallion . . . whoever and whatever you are."

"When you say you are not whole, you are speaking as if you are crippled, Maggie, but you are not, not where it counts. *I* am the one who is crippled, lame, blind. . . . You are perfection, all a man could want in a woman, except you are born of the wrong people."

"I don't care! Did you think to destroy my love by coming to me as an Indian? Shall I want you less now? That's not the way it works, Joe! You can't make me hate you. . . ."

He drew back slightly and held her at arm's length. "I don't want your hatred, but neither can I accept your love, Maggie. I come to you like this because this is what I am—what I have been denying in myself. I can deny it no longer."

Alarm clanged through her. "You must deny it! No one but me must ever see you like this. Indian or not, you belong to me; I love and accept you. But others won't. It can be our secret, Joe, ours alone!"

"No, Maggie," he said sorrowfully. "Were you not listening? Do you not understand? Joe Hart is dead. He is no more. Heart-of-the-Stallion is my only name. But I have not behaved as a stallion should. I have not fought for my herd or my heritage or my right to live on our ancient lands. I have been too weak, angry, and afraid. Now I am finally ready to reclaim my birth-right and accept the consequences of who I am. I will go to Lapwai and reveal my true name. I will stay there and aid and advise my people in their continuing fight to gain their free-dom. . . . I cannot live as a white man any longer and still feel good inside my skin. I cannot turn a blind eye to my people's suffering."

"But you *are* half white! How can you reject *that* side of you and still feel good about yourself!"

His mouth settled into a grim line. "I will use that side of me to help my people. All I have learned from the whites will enable me to better serve the Nez Perce."

"What if the Nez Perce don't want you? What if they reject you because you *have* lived as a white man and learned all our ways?"

For the first time, he smiled. "They will not, Maggie. Espe-cially when they realize that I have come to join them. They will embrace me as a long lost brother."

"And whom shall I embrace?" Maggie bitterly demanded. "You refuse to stay with me, but you have made it impossible for me to give my love and loyalty to any other man. You call me here, raise my hopes, make me think you are ready to admit you were wrong about us . . . only to shatter my dreams and ruin my life with yet another rejection."

"Do not say that, Maggie. Do not speak as if your life is over. If you cannot love Rand, you will find another."

"No, Joe. For me, there will never be another." Maggie held herself stiffly apart from Joe, but she spoke to him from the furthest reaches of her soul. "Oh, Joe, give me another memory to cherish in the long years ahead! Give me one more chance to love you—and *then* see if you can still walk away from me and all we might have together."

A tiny voice inside Maggie demanded to know what had happened to her pride—that she should shamelessly *beg* like this! But she paid it no heed. What did pride have to do with love anyway? The strong and the proud had no need of love;

they could survive without it. Only the flawed and the weak craved love as if it were life-giving air. Whatever she was capable of becoming apart from Joe, whatever heights he might attain without her, could never equal the splendor of what they could be together. If only she had more time to convince him of that truth . . .

"Are you afraid to love me? Is that it? Do you think if you do, I'll never let you leave me? You're right, Joe. I won't play fair. I'll use whatever I can to hold you here—to keep you from going to Lapwai."

"Ah, Maggie . . . ," Joe uttered a low groan and suddenly pulled her tight against his half-naked body. His breechcloth did nothing to hide his desire for her, and having enticed him this far, she boldly pressed herself against him. One of his hands moved up to entwine in her hair while he ravished her mouth with kisses. The other pinioned her to his hard strong body. As one, they dropped to their knees in the grass—mouths already joined, bodies straining to be closer.

As always happened when they were together, as Maggie had known would happen, their love-making flowed in a natural progression that made it all seem so right, easy, and effortless. One moment she was fully clothed and the next, she was lying naked in Joe's arms, twisting, turning, and writhing in an increasingly intimate, almost desperate dance of love.

Tongues mated, hands and mouths found all the most sensitive spots, flesh slid across flesh, skin tingled with awareness, arms and legs entwined. Maggie knew no embarrassment, no hesitation, in giving herself to the man she loved. If this was to be their final joining, it must be fulfilling enough to last a lifetime. It must be so perfect and complete that she would remember and cherish it always . . . but maybe, just maybe, it would be so perfect that she would not have to say goodbye when it was over. She would have changed Joe's mind about leaving her.

Joe entered her in one swift sure thrust, and she lifted herself to take him more fully, more deeply into the core of her. She ceased to be white, and he ceased to be Indian. Now they were only man and woman, male and female, two halves of a magnificent whole, indistinguishable one from the other.

The moment of fulfillment shattered Maggie's senses and sent her spinning through time and space. She forgot where she was, what day it was, even why she was doing this. There was only the glorious burst of pleasure and rapture . . . the sense of exquisite oneness, rightness, and fulfillment of destiny. She was where she belonged, and Joe was there with her, sharing one of life's grandest miracles.

All too soon, the ecstasy faded, and she became conscious of the dry grass abrading her sensitive skin, the sunshine burning it, and a general itchiness all over. Joe smoothed back her hair and nuzzled her ear.

"What are we doing, Maggie—lying out in the open like this, where anyone could come along and see us? Why have we even done this, today of all days?"

"Because it should be *us* getting married, Joe. Because we belong together . . . don't you feel it? Say you do. Say it, Joe."

In answer, he kissed her cheek, nose, and eyelids. "Maggie . . . my Maggie. . . . After all this, don't you understand yet? It's only because I love you that I have the strength to leave you. I cannot subject you to what lies ahead for me. . . . I will not have you become outcast from your own people, your own family."

"Then why did you bid me come to you? Was it to tear out my heart and give it back to me, lacerated and bleeding? Why, Joe? Tell me why."

"It was to bid you to be happy in your marriage and to give you something precious to me," he said. "Wait here a moment while I get it."

He rose from her, strode to Loser in all his wondrous nudity and returned bearing a sheaf of papers. She sat up, wrapped her shirtwaist around herself, and took them as he wordlessly held them out to her. More papers. Instinctively, she knew what they were. Her fingers shook as she opened them, and the print blurred as she tried to read the first sheet.

As her eyes filled with tears, she murmured: "I can't read it. Tell me what the paper says."

"It is the deed to the land I bought. I am giving it to you. It is my wedding gift. I will not be permitted to keep the land once it is known that I am Indian. The authorities at Lapwai will take it from me."

Tears scalded her cheeks. Her throat burned. She very well knew what this meant to him. "What about the cattle you bought—and the horses I was going to sell you?"

His voice was flat, emotionless. They might have been discussing the weather. "They will not let me keep them either. I pray you will hold them for me until the day I can claim them as an Indian, until the day *all* my people gain the right to once again raise horses and cattle, and freely roam the lands of their forefathers."

"And if that day never comes? What then, Joe? You will have thrown away all you have ever wanted for the sake of an ideal—a hopeless dream. How much land does this paper represent?"

She scrambled to her feet and faced him squarely, the two of them as naked and vulnerable as babes newly arrived in the world. He gazed at her dispassionately, his face a mask. "More than four times the amount of land I will be permitted to own as an Indian."

"I don't understand! Why would you do this?" She shook the papers in his face. "I don't want your land—I want you, Joe! The land means nothing to me without you."

"There is no way to explain, Maggie. You are white; therefore, you cannot possibly understand. I can find no words to tell you. I only know I must do this. It is . . . my fate."

She tried one last time to reach him. "Joe, before I met you, before you taught me that I was capable of galloping across a meadow, I dreamed of being whole and perfect. But I allowed the perceptions and fears of others to shape my view of myself. I *was* a cripple, in my mind if not my body. I was afraid to try new things for fear of failing. . . . Is that what *you* are doing?

Are you afraid you will fail as a white man, so you're seeking refuge among the Nez Perce?"

"It's not that!" he harshly denied. "It's . . . the guilt. The knowledge that I can have everything and my people nothing. That I can own hundreds of acres, and my brothers only eighty. That I can ride spotted horses, while they must walk. That I can seek the mountains or the sea whenever I wish, while they must go where they are told. . . . Maggie, I met an old Indian and a boy on my land. They were breaking the law by being off the reservation, and some white men came to take them back. The white men drew their guns on them and forced them to return. Your laws allow this, so I could do nothing to help them . . . nothing but watch as they were led away. It came to me then: I have abandoned my people when they need me most."

"Joe, you can help your people much better *off* the reservation than you can ever hope to help them by becoming a hated Indian yourself. In the years to come, *I* can help them. As my father is fond of pointing out, the Sterlings will be an important family in this region."

"Get dressed," he snapped, abruptly jerking away from her. "I will not allow you to weaken me and sap the strength from my resolve."

Angrily, he put on his scanty garments while she struggled back into her clothing. He finished before she did and went to get Preacher. He brought the old gelding to her side and said: "It is time for you to return. Before they come looking for you."

He lifted her up into the saddle before she could protest and handed her the reins. She still held the papers—the deed to his land—and she crumpled them in her agitation and waved them beneath his nose. "I don't want your papers. Don't make me keep them. I *won't* take your land from you."

He snatched the papers from her, lifted the flap of her saddlebag, and stuffed them inside. "They are of no further use to me, Maggie. You must keep them."

"I won't!" she cried, twisting around in the saddle to remove the papers. As she reached into the saddlebag, her fingers brushed something cold and hard—the six-shooter she carried with her, at Rand's insistence, everywhere she went. She had forgotten she had it in her saddlebag. . . . Would that she could turn it on Joe and make him see reason!

Yet no one ever saw reason by being forced into it; some lessons a person had to learn by himself, usually when it was too late to change things. Sighing, she left the papers where they were. By the time Joe came to his senses and wanted them back again, it would be too late. He'd be known as an Indian. If she did not accept his gift of the land, it would be confiscated and resold to a white man.

This was truly goodbye then. She would never see him again. Already he had started to walk away—heading in Loser's direction. She squeezed Preacher's sides and trotted after him, unable to let him go like this.

"Joe!"

He stopped and turned. She rode slowly up to him, her heart splintering inside her breast. She leaned down and touched his face, engraving his image forever in her memory. She would never forget his silver-gray eyes. Never. Nor his finely chiseled, sensual mouth. How could she forget what that mouth had done to her—the way it had kissed her and moved across her naked body, loving every inch of her?

She bent down for one last kiss. He allowed her to kiss him but would not respond. He was holding back, trying to make the parting easier. Wrapping her arms around his neck, she deepened the kiss . . . demanding his acknowledgement of the feelings that existed between them.

And that was when she heard the sudden loud click, the unmistakable sound of a hammer being cocked. A horse whinnied in the background, and a familiar voice said: "Git away from 'im, Maggie, so's I kin shoot the son-of-a-bitchin' Injun. There's nothin' I'd like better than plantin' 'im in the ground on mah weddin' day."

Twenty

"Rand, no!" Maggie cried, reining the old gelding around so fast that he almost lost his footing and fell over.

Fifty paces away, Rand sat on Cricket. He was alone, which made her all the more nervous; there were no witnesses, no one to take her side and calm down her fiancé, whose anger had never been more apparent. Rand held not a six-shooter but a long Winchester, and as Maggie watched, he raised the rifle and took careful aim at her—rather at Joe, who stood behind Preacher.

"Ya' gonna hide b'hind some calico's skirts, Injun? Git out here so's I kin git a bead on ya'."

Despite Maggie's efforts to keep Preacher between Rand and Joe, Joe calmly stepped out from behind the horse. "If you want to fight, Rand, get down and fight. But you should know that you've already won. Maggie's headed back to the ranch to marry you, and I'm on my way to the reservation."

Maggie succeeded in maneuvering Preacher between Joe and Rand again. "Only part of that's true, Rand. Joe's going to the reservation, yes, but I'm trying to talk him out of it. He's not really an Indian, you see. He's only *part* Indian, and that's no reason why he should have to stay on the reservation for the rest of his life."

"Part Injun's good enough fer me, Maggie. Only I ain't killin' him jus' 'cause of that. I'm killin' him fer darin' t' put his hands on ya'. Git out from b'hind that hoss, ya' stinkin' coward."

"Put down that rifle, Rand! If you shoot Joe, I'll see that you hang for it. He's an unarmed man."

"I ain't gonna hang fer shootin' no Injun that touched my bride," Rand growled. "Ain't a jury in the state that'd convict me."

"But I'm not going to marry you, Rand! I've changed my mind. Even if I hadn't, you can't kill a person like this, with no means of defending himself. It isn't right. You know it isn't right."

"I can do any damn thing I please t' a runaway Injun who's been messin' with my woman. I know whut happened, Maggie. He lured you up here t' try an' stop this weddin', though why you didn't turn tail an' run when you saw how he wuz dressed beats me. I cain't b'lieve you've gone partial t' redskins. . . . Anyway, it wuz jus' pure luck I noticed Preacher wuz missin an' guessed where you had gone."

"You *guessed* I came up here to the meadow?" Maggie was incredulous. She would not have given Rand credit for that much intuition.

"Yeah, I guessed. It wuz easy after I saw Lena's face when I asked her if she knew where you wuz. B'sides, this is where you always come when you light out on yer own, ain't it? Here an' town, an' I didn't think you'd be goin' t' town this mornin'. . . . Now, come on, Injun; yer wastin' my time."

Preacher broke into a trot as a result of Maggie's frantic efforts to shield Joe; while she struggled to control him, Joe again stepped into the open.

"The way to settle this is with our fists—unless *you* are too much of a coward," he taunted Rand.

"Aw, what the hell!" Rand snarled, shoving the nose of his Winchester back in the leather case attached to his saddle. "I'd rather kill you with my bare hands anyway than shoot you. Shootin's too quick an' easy."

He slid off Cricket's back, flung his Stetson to one side, and tore off his shirt. Joe, meanwhile, circled him, half-crouching and watching the blond man with narrowed eyes.

"Please don't do this!" Maggie begged. "One or both of you may get hurt. There's no need for this violence. It won't change anything. . . . Win or lose, I'm not going to marry you, Rand. Joe, if you fight him, you'll only make trouble for yourself. Let's stop this while we can. Please, I'm begging both of you. . . ."

"Maggie, get back," Joe warned. "Stay out of the way."

"Yeah, git back," Rand agreed. "Ya' don't wanna git spattered with Injun blood."

"No blood-letting! There mustn't be any blood-letting!" Maggie pleaded, but both men ignored her. She suddenly realized that this moment was inevitable. They had been heading toward it for a long, long time. She was the only one seeking to avoid the fight; Joe was resigned to it. . . . No, he was *eager* for it. But even if he won, he'd actually be losing. Indians didn't win fights with white men anymore; whatever they did, they lost.

While Rand's horse moved off to graze with trailing reins, Rand and Joe circled each other—both of them watching for the unguarded moment, the slightest hesitation, the tiniest weakness in the other. To Maggie, they looked well-matched. Joe was taller by several inches, but Rand was heavier, his body more muscular. They were a study in contrasts—one blond, fair-skinned, and blustery, the other dark, lithe, and lean, moving silently as a cat.

"Whatcha waitin' fer, Injun?" Rand panted. "Come an' git me. You think yer a better man than me? Well, prove it. I been lookin' fer a chance t' show ya' whut I can do, one on one. Ya' may be able to ride better'n me—an' rope, an' break hosses. Ya' may even be able t' *kiss* better'n me, but I bet ya' can't fight better. Ya' know why? Cuz' ya' got goose feathers where yer liver oughta be. Yer spine is made of calf's foot jelly. When ya' piss, it comes out water; only when ya' crap is it yellah."

He can't augur as well as you, Rand, Maggie thought. *That's one thing he can't do nearly as well. Augur and boast. That's where you excel.*

She had regained control of Preacher and now sat astride him twenty feet away, her heart in her mouth, her hands damp and clammy. Rand kept up a steady stream of insults—while Joe said nothing, nothing at all. But suddenly, he lunged at Rand. The two men grappled, their muscles straining as each sought to throw the other. Rand succeeded in breaking Joe's hold and managed to land a couple of fast punches.

Joe did not punch back. Rather, he dodged so that the punches fell harmlessly on his shoulders. Rand went after him like a battering ram, but most of his blows did not connect. Then Joe caught Rand in a hold around the neck and again, the two men strained, pitting their strength against each other.

Rand's bulk gave him the advantage, and once more, he broke free—but Joe's speed enabled him to get in a few quick jabs that Rand wasn't expecting. Thud, thud, thud! With a roar of outrage, Rand threw himself at Joe, and the two went down, rolling over and over in the grass at Preacher's feet.

First, Rand was on top, his huge fists pummeling Joe's face and shoulders. Then Joe was on top, then Rand again. Maggie couldn't tell who was winning. Both men were sweating, and Rand's skin was darkly flushed. There were grunts and curses—the latter from Rand. Joe continued to fight silently, and it began to look as if he were winning. Fewer punches landed on him. He couldn't pin Rand in an unbreakable hold, but he could deliver some punishing blows that the blond giant could not avoid.

Of the two of them, Rand was breathing more heavily and moving more slowly. Getting to their feet, the men circled each other again. Lightning-swift, Joe stepped behind Rand and twisted one arm behind his back, forcing the bigger man to his knees. Bellowing with pain and outrage, Rand tossed Joe over his head.

Joe rolled and sprang to his feet, but when Maggie glanced back at Rand, she saw that Rand had drawn a knife. "You asked fer it, Injun. Now, yer gonna git it. I quit tryin' t' fight fair with ya'—ya' slimy bastard. Now I'm gonna carve up yer guts."

It was too much for Maggie. "Rand, stop! You mustn't use that knife! You can't. Please, Rand, I'm begging you."

She swung down from Preacher, entangling her bad leg in her skirt. Awkward and ungainly, unable to keep her balance in her haste, she sprawled on the grass near Preacher's hooves. Tears of helplessness stung her eyes; never had she felt so useless and inept! Snorting, Preacher backed away from her. She had just enough presence of mind to grab his reins before he bolted.

When she looked back at the two combatants, she froze in horror: Blood was dripping from two long red scores on Joe's chest, and Rand was slicing at him with the knife. Rand had long arms, and the knife in his hand made his reach even longer. Joe kicked at the weapon, but Rand held tight to it. Another good swing, and he cut Joe again.

Intent on stopping Rand before he killed Joe, Maggie shrieked and scrambled to her feet. Preacher pulled back on the reins, dragging her away from the fight. She was about to let the panicked horse go when she remembered the six-shooter in her saddlebag. It was her only hope for making Rand see reason!

"Easy, boy. Easy now," she crooned to the old gelding, while the men scuffled behind her.

Preacher stood still, his ears pricked toward the commotion. Snorting his uneasiness at the scent of blood, the old horse allowed her to approach and fumble in the leather saddlebag. Joe's papers—the deed to his land—scattered and drifted to the ground as Maggie's shaking fingers found the gun. Holding it in both hands, she turned back toward the two men.

"Rand! Get away from Joe. Leave him alone now. Dear God, he can barely stand as it is."

She uttered a strangled cry of anguish, for in the few brief moments when she had been retrieving the six-shooter, Rand had cut Joe badly. His entire torso was criss-crossed with cuts, yet he was still standing, his gray eyes shining with a determined light. Yet he was swaying, too, the blood running in rivulets down his body, and Rand was grinning triumphantly.

"Keep comin' at me, Injun. Every time ya' do, I git another slice o' red meat." He laughed a terrible laugh, wild and maniacal, which sent a shudder down Maggie's spine. What was going on here? Why hadn't Joe used his superior speed and agility to keep *away* from Rand? It was almost as if . . . as if . . .

She pointed the pistol at Rand. "Get away from him, Rand. You've hurt him enough. Any more and you'll kill him."

"Hell, Maggie, that's whut I intend. Why, I ain't even scalped him yet. An' I gotta scalp him—jus' like his folks used t' scalp us white folks. 'Member, Maggie? I gotta do it—fer my Pa an' Ma. Fer yer uncle. Fer you, too, Maggie, an' fer yer Ma. . . ."

Rand turned toward Joe who was watching him intently. Joe stood absolutely still, doing nothing to defend himself or get away. Rand raised the knife to deliver the killing blow, swinging his arm high above his head. Maggie didn't have time to think; she only reacted. She lifted the pistol and aimed it the way Rand had shown her. She sighted down the barrel at Rand's hand clutching the knife, held the weapon steady exactly as he had taught her . . . and then she fired.

The retort drove her several steps backward and scattered the horses. A puff of smoke momentarily obscured her vision. Her nostrils stung with an acrid odor. As the smoke cleared, she saw what she had done. Rand lay crumpled on the ground, holding not his hand but his bloodied head, and groaning. Unfortunately, the knife he had held but a moment before was buried to its handle in Joe's upper chest. Joe himself had fallen. She had fired too late . . . too late to save him.

"Joe!" she screamed. "Joe!"

Flinging aside the pistol, she rushed to Joe's side. He lay on his back, his face ashen, blood pouring from his many wounds, but especially the one in his upper chest, near his collar bone. Dropping to her knees beside him, Maggie grasped the handle

of the knife which was slippery with blood. It took all her
strength to pull it out. When she did, a red fountain immediately
spurted.

Panic-stricken, she lifted her skirt and frantically began tearing at her petticoat. The thread resisted her efforts, but she
finally managed to rip off a strip of fabric which she pressed
to Joe's wound to staunch the flow of blood. There was so
much blood! He was bleeding to death before her very eyes.

Joe's teeth were set in a grimace, and his eyes were closed,
but as she worked over him, he stirred. "Is he dead?" he demanded in a raspy voice.

Maggie did not immediately understand the question. In her
zeal to save Joe, she had all but forgotten Rand. The inquiry
finally penetrated her befuddled brain, and she answered soothingly. "I don't think so. I'll look later. First, I've got to stop
this bleeding."

She made a make-shift bandage out of pieces of her petticoat,
then tore off the hem of her skirt to bind the bandage more
securely around Joe's wound. Winding the strip of fabric over
his shoulder and under his armpit, she was able to fasten the
bandage in place well enough that he ought to be able to make
the ride back to the ranch—she hoped.

However, when she tried to get him to his feet, she was
forced to acknowledge the full extent of his wounds. Weakened
by blood loss and gritting his teeth in pain, he leaned on her
heavily. No sooner had he risen when he fell back down
again—this time, unconscious. Swept with anxiety, she leaned
over him in the grass.

"Joe . . . Joe, can you hear me?" Gently, she slapped his
face but got no response.

He was still breathing but his skin was ashen. If she did not
get help for him soon, he would die. She scrambled to her feet
and started to fetch Preacher, stopped halfway to the horse and
decided she had better check on Rand instead. Both men were
probably in dire need of greater medical expertise than she was
capable of providing. If she could just get them to the ranch,

Lena would help, and someone could go for the doctor. Maybe Doc Rawson was already there. She had sent him an invitation to the wedding.

Rand hadn't moved from where he had fallen, and she hurried over to examine the extent of the damages wrought by her six-shooter, the gun he had insisted she carry at all times and then taught her how to use.

Kneeling down beside Rand, she became conscious of the enormous anger she still felt for him. It welled up in her, so that she felt no pity for his suffering and indeed wished that he was injured so badly that he had surely learned his lesson.

"Rand, wake up!" she harshly commanded, noting that his eyes were half-closed, and he seemed to be dozing or in a daze. Blood was oozing from a long crimson crease on his forehead, and he wore a stunned expression.

"Rand? Damn it, Rand, wake up! Joe is dying, and I need your help getting him up on Preacher or Loser, if I can even find Loser. He's around here someplace; he *must* be." She took hold of Rand's shoulders and shook him, causing his head to roll to one side.

"Rand! Damn you, don't do this to me! You can't die on me. I'm angry with you, yes, and I'll never forgive you for what you did to Joe—but I don't want you to *die!* Do you understand me? You have to live and say you're sorry, and then I'll forgive you because I know how much you've been hurt by Indians in the past. You just went too far, Rand. You got carried away . . . but you're not a bad person, really you're not. I'm sorry I couldn't love you like you wanted, like my father wanted . . . I'm sorry I shot you. Sorry this happened. . . . It *shouldn't* have, really . . ."

She realized she was babbling hysterically, and she stopped abruptly as Rand's eyes opened, and he turned his head to look at her. "M-Maggie?"

Her name came out as a croak, but at least, he was alive and talking. Quickly, she tore another strip off her petticoat and tied it around his forehead. The wound appeared superficial.

The bullet had left a deep crease and probably knocked Rand silly, but she didn't think he would lose his life because of it—not like Joe.

"Rand, you've got to get up now and help me with Joe. If we don't get him to a doctor, he'll die."

Rand's face hardened. "So let him die. I ain't helpin' no Injun."

"Rand, you must! I can't manage by myself. I need you to help me. . . ."

To her surprise, Rand pushed her aside and sat up. "Where's that six-shooter? I'll finish off the son-of-a-bitchin' redskin, once an' fer all."

"No!" Maggie scrambled to her feet and retrieved the gun before Rand could get to it. With trembling hands, she again aimed at the man she had once intended to marry. "I won't let you kill him. You may already have wounded him fatally, but I won't let you harm him further. I don't want to, but if I must, I'll kill you, Rand."

Unsteadily, Rand rose to his full height and towered over Maggie, his face contorted with pain and loathing "So yer choosin' him over me, is that it, Maggie? Yer choosin' a god-damn Injun."

"I never meant to choose him—never meant to fall in love with him. It just happened. I fought it, and *he* fought it. Neither one of us wanted it. Can't you understand?"

"What I understand is that I shoulda killed him a long time ago. Gimme that gun, Maggie."

Swaying where he stood, Rand reached for the six-shooter. In his dizziness and disorientation, Maggie found it easy to avoid him. She merely backed up a couple of steps and kept the pistol trained on Rand's midsection. "Get out of here, Rand. Get off Sterling land, and don't ever come back. If you do, I'll tell everyone how you tried to kill Joe. How you pulled a knife when he was unarmed, and then tried to shoot him as he lay bleeding to death. You may already be guilty of murder. If Joe dies, you will be. . . . Is that what you want, Rand? To be hanged for murder, or at the very least, to have to spend the rest of your life behind bars?"

Rand's eyes widened. "You'd do that t' me? All on account of some Injun?" He seemed unable to believe it, so great was his hatred of Indians and his certainty that she, too, must hate them.

She nodded. "I'll do it, Rand. I'm sorry, but as God is my witness, I'll do it." She motioned with the pistol. "Go on now, go. I can't look after Joe properly while you're still here, arguing with me."

Rand stared at her a long moment. Then he put his hand to his temple and touched the bandage there, as if needing the reminder that she had shot him once and might actually do it again. "G'bye, Maggie," he said in a raspy tone. "I guess this is g'bye for real, ain't it?"

"Yes, it is. Goodbye, Rand." She didn't lower the pistol, but kept it trained on him as he turned, grabbed his hat off the trampled ground, and began to stomp in Cricket's direction. As if nothing had happened, the big horse was grazing not far from Preacher.

She waited until he reached Cricket, mounted, and had ridden a good distance in the direction opposite from the ranch before she returned to Joe. As Rand disappeared over the horizon, she dropped to her knees beside Joe who was still alive but unconscious. She would have to ride back to the ranch and get help— bring the cart or a wagon. Send someone for the doctor. Call off the wedding . . . *the wedding.*

By now, the guests should be arriving. Lena would be growing anxious that she had not yet returned. Her father was probably pacing the floor and cursing, wondering what had happened to the bride and the bridegroom. How could she ever explain all this? How could she tell her father that Rand was gone for good and Joe in danger of dying—and all because of her?

Dear God in heaven, what had she done?

Blinded by tears of regret and anguish, condemning herself

for having responded to Joe's summons in the first place, she sat back on her heels and succumbed to the overwhelming urge to weep. This was all her fault. She had no one but herself to blame. On the very morning of what was supposed to be her wedding day, she had shamelessly lain in the arms of another man; what sort of woman was she—to behave in such a scandalous, incomprehensible fashion? No wonder this tragedy had resulted!

Choking back her tears, she wiped her eyes with the palms of her hands. Weeping wouldn't solve her problems. It was time to leave Joe and ride for help. Bending over Joe, she gently touched his cheek. "Joe, I'm leaving you now, but I'll be back soon with a doctor. Can you hear me?"

There was no response. Barely any indication that he was still alive, except for the slight motion of breathing. As fast as she could, Maggie caught Preacher, climbed on his back, and urged him into a lope.

She rode at breakneck speed back to the ranch and straight up to the house. There, she slid off Preacher who was winded and drenched in sweat from the long, fast ride. Dimly, she noticed the wagons, carts, and carriages drawn up in front of the house, the tables and benches set up in the side yard for the feasting after the wedding. . . . *Yes! There was Doc Rawson's horse and buggy.*

At least, no one would have to ride into town to fetch him; no emergencies there or elsewhere had side-tracked him from the festivities. Immensely relieved, she started up the steps in search of Lena and her father. Just then, the door to the house flew open, and a red-eyed, swollen-faced Lena emerged. She failed to notice Maggie's torn clothing and blood-spattered shirtwaist.

"Maggie! Oh, *Madre de Dios,* I am so happy you have come at last. I looked out the window and saw you riding toward the house. Hurry, *querida,* come quickly. Your Papa . . ."

"Papa? What about Papa? Where is he? I must see him at once."

"This morning after you left, he came downstairs for breakfast and collapsed, *querida*. The doctor says he is dying. He is with him now. Hurry, Maggie. Your Papa has been asking for you, and I did not know what to tell him. *Señor* **Rand** is not here either, and Nathan has been asking for him, too. Did you see him? Do you know where he is? He was looking for you before all this happened. I did not tell him where you went, but he rode off as if he *knew*. . . . Oh, *querida,* this is a terrible day—a terrible, terrible day."

You don't even know yet how terrible. Maggie rushed past Lena and into the house. A bunch of women, dressed in gay colorful gowns, milled in the hallway in front of the stairs, but silently parted to let her pass as she limped through the middle of them and started up the steps.

"Dear Maggie, we're praying for you and your poor, poor father!" one woman called out, and Maggie nodded her thanks and kept on going.

Joe's flesh was on fire. His entire body burned, and it seemed too much of an effort simply to open his eyes. But he forced himself. He gazed up into bright hot sunlight and an intensely blue sky. Where was Maggie—and Rand? Was Rand dead? Ignoring the pain lancing through him at each tiny movement, he lifted his head and looked around.

He saw no one—not Maggie and not Rand. Neither did he see Preacher, Cricket, or Loser anywhere nearby. He surmised that Maggie had gone to get help. It would be awhile before she could return—plenty of time for him to pull himself together and leave.

Groaning against the pain, he rolled onto his side and managed to rise on one elbow. He had to get up. Had to. It was either that or die out here in the sun. Die waiting for Maggie to return—and if she did return before he died, what then?

Maggie would try to save him and then to convince him to marry her, which he still wasn't prepared to do. Indeed, sometime during his fight with Rand, rather than take the knife from the blond foreman and be forced to kill him, he had decided to let Rand do his worst and end the whole miserable situation. Rand would not have been satisfied with anything less than a fight to the death anyway, and if one of them had to die, it would be better for Maggie if *he* died than if Rand did. But Maggie had interfered, and as a result, he hadn't died, after all . . . though he felt he was close to it.

Now he had to flee before Maggie returned with half a dozen cowhands and her father to save him. All of them would see him dressed as an Indian, and if he did by some chance manage to survive his wounds, he would soon be on his way to the reservation anyway. . . . And Maggie, sweet, stubborn Maggie, might insist on defying her father and accompanying him. Or else her father would shoot him right before his daughter's eyes. Or Rand would simply finish what he had started.

At the very least, Maggie would be disowned. Her family and her neighbors would shun her. He couldn't let that happen. He must get up and flee before she returned. But where could he go? . . . Did it really matter? He could seek refuge in the mountains, perhaps . . . or he could try and make it to the reservation. At the moment, he couldn't even remember the direction of Lapwai. The important thing was simply to get out of there.

He looked around for his horse and saw a tiny speck in the far distance. . . . Ah, there was Loser, taking advantage of temporary freedom by seeking the sweetest grass. Now, all he had to do was whistle and call the horse to him. The simple act required a supreme effort of will, but even then, Joe's signal was thin and weak.

The tiny speck lifted its head and glanced in his direction, and Joe tried again. On the third effort, Loser finally came— trotting warily toward him and snorting at the scent of blood. The horse came close to him, lowered his head, and nuzzled Joe as if wondering what he was doing down there.

"Good boy," Joe murmured. "Now, if I can just get up on you. . . ."

He rose to his feet by clutching Loser's leg and pulling himself upward. Loser nosed him several times, sensing he was injured, but otherwise stood rock-still while Joe labored to stand and then swing his leg over the horse's back and climb aboard him. Twice, he fell and had to start over, but Loser did not abandon him.

Joe was reminded of the time he had found Loser near death in the snowdrift and rescued him. The horse seemed to realize it was time to return the favor. Patiently he stood with head lowered and legs firmly planted while Joe struggled to get on his back.

By the time he had made it, Joe was perilously close to unconsciousness, his body incapable of directing the horse and telling him where to go. Leaning forward, he wrapped his arms around the stallion's neck to keep from falling off and surrendered himself into the keeping of his *wy-a-kin*, the spotted horse, now personified in the best friend he had ever had— Loser.

"Take me where you will, old friend. I can do no more," he whispered, and the stallion began to walk and then to lope, carrying Joe away from the meadow.

Maggie stood by her father's bedside and knew that she had never faced a worse conflict: to stay and keep watch over her dying parent or to return immediately to the meadow with help for Joe.

Nathan had fallen into a state of gray-faced half-awareness, in which sometimes he roused and made perfect sense and other times he appeared to drift in a world of his own making. Doc Rawson was with him but shrugged helplessly and shook his head at Maggie's look of inquiry. She understood perfectly. The doctor had done all he could, and it wasn't enough. Her father was slipping away. In a short time, he would be gone.

Lena hovered near the bed, straightening a linen sheet that did not need straightening, plumping an extra pillow that would probably never be used. . . . She was surprisingly calm and composed, not in the least hysterical as she had been that first time when Nathan took sick. Only when Maggie caught her friend's eye could she see the suffering and inner turmoil, the wordless grief and sorrow. Lena still had not noticed her dishevelment—but Doc Rawson did.

"My dear girl, are you all right?" he inquired in a low, concerned voice. "What has happened to you?"

Maggie glanced down at her torn, stained garments. "This isn't my blood. It's Joe Hart's. He's up in the high meadow dying from knife wounds inflicted by Rand. I rode back to get help for him."

"Madre de Dios!" Lena exclaimed, while Doc Rawson's eyes widened behind his spectacles.

Maggie had thought her father couldn't hear; he had shown no recognition of her presence, but suddenly, he stirred. "Rand! Where's Rand? Didja fetch him fer me, Maggie?" Her father's eyes opened, and he stared up at her. "Where's Rand, Maggie? Didn't anybody tell 'im I'm gittin' ready t' go up yonder an' fork a cloud?"

Maggie didn't know what to say. She glanced helplessly from Lena to Doc Rawson. They didn't know the whole story, so they couldn't lend any assistance. "I . . . I don't want to upset you, Pa. We . . . we can talk about it, later."

"Later?" Her father gave a weak but derisive snort. "I ain't got no more laters. Tell me now. Whut's happened t' Rand? I kin take the truth better'n I kin take not knowin'."

Doc Rawson gave an almost imperceptible nod, and Maggie decided that it was too late to spare her father the truth anyway. He would only guess she was evading or outright lying, and that *would* make him very upset. . . . Besides, if he was really dying, he deserved the truth. There was nothing to be gained by concealing it from him.

"I-I went up to the high meadow to meet Joe, and Rand

followed me. Rand and Joe got into a fight. Rand pulled a knife on Joe and cut him up badly. He was just about to kill him, when I . . . I got out my six-shooter and shot him."

"You shot Rand?" her father croaked. He gave her a long incredulous look.

"Yes, and I . . . I sent him away," she finished in a hoarse whisper. "I told him never to come back, or I'd see that he winds up paying for what he did to Joe. Rand wasn't hurt that bad, and I made sure he left before I rode back to get help for Joe."

"Oh, I *knew* something like this was bound to happen!" Lena uttered a single choked sob, then stuffed her fist into her mouth to silence herself. Doc Rawson sighed. Her father simply stared at her, a deep frown wrinkling his forehead.

"It's my fault—all of it," she continued. "I should never have gone to meet Joe, today of all days, but I did. The men will have to go up and get him. Doc Rawson, too. Joe was unconscious when I left him, and he's lost a great deal of blood. Doc . . . can you leave my father long enough to tend to Joe— or should I have the men bring Joe here in the cart first?"

"Did you bind his wounds tightly?" Doc Rawson asked.

Maggie nodded. "As tightly as I could, the deepest one especially. Still, it will be hours before you can tend to him if you wait until they bring him here."

"I don't imagine I can tend him properly up in some meadow," Doc Rawson said. "I may have to stitch him up. Better have the men go get him."

"I'll go and tell Gusty," Lena volunteered. "The men should leave immediately. Maggie, will you be staying here with your father—or going with them?"

Again, Maggie felt the pull of conflicting emotions—love and concern for *both* men, only one of whom she could attend. "There's nothing more I can do for Joe," she reasoned sadly. "I already did all I could. So I might as well wait here."

She gazed down at her father's face; it seemed carved of

clay, the face of a man already dead. But his eyes were still alive, and sorrow burned in them.

"Let me go downstairs a moment and give the men some instructions for moving Joe Hart," Doc Rawson said. "I will not be gone long."

"I will go with you," Lena announced. "They should take some blankets with them—and a canteen. You stay and keep watch over your father a moment, *querida*. Yes?"

"Of course," Maggie murmured.

No sooner had Lena and Doc Rawson left the room when Nathan tried to lift his head from the pillow. "Maggie?"

"Don't try to move, Pa. Lie still and conserve your strength."

"Fer whut, Maggie? I know I'm dyin'. The end's comin' fast; I kin feel it. But b'fore it gits here, I wanna ask ya' somethin'. They wuz fightin' over you, wuzn't they?"

Maggie smoothed back his silver-streaked hair. "Yes, Pa. They were fighting over me. And also because Joe's an Indian. . . . But you knew that, didn't you? And you threatened him because of it."

"I wuz jus' tryin' t' pertect you, Maggie. Whut kinda life could you have married t' an Injun?"

Maggie's vision blurred with tears. "I don't know, Pa, but I would have appreciated the chance to find out—to make my own mistakes and decisions. . . . Oh, but I'm not blaming you! I let this thing with Rand go on too long. I should have confronted you sooner, called off the wedding, done what I knew to be right—but I didn't. I allowed you to manipulate me, and everything that's happened is the result of it."

"Yer too easy on yer ole Pa, Maggie. One thing dyin' does fer a man is t' clear all the cobwebs outa his head. I wuz plumb wrong t' do whut I did—plumb wrong t' try an' run yer life, Rand's, an' Joe Hart's. Whut happened t'day is *my* fault. Don't take the blame on yerself. I hate Injuns, so I hated Joe and schemed t' keep you from marryin' him. Truth is I admired him, too. He's got plenty of sand, jus' like me at his age."

Maggie sat down on the edge of the bed and held her father's cold hand. "You needn't have worried so, Pa. Joe would never have married me anyway. He thought I belonged here on the Broken Wheel with you. And today, he . . . he asked me to come to him only so he could say goodbye. He was dressed as an Indian and was planning on turning himself in at the reservation. We . . . we were just saying our farewells when Rand found us."

"He wuz plannin' on turnin' himself in! But what about the land he bought and the cattle I sold him?"

"He . . . he gave them to me as a . . . a wedding present." Maggie managed to choke out.

"A weddin' present. . . . Well, I'll be damned. Don't that beat all? . . . Only now, there ain't gonna be no weddin'."

Her father fell silent for a few moments, and his breathing seemed to grow more labored. Watching him struggle to draw breath, Maggie became alarmed. "Shall I call Doc Rawson back in here, Pa? Just nod your head yes or no."

Nathan shook his head no, and when he could manage it, muttered: "What fer? He cain't do nothin'. The ole ticker's jus' windin' down; too bad it ain't a clock ya' kin just wind back up again."

"Oh, Pa!" Maggie smiled through her tears. "You're the only man I know who can joke on his death bed."

"I'm . . . jokin' so's I . . . I don't cry, Maggie. When I think of all the bad things I've done an' how jus' plain stupid I've been. . . ."

He trailed off, and two tears trickled down his sunken cheeks. Maggie wiped them away with her fingertips. "I know, Pa. I feel the same way. I . . . I actually shot Rand and might have killed him, and I don't know how I'll ever live with that. I never knew I was capable of such violence, just as Rand probably never knew *he* was capable of trying to kill Joe. If Joe dies, Rand will be a murderer. And I . . . I . . ."

The thought of Joe dying was too terrible to contemplate, and Maggie could not go on. She didn't know what she would

do if Joe died. It would be as if a part of her—the best part—
died with him.

"You . . . you really love that Injun?"

For her father's sake, Maggie wanted to deny it. Old habits
were hard to break. Please your father. Make him happy. Let
him decide what's best for you. But she *had* to tell the truth
finally; it was long past time.

"Yes, Pa, I love him. And he loves me, which is why he was
letting me go, because he, too, thinks he knows what's best for
me."

Her father gripped her hand with surprising strength. "Then
don't let him do it, Maggie. If he lives, make him marry ya'.
That's whut's best fer ya'. Convince him he has t' live as a
white man, and if he wants t' better the lot of his people, he'll
have t' do it from outside the reservation, not in it."

Maggie was stunned. Was this really her father giving her
this radical advice, telling her to go marry an Indian?

"Pa . . . do you really mean it? You don't sound like yourself."

Nathan sighed, a long rattling sound, as if he were drowning
in his own liquids. "I'm thinkin' of me an' Lena—an' how I
hurt her an' myself by bein' too proud t' publicly take up with
a bean-eater. I broke her heart, Maggie, an' made her miserable,
and that made *me* miserable. I cain't tell ya' how much I regret
it. . . ."

He lifted his hand and shook his finger at her in a scolding
gesture. "An' one day, I don't want you t' be lyin' on yer deathbed kickin' yerself in the ass fer not havin' done the one thing
that would've made you the happiest while you wuz alive. If
marryin' an Injun is whut it takes t' make ya' happy, Maggie
honey, then go marry him an' tell everybody else t' go soak
their heads in the hoss trough if'n they don't like it—me included, 'cept I won't be here t' see it."

"Oh, Pa!" Maggie sobbed, torn between laughter and tears.

"I don't guess it's too important whut a person is—Injun,
white, Mexican, or the color of the ace of spades. It's whut's

in his heart that counts, Maggie. I kin see now that Rand let jealousy and prejudice rule him, while yer Injun was thinkin' of you with love. That's more'n I did fer Lena, an' it's my one big regret when I look back at all I done in life."

"It's not too late, Pa. You can tell Lena you're sorry. You can still apologize for being so mule-headed.

Her father's face brightened. His eyes lit up, and his color actually improved. "I can, cain't I? I guess I still can. . . . Go git her, will ya', Maggie? 'Fore I'm too blamed weary t' keep a-jawin' like this."

"Yes, yes, Pa, I will. I'll be right back."

"Wait a minute—fetch the preacher, too. Send him right on up here. We done told him there was gonna be a weddin' t'day, and there's still gonna be one . . . only it'll have t' be short an' sweet."

"Of course, Pa! I'll fetch him directly."

Maggie all but ran from the room. She met Lena, Doc Rawson, and of all people, the preacher himself coming up the stairs.

"Maggie, how is he?" Doc Rawson asked when he saw her in such a hurry.

"He's . . . he's still alive and giving orders. He wants Lena and the preacher to come up right away."

"Ah, yes," the preacher intoned in a sonorous voice. "When they're dying, they *all* want to see the preacher."

"No, you don't understand. He doesn't want to see you because he's dying, he wants you to marry him. I mean, marry him and Lena—perform the ceremony, that is. Witness their vows."

"He wants to marry me?" Lena cried, joy flooding her features. "Oh, my dear *Señor* Nathan!" She picked up her skirts and flew up the steps.

"Dear me," the preacher said. He was a tall fencepost of a man, with an enormous Adam's apple that was bobbing in agitation. "I'll have to get my book first. I left my book downstairs in the parlor."

The preacher turned around and descended the stairs, disappearing into the midst of a horde of fluttering women all wondering what was happening. Maggie realized that they had overheard some of her conversation, and she wondered what she could do to distract them while Lena and her father were quietly married in the upstairs bedroom.

"Mrs. Potts!" she called out over the din of murmuring voices. "Mrs. Potts, will you take the ladies outside and see that they are served some punch or tea, please, around the tables? Reverend Simpson is just going to look in on my father, that's all."

"Of course, dear." Mrs. Potts, an enormous woman with a bosom the size of a chuck wagon, began herding her charges out of the front door of the house. "Come along now, everyone. Let's give the Sterlings some privacy in their hour of need."

Maggie and Doc Rawson waited a few moments on the steps until Reverend Simpson returned, clutching his black book importantly to his scrawny chest. The three of them mounted the remaining stairs together. However, when they pushed open the door to the bedroom and went inside, they saw Lena kneeling at the side of the bed, her shoulders shaking, as she clutched Nathan's hand to her cheek and silently wept.

On the bed itself, Maggie's father lay perfectly still, his eyes slightly open, his features frozen in that look of joy Maggie had witnessed but a few moments before. . . . It was too late. He had waited too long. Now there would be no wedding on the Broken Wheel ranch. The preacher would have to conduct a funeral instead—at least one, and possibly another.

Dear God, please. Don't let Joe die, too! Maggie prayed from the depths of her heart.

Twenty-one

Nathan's abrupt death freed Maggie to return to the high meadow to help Joe. However, by the time she achieved sufficient control of her emotions to realize it, the men had already left, some on horseback, with Gusty driving the cart and taking the longer route to get there. Determined to join in the rescue one way or another, Maggie was in the midst of saddling Dusty when one of the wedding guests intervened.

"Miss Sterling?" Augustus Potts, Mrs. Potts's husband, laid a hand on her arm to prevent her from mounting the colt. "I don't know what all is a-goin' on here, but I'd like to offer you the use of my horse and buggy t' git wherever it is you're goin'."

Maggie dashed away the tear tracks on her cheeks. "Thank you, Mr. Potts. I believe I'll take you up on your offer as my colt is only greenbroke, and the only other horse I know how to ride is gone—pulling our cart."

"I'd be much obliged if'n you'd permit me t' drive ya', Miss Sterling. Mrs. Potts wouldn't like t' see you go off all by yerself—an' upset t' boot."

"All right," Maggie agreed.

Another man came up and took charge of Dusty while Mr. Potts led Maggie to his horse and buggy, which reminded her of the doctor's rig. She climbed up to sit on the shaded seat and gratefully leaned against the cushioned backrest, while Mr. Potts climbed up beside her.

He clucked to his horse. "Now then, Miss Sterling, where are we goin'?"

She gave him a few brief directions, and they started out. On the ride there, she briefly explained what had happened, leaving out only the part about Joe being an Indian. She was afraid if she told anybody about that, they might refuse to go to his aid—another reason why she was so anxious to be there when the men found him. Their reaction to the fact that he was Indian might be to let him lie there and die—though she didn't think Curt Holloway could be so cruel.

Curt seemed to idolize Joe; indeed, now that she thought about it, she realized that all the men liked him except Rand . . . but then they hadn't known that he was an Indian.

Halfway there, they caught up to Gusty trying to get Preacher to trot a little faster. The old horse was simply too tired and would do nothing more than plod along slowly, no matter how much Gusty urged him onward.

"If 'n you don't move on out, boy, I'm a-gonna have t' resort t' the whip," the old man was threatening.

"Leave him be, Gusty. We'll go on ahead," Maggie told him. "Just come as soon as you can. We'll need the cart to bring Joe back; it's a little bigger than this buggy."

"I still cain't git it through mah noggin that Rand done a thing like that t' Joe." Gusty shook his head and sighed.

Lines of sorrow seamed his face. He had been close to Rand, friendly to Joe, and never had approved of violence or confrontation of any kind. Though he sometimes stuck his nose where it didn't belong, he tried hard to make sure everyone got along.

"I don't think he meant to hurt him quite as badly as he did," Maggie defended, though she knew very well that Rand had intended to kill Joe, if he could. She wondered where Rand had gone and what he would do now—and what version of the fight he would give if he had the chance. If he was smart, he wouldn't talk to anyone. He'd leave the territory and never look back.

"Things just got out of hand, that's all," she offered by way of explanation, then wondered why she was even bothering to try and explain Rand's violent behavior. He didn't deserve to be protected from the consequences of his actions—but then he hadn't deserved her treachery either. She supposed that what she had done to him, on their wedding day, no less, had been enough to incite him to boundless rage, and in his rage, he had behaved abnormally. She couldn't quite forgive him, but neither could she condemn him—especially since she herself bore a healthy share of the responsibility for what had occurred.

"How's yer Pa, Maggie?" Gusty belatedly inquired. "He must be doin' better or you wouldn't be here—right?"

Maggie had forgotten that the men didn't know yet that her father had died. They had left right before it happened. "No, Gusty. I'm sorry. He's not doing better; he died a short while ago, just before I left."

"He died! Why, I cain't b'lieve it, God rest his soul." Gusty's composure shattered. Tears welled in the old man's eyes, and the tip of his nose turned bright red. "Well, I'll be hornswoggled. He went jus' like that, did he?"

Maggie nodded. "He had sent me to get the preacher so he could marry Lena, and while Reverend Simpson was fetching his black book, Papa died. It happened very quickly."

"Goddam, Maggie . . . I'm plumb sorry. This is one hell of a day, ain't it? First, Joe gittin' stabbed, then yer Pa dyin' . . . an' who knows if poor Joe will still be alive when we git there?"

"He'll still be alive. He has to be," Maggie murmured, more to herself than Gusty. "Could you drive a little faster, please, Mr. Potts?"

Augustus Potts put his sleek little black mare into a sprightly trot, and they drove around Gusty and Preacher. Still, it was late afternoon by the time they arrived at the high meadow. As soon as the men saw Maggie in the buggy, they rode over to greet her.

"Where's Joe?" She stood up in the buggy to peer ahead toward the spot where she had left him.

Curt Holloway politely tipped his hat to her. "We've searched this whole meadow, Miz Sterlin', but we ain't found 'im. The grass is all soaked with blood where he musta been lyin', but Joe himself ain't here, an' neither is his hoss."

"He *must* be here! He was unconscious when I left him. Why, I was afraid he might die before I could return. Have you searched the surrounding area? Maybe he was trying to get help for himself."

Down at one end of the meadow, the herd of spotted horses was still grazing, but the herd stallion, upset by the commotion of so many people, was trotting up and down and snorting.

"Yes, ma'am, we did," Curt said.

Burt Lyman rode closer and offered his opinion. "We been all over this meadow an' even up inta the nearest mountains. He ain't here, or else he jus' don't wanna be found. You sure it wuz Joe that got hurt an' not Rand? Seems mighty strange they've both disappeared."

"Of course, I'm sure. Didn't Lena tell you?" Maggie repeated her story of how Rand and Joe had been fighting, and she had had to draw her six-shooter to keep Rand from killing Joe. "But Rand wasn't badly hurt," she finished. "The bullet only creased his forehead, and after that, I ordered him to leave. That's why he's not here. I told him never to show his face at the Broken Wheel again. Then after he had gone, I rode back to the ranch to get help for Joe. Joe was the only one in danger of dying; Rand was fine when he left. . . . You don't see *his* body around here, do you?" she demanded, anxious to quell any suspicions regarding Joe.

"We ain't disputin' whut you say, Miz Sterlin'," Curt hastened to assure her. "Hell, you wuz s'posed t' marry Rand t'day, so it only stands t' reason that he musta been at fault for whutever happened, or you wouldn't be so upset with him. We all know Rand's been spoilin' t' fight Joe fer a long time, so I guess we ain't too surprised it finally happened. . . . All we're sayin' is that neither Joe nor Rand is here, an' they didn't leave good enough tracks fer us t' follow. Could be Joe's passed out somewhere, but then it's kinda suprisin' we ain't found his hoss, at least."

"Hell, we ain't no good at followin' tracks anyway," Burt complained. "I mean, this meadow is all marked up with horse tracks goin' every which way. Can't none of us pick out a single set an' say who it b'longs to."

Joe could have picked one out . . . and he could just as easily have hidden his own tracks if he didn't want to be found. That is, if he was conscious and able to ride.

He must have been, Maggie realized. He must have regained consciousness, mounted Loser, and ridden away. His message couldn't be clearer: He had made his choice, and she wasn't to interfere. He wanted to be an Indian, and she would probably never see him again. Even if he managed to survive his wounds, he wouldn't return to the Broken Wheel.

"If Joe's horse isn't here, *he* isn't here. Let's go home," she murmured in defeat. A small sob burst from her throat. "We've got to bury my father who died just a little while ago."

"Yer father's passed on, Miz Sterlin'?" Curt inquired. "I sure am sorry t' hear that."

The faces of all the men who had ridden up to meet her radiated sympathy, shock over what had happened, and that curious acceptance of sudden violence and death with which most cowboys seemed to be born. Suddenly unable to speak, Maggie could only nod.

"Don't you worry none, Miz Sterlin'," Burt Lyman consoled her. "We'll take care of everythin' fer ya'. Ya'll go ahead an' start back t' the ranch house."

"Good idea, gentlemen." Mr. Potts looked greatly relieved. "We'll leave immediately. I don't relish drivin' an unfamiliar trail in the dark."

He turned the buggy around and started to head back the way they had come, when Maggie suddenly spotted a piece of crumpled paper lying in the grass in front of them and about to be trampled beneath the mare's hooves.

"Wait," she pleaded. "Wait a minute, Mister Potts."

"Whoa!" he called to his mare, and after the horse had come to a standstill, Maggie climbed down from the buggy and picked up the piece of paper. It was the main sheet of the deed to Joe's land that he had signed over to her.

"What is it?" Mister Potts asked.

"Nothing important," Maggie answered, but she folded the paper and stuck it in the sleeve of her shirtwaist. It *wasn't* important, she told herself, but still, she would keep it—if for no other reason than to hold onto something Joe had cherished.

Maggie and Mister Potts rode in silence all the way back to the ranch. Maggie's grief and sorrow were too deep for conversation—too deep even for any more tears. She had already shed a bucketful; it seemed that her life was surely over. The worst that could possibly happen had happened. She had lost her father, Rand, and Joe, all in one day. Now there was nothing left to do but bury the dead, try to console Lena . . . and then to get on with her life, whatever was left of it. She couldn't even think about the future at the moment.

The next couple of days passed in a dull haze of activity—greeting people, explaining what had happened, planning the burial, enduring the sympathetic utterances of one person after another. . . . A deputy marshal even rode out from town to investigate the incident. Once again, Maggie had to explain, which she couldn't do without telling the truth about Rand's motives.

However, without a body to provide evidence of a murder or severe assault, the deputy quickly lost interest in the case. "Let me know if either man shows up, Miss Sterling, so I can verify exactly what happened and determine for myself who was at fault."

"I will," Maggie lied, intending to do no such thing. As far as she was concerned, the whole thing was over, and she very much doubted she would see either man again. . . . But, oh how she ached for Joe and wished she knew where he had gone and how he was faring!

Maggie managed to survive those first few days after the

incident, but without Lena, she would not have. Lena made it all possible. From some deep well of strength, the little Mexican woman never faltered as she stood at Maggie's side while her father was buried beside her mother far up on a little hill overlooking the ranch. Afterward, Lena fed everyone her famous tortillas, *frijoles,* and other foods Nathan had loved, and then labored far into the night cleaning up the mess after everyone had left.

Maggie finally had to urge her to quit and go to bed, for it had grown quite late, and Lena had dark circles under her eyes. "Lena, sleep late tomorrow. We've nothing until the afternoon when Mr. Glover comes out from town to read Pa's will. I already know what it says: Pa left you enough money that you will never have to worry where your next meal is coming from. And anyway, you know you'll always have a roof over your head. This is your home as much as mine; I just want you to know that I cherish having you here, and I just hope you won't be too lonely now that Pa's gone. At least, we'll have each other."

Lena paused in the act of wiping off the table in the kitchen yet again. "Oh no, *querida.* I will not be staying here. Now that your Papa is gone, I am going back to Mexico."

"Back to . . . ? Lena, what are you saying? You can't leave the Broken Wheel. Didn't you hear me? This is your home, too. And I . . . I *need* you. Who will help me run the ranch? Who will keep house now that I have so much responsibility resting on my shoulders?"

Lena regarded her sadly. "I do not know, *querida.* If Joe Hart is still alive, perhaps he will come back to help you one day. If he does not, there is still Gusty and Will . . . and you can always hire someone from town to cook and clean for you."

"Joe's not coming back. Not ever, Lena. I . . . I can't tell you why, but I know he isn't. Trust me on this. And in case you're wondering, Rand isn't coming back either. If he did, I'd send him away again. But he won't. No one's even seen him in town. He seems to have disappeared entirely. . . . As for someone else cooking and cleaning, I . . . I couldn't bear to share the house with anyone else. You are my friend, Lena—the only person I love whom I still have left. Surely, you can't abandon me. Why, I don't even know if I can run this ranch yet—or if the men will take orders from me. You *can't* leave, Lena!"

Lena shook her head, her dark eyes glistening. "Forgive me, *querida*. But I have wasted half my life waiting for your Papa to admit his love for me. When he finally did, well, it was too late. There is nothing here for me except memories, some happy, some sad. I want to go home—back to Mexico. I want to see if any of my family is still alive. I . . . I want to make a new life for myself. I have thought it all over, and it is time for me to return to the land of my birth. By now, they will surely have forgiven me for one youthful mistake."

"But Lena! What will I do without you?" The tears Maggie had been suppressing, tears she had refused to shed for the last several days, now erupted. "I can't go on if you leave!"

"Yes, you can, *querida*. I have seen such a strength in you— everyone sees it. You are much stronger than anyone ever thought you were. Why, you can even ride horses now. You never stop to think of your bad leg; you do everything a woman with two good legs could do. . . . No, you do more. And you will learn to run this ranch. No one doubts it—except you yourself, *querida*. You do not need an old bean-eater to help you."

"That's not true! I do need you! I've lost everyone, Lena."

"Then stand on your own two feet, *querida*. You can do it. You are no cripple. Joe Hart could see that; now so can I. So can everyone. Why can't you see it?"

"But I . . . but I . . ."

Maggie swallowed her protests. Lena was right. She wasn't a cripple any longer, and she *would* somehow manage to run the Broken Wheel. She knew what needed to be done as well as anyone. Hadn't she watched her father and Rand all these years? Hadn't she participated to the best of her ability? First, she would hire a few more men—the best riders and ropers she could find. Young men to help Gusty, Will, Curt, and the others. That very night, she would get out the ranch books, where her father had kept track of everything. She had often helped him—recording figures, planning for the future, figuring what prices they could get for their cows. . . .

Rand had had no aptitude for figures and this side of ranch work. But her father had discussed these things with her often. Sometimes, he had even sought her opinion. . . . Yes, she could do it. But to have to attempt it without Lena . . .

"Oh, please, Lena. Won't you reconsider? I . . . I'll miss you too much!"

The older woman burst into tears. "And I'll miss you, *querida*. But surely you can see why I must go? This was never really my home; I only stayed here so many years because of your Papa. I have family in Mexico. Cousins, aunts, nephews, nieces I have not seen in years. With your Papa's money, I will be rich and independent—no burden to my family. Perhaps I can even help them. I *must* return, *querida*. When I left, I . . . I did not do so in the best of circumstances. I hurt people I love. I myself was hurting. I must make things right again, before I die—as your Papa tried to do when it was too late. I don't want it to be too late for me."

Put that way, Lena's arguments made sense, and Maggie knew she couldn't stop her friend from going—but it would be so hard to say goodbye! Now, she would not even have Lena; except for the ranch hands, she was truly alone. And she was not as close to any of them as she had been to the people she had just lost. What she needed just to survive was . . . the heart of a stallion. But that was the *last* thing she could ever have. So she embraced her friend and prepared herself for yet another dismal leave-taking.

Lena departed, the fall round-up came and went, and somehow Maggie endured. The men were wonderful—working long hours, offering suggestions at her request, and helping to make certain everything was done properly. Without Lena, the food was not as good, but no one complained, and Curt Holloway began to emerge as a leader. Maggie asked him to be trail boss, a position akin to foreman, but he never ordered anybody around, as Rand had done. Instead, he won the men's respect by asking politely and thanking profusely. He was never afraid to admit when he was wrong or uncertain about the best way of dealing with a potential problem. For the most part, his decisions were excellent, and he learned fast.

Maggie was learning fast, too. Everyday she rode Dusty, for Preacher was getting too old for such strenuous exercise. Gaining confidence in the round pen, she soon graduated to riding all around the ranch and then further out onto the range. Day by day, her leg grew stronger, and she relished the long hours in the saddle. It was an achingly beautiful autumn, with brilliant blue skies, splendidly colored foliage, warm days, and chilly nights. At least once a week, she visited her father's grave and talked things over with him as if he were still alive and able to hear her. Somehow, just by articulating her problems and accomplishments, she felt better about everything.

On one such visit, she was startled to see a wagon parked out of sight from the grave around the side of the hill. In it sat the lone figure of a woman, her face hidden by a bonnet as she sat patiently waiting for someone or something. As Maggie continued around the side of the hill, she spotted another figure. Beside her father's grave stood a man respectfully holding his Stetson and gazing down at the headstone Maggie had placed there, next to the headstone of her mother.

For a moment, her heart leapt in anticipation and eagerness, but then, riding closer, she recognized Rand. So absorbed was he in his own thoughts that she rode right up to him before he noticed her. He looked up suddenly, and a dark flush spread across his tanned face.

"Maggie! What're you doin' up here?" His gaze swept her and Dusty, registering surprise at the fact that she was riding so confidently, and as well as anyone else on the ranch.

"Yes," she said, in answer to the question he hadn't asked. "I ride everywhere now. And I'm running the ranch by myself. Since my father died, I've learned to do all kinds of things . . . but that's enough about me. What about you, Rand? What are *you* doing up here? I thought you had gone someplace far away. No one's seen or heard anything about you."

"I been at a . . . a friend's," he said in a low voice. "When I left you that day—the day I fought Joe—I went to a friend's house. It was the only place I could think of to hole up until I found out if Joe was dead or not."

"A lady friend's? Is that her in the wagon on the other side of the hill?" Maggie jerked her head in the direction of the vehicle which was out of sight—and probably out of hearing—from them.

Rand lifted his head, his manner almost belligerent. "That's her, and you know her. She's Victoria Gottling, from the Lazy G."

"Victoria!" Indeed, Maggie did know her. She was the young woman who had long had her eye on Rand. Victoria had come to her father's funeral, and—Maggie now recalled—asked all sorts of intrusive questions. "You've been at the Lazy G all this time?"

"I didn't have no place else to go. Victoria was always sweet on me, so I thought I'd go there fer a spell. She welcomed me with open arms," he smugly added. "Then she hid me in a line shack 'til we could figure out what t' do next."

"So—what is it you're going to do?"

"We're runnin' away t' git married. I figure we'll take up ranchin' someplace in Oregon or Californy. I got some money saved, and so does she. She got it from her Grandma Gottling who died and left it to her in a gunny bag."

"Well . . . I'm glad to hear that you've found someone else to love, Rand—and that she loves you. But you don't have to leave the territory, you know. Joe's disappeared, so there's no proof that you tried to kill him. Except for my word. As long as you stay away from the Broken Wheel, I'm willing to let the matter drop."

"I'm leavin' anyway. I got no stomach t' stay in this territory now. All I wanted was t' visit Nathan's grave an' say g'bye t' him b'fore I went." His gaze returned to the headstone, and Maggie read genuine sorrow on his sullen features. Her compassion stirred. No matter what he'd done, she couldn't hate Rand. Her feelings for him were much like that of a sister toward an exasperating brother.

"Pa asked for you before he died, Rand. He cared for you a great deal."

"I s'pose you blamed everythin' on me," he growled. "You probably told him it was all my fault."

"And I suppose you've told Victoria and whoever else you've confided in that Joe's an Indian, and therefore it was all *his* fault."

"Hell, no. I ain't told another livin' soul that Joe's an Injun. You think I want folks t' know that you threw me aside 'cause of a *redskin?* I got more pride than that, Maggie. Whut happened to him, anyway? I thought he'd be livin' in yer house by now, sleepin' in yer bed, and runnin' the Broken Wheel."

"You thought wrong. I told you then that Joe had decided to return to his Indian ways. That was the truth. He disappeared the day you two fought, and I haven't seen him since."

Rand glanced away from her, his eyes troubled. "You reckon I really did kill 'im? That he died somewhere up in the mountains where he musta gone?"

"I . . . I think I would know it if he were dead. But I can't be sure, Rand. Wherever he is, he, too, is gone for good. I don't expect him to ever return."

Rand's gaze came back to her. "I'm sorry, Maggie. I . . . I've thought a lot about whut I did—an' how I acted. It scares me t' think I could've done somethin' like that. I . . . lost control, y' know? I don't know whut got inta me. I only know I don't wanna feel such hatred ever again. I don't wanna let go like that again. Victoria . . . she's made me see . . . she's helped me t' understand. . . . Hell! There's no way t' explain it."

"You don't have to explain, Rand. I know what you're trying to say. We've all . . . grown . . . because of this. Joe helped me to understand that prejudice and hatred are wrong. Lena helped Nathan to understand it. Now, Victoria's helping you. Do you know that my father asked Lena to marry him just before he died?"

"I'll be doggone. Ya' mean it? He married the l'il bean-eater?"

"No, he never had the chance. He died before he could do it. But he made Lena very happy just by asking her. She's not here anymore either. She left the Broken Wheel and went back to Mexico.

"So yer all alone, huh?" Rand's mouth had a rueful slant.

Maggie nodded. "But I don't mind. I love running the ranch, and the boys are all helping me. I'm . . . content, Rand."

"Well, that's good, Maggie. That's real good." He cleared his throat and jammed his hat back on his head. "Guess I better be gittin' back t' Victoria now, or she'll be wonderin' whut's keepin' me."

"I guess you better."

He nodded and walked past her, but Maggie stayed for awhile at her father's grave. She hoped he knew that Rand had come to pay his respects and was going to try to be a better man from now on. She was glad she had seen him again. Now the only thing left unfinished in her life was the matter of Joe.

The good weather held until just after Thanksgiving, when cold winds brought the first breath of winter and two days of sleet. On the first nice day after the surprise storm, Maggie drove into town to stock up on supplies. At Magruder's Mercantile, she overheard some disturbing news. Two women were discussing the situation at Lapwai, and the shop owner's wife, Martha Magruder, was saying: "Yep, it looks like it's gonna be a cold hard winter fer them Injuns. Guess they didn't get their government allotments in time this year—and they ain't got no blankets, warm clothes, or much in the way of food supplies. Now that cold weather's set in, they likely won't git 'em 'til spring. Y' know how it is with the government."

Maggie's ears pricked at the mention of Lapwai and Indians, and she unashamedly strolled closer to eavesdrop.

"Well, I don't feel a bit sorry for them murderin' scoundrels," one of the women—sour-faced Mrs. Cleaver—responded. "If they're sufferin', it's only 'cuz they deserve it—considerin' all they've done in the past."

"I agree, Letty," the second woman chimed in. "They sure ain't learned nothin' in all the years of their captivity. Why, if they farmed and made ready for winter like white folks, they wouldn't be in this predicament. I don't see why the government should have to be lookin' after 'em anyway. Let 'em shift fer themselves like we hafta do."

"At least if a few of them starve this winter, there won't be so many at Lapwai." Martha Magruder shivered in a delicate, exaggerated manner. "Personally, I'd sleep better at night if there weren't any more Injuns in the entire state of Idaho."

Maggie had heard enough. She couldn't believe that these women—none of whom had ever missed a meal in their lives—could be so hard-hearted. Limping over to them, she made no effort to conceal her dismay and anger.

"There are women, children, and old people at Lapwai. How can you sleep soundly at night knowing that the innocent are suffering right along with the guilty? Imagine not having enough blankets during that ice storm—and going hungry. Picture your babies crying in misery. What's the matter with you ladies, that you can't feel any compassion for those less fortunate than yourselves?"

Martha Magruder drew herself up tall and fairly bristled with indignation. "Excuse me, Maggie Sterling, but we were havin' a private conversation here. And anyway we were discussin'

Injuns. Have you fergot whut Injuns have done to folks around here—includin' yer own family?"

"No, I haven't forgotten," Maggie said. "But we're also discussing human beings. Just how much of the reservation land is fit for farming? Do they have the proper tools and equipment? And if farming isn't possible, how much land is good for grazing? Are the Indians permitted horses and cattle? Are they even allowed to become ranchers?"

"Ranchers! You mean like us—and like your father, God rest his soul?" Mrs. Cleaver asked in a shocked tone.

"Why not?" Maggie demanded. "How can they provide for themselves if they aren't permitted to do what we do—and if they have to stay on the reservation all of the time? As you well know, much of the land around here is suitable only for mining or ranching. Just how do we expect them to survive—or don't we? Maybe this oversight of the government is deliberate. Maybe the Indians *never* receive their allotments on time."

"Well, I certainly never expected to hear *you* defendin' Injuns, Maggie! Why, if yer poor Pa could hear you, he'd be spinnin' in his grave." Martha Magruder folded her arms across her flat bosom and glared at Maggie. She was a tall, angular woman with a prim mouth and a perpetually sour expression—much like Mrs. Cleaver.

"Maybe Maggie's right," the second woman, Effie Lathrop, opined. "I certainly don't like to think of little children goin' cold and hungry."

"Little children grow up to be adults, Effie—and it's the adults we don't need around here," Mrs. Cleaver sniffed.

Maggie decided not to waste any more time. Inspiration had suddenly struck, and she was eager to put her thought into action. "Martha, do you have any blankets for sale?" she asked sweetly.

Martha blinked at the sudden change of subject. "Of course, right over there." She pointed to a pile stacked on a table near the wall.

"I'll take all of them," Maggie told her. "And then I want a half dozen sacks of flour, a keg of dried beef, several sacks of dried beans. . . ."

"What on earth . . . ? What are you up to, Maggie Sterling? That's far more than you usually buy—even at this time of year."

"Could you have your husband fill up a wagon with staples and deliver it to me at the Broken Wheel?"

"Well, yes, but . . ."

"But nothing. Just do it, Martha, and have him bring me the bill. I'll pay it immediately."

"You ain't fixin' t' take all that stuff over t' Lapwai, are you?"

"That's *my* business, isn't it? I believe I can do whatever I want with it. However, if you ladies have any donations you'd like to make to assist the starving Indians, I'd be happy to see that they get them."

"Donations! Not me . . ." Martha Magruder and Mrs. Cleaver jointly declared.

But little Effie Lathrop said: "I . . . I might have some old clothes that my kids have outgrowed, Maggie. Do you think the Injun children could use those?"

"I'm sure they could," Maggie said. "When I finish my shopping, I'll stop by your house on my way out of town and collect them."

"Effie!" Martha hissed. "How could you?"

Effie squared her slender shoulders and looked her friends straight in the eye. "Them clothes are well-patched, and some even have holes in 'em—but if they can help keep little bodies warm this winter, why, I'm happy to part with 'em."

"Thank you, Effie," Maggie sang out, and for the first time in a long time, she actually felt happy.

Maggie spent the rest of the day gathering items she thought the Indians could use. It was a daring, difficult task going house to house and business to business, asking for donations to help the Indians survive the winter. Some people were greatly offended and threatened to toss Maggie off their properties, but others thought for a few moments, frowned, wrestled with their consciences and came up with old clothing, a much-mended harness, a bushel of dried apples, or some other such thing.

Maggie was delighted with the response and got to know more about her town neighbors in that single afternoon than she had known in her entire life up until now. She made enemies, but she also made friends, such as tiny, petite, blond Elsie Whitcomb, who exclaimed: "I think it's just wonderful what you're doin', Maggie. I'm fairly new to these parts so I don't remember all the troubles folks had with the Indians, but I say it's time t' bury the hatchet, so to speak, and learn t' get along t'gether like good Christians should. Most of those Indians at Lapwai have been converted, haven't they? So why *shouldn't* we give them an example of what religion is all about? Neighbors helpin' neighbors in time of need is a good place t' start."

Maggie invited Elsie to come for a visit sometime soon and returned home with a warm feeling in her heart and a sense of burgeoning anticipation. She would drive the wagon loaded with supplies over to Lapwai in time for Christmas—on the first available day of fine weather. While she was there, she would inquire after Joe. At least, she hoped to satisfy herself that he was still alive. Knowing that much would ease her mind considerably.

Then maybe she could devote herself whole-heartedly to running the ranch. She could live her life without regrets, without wondering, without dwelling on the tiny spark of hope that occasionally flared up within her. She could be *content,* as she had told Rand that she was. She just wanted to know if he was alive and well. That was all. Then she would force herself to forget him.

Twenty-two

Less than a week before Christmas, Maggie set out for Lapwai with her wagonload of supplies, drawn by Preacher and Nip, the other old gelding occasionally used for driving. Nip did not pull well by himself, but he could do the job with a buddy, and Preacher couldn't manage such a load by himself.

It was a beautiful frosty morning with the sun shining brightly. The frost soon melted, leaving the land new-washed and somber in its varying hues of brown, tan, and ocher.

It took several hours to get to Lapwai, plenty of time for Maggie to prepare herself to see Joe again, if indeed he had gone to the reservation as he had said he would. Nevertheless, when she finally drove onto reservation land, she realized how slim was the possibility that she would encounter him. Indeed, she saw no one. Not a soul was in sight.

Lapwai, which meant "place of the butterflies," was located on the Clearwater River about twelve miles from the river's confluence with the Snake River at Lewiston. A small stream flowed into the river here, and bare brown hills surrounded it. A scattering of log houses in the Lapwai valley beckoned to Maggie, and she set out for them.

Halfway there, she met a young woman also driving a wagon—this one empty. Maggie exchanged greetings with her, and they stopped to talk. The red-haired, brown-eyed young woman turned out to be a missionary who worked with Indian youth, trying to introduce them to reading, writing, and religion . . . not necessarily in that order, she laughingly explained.

When Maggie asked her name, she said: "Well, it isn't Spalding," which Maggie knew was the name of the first missionaries who had tried to convert the Indians long ago. "Just call me, Anna," the girl said with a broad smile. "And you are Miss or Mrs. . . . ?"

"Oh, I'm not married!" Maggie exclaimed. "Please call me Maggie."

"All right, I will."

Anna was delighted to learn that Maggie was bringing supplies, although she cautioned that the Indians might be unwilling to accept them. "They're a proud people no matter what anyone says about 'em being lazy or slovenly. I've seen no proof of those accusations. However, they're desperately poor and possess little in the way of the white man's comforts, and this, as you probably know, is rather harsh terrain. They live scattered across it in their own rude shelters, and all they seem to want is to live their own lives in their own way. Unfortunately, the old ways are forbidden to them, and without basic necessities—and a helping hand now and then, they find it difficult to survive."

"I hope they will accept what I've brought," Maggie said. "It isn't much, but it may help them survive the winter. . . . By the way, do you happen to know of an Indian named Heart-of-the-Stallion?"

Anna shook her head. "No, that name is unfamiliar to me. Does he have a white name?"

Maggie hesitated, then blurted: "Joe. His name is Joe."

"There are many Indians who took the name of Joseph," Anna pointed out. "Can you describe him?"

Maggie did her best to describe Joe without mentioning his eye color. She was reluctant to say too much, for fear of exposing him if he had decided *not* to reclaim his heritage after all.

"I'm sorry, but I can't help you," Anna apologized. "You should speak with old Charlie. He knows everyone. He and his grandson just happen to be here today. They live quite a way from here, in a lonely little cabin in the hills, but they came down to the valley a few days ago in the hope of receiving their government allotments. Come with me, and I'll find them for you. Sad to say, the allotments still haven't arrived, and I don't think they're coming—so your supplies are badly needed. If folks will just accept them . . ."

Anna turned her team around and drove ahead of Maggie toward the log houses. It was so quiet. There were not even any barking dogs—and no sign whatever of Indians. As they drew closer to the cluster of buildings, a single young boy stepped out from a doorway and silently watched them approach.

Anna called out a greeting to him in a language Maggie surmised was Nez Perce. "That's Matthew," she explained to Maggie. "I sent him inside to fetch his grandfather."

"Matthew," Maggie repeated. "I once had an uncle named Matthew." She did not add that he had been killed by Indians. She noticed that the boy wore moccasins, not shoes, and was ill-clad to face anything but warm weather. She herself had dressed in heavy clothing in case an unexpected storm swept out of the mountains. Matthew appeared to be the size of the garments donated by Effie Lathrop, and Maggie hoped they would fit him.

Matthew raced inside the house and returned a few moments later leading an old Indian with long white hair secured by a faded bandanna around his forehead. Maggie's first thought was that he must be blind, for a milky white film covered both eyes. But then, he raised his head and looked at her, peering through the film, and she realized he could still see a little.

"Ask him whatever you'd like," Anna invited, still sitting in her empty wagon. "I'll translate for you. He speaks a little English, but there will be less chance for misunderstanding if we use his native language, instead of ours. Besides, I need to practice my Sahaptin dialect."

"All right," Maggie agreed. She boldly inquired if he knew of an Indian named Heart-of-the-Stallion.

Upon Anna's translation, the old man looked surprised and then conceded that he might. Why did she want to know about him?

Maggie was in a quandary. She feared saying too much, but if she said too little, she would never learn anything. "I . . . I had heard that he was hurt—wounded in a . . . a fight. I just want to know if he is all right."

Anna translated, the old Indian responded, and Anna said: "He says he still lives—this Indian who was hurt."

"Is he here on the reservation? C-can I see him?" Maggie was so excited, she stammered the requests. She had no idea what she would say to Joe if she saw him, but she wanted to reassure herself that he had actually recovered from his wounds.

The old Indian answered, and Anna translated. "He's not here. He's somewhere up in the hills. Still recovering, I gather. It's amazing I haven't heard of him. I've made it my business to try to get to know as many of the Indians as I can. Of course, some of them avoid the missionaries; they don't *want* to be educated. They still think that one day Chief Joseph will win permission to take the Nez Perce back to the Wallowa Valley in Oregon. It will never happen, but they won't give up the notion. They just keep hoping."

"Will you ask him if Heart-of-the-Stallion is happy now?" Maggie had to know if Joe had at last found peace of mind here among his own people. She only realized what an odd question it was, when Anna's brows lifted in surprise. Before the young woman could even ask the question, old Charlie answered it.

"No. Not happy," he said, lifting his head and directing his milky-eyed gaze straight at Maggie. He then lapsed into his own tongue and spoke at length for several moments.

"Charlie says this Heart-of-the-Stallion is very confused. Very sad and worried. Like a half-blind man trying to find his way in the dark. He does not know his rightful path in life and must keep praying he will somehow stumble across it," Anna explained. "I just hope he's praying to the right God, the one we've been trying to teach the Indians about. If he is, he'll realize soon enough that brooding will avail him nothing. He should take up farming instead."

"Farming?" Maggie glanced around at the barren hills, where there was little space for proper cultivation and small chance of success if one did try to grow things. She did not know whether to be glad or depressed by the news that Joe was up in the hills, brooding. "Will I ever see him again?" She was unable to keep herself from asking the question.

This time, Anna gave her a sidelong glance, as if wondering why she would want to see this man. Still, she translated, and the old man sighed in response. "Charlie says he doesn't know. Heart-of-the-Stallion must find his own way to live in the world. When he is ready, he will come out of the hills and tell his friends what he has decided. . . . That's not really an answer, is it? How did you ever manage to meet this Indian in the first place? I don't recall you visiting the reservation before today."

"I . . . I've been here before," Maggie lied. "Not often, but a few times. I'm finished now. That's all I wanted to ask the old man."

"This Heart-of-the-Stallion . . . you said he was wounded in a fight. When and where did that happen? Fighting is forbidden on the reservation."

"It wasn't his fault," Maggie insisted, fearing she had said too much. "Anyway, it happened some time ago, and I've learned what I wanted to know. Now, we must see about distributing the supplies I brought."

"Oh, yes, the supplies! We'll take them to my husband who will see that they are divided equally. . . ."

"Wait. Ask the boy—Matthew—if he wants some warm clothing first. It's right on top here in my wagon. We won't have to unload to get to it."

Anna made the inquiry, but Matthew stiffened and shook his head in a violent manner. "I think we can take that as a no," Anna told Maggie. She smiled sadly. "I believe he wants nothing from white people except his freedom to leave the reservation and go wherever he wishes, and that he can't have."

Maggie studied the young boy who very much reminded her of Joe. His eyes were black, not silver, and his hair was darker, without Joe's reddish glints, but he possessed the same lithe grace, arrogant posture, and unbending pride. He returned her gaze with the same hostile, slightly wary, doubting expression Joe had worn in the early days of their acquaintance.

It wrenched Maggie's heart just to look at him. "Tell him I will leave the clothing here anyway, in case he changes his mind."

Anna nodded. "A good idea. He may not be so proud when the snow is up to his knees."

Yes, he will be, Maggie thought. *If he's anything like Joe, he'll stubbornly refuse even when he's freezing to death.*

Joe had given up more than a warm shirt and pair of trousers for the sake of being Indian. Where was he now? Up in the hills, the old man had said, trying to decide what to do with his life. Had he finally realized that the Indians' situation was hopeless? One would need to own far more than eighty acres of land in this region in order to prosper at farming or ranching—and from what little Maggie could see, not much of either was being done on the reservation. Even the Broken Wheel had to depend on the open range to support its cattle, and the soil and rainfall here obviously would not support farming.

She sighed deeply. *Oh, Joe! You've made a big mistake, but will you ever realize it? And if you do, is it too late to change your mind?*

She feared it was, and as she had promised herself, she must forget him. As soon as her wagon was unloaded, she left Lapwai and returned to the ranch.

Christmas passed quietly, snow buried the Broken Wheel in pristine whiteness, and the lonely winter slowly slipped by. In early spring, before anything budded, Maggie heard that the small ranch next door was for sale. Her nearest neighbors had given up on wresting a living from the harsh landscape and gone to California.

Maggie visited a banker in town, raided her precious financial reserves, and bought the place for no other reason than that it abutted Joe's land. It also gave the Broken Wheel additional grazing land, a portion of which could be planted in hay, but she counted the second reason as less important than the first. It was land Joe himself should have bought to extend his own holdings, and for some reason, she wanted no one else to own it but herself.

In mid-April, Maggie received a letter from Lena saying that she had met a Mexican rancher, they had fallen in love, and were soon going to wed. The news brightened Maggie's dismal spirits and gave her the impetus to cast off her gloom and ride up to the meadow to check on her horses.

Three days of rain prevented her from doing it immediately, but at last, the sun came out, the air shimmered with golden warmth, and Maggie felt it was time. Today, she would saddle Dusty, ride up to the high meadow, and greet her new foals. Perhaps in the high country, she could finally accept the idea that she was never going to see Joe Hart again.

As Maggie rode up to the meadow, she knew a contentment and peace she had not experienced in a long, long time. It was as if she were coming home, for aside from its being the location of the fight between Joe and Rand, the meadow recalled hours of happiness, escape from problems and responsibilities, and a simpler time in her life, when the only thing she had to worry about was the well-being of her precious Appaloosas.

Today, she felt much as she had a year ago, when she was still a sheltered, pampered young woman, taking pleasure in stealing an afternoon of sunlight, blue skies, and the company of her horses. A year ago, she had been looking forward to marriage—though dreading it too, she now conceded—and she had been assuming that her father would live forever, and someone would always take care of her.

Now, she was a woman, no longer dependent on others to

make her decisions for her, and indeed, others now depended upon her. She had left instructions for the day's work with Curt, told him where she was going, and then saddled Dusty and ridden off alone as she would never—could never—have done exactly one year ago. She had grown up, matured, blossomed . . . but no one she truly cared about was there to appreciate her transformation. Ah, well . . .

Suddenly unbearably eager to see the herd, she urged Dusty into a canter. The warm wind loosened her hair so that it streamed out behind her like a banner, and she reveled in the sense of freedom and flight as Dusty carried her far and fast. With a sharp stab of nostalgia, she remembered her first gallop held tightly in Joe's arms. . . . What she wouldn't give to feel those arms around her again!

Only now she didn't need him to keep her from falling off the horse; she had grown secure and confident in the saddle. Her leg would never be normal but it no longer kept her from doing anything she wanted to do. If she chose to ride like the wind, she could. She let Dusty out for a short gallop and savored every moment of it, then slowed him to a trot as she approached the meadow and the herd.

Sensing he was near the place of his birth, Dusty gave a joyous nicker, which several of the mares answered. However, Maggie carefully dismounted some distance away from the main body of the herd. She did not trust the herd stallion not to challenge her younger horse, even though Dusty was now a gelding, and therefore no real threat to the stallion's supremacy. Dusty still had no manners where other horses were concerned; plowing into the middle of whatever bunch he encountered, he usually earned himself a few kicks and bites before he figured out that his place was at the bottom of the pecking order.

Maggie removed his bridle, slipped on the halter she had brought in her saddlebags, and tied him securely to a tree, leaving only enough rope for the colt to graze while he waited for her return. Distracted by the new green shoots of grass, Dusty promptly forgot his excitement at being back in the meadow.

But Maggie maintained hers. She walked slowly toward the grazing horses, her eyes eagerly searching for the new foals. Three of them were prancing about on their spindly legs, and last year's foals, yearlings now, were so big she hardly recognized them, except for their markings. Then she froze—staring—at a horse she was sure she had never seen before.

It was a young Appaloosa mare, thin but with pretty markings in a loud leopard pattern. Quickly, she scanned the herd for other strange horses, for it suddenly occurred to her that there were too many for the small bunch she normally kept here. *Yes, there was another new one!* And another and another—all young mares—each a particularly fine specimen of the breed.

They all shared the common trait of being thin, as if they had traveled a far distance to get here. Quite proud of his new additions, the herd stallion trotted up to one and nosed her flank as Maggie watched. The mare squealed and kicked at him, but Maggie knew that this was just a preliminary rejection. In time, perhaps by next year, another foal would be running about and playing in the meadow.

Where had the four new horses come from—and who had brought them? Her eyes traveled to the high ridge overlooking the meadow, to the very spot where she had first seen Joe. She blinked rapidly several times, sure that her imagination and memory were playing tricks on her. Because she so much wanted to see him, *Joe was there.*

Motionless as a statue, man and horse stood silhouetted against the sky, and it was so very nearly the exact same stance, the exact same clothing even—Stetson, vest, spurs, and so on— that Maggie was sure she must be mistaken. She stared at the apparition for a full minute, and then it moved. The man lifted his hand and brushed the brim of his hat in that old familiar gesture that only Joe Hart knew how to do. Then, with invisible signals, he turned his horse and began riding slowly out of sight down the ridge.

Maggie just stood there, unmoving, her heart pumping madly

inside her chest. This couldn't be an apparition; Joe was real, and he was here, dressed as a white man . . . and oh, she looked a sight! Her hair was all windblown and disheveled, she was wearing her oldest, shabbiest shirtwaist over a patched, faded skirt she had altered just for riding.

She smoothed down her hair and garments. Bit her lips and pinched her cheeks. Knowing that nothing would help much at this point, she gave up trying to primp and simply waited for him to appear in the meadow. A few moments later, he did.

He rode straight up to her, swung down from Loser, and without saying a word, took her into his arms. Returning the embrace, Maggie reveled in the sight, feel, and leathery scent of him. So much needed to be said. So much to be explained, but for now, all that mattered was to hold him and be held by him. He was whole and alive, looking older perhaps, the lines in his face a little deeper, but he was here . . . and for the moment, he was her's.

At long last, he drew back and studied her face, his silver-gray eyes hungrily consuming her. "You are more beautiful than I remembered . . . ," he murmured huskily.

She laughed. "I'm not beautiful; you are!" She lifted her hand to remove his Stetson so the sun shone full on the chiseled planes of his face and revealed the red glints in his dark hair. "You look well," she whispered. "Better than *I* remember."

"I am well," he agreed. "Better, perhaps, than I have ever been in my life. Rand may have done me a favor carving me up the way he did; I was a long time recovering during which I had nothing to do but think."

"Tell me about it, Joe. Where have you been? Why are you here?"

"Didn't you notice the new horses?" He nodded toward the herd.

"Of course, I did. Four beautiful young mares. I'll ask you later where you found them; for now, I want to know why you brought them here."

"I brought them for your father. They are a gift. I know he

does not value them as you and I do, but I thought they would be an appropriate bride price."

Her heart hammered even louder than it had already been doing. "Bride price? What do you mean?"

He took her hand and squeezed it tightly against his chest. "Maggie, I heard that you were still unmarried, which gave me hope I might still have a chance with you. Therefore, in the time-honored fashion of many Indian tribes, I have brought horses to your father. That's what an Indian brave does when he wants to marry a beautiful maiden; he brings horses to her father. I want both of you to accept me for what I am—an Indian, even if no one else ever knows my secret."

His words thrilled her, though his timing left much to be desired. "My father is dead, Joe. He died the same day you and Rand fought, and you disappeared. But before he died, he . . . he said I should convince you to live as a white man and to help your people from outside the reservation, not on it. . . . Your coming here like this, dressed as a white man; does it mean you have changed your mind about claiming your Indian heritage?"

Joe drew her to him and rested his chin on top of her head. "Oh, Maggie, I've been so blind. But I didn't know it, until I lay near death and was forced to think long and hard about my life and all I have and have not accomplished."

"It seems you and my father went through very nearly the same process—only he did not survive to benefit from the experience. He did try to right some wrongs before he died, but his wisdom came too late, and he was unable to act on it."

"You do not know how I prayed to *Hanyawat* that it was not too late for me, Maggie. . . . I have been wrong about so many things. I was wrong, and you were right."

"Start at the beginning," she urged. "Tell me where you went when you left here. You were unconscious, when I last saw you. I ordered Rand to leave the Broken Wheel, and after he did so, I rode back to the ranch to get help but couldn't return as soon as I had intended because my father was dying. As soon as he died, I came back here, but by then, you were gone. The men searched everywhere and couldn't find you. . . ."

Joe sighed and gazed off into the distance, his eyes clouded with remembrance. "Loser took me up into the mountains where I lay in a fever for several days. During one of my brief bouts of consciousness, I was able to find herbs and make a poultice for my chest wound. Finally, I realized that if I didn't get help, I was going to die. I figured I was dying anyway, and I wanted to do it on my own land. So I rode there, where I collapsed from weakness, blood loss, and hunger. Man-Who-Dreams and Red Fox found me. They are the two Indians, the old man and the boy, I told you about. I had first met Red Fox hunting on my land. Hoping to see me or at least to leave a sign of their presence, they had gone there again to let me know they were all right after being locked up for a time on the reservation as punishment for leaving it."

"The old man and the boy," Maggie interrupted. "What are their white names?"

"Charlie is the old man and Matthew the boy."

"I met them. I went to the reservation and asked the old man if he knew you. He told me you were up in the hills. I couldn't question him further because one of the missionaries was with me."

"I know. It was Man-Who-Dreams—Charlie—who told me that a pretty unmarried lady named Maggie brought a wagon-load of supplies to help the Indians through the winter. Thank you for that, Maggie. Had you not done what you did, the Nez Perce would have starved. Some did not survive as it was, for the government allotments never did arrive."

"I'm so sorry to hear that. But go on, please! Tell me what happened next."

"Man-Who-Dreams and Red Fox took me back to the reservation and hid me in their little shack. They cauterized my worst wound, cleaned and stitched up some of the lesser ones, and nursed me back to health. The one thing they would not do was allow me to surrender myself to the authorities."

"The authorities never knew you were there? No one ever discovered it?"

"Oh, some of the Indians knew, but the whites never found out. Their greatest concern is keeping Indians from leaving the reservation, not preventing new ones from entering. Man-Who-Dreams and his grandson have their own little shack up in the hills, and as long as they appear for the occasional counting of heads, no one bothers them. The trouble is they never know when a head count will be done, and then, they had better be there."

"You stayed the winter with them?"

Joe shook his head. "No, as soon as I was able, I left and returned to the mountains. I needed time alone—to think, pray, and meditate. I spent much of the time not far from here, for this meadow is a good place to pass the winter. I figured if the horses could survive here all year and bear their young even during the cold months, a man could do so, too. I built myself a small shelter and lived off the land, hunting small game and fishing through the ice on the river."

"Oh, Joe!" Maggie thought of him all alone during the winter and could not imagine how he had survived. But he had— Oh, thank God, he had!

Joe grinned—that dazzling grin that lit up his face and eyes with a warm radiance. "It was a . . . a time of learning and . . . and reflection. A good time. A hard time. I truly had to live as my ancestors did. And do you know what? I found that I missed certain things I had known in the white world: the companionship of the other cowhands—their arguments and endless augurin'. I missed hot coffee simmering on the stove—and biscuits, beans, and bacon. I missed having a real roof over my head. Luckily, I had my soogan, and some of my clothes and other belongings, which I had kept up here for line riding, but I missed books, newspapers, card-playing, and lots of other things like that. Most of all, I missed you, Maggie. . . . I would dream of you at night and wake up hearing your name on my lips. You were the only thing that kept me sane. For your sake,

I stayed alive, though sometimes I despaired and wanted to die."

"Oh, Joe . . ." Tears filled her eyes at the thought of what he had endured, the inner struggle as well as the fight for mere survival. Her own loneliness and bouts of sorrow and depression were nothing in comparison. "I dreamed of you, too," she shyly confided. "And I kept wondering where you were, what you were doing, and if you had finally found peace and happiness. . . ."

"What I found is that I don't want to live life without you, Maggie. And I don't want to stay on a reservation, growing older and more bitter with each passing year. . . . I want to help my people, yes, but I don't want to see my children suffer or go hungry. I guess I'm not as . . . as idealistic and committed as I thought I was."

"Is suffering the only way to be committed to a cause? To prove to yourself that you care, Joe? I don't think so."

His grin flashed again. "Man-Who-Dreams said very nearly the same thing to me. When suffering comes unsought, the man who endures it bravely is called courageous. But to seek suffering for its own sake—to *prove* one's courage or dedication—is only a form of self-conceit, especially if it benefits no one. *Hanyawat* gave us this beautiful earth to enjoy and put upon it all that man needs to survive and prosper. Indian or white, we share this land together. I must find a way to live in *both* worlds, Maggie. The reservation land can be made more fruitful—just as land in other places can be coaxed to yield more sustenance. White men are doing it all over the state of Idaho; why can't Indians?"

Maggie suddenly remembered something she had been reading in a newspaper just the other day. In Moscow, a mining town not far from the Broken Wheel, a university had been founded several years previously. Now flourishing, it was conducting studies to improve farming methods in the region and discover which crops grew best locally. Just south of Moscow, for example, along the Palouse River, were meadows filled with camas bulbs which the Indians had long harvested. The soil there was said to be a hundred feet deep and was called Hog Heaven. Other areas were less blessed, but researchers believed they could be made more productive through better utilization of existing water sources, such as the rivers and the run-off from the mountain snows.

Perhaps Joe would be interested in finding out what was happening right there at the university. Maggie said as much, briefly explaining what she had read, and Joe looked thoughtful, then began to grow excited.

"Do you mean I could go to this special white man's school and . . . and they would teach me things that could perhaps benefit the Nez Perce?"

"Why not?" Maggie questioned. "The idea's certainly worth considering. We need to keep discovering new ways to better run the Broken Wheel, too. And to make *your* ranch profitable. I still have the deed to your land, Joe—and I bought the small ranch in-between. Between us, we now have plenty of land, but there's only so much of it to go around. The days of the open range are ending, and more and more people are coming here each year; Moscow is growing, and so is Lewiston. The mountains are being mined, the forests cut, and . . ."

"Mother Earth is slowly being destroyed." Joe's eyes darkened, and the radiance faded from his face. "The Nez Perce never cut the forests nor raped the mountains nor destroyed the wild herds of animals who once roamed these lands. Only white ranchers, miners, and farmers do these things."

"I know," Maggie said. "So perhaps Heart-of-the-Stallion will have something to teach the teachers at the university, too."

The fire rekindled in Joe's eyes. "Perhaps . . ." he whispered.

Maggie linked her arm in his. "Now, tell me where you found those four lovely mares. . . ."

The corners of Joe's mouth twitched. "I didn't find them; they found me."

"I don't believe you. Oh, there might be a few around here

still, but . . ." She paused and studied him with growing suspicion. "Usually, when people come across Appaloosas roaming wild, they sell them to Wild West Shows or as curiosities to people back east, as I sometimes do with my babies. Where *did* you get these horses, Joe?"

"All right, Maggie, I'll tell you, for there must be no more secrets between us ever again. I stole them from a couple of men who were taking them back East. Only it wasn't really stealing, was it? Since *my* people owned them before *they* did. I was just reclaiming them."

"But Joe! What if someone saw you? What if they come after you and find the horses here?"

"They won't, Maggie. Trust me to have done the job properly. The mares were with a herd of mixed-breed horses a couple of wranglers were taking back East to sell. When the men woke up one morning, four were missing—the *best* four for our purposes, the purebred spotted ones, those who will cross well with Loser or your stallion. I doubt they will be missed, since they're just skinny, pestle-tailed Appaloosas. Now, if I had taken the solid-colored ones, that *would* have been stealing, and the men might have been angry. As it is, they probably just figure the horses wandered off somewhere. . . . Anyway, it was a long way from this meadow. By then, I was deliberately searching for wild horses to capture for your father. I wasn't necessarily looking for spotted ones, but when I saw them. . . . Well, the opportunity was too good to let pass."

"I'm sorry my father isn't here to accept them. Or perhaps he is here—in spirit. He loved this land and never wanted to leave it."

"I don't blame him. I don't want to leave it either. Will you marry me, Maggie? Will you help me raise horses, cattle, and . . . children? Will you also help me find a way to help my people?"

"Of course!" she cried joyously, tossing his Stetson high into the air, then hugging him enthusiastically. "And I'll live anywhere you want to live—on your ranch, on my ranch, in Moscow, Bitterroot, on the reservation, or . . . or wherever. You name the place."

Joe let out a wild Indian war whoop, lifted her up, and spun her around. Such an unfettered display of emotion was so unlike him that she burst out laughing. "Just where do you intend for us to live, Joe Hart?"

"Wherever *you* want," he gallantly offered, setting her down on her own two feet. "Or let's live here in one end of the meadow itself. We can build a new house that no one else has ever lived in before."

Maggie thought of the long cold winters and shivered. Even the prospect of spending the nights in Joe's arms could not banish the specter of how cold and inaccessible the high meadow could be in winter. "Well, perhaps we can live here part of the year, at least."

"That sounds good to me. It can be our own special place— where we can come to be alone, and I can live like an Indian when I feel the need. . . . Maggie, I want to help Red Fox— Matthew—to get an education, too. One day, the Indians will be permitted to leave the reservation. Before that happens, the boy must learn how to survive in the white world. I can teach him. I know from experience that it is not an easy path to walk—but at least, he will have me to show him the way."

"And me," Maggie corrected. "I'll be there walking the path with both of you. We'll all walk it together."

"Maggie, my Maggie . . ." He enfolded her in his warm, strong embrace. "I pray we will not be disappointed in what we hope to accomplish. Whites and Indians may never learn to set aside old wounds and conquer their mutual hatred."

"But I've already made some progress in that direction! Many of the townspeople in Bitterroot donated items that were in that wagonload of supplies I took to the reservation. Of course, some thought it was terrible I was trying to help the Indians—and some of the Indians wouldn't accept my donations—but at least, it was a beginning."

Maggie thought of another problem. "Joe? What will we tell

the ranch hands about what happened that day when you were wounded? They searched this whole area for you. Your disappearance was very mysterious and made them question what really happened up here."

He smiled down at her, and a sly twinkle lit his eyes. "Why don't we tell them I was rescued by an old Indian who took me deeper into the mountains to heal? That would explain our sudden concern for Indians and our desire to help them in return."

Maggie smiled back at him. "Joe Hart, you are positively brilliant, not to mention devious."

"I am also badly in need of a kiss from my future wife. Do you think you can manage to stop talking long enough to give me one?"

"Oh, I can manage more than a kiss, Mister Hart."

She wound her arms around his neck and pressed closer to him, and he uttered a small growling sound and lowered his mouth to hers. The kiss awoke all their slumbering, long-denied desires for each other, and it wasn't long before they were searching for a clean spot a safe distance from the horses. Between heated kisses and caresses, they finally found a patch of tender young grass where they could lose themselves to the joy of rediscovering one another's bodies. They came together in a surge of passion so strong that they had no time to remove all their clothing, and even their surroundings ceased to matter.

Following that first exquisitely satisfying and tumultuous reunion, they dozed in each other's arms, then awoke to discover a curious foal nuzzling them then leaping back in surprise as Joe sat up suddenly. The herd had closed ranks upon them, and they were now lying squarely in the middle of the grazing horses.

Joe started to laugh, and Maggie joined him, then she rolled over on top of him, and kissed him long and lingeringly. Only the curiosity of all three of the new babies roused them to a realization of their vulnerability. One of the foals, a little filly, found it necessary to leap over them to rejoin her dam. Sighing,

Maggie decided they had best get up before one of them got kicked in the head.

Pulling together the two halves of her shirtwaist, she set out to pick the perfect spot for their house, which she envisioned as a small cabin with just enough room for the bare necessities. A place to shelter when they came to check on the horses. A place for only the two of them—safe from curious foals wondering what two humans were doing rolling around together on the grass.

When she had found what appeared to be the perfect location, she called to Joe who had enticed one of the foals into submitting to its first grooming. Rubbing and scratching the little fellow's itchy spots, Joe had already won the baby's trust, and he gave Maggie a broad, triumphant smile before rising from the grass and coming toward her wearing only his boots and denim pants. The rest of him was magnificently bare, and the sight so distracted her that she almost forgot what she wanted to tell him.

"Oh, Joe! I love you so much!" she exclaimed, bursting with joy and flinging her arms around him.

"And I love you, Maggie Sterling."

They clung to each other and kissed once more beneath the blue Idaho sky, secure in the knowledge that whatever problems or adjustments awaited them in the future, they had found home and happiness . . . at long last.

Epilogue

This story is fictional, as is the town of Bitterroot, but the history is all true. In 1900 and 1904, Chief Joseph was allowed to visit his father's grave in the Wallowa Valley in Oregon. He begged the ranchers there to sell land to the Indian Bureau, so that he and his tribe could return to the valley to live. They refused, and the old chieftain reportedly died of a broken heart on September 21, 1904.

Despite the tragedies that haunted the Nez Perce, Maggie and Joe's dream of preserving the Appaloosa as a distinct breed of horse did come true. The compassion of the occasional rancher who recognized the value of the spotted horse saved the breed from extinction during the bitter years following Chief Joseph's surrender. Today, Appaloosas can be found across the United States and elsewhere serving mankind in every equine capacity. The headquarters for the Appaloosa Horse Club and a museum dedicated to the spotted horse is located in Moscow, Idaho. Not far away, the descendants of the Nez Perce Indians at Lapwai still ride Appaloosas across their ancestral lands just as Joe envisioned.